A CURSE OF
ASH AND IRON

Christine (signature)

CHRISTINE NORRIS

PAPER
PHOENIX
PRESS
Pennsville, NJ

PUBLISHED BY
Paper Phoenix Press
A division of eSpec Books
PO Box 242
Pennsville, NJ 08070
www.especbooks.com

ISBN : 978-1-956463-29-3
ISBN (eBook): 978-1-956463-28-6

A previous version published by
Curiosity Quills Press in 2015.

Cover Images:
Rusty steampunk background with clock
and different kinds of gears © Ellerslie

Jewelry, patterned banner with antique watches,
decorated with gold and brass gears on dark blue,
textured, striped background, drawn in steampunk style. © Black moon

Cover Design: Mike and Danielle McPhail, McP Digital Graphics

Interior Design: Danielle McPhail, McP Digital Graphics

DEDICATION

For Rebecca, Cora, Dorothy, Patricia. For Oscar, Clarence, Ben, and Harry. You haven't been forgotten. And for Karen, Sarah, Jason and Uncle Michael. We carry them with us.

PROLOGUE

1869 – Seven years earlier

GRAY LIGHT FILTERED THROUGH THE HIGH WINDOWS OF THE THIRD floor hall. Ben tiptoed across, though he really needn't have bothered — the carpet was thick, the rain pounding, and the argument downstairs loud. He wasn't exactly *allowed* on the third floor, but that had never stopped him before. Tiptoeing was just habit.

He pushed open one of the doors and peered inside. The only eyes that returned his gaze belonged to the collection of stuffed bears and porcelain dolls arranged around the small table in one corner of the nursery, in the middle of their perpetual tea party. They all seemed to give him the same accusatory stare, which, when combined with the dim light and the sounds of the storm, made him shiver. He never liked being alone with Ellie's menagerie; he got the distinct feeling they moved on their own when he wasn't looking, and talked about him behind his back.

"Ben."

The whisper tickled the back of Ben's neck, and at first he was afraid that one of the dolls *had* called. Then he realized it had come from behind him. He pulled his head from the nursery doorway and turned around. He didn't see anyone, so who had called? A ghost, perhaps? A Fae spirit? Another shiver ran down his spine at the thought. No matter how many times his mother told him that bogeymen, ghosts, and fairies were only real in storybooks, he took no chances. He kept still as stone and waited to see if the voice would call again.

"Ben. Over here."

Only his eyes moved, searching the gloom. Thunder rolled above his head, which did nothing to discourage the idea that something otherworldly called him. Then he spotted a small, pale hand emerging from the partially open attic door. One finger beckoned him forward. For a moment Ben was sure it was the hand of a ghost, and the look on his face must have given him away, because a familiar giggle snuck from behind the attic door.

"Ellie!" His shoulders slumped as the fright *whoosh*ed out of him. He tromped across the hall. "What are you doing?"

"Hiding."

"From what?"

The sound of two women's voices floated up the stairs, sounding like screech owls fighting over a squirrel. A baby's cry mixed with the shouting—Ben's little brother, Harry, not two years old, howling from his playpen. Ben had no idea what the argument was about; he had run as soon as the yelling started. This was not the first time he had heard his mother's voice raised to the level of a train whistle. Yelling like that, in his experience, was usually followed by throwing things. He wanted to be well clear if she got her hands on one of the cast-iron frying pans.

Hiding sounded like a good idea.

The attic door swung open, and a small, dark-haired girl in a crisp and frilly blue dress appeared. She beckoned him again.

"Come on, quick."

As soon as Ben came close enough, Ellie clamped her hand around his wrist and dragged him up the dusty stairs to the dustier attic. A candle sat in a silver candlestick at the top of the stairs, its light guiding them like a Christmas star. The rain was louder up here, pounding against the peaked roof, shutting out all other sounds. Ellie scooped up the candle, holding it at arm's length so that the tiny pool of oily light fell over the silent specters of sheet-covered furniture, old steamer trunks, a wardrobe, and moldering dressmaker's dummies.

Although it looked like a hodge-podge of junk, there was an order to everything that only Ben and Ellie understood. They had spent weeks quietly arranging the junk, choosing the best of the furniture and placing it in the center of the room, where they had made a clearing. It was lined with an old threadbare rug, the loveseat and chairs gathered around a chipped marble-top table. They spent many afternoons here, playing games and making up stories. The space was stifling in the summer and freezing in the winter, but it was theirs and theirs alone.

Ellie picked her way through the clutter, her feet finding the winding path that led between strategically placed items. She had to release him when they came to the place where the only way forward was to crawl beneath a stack of precariously arranged books piled atop an old ironing board that was laid across a gap between two trunks. Ellie had gotten the idea for the crawlspace after reading *Alice's Adventures in Wonderland*. She called it their "rabbit hole".

They emerged in their little oasis, tucked away behind years of forgotten things, and Ellie set the candle on the table. Then she began pacing. There was only room for three or four good steps, but she took every inch of it, spinning on her heel to go back the way she had come.

"Ellie, what is it?" Ben flopped onto a moth-eaten armchair, chosen for its squashy, comfortable cushion. "What's wrong?"

Ellie stopped pacing and looked at Ben. The flickering candlelight reflected her eyes, and Ben's stomach flipped. She looked as if she would burst into tears at any moment, which frightened him. She didn't cry often. Ben thought it was brave of her not to cry at the drop of a hat, like some girls did. Even though lately she had plenty of reason to cry, she hadn't—at least not in front of him.

"Are you missing her?"

Ellie shook her head. "I miss her every minute of every day. But that's not it."

"So, what then? Something your stepmother did?" He stood up and slipped his hand behind her ear. "I thought we had decided she's a ridiculous troll. You are the princess of this house, and she can't do anything about it."

When he pulled his hand out again, a penny had appeared in his fingers. The trick always made Ellie smile, even if she had figured out how it was done after only the fifth time he had performed it for her. But her face remained all downward lines, her worried gaze boring into him.

"You're my very best friend, aren't you, Ben?" she asked, as if the sun coming up tomorrow depended on his answer.

"You know that I am. What kind of a silly question is that?" Ben was confused and a little insulted. They had been best friends for years, even though Ellie's governess, now her stepmother, often stated that it was inappropriate for a girl of Ellie's status to "fraternize with a common boy". That was part of the reason they had made their hiding place in the attic. Neither of them cared a whit about common or rich or any of it. They had both decided it was stupid to not talk to someone just because how much money they had in the bank or didn't, or if they rode in a carriage or walked. Why was this coming up all of a sudden?

"And you'll be my friend always? No matter what happens?"

Ben's insides turned icy. "Do I really need to say it?"

Ellie's eyes pleaded. "Please."

"Of course I'm your best friend. We'll be friends until we're old and gray and have no teeth left in our heads." It was a pledge they had made up years ago, repeated often and usually accompanied by giggling at the thought of the two of them in their old age, gumming their food while they sat in matching rocking chairs. Ben felt a smile creep onto his face, but there was no laughter from Ellie.

"Promise me you'll remember?" She wrung her hands, then grabbed both of his and held on as if she were hanging from a cliff. "Swear you'll never, ever forget! Even if we live on opposite sides of the world, and don't speak for years and years, promise you'll still be my very best friend."

"Of course I won't forget! Ellie, will you *please* tell me what is going on? Are you going somewhere?" The idea popped into his head that her stepmother and father had decided to send her away to some snooty boarding school far away where he would never see her. His insides quivered like cold gravy. He gripped Ellie with as much force as she gripped him, so that even a hurricane couldn't tear them apart.

Thunder rolled again in the form of stomping footsteps below, followed by angry voices. "You have been dismissed, and you will leave immediately." There was a dangerous edge to the unmistakable shriek of Ellie's stepmother. "If you do not leave I will call the police to have you bodily removed from my home. It's time you learned to respect your betters."

"You may have the power to toss me out, Olivia Banneker, but you will never be my better." Ben's mother gave as well as she got when it came to attitude. "Respect is earned, a lesson you should have taught yourself."

Ben could barely hear Olivia's reply; it was so low it was almost a growl. "You will get your brat and leave *my* home this minute. And do not expect me to supply you with references to your next employer, you spiteful woman."

"Oh, I'm spiteful, am I?" Ben's mother's voice was just this side of shouting. "Don't worry, I would never dream of asking you for anything. Ben! Ben, come here this minute! And you never, *ever* call my child a brat. He's better behaved than half the ungrateful spawn of your so-called 'better class'. I only wish I could take sweet Ellie with me, and away from this house."

Ben gasped as he realized what was happening. He gripped Ellie's hand tighter and saw the tears begin to run down her cheeks. She had known, and that's why she had dragged him to the attic.

"Don't answer," she said in a damp whisper. "If they can't find us, maybe they'll give up looking and you can stay. You could live here."

It was a desperate wish. Ben's mother would never give up, would never leave him behind, even if he begged her. And as much as he loved Ellie, he didn't think he could bear to be separated from his mother, brother, and father. He would miss his home, so different from this big house full of fancy things. It was almost as much a home to him as his own little one in South Philadelphia, but only because of Ellie.

His mother called again, and it was all he could do not to return the call as he struggled between Ellie's pleading face, and the automatic pull of his mother.

"Benjamin Grimm, if you do not appear before me this very instant, you are in for the beating of your life!"

Ben was not frightened by this threat; his mother was full of bluster but would never really beat him. At least, not terribly. But he would take the paddling, because he could not abandon Ellie.

The shouting came very close to the attic door, and it was Ellie's turn to gasp.

"We forgot to lock the door!"

The knob rattled and the door flew back against the wall, banging louder than the thunder. Ben and Ellie turned their heads toward the sound and froze.

"Ben, are you up here?" Feet stomped up the stairs and across the attic's bare floorboards. They came straight toward where the children hid, and too late both of them realized that the candle had betrayed them.

"There you are! Didn't you hear me calling you?" Ben's mother's face floated out of the gloom. At any other time it would have been a huge laugh to see her trying to fit her adult shoulders through the child-sized space of the rabbit hole, but all amusement seemed to have been sucked from the world. Their safe place had been invaded. She stood, irritation etched on her face, but as she looked from one child's face to the other, her anger fell apart.

"I'm sorry, Ben. I don't have any choice." She knelt beside the pair, her full skirt billowing around her. She looked at Ellie and stroked her hair, as if she were her own daughter. "I am so sorry that we have to leave you."

"But you... can't go, you can't." Ellie's words came out between gulps of air as she fought the sobs that threatened to overcome her.

"It's not fair, I know. First your mother, and now us. But your father is still here for you, my love. You must be brave, now. Be brave and strong, and remember who you are."

She kissed Ellie on the forehead, and as she did she grabbed Ben's hand and gently slid Ellie's from its grasp.

"No! Please don't!" Ellie cried. "Please!"

Ben tried to hold on, but his mother grasped him by the shoulders and pulled him toward her. He watched Ellie as his mother dragged him away, tears streaming down his own face.

"Ben! Don't forget your promise!"

"I won't! Ellie!" He struggled against his mother's grip, but knew it was a pointless battle. She pushed him down and through the rabbit hole, into the darkness beyond. His best friend was gone, swallowed by the dusty attic clutter.

CHAPTER I

1876

I F BENJAMIN GRIMM'S SHORT YEARS WORKING IN THE THEATER HAD taught him anything, it was that the stage was not all that different from reality. People played their parts in life, just like on stage, at least according to old Will Shakespeare. Pretending was something some people did all too well; like magicians, never revealing their secrets.

Ben had been working for the Walnut Street Theater for over two years, and yet everyone still treated him like a new apprentice. He had spent the entire afternoon rooting through the storage closet in the loft over the lobby, searching for a stupid hat that the Wardrobe Mistress had insisted, in no uncertain terms, existed. It wasn't until he heard voices in the lobby below that he realized how late it was. He emerged from the closet, hot, coated with dust, and empty-handed. His heart plummeted when he saw the people milling about below.

"Damn it, I'm trapped." The stage crew must never be seen, and if he left the loft now, that was a given. The official reason for such a silly rule was that it spoiled the illusion, but Ben thought it more likely that seeing the lowly stagehands would insult the delicate sensibilities of the fan-fluttering, top hat-wearing patrons. Ben snorted a laugh as he imagined himself strolling through the lobby in his braces and shirtsleeves, leaving a trail of dust. While the looks on their faces would be terrific for a good laugh, it wasn't worth losing his job to see. At least, not today.

So Ben watched the crowd below, debating the best way to get out of his tricky situation.

When a girl he thought he knew entered with the rest of the audience for the evening performance, he leaned on the railing and stared, his crisis forgotten. He leaned over a little further and squinted, but the girl was too far away for him to be sure it was Eleanor Banneker. Memory, or maybe the flickering gas flames that lit the lobby, could be playing tricks with him. No, it was more than faulty recollection or bad illumination that caused him to doubt his eyes. The girl he watched from the shadows wore a lavender and green silk gown that hugged her frame, revealing the curves of a grown woman. It couldn't be Ellie, then. She would have just turned seventeen, and it was impossible she would look like that.

Ben kept his gaze on the mystery woman and tried to remember how many years it had been since he had seen Ellie, using his fingers to count backward. He remembered the last time with absolute clarity. But time was being slippery with him and he couldn't remember how old he had been then. Nine or ten? Did that make it six or seven years ago? He leaned over the rail as far as he dared to get a better look. If the stage manager caught him he would get a whipping, which was the price of working for his father.

The girl that might be Ellie turned away from him. *Damn it.* He still wasn't certain, and now that the idea it *was* her had wormed its way into his head, it wouldn't leave him alone. He dashed to the top of the steps that led to the loft, but she slipped inside the theater with the rest of the audience. The ushers closed the theater doors and Ben had his chance to escape. He raced backstage to his place at the ropes of the main curtain, and made it just in time, ignoring the scathing looks from the other stagehands. Fortunately, his father was in his own place on the far side of the stage, unable to witness Ben's tardiness.

Ben tried to concentrate, but it was no use; his mind was full of Eleanor. His distraction caused him to run into the lead actress during the first scene change, and he almost missed his cue at the end of Act One. When intermission was nearly over, he peeked out from behind the curtain to try and get another look at his mystery girl.

Someone tapped him on the shoulder.

"Hey, Ben," the tapper whispered. Ben looked over his shoulder at a short, stocky man in his early twenties. Ronald, a fellow stagehand. "What are you doing? Are you going to help me lift this fly or not? The backdrop weighs a ton, you know. I can't do it by myself."

Ben waved him away. "I'm busy. Go find Artie, he'll help you."

Ron made an annoyed sound but cleared off. Ben returned to his people-watching. The audience trickled in, and Ben spied the girl in question on her way down the aisle, coming right toward him. His heart gave an unexpected leap and his throat went suddenly dry. It was definitely Ellie. She looked the part of the society girl she was born to be, lovely and graceful; certainly lovelier than the overdressed peacock beside her. Benjamin did a double take when he realized the peacock was Rebecca, Ellie's stepsister.

Ben remembered little of Rebecca, except that she was a plump little mouse of a girl who rarely spoke. She was still on the plump side, and wore a pained, uncomfortable look along with her emerald evening gown, as if her corset was laced too tightly. The expression was one she had inherited from her mother — Ellie's stepmother. The woman herself walked behind Ellie, shepherding the two girls down the aisle toward their seats.

Ben stifled a laugh. The old crow had seen the bad end of the years since they had last met, her hair streaked with gray and her skin sagging around the jaw and neck. But her eyes, cold as the Delaware in winter, were exactly as he remembered. He wondered if the second Mrs. Banneker could feel the heat of his glare.

The roar of applause jolted Ben out of his reverie. The lights lowered, he raised the curtain, and the second act began. In-between set changes, he dashed back to his place to look at Ellie. The performance ended, and Ben couldn't let her go without one last look. He lowered the main curtain, apparently a bit too quickly for the lead actor.

"Excuse me, but I was not finished with my curtain call!" he shouted at Ben as he dashed toward the stage door. Ben tumbled out onto 9th Street and charged toward the corner. Breathing hard, he peeked around to Walnut Street and the theater's entrance. A line of horse-drawn carriages waited by the curb, ready to take the audience members home, or to a late supper, or to various clubs to drink bourbon and gin. Ben reached into his pocket, his fingers finding a brass gear — his lucky talisman. He rubbed it between his forefinger and thumb, trying to calm the unexpected swell of conflicting emotions that seeing Ellie had stirred in him — curiosity, excitement, anticipation. Did she still love to sing and dance, or to read everything she could get her hands on? The space of the years between then and now called to Ben, begging to be filled.

He scanned the stream of bodies that emerged from the theater's polished wooden doors and spilled onto the sidewalk. Ladies pulled their wraps snugly around their shoulders against the October chill, and men checked their pocket watches before buttoning up frockcoats and securing silk top hats. Ben shook his head — they looked like a bunch of overstuffed turkeys ready to roast. He had never been fond of fancy dress, not that he had the occasion or the means to wear any. It looked uncomfortable, and also like it would get dirty easily. Ben was nearly always dirty in some manner, with some speck on his shirt collar or grease beneath his fingernails from working or building something in his workshop.

Ellie, Rebecca, and Mrs. Banneker appeared on the sidewalk, and Ben had to remember to breathe. Ellie's cloak covered her gown, but she stood tall, moving as if her feet barely touched the ground. She had always been graceful. Dancing lessons, insisted upon by her mother since she was young, had probably helped. Ben smiled as the younger version of the girl he saw before him appeared in his mind, twirling and curtseying in time to her governess' tapping on the floor with a cane while Rebecca served as her dancing partner. He hadn't been allowed to watch, of course, and Ellie's governess would rather have set her hair on fire than let Ben stand in for Rebecca. But he had sneaked a peek now and again, just like was doing now.

Ellie looked over her shoulder in response to her stepmother's call, and Ben got a glimpse of smooth, unblemished cheek and kind, soft eyes. Ben noticed it again, the same something he had seen in the lobby that made her appear older, more careworn. He wasn't sure what it was, but he recognized it—he had seen the same look in his mother's eyes once in a while, when she thought Ben wasn't paying attention.

He wanted to call out to Ellie, to shout his joy and surprise over seeing her, but of course he could not. The social gap between them was too wide for sidewalk greetings outside the theater.

"Where is Mr. Banneker this evening?" one of the stuffed turkey-men asked Ellie's stepmother. "I've not seen him in months. Not working late on a Friday evening, is he? The banks are all closed!" He chuckled at his own joke.

Mrs. Banneker stiffened beneath her fur wrap. "He is on sabbatical in Paris, Mr. Van Wyck. I thought you knew? Then he's taking some time along the French coast. We went there on our honeymoon and, ever since, he's just loved France. The sea air is so good for him, and these city winters are so terrible." She twittered a girlish, high-pitched laugh. Ben fought the urge to vomit. The woman he remembered was neither stupid nor girlish. More like a demon stuffed into a dress.

He was so focused on Mrs. Banneker that he almost missed when Ellie spotted him. Her wide-eyed, puzzled expression shifted to recognition and surprise, and she moved half a step toward him, then stopped. She must have been thinking the same thing as Ben—that she could not just walk around the corner unescorted. But she held his gaze for moment and then glanced to her left and right. Turning herself away from the crowd, she pulled off one of her gloves and shoved it into her reticule. What in the world she was doing?

"Excuse me, Ste... ma'am? I seem to have lost one of my gloves."

Mrs. Banneker turned away from Mr. Van Wyck and faced Ellie. Her face puckered for a split-second in irritation, smoothing quickly into a look of benevolence. "Lost a glove, my —"she swallowed, her lip twisting up as if she had tasted something bitter " — dear?"

Ellie's smile never faltered. "Yes. I'm such a goose. I must have dropped it inside. I'll just go and look for it. I won't be a moment."

She excused herself and walked into the theater, leaving her step-mother standing with her mouth open. Ben remained for a second longer before he realized what was happening and dashed back through the stage door.

"Hey, Ben, where ya been?" Ronald called out as Ben rushed by. "And just where are you going? Just because your dad's the stage manager doesn't mean you get to slack off."

Benjamin ignored Ronald and dodged the obstacle course of the backstage area toward the curtain, nearly tripping on an overstuffed chair. The auditorium was empty. The footlights were dark, but the lights from the chandelier above the audience area glowed brightly, the crystal throwing rainbows around the room.

Ellie entered. She stopped for a moment, her eyes wary and her hand against her stomach as if she were holding in her breath.

"Ellie?" Ben called her. "Ellie Banneker?

Her shoulders relaxed and her breath came out in a *whoosh*. She paused for another breath before making her way down the center aisle toward Ben. The door closed behind her with a muffled thump, shutting out the murmurs of those who remained in the lobby. The theater dropped into an eerie quiet. Now that they were face-to-face, over-whelming self-consciousness replaced Benjamin's excitement. He ran his sweaty palms through his hair, smoothing the runaway brown locks his mother would say needed trimming. He was suddenly aware of the way he was dressed—he looked like a ragamuffin compared to the upper-class men Ellie must be used to. Her chestnut hair shone in the light, her green eyes wary but bright. Ben stopped near the first row, a lump in his throat, hoping she wouldn't notice the scuffed tops of his shoes and his frayed shirt cuffs, and let her approach him.

"Benjamin Grimm? It *is* you." Her smile widened, and it was as if the curtain had gone up in her eyes. The sadness Ben had seen before lifted, and she became a girl of seventeen. She reached out to him with her bare hand. His nervousness evaporated like morning fog. He wiped his hand on his pants and then grasped hers tightly, catching the slight scent of soap and rose water.

Ben had expected the soft hand of the daughter of a prominent banker; hands used to doing embroidery and playing the piano. But there were calluses on her palm, the nails short and ragged. Her skin was pink and chapped. His expression must have given away some of his surprise, because when he released her hand, Ellie tucked it into the folds of her skirt. "I can't believe that you... It's been so long, Ben. You've grown."

The look in her eyes made Ben decide to keep quiet about her hands. He was glad she had come in to see him. Having spent years under her stepmother's care, he had worried she might have turned into a snob. "As have you, my lady." His grin was large as he bent over in an exaggerated bow.

"Oh, please don't. Ben, stop it this minute." Ellie put her hands to her blushing cheeks, as if trying to hold back her smile.

Ben stood, laughing, and thrust his hands in his pockets. "I was hiding in the loft above the lobby and saw you come in tonight. I... didn't recognize you at first. You've, uh, changed." It was his turn to blush again as he remembered what he had been thinking about her curves.

"You've changed too." She squinted and looked closely at his face. "I can't see any dirt. So your mother finally wrestled you into submission about keeping clean."

Ben didn't answer, only smirked and scratched the back of his head. "I tried to think how many years it's been since I saw you last."

"Seven." Ellie's reply was so soft he almost didn't hear it. "Seven years. The last time I saw you, we were both ten, after..." she hesitated. "After my mother died."

Ben's smile faltered. "Yes, that's right." He felt stupid for forgetting, even more stupid for making her bring up something so obviously painful. His own mother had cried for days after her employer's passing. Ellie's mother had been a lovely woman, who had provided him with a seemingly endless supply of sweets.

Ellie shook her head as if shaking herself free of the edge of melancholy that had dropped over the conversation. "How is your dear mother? And your little brother? I'm sure he's no longer the chubby-cheeked baby I remember."

Ben shrugged. "Mother's fine. She keeps busy running the bookshop. Harry is… he's a little brother."

Ellie wrinkled her nose and narrowed her eyes. "Being as I have no little brothers, I'll have to assume that you mean you love him dearly and can't imagine life without him."

"Not exactly, but I don't want to ruin your image of me as a wholesome young man, so I won't tell you what I really think about him. It wouldn't be proper for me to say in front of a lady, anyway."

"You think I'm a lady, do you? You might be surprised at some of the words I've used when no one is listening." Ellie's gaze wandered over the theater's ceiling. There was a teasing note in her voice. "I never thought I'd see you working here. If I remember correctly, you said that if you were going to be in the theater, it would be in *front* of the footlights. A magician, I believe it was?"

"I'm still working on that," Ben's reply was touched with defensiveness. "But now it's illusion instead of straight magic, don't you know that? It's all the rage in Europe. Until I can find a backer, I need to work. My father, he's the stage manager now. He got me the job, said it would do me good to learn a real skill." He rolled his eyes.

Ellie raised an eyebrow. "He doesn't approve of your career aspirations?"

Ben shook his head. "He lets me keep my workshop, but thinks I'm wasting my time." He shrugged. "It's better than the brickyard."

Ellie laughed out loud; a pretty sound that rolled around the inside of the theater. She covered her mouth and glanced over her shoulder to make sure no one else had heard. When she stopped giggling, she looked at Ben and sighed. "I can't stay, I don't want to keep my stepmother waiting." She glanced over her shoulder and back to Ben. "It was so good to see you again."

Ben felt the words were weighted somehow, like a current pulling beneath the calm surface of a river. "It was good to see you again too, Ellie." There was so much more Ben wanted to say, seven years' worth.

He didn't dare ask to see her again, though, and resigned himself to only having this stolen moment.

Ellie pulled on her "missing" glove and took Ben's hand once more. "Goodbye, Ben." She released him, but did not turn and leave; instead studying him as if he were an interesting painting, her eyes glowing. The look brought on a sudden rush of memory. Ellie was up to something.

"Do you remember your promise?"

Ben was puzzled for a moment, and then he remembered. "Of course."

"And are you still my friend?"

"Until we're old and gray and have no teeth in our heads." Ben smiled, waiting for her to laugh like always. But, just as the last time he had said it, up in the dark attic on their last meeting, she remained serious. With a bob of her head she turned and was gone.

Ben remained frozen in place. Something wasn't right with Ellie, he could feel it. There had been a darkness behind her smile he couldn't place. Ronald poked his head from between the curtains, jarring Ben from his thoughts. "If your clandestine rendezvous is over, boy-o, could you *possibly* find a moment to, I don't know, do your job? Come on, we have to reset everything for tomorrow night."

Ben stared at the door a moment longer, his body in the present but his mind following Ellie out the door. He rubbed his thumb over his lucky gear. "Yeah, yeah, hold yer horses, Ronny boy. I'm comin'."

Eleanor hurried through the empty lobby and out onto the sidewalk. She was going to pay for making her stepmother wait, but it had been worth it. Of all the people in the world, she never expected to see Ben tonight. He had been her best and only real friend, and she felt the loss of him almost as deeply as her mother's. Perhaps finding him again had been mere coincidence, perhaps it was Fate's doing. Her heart pounded so loud she was sure it would be heard blocks away. A plan had begun to form in her head, months ago, but she could never succeed alone. Meeting Ben tonight had rekindled both the idea and her hope. She wasn't going to pass up this chance, not when it had dropped in her lap.

Ellie stepped onto the sidewalk and into the carriage, which was one of the few remaining on the street. The door was open, her stepmother and stepsister inside, waiting. She forced herself to remain calm. If her stepmother saw her looking so happy, she would want to know the cause, and Ellie could not let anything spoil her good mood. The second the footman closed the door, her stepmother began her lecture.

"You foolish girl, making us wait for you." Any trace of the genteel woman on the sidewalk had vanished. "You're very lucky the carriage was here at all. I had half a mind to leave you here."

Ellie formed a scathing response in her head but left it unspoken. She had vast personal experience to attest to the fact that it wasn't a good idea to provoke Olivia Banneker. She imagined the look on her stepmother's face if she *had* said it, and that was enough.

Olivia continued, "The only reason I waited was because of the scandal leaving you would have caused. People would talk, and there can't be even the slightest hint of impropriety cast upon us, not now, at this crucial time."

She's so worried about scandal, Ellie thought. *What would she do if the gossips knew what was really going on behind the closed doors of the Banneker house? Tongues would wag in every parlor of the city.*

Her stepmother sat back against the seat and looked out the window, speaking to herself. "We need to be especially careful now." She turned to the window and spoke softly, as if her words were only for the streetlamps, their oily pools of light floating by the carriage windows like phantoms. "We all make our bargains, do what we have to, and sometimes the things we want come at a cost dearer than we know. I refuse to let a silly girl like you get in my way."

Ellie had no idea what she meant, and no intention of asking—she was rebellious, not stupid. Rebecca remained silent, trying to stay out of her mother's field of fire. Ellie closed her eyes and held onto the hope she had felt a moment before. "I am sorry, *Stepmother.*"

Olivia gave Ellie a pointed, venomous glare. She snaked her fingers around the younger girl's wrist, squeezing so tightly the bones ground against one another, and it was all Ellie could do not to cry out.

"If you ever do anything like that again, you will be."

CHAPTER II

BEN STUDIED THE BIRD CAGE ON TOP OF THE TABLE, NERVOUS. HE crossed his fingers that this time it would work, then leaned on the table with one hand and pushed a small button on the underside of the tabletop with the other.

"Ben! What are you doing down there!"

Three things happened at once: the metal cage collapsed into a hidden chamber beneath the table, Ben twitched, and the cage pinched his thumb on its way down. All of which was followed immediately by a curse word as he jammed his thumb in his mouth. His triumph at finally getting the cage to work was dampened by irritation at himself. The collapsing part went exactly the way it was supposed to. The rest was unexpected. He had allowed the call to shift his focus, something he couldn't do when he did this illusion in front of an audience. In his frustration and pain he kicked the table, which caused the hammer he had been using to fall from the top. As if its purpose was to add insult to his injury, the hammer landed on Ben's foot, causing another word to fly from his mouth that would make his mother scrub the inside of it with soap.

A series of thumps on the stairs preceded a small boy with shaggy hair that hung in his eyes. "Ben? Are you busy?"

"I was," Ben mumbled around his sore thumb. It was no use trying to do anymore today. He wasn't able to concentrate. If his pesky younger brother wasn't getting underfoot, his own wandering mind dragged his thoughts away. His conversation with Ellie nagged at him, and he wished there was some way for him to talk to her again, even just for a few minutes. He knew he could draw out whatever she was hiding.

The impatient boy jumped the last few stairs and landed on the dusty floor of the basement workshop. "Come on, Ben, what are you doing down here?" His eyes went to the table. "It works? Terrific! Can I help?"

"I'm busy, Harry, and no." Ben picked up the offending hammer and walked to the other end of the musty, low-ceilinged room. An open notebook sat on the long workbench. If he wasn't going to build any- more today, maybe he would have better luck with brainstorming. He hunched over the page and studied the drawing, which showed the plans for the table and cage apparatus that had tried just moments ago to eat Ben's hand. The sketch was surrounded by notes in his slanted, scratchy handwriting, denoting the levers, gears and pulleys that caused the cage to collapse into the table. When it worked properly the bird cage, with two birds inside, would seem to vanish into thin air.

He turned the page, to a drawing of a cabinet that would cause an entire person to apparently vanish without a trace, and studied it. His thumb, which had begun to turn a terrific shade of blue-black, throbbed. *Small price to pay, I guess.* It had taken him three months to get the cage table to operate properly. He had learned a great deal about construction (and safety), so the next project would go much more smoothly. Hopefully.

Harry whipped the book from under Ben's nose. "Have you come up with any new magic tricks?"

Ben pulled the book from his little brother's fingers before he could smudge the drawing. "Harry, watch it, will you! They're not tricks, you nitwit. I've told you a hundred times I don't *do* magic tricks anymore." Ben gave his brother a small shove and held the notebook against his chest. He scanned the page — the pencil lines were smudged in one or two places, but no real damage had been done.

"Watch it!" Harry shouted up the stairs. "Ma! Ben pushed me."

Cora Grimm's stern but weary voice floated down. "Harry, leave your brother alone while he's working."

Ben stuck his tongue out at his brother, grateful that at least his mother understood how important his work was to him. Harry crossed his eyes, gigantic behind a thick pair of spectacles.

"Can't you go stick your nose in a book or something?" Ben loved his brother, but there were times when he wanted to box his ears. "This is important work, and I can't have you mucking it up."

When he had told Ellie he wanted to be an illusionist, he wasn't lying to make a good impression. He had been fascinated with magic ever since his mother had shoved a book of magic tricks into his seven year-old hand one rainy afternoon. He practiced day and night — sleight-of-hand maneuvers, card tricks, making small items disappear.

His primary audience had been Ellie. He must have driven her mad, always clumsily pulling pennies from behind her ears, stuffing her pretty linen handkerchiefs up his sleeves over and over. She had been a good sport, smiling and laughing at his feats of prestidigitation, especially when he muddled them.

He shook his head — Ellie was suddenly in his every thought. When they had first been separated, so violently and with no time to say goodbye, he had been confused and upset. Though he would deny it publicly until the day he died, he had cried for days, begging his mother to take him back to the fancy house on Delancey Place. He had even gone so far as to sneak out. But he had only made it halfway when his father caught and scolded him. And though he hadn't thought of her as often in recent years, until the night at the theater she had remained the girl with short dresses and bows in her curled dark hair.

An image of the Ellie he had seen last week floated through his thoughts and a small smile crept onto his face as he recalled the curve of her slender neck, tendrils of her chestnut hair whispering against it, her sparkling eyes and full laughing lips. She was definitely no longer a little girl.

"Important?" Harry huffed, and for once Ben was grateful for the distraction. "What's so important about a bunch of magic tricks? Now, astronomy is important. Medicine, that's important. Science is important. They help people. Ideas are important, because they lead to great inventions."

"But these *are* ideas," Ben said with an exasperated sigh. "*My* ideas and *my* inventions. I'm so sorry they don't meet your lofty standards." He only half-listened to his brother — his thoughts torn between the last wisps of Ellie that clung to his mind and the sketch of the vanishing cabinet. He pulled his lucky gear from his pocket, tossed it into the air, and caught it. The workbench was scattered with its brothers and sisters, a motley assortment of gears and springs. Most of his construction materials had been given to him by Mr. Rittenhouse, the kindly watchmaker who occupied the shop next door to his parents' bookshop, beneath which he kept his workshop. Other parts he had salvaged from the local scrap yard. Ben rubbed his gear again thoughtfully, then stuffed it into his pocket and grabbed a rickety wooden stool, settling himself onto it.

Harry plopped onto the floor, adjusted his glasses, and leaned back on his hands. "I'm going to be a great scientist when I grow up. You'll see. People all over the world will be reading about my accomplishments. Maybe I'll cure an incurable disease."

"How can you cure an incurable disease? By definition, incurable means it can't be cured."

Harry rolled his eyes. "And what about you? Are you going to be the next Houdini?"

"His name was Robert-Houdin, not Houdini, you loony-bird." Ben left the cabinet design and flipped to the next, which showed a gadget that would make it look as if he were sawing a person in half. "And what kind of a name is 'Houdini', anyway? It sounds ridiculous."

"Boys, that's enough," their mother called, a bit more sternly.

"Sorry, Mother," the boys chimed in chorus.

"That'll be you, though," Harry whispered. "The Great Houdini, making birdcages disappear for all the crowned heads of Europe." He giggled at his own joke.

"You're a real inspiration." Ben said in an offhanded way. "For your information, I can do a whole lot more than make birds disappear. Look at this one." He turned the page and held up another sketch, one he hadn't quite completed. It looked like a tree, but, like the birdcage-table, contained hidden gears and pulleys.

Harry sat up and put his nose close to the book. "That's an odd-looking thing. What does it do?"

"It's supposed to be like Jean Robert-Houdin's famous illusion. I'll use a handkerchief from the audience and hide it inside an egg, and then I'll put them both inside a lemon, and all three inside an orange, and I'll bury it in the pot." He tapped the sketch. "Then just like that, I bring everything back by way of this mechanical orange tree. It'll blossom before their very eyes, and they'll all be amazed."

The orange tree trick held a special place in Ben's heart. It was the one that had turned his attention from simple sleight-of-hand to the realm of illusion. He had been twelve when the famous European illusionist Jean Eugene Robert-Houdin came to Philadelphia. The great man had agreed to perform at the Walnut—for a single night. Ben's father had taken Ben to the theater, as he had dozens of times before, but this was a performance that would change Ben's life. He had watched with wide eyes, trying to figure out exactly how the man had made a tree grow before their very eyes. Listening to the gasps of the audience's amazement and the thunderous applause of their approval, Ben imagined himself taking the curtain call to a standing ovation, and knew this life was what he wanted.

His father had taken him backstage to meet Robert-Houdin. He was soft-spoken, with a full white beard and a thick French accent. There was something mysterious about him, a twinkle in his eye as if he knew the secrets of the universe.

"Here, this is for you." Into the wide-eyed boy's hand he slipped a small brass gear. "It has always brought me luck. I hope it will do the same for you."

The orange tree had taken Ben years to puzzle out, but so far it was just a drawing. He turned to the last page. It looked like a simple sketch of two people positioned to dance.

"Playing with dolls?" Harry looked over Ben's shoulder. "Planning on a career in toymaking if your life as a vagabond prestidigitator doesn't work out?"

"Oh, will you please shut up, Harry." Ben showed the book to his brother. "These are automata."

"Auto-whats?" Harry scratched his head.

"Mister Robert-Houdin made dozens of them. They might look like dolls, but they move like they're alive. Some can play a song on the piano, some can draw a picture, and others can write their name."

Harry's eyes grew wide. "How do they do that? Magic?"

Ben winked, amused by how quickly Harry's attitude had changed. "Maybe. It's a secret, and a magician never tells how the trick is done." Unlike the orange tree, Ben knew exactly how the automatons worked. Mister Robert-Houdin had told the young Ben, in a conspiratorial whisper, that he had been a clockmaker before he had become a magician, and that inside all the automatons were clockworks that made them move, wound with tiny silver keys.

Harry's eyes narrowed with suspicion. "So how did *you* figure it out? I know you didn't come up with it all by yourself."

"No, that's true. Someone told me the secret, but only if I promised never to tell, not even my brother." Ben understood Harry's sudden captivation. His younger self had been even more fascinated by the mechanical people than by the magic orange tree. The way they moved was mesmerizing, as if they were enchanted.

"Watch this. Mister Robert-Houdin gave it to me." He went to the end of his workbench and lifted up a ballet dancer automaton. It was the most precious thing Ben owned. He placed the dancer, which stood on a wooden box, onto the floor in front of Harry. He reached into the slit at the back of her pink satin dress and turned the tiny key. She lifted her head, as if waking from sleep, and then raised her arms over her head, forming a circle. She lifted herself onto her toes and began to twirl and spin in a perfect recreation of her human counterpart. Finally, she dropped into a curtsey before returning to her original position.

Harry sat there, mouth open. "She's amazing, Ben." He looked up at his big brother with newfound admiration. "You're a good builder, but can you really make one like this?"

Ben took the rare compliment from his brother with a smile and a nod. He had studied the ballet dancer for years, taking copious notes before attempting to create anything of his own. He had made dozens of clockwork toys, starting with wind-up mice. Then he had taken the ballet dancer apart and put her back together again. The dancers in Ben's sketch were the next step, but they would be difficult. He imagined the two puppets dancing a waltz, just as he imagined real dancers did at fancy balls. Ben turned to the final page of the notebook.

"What in the heck is that?" Harry cried.

Ben didn't answer, because he didn't have a name for what the sketch depicted. The idea had come to him in a dream a year ago. When he woke he had snatched up his pencil and begun to draw, before the image could fade. From his mind to the page was as far as the idea had gotten. In the clear, harsh light of day, the idea seemed impossible.

He didn't doubt he could build it, if he had the materials, though he would need a bigger workspace than this little basement. The bigger problem was how to make it run. There weren't clockworks or springs large enough for it to work like an automaton, except in one of those huge clocks like Big Ben in England. Clockworks weren't practical for this... whatever it was.

"It's... none of your business." He grabbed a pencil and quick-sketched some more of the machine.

Harry squinted at the page, turned his head one way then the other, and then shrugged. "I can't make head nor tail of it."

"That's because *your* head is stuffed with straw." Ben shut the notebook with a snap and put it aside.

Harry opened his mouth, one finger poised for a rebuttal, when Mother's voice floated down the stairs. "Boys, I need your help with customers. Come up out of that cave, the both of you. Now."

Ben secured his notebook in a drawer and followed Harry up the stairs and into the back room of the bookshop, where the oddly comforting scent of paper and binding glue welcomed him. The shop, which bore the obvious-yet-charming name of Grimm's Tales, had belonged to Ben's great-grandfather, then his grandfather, who had passed it to Ben's father, Oscar, who bore the surname like a badge of honor. Whenever someone asked him if he was related to the famous Brothers Grimm, he always replied, "of course!" Whether it was true or not, Ben wasn't certain, but it made his father happy and helped to sell books. His mother was in charge of the store, and Ben helped her during the day, when he wasn't needed at the theater. When the season ended, his father would spend his time here as well.

"Make sure you wash your hands before you touch anything," Ben's mother warned. "And *please*, for pity's sake, clean under your nails. No one wants to see a bookseller with grease under his fingernails." She walked out of the room and into the front of the store before Ben could remind her that he was *not* a bookseller. He went to the rear of the room, which had been turned into a cozy little kitchen area. At the sink he rubbed coarse but sweet-smelling soap over his hands. Then he took a boar's hair brush from a small shelf above the sink and scrubbed until his fingers turned red.

His mother bustled into the back again. "Harry, dear, will you please get that crate and bring it out front?" She pointed to the one she wanted, filled with new books packed in muslin. "Yes, that's the one. I just can't keep enough copies of that new Mark Twain book on the shelf." She lifted one from the box and inspected it. "I wish I had time to read it—Tom Sawyer sounds like a very interesting character."

Harry grumbled as he lifted the crate and hauled it to the front. Ben dried his hands and followed. His mother hadn't been kidding— the shop was full of customers. The bell above the door sang a cheery welcome as another entered. He scanned the crowd and chose to approach a group of three young, attractive women who were accompanied by another who was not young but might once have been attractive. He put on his most trustworthy expression. "Can I help you find something?"

One of the girls giggled, but quickly stifled it with her gloved hand. Ben thought she was lucky she didn't freeze where she stood under the older woman's icy glare. She turned to Ben and managed to un-pucker her lips enough to speak. "Yes, we are looking for the newest edition of *Godey's Lady's Book*, if you please, young man."

Ben bobbed his head. "If you'll follow me?" He led the group to where the magazines were located and extracted a thick, hard-covered volume from a shelf. He placed it on the counter and the girls surrounded it, a look of hungry anticipation in their eyes. All three of them grabbed it at once, threatening to rip it to pieces as they pulled in different directions.

"Ladies, please," the older woman admonished. "We do not snatch like street urchins. People will think you were not raised well." She gave Ben a glance that said he did not really count as "people," but that he would do for the purpose of teaching the girls a lesson in manners.

The girls stopped their tug-of-war and dropped the magazine, which hit the counter with a dull thud.

"Mother," the tallest of the girls said. "I should be the one to look at it first. After all, I am the one coming out this year. I need a gown for the Assembly Ball." She looked at the other two. "While *they* are still too young and will be at home, sitting with Nurse like the children they are."

One of the other girls, who looked enough like the first to be her sister, pouted. "I'd still like to see."

The girls' mother closed her eyes, praying either for patience or her daughters to suddenly be struck dumb. "*I* will take the magazine, thank you. There's an article by Mrs. Hale about women's education I'd like to read. She's been talking of nothing else at the club, and I simply must see it for myself." The woman reached into her purse and handed Ben some money.

Ben's mother appeared behind him. "If you like the *Lady's Book*, Mrs. Purcell, we also have the newest *Harper's Bazaar*." That was his mother, always the saleswoman. "It has some wonderful color plates of all the latest fashions from Paris."

The girls perked up at the mention of the French capital.

"Oh, Mother, please, can we?" the smallest girl, who looked about thirteen, pleaded. "I'm sure there will be new recipes, too. Perhaps we could have Cook try something for Sunday supper?"

The girl's mother looked at her youngest daughter, then at Ben's mother; the decidedly unladylike words the woman had for Cora Grimm were practically written upon her face. The woman relented with a sigh and fished in her reticule for more money, while Ben's mother reached behind her and fetched the other magazine from the shelf.

"Ben will be happy to wrap those up for you."

The woman handed over a piece of paper scrip and Ben's mother went to the cash register to get her change. Ben pulled some brown paper and twine from beneath the counter and wrapped both magazines.

"Your shop seems to be very popular," the oldest girl said lightly. "Is it always this busy?"

"It has been this year." Ben replied. "The Exposition has brought in a lot of tourists."

The girl's eyes widened, but there was mischief behind them. "Have you been to the Centennial Exposition?"

Ben paused in his work and looked up. The girl was pretty, blonde with bright blue eyes, but he thought her nose was too small and her eyes too wide. He preferred green eyes, though he couldn't say why.

She smiled. "I've been meaning to go all year, and haven't made it yet. And it's going to close soon."

"I haven't been either." The girl looked over her shoulder at her mother, who was getting her change. "I hear it's full of marvels. Did you know a Mr. Bell has invented a contraption that will allow people to talk to each other over long distances, using only wires? There is also supposed to be a giant steam engine, like the one in a train, but that stays in place and can run a hundred other machines at once." She gave a little shiver. "It all sounds perfectly strange and impossible."

Ben had not heard about the marvelous machines, but was instantly intrigued, particularly at the idea of the steam engine. The last sketch in his notebook flitted into his mind, and he was suddenly overcome with desire to run clear across the city.

"It does sound impossible. And wonderful. You've convinced me. I will have to go before it closes." He had the brief but insane thought to ask the girl to accompany him, but her agreeing was almost as impossible as talking to someone miles away over wires.

"Katharine," the girl's mother called. "Come along now, we have three more stops to make, and I'm afraid we'll be forever at the milliner's. You know how she likes to chat."

Katharine took the package from Ben and clutched it to her chest. "Good day to you, sir. Thank you for all your help."

"My pleasure." Ben nodded his goodbye and watched the girls and their mother leave the shop. She was a nice girl, for a socialite, and it was no use thinking anything beyond that. Ben returned to mingling among the customers. He came upon a solitary woman in a shabby coat too big for her, with a bonnet that covered her face. Ben wondered if she was an actual customer or a poor woman just looking for a place to get out of the cold.

"Can I help you find something, ma'am?"

"Yes, I'm looking for a copy of the new book by Miss Louisa May Alcott. *Rose in Bloom,* I think is the title?" The voice was familiar, and when the woman turned, Ben nearly jumped out of his skin. It was Ellie Banneker. She grinned at Ben's surprise. Ben peered around, in search of Ellie's stepmother and stepsister, but she appeared to be alone.

"What are you doing here?" Ben whispered, dumbfounded by her sudden appearance. "Without a chaperone and dressed like a… maid?" If he hadn't seen it with his own eyes, he wouldn't have believed it. Her disguise was complete, down to the worn edges of her coat.

Ellie waved the question away. "Never mind. No one will miss me." She scanned the shelves, running a gentle hand along the books. "Oh, how I love the smell of books. I can't remember the last time I read one."

Ben leaned over, pretending to be helping Ellie as if she were a customer. "How is that possible? You always had your nose in some book or other. I thought ladies of leisure were all well-read?"

Ellie stared at the shelf longingly and sighed. "That's a long story." She glanced over her shoulder, and then her hand slipped from beneath her cloak. In it was a piece of paper, which she handed to Ben.

Ben, both puzzled and intrigued, slipped the paper into his pocket. "Why don't you come and say hello to Mother? She'll be so happy to see you." Ellie was close enough that he could again smell her rose water. It made him dizzy.

"No, no. She won't recognize me."

"Are you kidding? She could never forget you."

Ellie's expression turned sad, with such pain in her eyes Ben could almost feel it. "I have to go." She turned toward the door.

Ben caught her by the arm. "Wait."

The wide-eyed look of shock on Ellie's face, and the shocked looks the two of them received from the customers pressed upon him like a lead weight, and he realized what he had done. Laying his hands on a woman in public was well past inappropriate. His mind whirled, looking for a half-believable excuse.

"I'm, uh, so sorry, but you forgot your book, miss." Ben released Ellie and grabbed the first book he touched. As he put it into Ellie's hands he glimpsed the title — *Jane Eyre*.

Ellie gave a sidelong glance at the patrons, several of which had stopped what they were doing and stared openly at her and Ben. Ellie studied the book, and then looked at Ben with an understanding smile.

"Thank you, sir." She took the slim volume and whisked it beneath her cloak. "Some days, I do believe I would lose my head if it were not secured to my shoulders."

"I hope you enjoy it," Ben replied sincerely.

Ellie tilted her head, her smile mischievous. "I think I shall enjoy it very much. Good day to you." And with that, she turned and left the shop. The diversion ended, the customers returned to their shopping. Ben strode through the curtain and into the back room, his heart racing. He flopped in one of the chairs around the small kitchen table in the corner with a whoosh of breath and pulled Ellie's note from his pocket.

Ben,

If you really have kept true to your promise and are still my best friend, please meet me next Tuesday at midnight in the Christ Church burial ground at 5th and Arch Streets. I am in need of help only you can give.

E —

Ben stared at the paper, willing it to give him more information. *Ellie should become a spy.* Her ability to appear from nowhere and gift for utter vagueness made her a perfect candidate. Of course he would meet her — not only had she made him insanely curious with her cryptic note, but it was another chance to see her again. Three days until Tuesday. He could wait that long.

"Ben?" His mother appeared in the doorway. "Come on out, we've more customers to take care of." She must have seen something in his expression, because she stepped into the room. "Everything all right, dear?"

Ben stuffed the note in his pocket and stood, hoping his open smile revealed nothing. "I'll be right there."

Ellie slammed the door, her heart pounding like a drum and not only because her stepmother and stepsister could be home any moment. After all these years there was finally a chance for her to break free. She set the groceries on the kitchen table, her mind whirring. Since the night she had seen Ben at the theater, she had used every spare minute to think of a way she could ask Ben for help. Being left alone in the house today had been a stroke of luck. She just had to hope Ben would come and meet her.

Ben was the perfect choice. He had recognized her at the theater, which besides being an unexpected but welcome shock, was also a relief. She had spent so long not being herself she thought she might go mad.

Her mind continued to work as she prepared a tray for tea. She needed to think about exactly what to say to Ben when she saw him next.

She added a bowl to the tray and ladled soup into it from a pot on the stove. With the tray fully laden, she carried it out of the kitchen, being careful not to spill the soup as she backed through the swinging door and into the hall.

Ellie's foot hit something soft and she tripped. A streak of gray fur bolted down the hall. It stopped at the end, gray fur resolving itself into a cat, who hissed at her. She found her balance, somehow managing to keep all of the china on the tray.

"Darn you, Clarence! Always underfoot. Why don't you go and find some mice!"

Clarence, his tail in the air, strutted into the parlor, a place the animal was permitted and she was not. *Except to dust and make the fire.* Not that she had the desire to sit on the ugly, stiff furniture that filled the room. She stepped a toe over the threshold, tempted to spill soup on the ridiculous carpet, but changed her mind. *I'd only have to clean it up anyway.*

She set the tray on the small table beside the coat rack, and caught a glimpse of herself in the gilded hall mirror.

Don't I look a fright! She was disheveled but not hopeless. With a little pushing around of her hairpins, her mop of hair returned to something presentable. Tray in hand once more, she ascended to the third floor. The hall was filled with a gray, unfocused light that brightened the space but did not make it warm or cheerful. It was as if the same cloudy skies outside today hung inside the house, darkening its spirit.

Ellie stopped at one of the four doors in the hall. She balanced the tray with one hand and opened the door. The room was dim, with heavy drapes drawn over the windows and low flames in the lamps. She set the tray on a table and turned the small knob on the wall. The room brightened as gas fed the fires, illuminating the stuffy space that smelled of camphor, sweat, and illness. There was movement in the large bed, making it seem as if the bedclothes had taken on a life of their own.

"Olivia?" moaned a voice. The light fell on the speaker as he struggled to sit up. The man seemed impossibly thin, with waxy flesh hanging from his face, as if he were a melted candle. His eyes, which looked large in his gaunt face, looked around the room but did not focus on anything. .

"Violetta, is that you?" he called again. Ellie's heart squeezed at the pain and confusion in his voice. She plastered on a smile as she gently pressed her father's shoulders down and pulled the blanket up over his chest, and choked back the tears that wanted to fall. He was getting worse.

"No, Papa, it's me. It's your daughter."

CHAPTER III

F ROST COVERED THE SPARSE GRASS GROWING IN THE SPACES BETWEEN the headstones of the cemetery. It glittered on the stones, making them appear as if they were covered with diamonds. Ellie paced between the graves, rubbing her hands together, trying to keep them warm in her thin gloves. She pulled her too-large coat closer around her and prayed that Ben would come. Once he was here, and she had told him her story, she had to believe that he wouldn't run away screaming. Or try to have her committed.

The bells of Christ Church, five blocks away, announced midnight. She was not afraid of the cemetery, not even at the so-called witching hour. Instead, the silent churchyard wrapped her in comfort like an old quilt. This place was as familiar to her as her own home. She had spent many hours here among the silent graves, pouring her heart out to the stones. Or, rather, one stone in particular.

A noise startled her. Her breath came in short puffs of white while she scanned the area. A shadow moved, but she couldn't tell if it was someone walking along the graveyard's wrought iron fence or a tree swaying in the wind. What would she do if Ben didn't come? What if he couldn't get away? What if he didn't *want* to come? *Ben, please come.*

As if willed into existence by her thoughts, a tall figure materialized in front of the cemetery entrance. The moon's half-full light shone on Ben's face as he pushed open the creaking gate and entered the graveyard.

"Ellie?" he whispered. "Are you here?"

"Over here," she whispered back.

Ben closed the gate with a clang and jogged across the graveyard.

"Sorry I'm late. I had to climb out the window and shimmy down a drainpipe, and my pants got caught." He showed her the small hole in the fabric of his pants. "My mother is going to have a fit when she sees it."

Ellie squinted at the tiny hole and rolled her eyes. Boys. Always so dramatic.

"You've only torn it on the seam. That's an easy mend." She was so pleased to see him that her smile was uncontainable. "I was so surprised to see you at the theater."

Ben's shoulders relaxed. "So was I to see you. At first I didn't think it was you, I thought... Never mind." He looked around at the scenery. "You couldn't have picked a cozier spot for a meeting?" He pulled the collar of his brown wool peacoat up around his ears. "Somewhere indoors, with a fire, maybe?"

"No, this is the perfect spot." Ellie turned toward a headstone that sat beneath a large hazel tree. Its branches stretched over the grave like a protective mother, and the few leaves left on its branches shook in the wind, sounding like a thousand whispers. A gray dove nestled in the crook of a branch, her head tucked under her wing in sleep.

The stone was large and smooth, a simple white monument with raised letters. It was whiter and looked newer than the others, some of which were over a century old. Ben read: "Violetta Schrack Banneker. Born 1839, Died 1869. Beloved Wife and Mother." He sniffed, and Ellie thought she saw a tear in the corner of his eye. "*Your* beloved mother. I'm sorry. I didn't know she was buried here."

"She's been the only one I've been able to talk to until now." Ellie crouched and stroked the stone. "I've always felt like she was watching over me. But now it's time that I took matters into my own hands."

"Ellie, I know something's wrong. " Ben inspected her clothing, the same plain blouse, skirt, and frayed coat she had worn to the bookshop. He looked her in the eye. "Whatever it is, you can tell me."

He's so sweet, Ellie thought. *When he hears my story, will he stay so loyal?* She took a deep breath and tried to slow her hammering heart. "Please, sit down."

She indicated a stone bench near her mother's grave. Ben sat, and she started to pace again. She twisted her fingers around each other, tying them into knots. *All I have to do is get the first few words out, and the rest will come.*

"It really is so good to see you, Ben." Ellie rubbed her fingers together, unable to keep her hands still. "You surprised me at the theater. More than you know. I..." She inhaled through her nose and pressed her lips together. "This is such a long story, Ben, and I want you to know all of it. I just don't know where to begin." She laughed, but tears burned behind her eyes. "Maybe I should have rehearsed it, like lines in a play."

Ben leaned forward, his arms on his knees. "Why don't you start with what happened after I last saw you. I mean, the night your stepmother fired my mother."

"That's as good a place as any, I suppose." She pulled her brows together in concentration. "First of all, you should know that your mother wasn't fired because of anything she did or didn't do."

Ben frowned a little and shrugged. "My mom is no layabout, and she worked really hard. But she loved it," he added quickly. "She was furious when she got sacked. I just figured your stepmother fired her to be mean. She never let my mother forget she was just a cook."

"She made the most wonderful meals, and she was always so kind." Ellie looked at her hands, the skin so chapped, covered by hand-me-down gloves. "At any rate, after my stepmother and father were married... it was so soon after my mother's death, do you remember?"

Ben nodded. "I thought he was loony to marry her, but then maybe that's because she was always so mean to me."

"She wasn't mean, exactly."

"Oh, you aren't defending her, are you?"

"Really, now, Ben. She was strict, but fair. You were always underfoot, whooping about like a wild animal and interrupting my lessons." Ellie tried to smother her smile, but it was impossible. "But it *was* strange, wasn't it? My father was grieving for my mother one moment and in love with another woman the next. He never even asked me how I felt about him marrying my governess. And then you were gone and then..."

Her lips puckered like purse strings. This wasn't the most difficult part, only the most embarrassing. The difficult part was yet to come. She took a deep breath, gathering her thoughts like dirty laundry. "After you and your mother left—"

"You mean after your stepmother tossed us out like the trash."

Ellie lifted an eyebrow, giving Ben a stern look. "Yes. After that night, everything was fine, or at least as fine as it could be. My father was inconsolable after Mother died, but when he remarried he was happy. My stepmother hired a new governess to teach Rebecca and me, and it was all perfectly normal. We went shopping and out to tea. She didn't exactly dote on me, not like she does Rebecca, which I suppose was to be expected. But she was kind enough, in her own way.

"About six months after my father and stepmother were married, something changed. My father came into my room that morning and kissed me goodbye, just like always. He left for work. He hadn't been gone more than a minute when Olivia came in and..." She waved her hand over her dress. "This happened."

Ben looked more closely at her clothing, and his eyes grew wide as realization struck him. "What are you saying, Ellie?"

Ellie closed her eyes and let the words pour out. "That for the last seven years I have been caring for my family. As their servant. I do the laundry, cook the meals, clean the house, and light the fires. All of it. I sleep in the attic."

Ben sat back, half-formed words falling from his mouth. "This doesn't make any kind of sense at all."

"I know it doesn't." Ellie knew how it must sound. What would he think when he heard the rest? "It's not as bad as all that. I'm lucky she didn't send me off to work in a mill, or to an orphanage."

"Your father wouldn't allow it." Something broke across his face. "And what about him? Why didn't he put a stop to it? I remember him being a good man." Ben jumped to his feet, angry. "How could he allow his wife —" he made a face, as if the word was bitter " — to treat you like this?"

Ellie crossed her arms over her chest, hugging herself tight. This was going to be more difficult than she thought. "He doesn't know."

Ben staggered backward, his mouth falling open. "Was he struck blind and dumb? How could he not know?"

Ellie could understand his anger. She had felt it herself, many times over. But now that he was on the path, she had to remain calm enough to lead him down it.

"I tried to tell him, that very first night. I didn't even cry, because I didn't want to seem like a spoiled child complaining about her wicked stepmother." A single fat tear rolled down her cheek. "But he didn't believe me. She had me cleaned up by the time he came home. He was so angry, said the most awful things — that I was jealous of my stepmother, making up stories so that he would send her away. I thought he didn't love me anymore." She wiped her eyes with the back of her hand, and forced back the rest of her tears. "After that he only had eyes for Olivia. I became invisible. Now he's... gone... most of the time."

Ben nodded. "He's in France, right? I overheard Olivia telling Mr. Van Wyck at the theater."

Ellie bit her lower lip, but said nothing. It was just one more complication, another distraction from the real problem.

Ben pounded one fist against the other. "Ellie, they're treating you like a slave! Why don't you just run away?"

Ellie pinned him with her clear, steady gaze. It wasn't like she hadn't thought of the same thing a hundred times. "Where would I go? I have no money of my own."

"To my house. My mother would be happy to see you. She would take you in, no questions asked. You can leave tonight." He paused, taking in Ellie's small, understanding smile before sitting on the bench again. "Of course you don't want to live in my drafty, cramped little house."

"Oh, Ben, no! It's not that at all." She furrowed her brow, trying to make him understand. "I appreciate the offer, more than I can say. But I can't leave Papa behind."

"Why not? He's ignored what your stepmother had done to you. Let you be turned into a servant. It's criminal. You don't owe him anything." Ben's voice rose.

"Shh!" She glanced toward the churchyard gate, but they were still alone.

"What about your father's friends? Surely one of them could help—"

She shook her head, stopping him before he could go any further. "My stepmother has, over the course the years, managed to remove me from the world. I never met most of my father's friends when my mother was alive." She was getting to the heart of the problem, but she wanted to ease Ben along, rather than spring it on him unawares. It was strange enough without being shocked with it.

Ben's anger deflated a bit. "I saw you at the theater."

"Yes, I go out, of course. I do the household shopping. And now that Rebecca's come of age, I accompany her as a lady's companion. My stepmother tells everyone I'm her poor niece that she's taken in out of the goodness of her heart. It makes her and Rebecca look good to those on the Philadelphia Social Register, and it gives Olivia a chance to rub in how she's destroyed my life. On the rare occasion anyone happens to ask after me, my stepmother spins a story about my being at a finishing school in Europe."

Ben only looked more confused. "How is she able to get away with these lies? You're right there in front of them, surely everyone sees how much you look like your mother."

The moment of truth had arrived. Ellie folded her hands and prayed for strength. "That's... complicated. I want to explain it to you, and I want you to listen to everything I have to say before you respond. Do I have your word?"

Ben sat back, his arms over his chest. "Ellie, what's the matter? You look terrified."

"Just promise me."

Ben nodded. "You know you can trust me, Ellie. "

There was no going back. Ellie steeled herself and forced the words past the lump in her throat. "It's the real reason I asked you here, Ben. I need your help."

"Whatever you need, you know you can ask."

Ellie held up her hand, reminding him of his promise to let her finish. "I need for you to help me... break the spell my stepmother has put on me and my father."

The words were like a steam train, starting slow then coming all in a rush. Ben stared at her for a moment, his wide eyes reflecting the moonlight. Then he narrowed them, looking at her as if she had spoken in a foreign language. But he remained silent this time, so she continued.

"Someone, most likely my stepmother, has placed a spell over me and my father. Bewitched me, in fact, and stolen my father's free will. And I need for you to help me release the two of us."

Ben's look of complete and total befuddlement continued, which did nothing to raise Ellie's hopes.

"The reason I was so surprised that you recognized me at the theater was because *no one* has recognized me for six and a half years." She paused to keep her voice steady. Turning into a hysterical madwoman would send Ben screaming into the night. "You said it yourself – why is my stepmother able to pass me off as her niece, when I look so much like my mother?"

Ben's nod was slow, his eyebrows creeping ever further up his forehead.

"You were absolutely right. Not one person has ever questioned my stepmother's story. Not once has anyone commented on how much I remind them of my mother, or asked if perhaps I was my own cousin, or suggested that Olivia's niece would be about the age of Ephraim Banneker's daughter."

She paused to let her words sink in. "At first I didn't recognize what was happening. When I was younger I didn't go out very often, and children are supposed to be seen and not heard. So it didn't seem odd that no one acknowledged me. But when I began to accompany Rebecca on outings, it became clear that no one could see my real face. I can't explain it beyond that. When I look in the mirror, I see my own face and for some inexplicable reason so do you. But I will swear to you that everyone else sees something different."

Ben inhaled and held up a finger, stopping Ellie's words. "But why don't you just *tell* people who you are?"

Ellie opened her mouth to remind him again of his promise, but stopped. It was a good question. "I've tried, Ben. Many times. But every time I open my mouth, the words will not come out."

"What do you mean? All you have to say is 'I'm Eleanor Banneker; please help me escape from this insane and evil woman'." The look on Ben's face almost made Ellie stop, take it all back. But she closed her eyes and pressed on.

"I can't. That is what I am trying to tell you. I hear the words in my mind, but when I try to say them it's as if I've been struck dumb. Watch." She cleared her throat. "My name is E… E–" She tried to cough up the rest of the words, but as always, they stuck in her throat like a lump of cold oatmeal. She threw up her hands in exasperation. "You see, I told you."

Ben scratched his cheek, and Ellie could almost see the gears of his mind turning, trying to come up with a diplomatic answer.

"All right, that's a problem. But it's not magic. You've probably been hypnotized, or mesmerized or something. I've seen it done on stage. A man waves his pocket watch, the girl falls asleep, and the next thing you know, she's clucking like a chicken. Your stepmother has hypnotized you so that you can't say your own name."

"This from the boy who used to believe in faeries and bogeymen?" Ellie's voice squeaked as she tried to keep her emotions under control. Ben used to be afraid of her dolls. What had caused such a change in him?

He solved the mystery with a dismissive wave of his hand. "All things in storybooks, meant to scare children. I've spent years learning about how the tricks are done, Ellie. There's no such thing as real magic."

This wasn't going as Ellie had hoped, but much closer to how she feared. "Hypnotism might explain how I can't say my own name, but it doesn't explain why no one recognizes me." She wished she could show Ben the cold but polite looks that her parents' friends gave her in the street or in the shops. Quiet nods when Olivia introduced Ellie as Ann Gibson, her niece.

"You said it yourself, I look exactly like my mother. How can anyone with eyes not see it? Did she manage to hypnotize the entire city, except for you?"

Ben pulled his brows low and then stood, taking her place in pacing along the path. "But, Ellie, be logical. I can wave a wand and make something appear or disappear, but it's only an illusion. There's always a trapdoor, or something hidden up my sleeve. Something to make you *think* what you're seeing is real. Remember when I used to pull coins out of your hair?"

Ellie was prepared for his objections. "That's a very reasonable thing to say, except that it's not only strangers who don't recognize me." Tears threatened and she pushed them back. Now was not the time to fall apart. "It's my father, too. Remember what I said about him not seeing me?"

That made Ben come to a stop, his mouth open, and Ellie knew she had his full attention. "You said you became... invisible." It was obvious he was connecting the points she had laid for him.

"It wasn't just him choosing his wife over me. After that argument, he drifted further away, and eventually he did not *see me* anymore. I could be standing right in front of him and he wouldn't acknowledge me." The tears fought their way through the carefully constructed wall she had built around her heart, remembering the pain of a ten year-old girl who lost one parent to death and the other to something she couldn't understand. "He hasn't said my name since. Not once."

Ben rubbed his forehead with his fingertips, as if he had a headache. "So Olivia hypnotized him too, then. Ellie, that's the only thing that makes sense. As for why people don't recognize you, well, I think people of a certain class can't be bothered to concern themselves with other people's problems. They're too busy caring only about themselves and how wealthy they are."

"You realize, of course, that *I* would be one of those same people if not for my stepmother's schemes?" This was going all wrong—she didn't want to fight with Ben, not when she finally had him to talk to. She needed him to listen and believe her.

Ben must have realized he had gone too far. He spluttered, his tongue tripping over his words. "Well, no, of course not. Your mother was an exception, you know. She was different. She wouldn't have let you turn one of those primped and pampered girls. Like Rebecca. I'll bet she's a real piece of work."

"Leave my stepsister alone," Ellie snapped. "She has been nothing but kind, and I don't think she's involved in any way." It wasn't the total truth. Rebecca and she weren't exactly friendly. Their relationship could be called carefully optimistic. But Ellie wouldn't let Ben tear down people who were unable to defend themselves.

"So, your father doesn't remember you, for whatever reason, and now he's halfway around the world, enjoying the high life in France. And you *still* want to stay?"

"Yes, I do. If he's under a spell —"

"Or, more likely, hypnotized," Ben interrupted. He had already made up his mind, and the conversation had already gone far off the rails. Ellie didn't want to argue the point any longer. "Either way, he didn't do it to himself. He isn't... ignoring me on purpose." She didn't want to explain about his illness today. Ben would be sympathetic, maybe even offer to take them both away. But there was nothing Ben could do for him. Even the doctor hadn't been able to figure out what was wrong. Moving him wasn't an option, her stepmother would never allow it, and besides, she wanted Ben's help, not his pity. It was her burden to bear, at least for now. If she could just get her father to recognize her, maybe he would improve. Maybe he would fight to get better. It was all she had to hold on to.

"I have proof."

That stopped Ben cold. He didn't suddenly believe Ellie was under a spell, but he was curious. She could see it in his face.

"I found this hidden under my stepmother's jewelry box." She pulled a sheet of paper from her pocket and handed it to Ben. "Actually it's just a copy. I couldn't take a chance she'd find it missing." In truth it had been stuck to the bottom of the box and Ellie had found it a month ago during her weekly cleaning. Her father's worsening condition had made her bold, and she had been searching for any money that her stepmother might have been hiding. If the worst happened, Ellie would need to make an expedient exit from the house. Ben was right about one thing—without her father, there was no reason for her to stay.

He unfolded the piece of flimsy, cheap paper. The pencil was smudged but readable. He scanned it quickly, then looked at Ellie, eyebrow raised in question.

"You see? The first one looks like a recipe for tea, but it's a love potion. The second one...

"Well, you can see for yourself it's a Bewitching Spell." She rushed the words together and went on before he had a chance to reply. "Both of them say you need something from the person that you are casting the spell on, to bind it to them. Look, I found this in the envelope." Ellie dipped her fingers into her pocket and pulled out a curl of chestnut hair, tied with a short length of crimson ribbon. "It's mine. I didn't find a lock of my father's but she must have it, or something else, somewhere that made the love spell work. She did this, Ben. She made my father fall in love with her, and then bewitched me to make me invisible to him and everyone else."

Ben, paper still in his fingers, pressed the heels of his hands to his eyes.

"All right, the tea I might believe. Not as a love potion," he said quickly. "But there are plenty of things in the world that can make people feel good and see things. Laudanum, absinthe, gin. Maybe there's something in that tea that makes someone feel like they're in love. As for the other, I'll say again that there's no such thing as spells and magic. You can't say a few words and tie a ribbon around a lock of hair and expect things to happen." He held the paper out to Ellie and shook it. "All this proves is that your stepmother is a lunatic."

The words stung like a slap to the face.

"And me too, I suppose?" She snatched the paper from Ben's fingers. She wasn't crazy. "I've proved to you that I can't even say my own name. That is real, no matter the cause." Her cheeks burned with embarrassment, tears she refused to shed stung the backs of her eyes. Despite her instincts, and her hope, maybe this had been a mistake.

"I didn't mean... Ellie, I just want you to be reasonable," Ben muttered.

Ellie needed to get out of there before she said something she would regret. "Fine, then. I'll just figure out a way to fix this on my own. All I want is my life and my father back." She pulled the copy of *Jane Eyre* he had given her from her pocket and shoved it at him. "And you need to take this back to your mother before she misses it."

Fuming, she left him standing in the cemetery, mouth open, the book clutched against his chest as she stalked away, leaving the gate clanking in her wake.

Ben stood for a moment in the graveyard, wondering what had just happened. One minute they had been having a conversation, the next she had gone. He had only been trying to make her see reason, so why had she gotten so upset? Part of him wanted to believe her, to go back to that childlike faith in fairies and magic beans. But the rest of him knew it just wasn't possible.

The one thing he did know for certain was that he couldn't leave things the way they were, with Ellie mad at him. He ran out of the churchyard and onto the sidewalk, looking right and left to see which way she had gone. He caught a glimpse of the tail of her coat as it whipped around the corner a block away. By the time he reached the corner, she was already two blocks ahead, her strutting form appearing and disappearing in the pools of light cast by the streetlamps. Ben started after her again, amazed at how fast such a slight thing could move.

CHAPTER IV

ELLIE DID NOT LOOK BACK AS SHE WALKED AWAY FROM THE CEMETERY. She was furious to the point of trembling, but with herself more than with Ben. What had she expected — that he would just believe her wild tale out of hand? While friendship counted for something, or should have, how could he be expected to just nod and smile and swallow such a story whole? She should have come up with a better plan, rather than just blurting it out the way she had.

She rounded the corner, her anger burning fresh. He *should* have taken her word for it, should have accepted that she had thought of all of the other explanations before coming to such an unbelievable conclusion. Maybe seven years was too long to expect a promise to last. Maybe she had been foolish to believe it would. They had been ten years old, just a pair of foolish children that believed the world was good.

The wind blew around her like angry spirits, ghosts chasing her down the sidewalk. Carved pumpkins smiled at her with wicked grins from several stoops. The festive gourds didn't frighten her — she lived with Olivia Banneker, after all. Neither did the sound of footsteps behind her. She stopped and turned, and there was Ben, running like the hounds of Hell were on his heels.

He skidded to a stop a few feet before he could barrel her over.

"Can I help you, Mr. Grimm?" She was still angry with him, but the sight of him standing there, red-faced and gasping for breath, made her want to smile. She held it in, however, not wanting to give him the satisfaction of seeing her anger so easily assuaged.

Ben leaned over, hands on his knees, trying to catch his breath. He held up a finger, asking for another moment before he answered her. At last, he stood upright, his face its usual color again.

He looked up at the sky and took a deep breath. "I shouldn't have said those things to you, Ellie. I'm sorry."

Ellie pressed her lips together and straightened her shoulders. "No, it's good that you did. At least I know how you stand, instead of having you lie to me to make me feel better, then treat me like I was made of glass because you think I'm not mentally stable."

Ben pulled his brows low and let out a long whistle. "That was a mouthful. But, no, I am truly sorry. What you told me was just... unbelievable. But, ah, that doesn't mean it's impossible." He gagged his brain, which wanted to add an, *I guess*. The only thing he knew for certain was that *she* believed every word. "I was just surprised. And, if you're still speaking to me, I'll help you."

Ellie's face brightened, but there was a hint of skepticism beneath. "Really? You're not just doing this to placate a girl you think has gone off her rocker? "

Ben held a hand to his chest. "Now I'm the one that's insulted. But I suppose I deserve it. I promise that this is a genuine offer of help."

"Well, then, in that case, you should take this." She pulled the sheet of paper from her pocket and handed it to Ben. "In all the stories, there's always a way to break a spell. We just have to figure out what it is."

Without warning, Ellie threw her arms around Ben's neck. "Oh, thank you. You don't know what this means to me."

Ben stiffened in her embrace, then wrapped his arms around her and squeezed her tightly, pulling her body against his. It was soft and pleasant, and he discovered that he would happily have stayed there until the sun rose. He inhaled her scent, wanting desperately to wind his fingers in her hair. He had just gotten comfortable when Ellie pulled away so quickly she almost tripped over her skirt.

"I'm so sorry, Ben." She held her hands to her mouth, her eyes wide. "You must think I'm the worst kind of girl."

Ben's voice got caught in his throat. "Please, don't be upset. I promise I don't think any less of you." He tried not to laugh at her look of consternation.

Ellie straightened her coat, her cheeks glowing in the lamplight. "I don't usually go around throwing myself at men." She pulled her brow low, reacting to his lifted eyebrows and open mouth. "What? What is that look?"

"You called me a man."

Ellie looked confused. "Well you are, aren't you?"

Ben crossed his arms over his chest. "I guess I am, sure. You're just the first person to ever say it."

It was Ellie's turn to look surprised. "Oh. I see. Well, good, then I'm glad I got to be the first, I suppose." She pulled away from him a little more, and shifted her feet, unsure what to say next.

"Oh, wait!" Ben reached into his coat pocket and pulled out a heavy bundle. "I almost forgot—I brought you a gift. I made it, actually." He held the small package wrapped in muslin and tied up with twine, out to her.

Ellie took it gently, her face still flushed. "Ben, you didn't have to bring me a thing. I don't have anything for you."

"Don't think anything of it. I just… it was in my workshop and I thought you should have it."

An awkward silence dropped over them. Ben, trying to lighten the mood, made a small bow and held his elbow out to Ellie.

"Miss Banneker, may I escort you home?"

Ellie said goodbye to Ben at her back gate, both the package and the copy of *Jane Eyre* tucked into her pocket. Ben had insisted that she keep it and that his mother would never miss it. She did not argue, because they had done too much of that for one evening. If the truth were being told, she wanted the book.

Such a good friend, she thought as she opened the back door. She unbuttoned her coat and hung it on the rack. Their brief embrace clung to her thoughts. Though it had been unbelievably forward it had not been unpleasant. And hadn't he looked dashing as he ran down the street?

She giggled and clapped her hands over her mouth, remembering that she was supposed to be sneaking. *Oh, you ridiculous girl! All you need is the white horse and a tall tower.* He was a friend, nothing more. The excitement of the evening drained away, slipping into the quiet and dark, leaving behind a drowsiness that made her feel as if lead weights had been tied to every extremity.

She crept up the servants' stairs toward the third floor. Her climb was practically silent; she had snuck out enough times to know each and every creaky board and step. She opened the door and found her way down the dark hall by touch.

"This is not what I asked for!"

Ellie froze, her hand poised on the attic doorknob. She turned in the direction of the scathing whisper. A thin band of flickering golden light peeked from beneath her stepmother's door.

Why in the world is she still awake? Olivia had been in the parlor when Ellie had pretended to go to bed. She had still been there around 11:30 when Ellie had snuck out to meet Ben. Her stepmother being up so late when she was not attending a party was unheard of. Usually she was snoring like a saw mill by 10:30.

Why couldn't she wait until morning to talk to Rebecca? Ellie's step-sister was the only one that would be in Olivia's bedchamber, especially at this time of the morning. *Unless...* the rest of the idea was enough to make her want to vomit. Her stepmother wasn't so callous as to have another man in her bedroom, with her ailing husband right across the hall, was she? Ellie wasn't naïve; she knew some ladies had dalliances with other men, for various reasons. Their husbands were always away, or simply neglected them, or they got bored. Servants talk, so she had heard all the rumors as she shopped in the market.

Ellie's queasiness turned to anger. She couldn't care less what her stepmother did in her bed — but her poor father! She stepped across the hall to her stepmother's bedroom door, ready to rip open the door and expose her stepmother's adultery.

"You got exactly what you asked for," someone replied, and Ellie put her hand over her mouth to stifle a gasp. The voice did not sound male. It barely sounded human. The only word to describe it was otherworldly. She leaned closer to better hear the conversation inside.

"You cannot think I wanted this." Olivia sounded furious and upset, a combination Ellie was well familiar with.

"That is not the point. You and I had an agreement. It is not my fault you did not understand it," the visitor said matter-of-factly. "There is always a price to pay. You said you would do anything to get what you wanted. I took you at your word, and you signed the contract."

"But why my husband?" Olivia's words came out as a strangled cry. "Why not his miserable brat instead?"

Ellie's ears perked up at the mention of her father. What did Olivia mean? She didn't even flinch at the rest. She had no idea what she had done to make her stepmother dislike her so vehemently, but her insults no longer stung.

Apparently, the visitor had no answer to Olivia's question. There was only the scuffle of feet, as if someone were rising from a chair. Footsteps moved toward the door, and Ellie backed into the shadows.

"I thought you did not really love him?" the visitor said with a touch of accusation. "When we made our bargain, you said he was merely a means to an end."

The bedroom doorknob rattled. Ellie quietly pulled open the attic door and hid on the bottom step. She peered through the crack between the door and the jamb. Something made her stay and look—she needed to see this mysterious person. The dark shadow of her stepmother's bedroom doorway turned lighter as the door creaked open. A lamp floated into the open space, illuminating the hand that held it. Ellie's stepmother walked into the hall, the light glittering on the gold locket she always wore.

Olivia stumbled over her words for a moment. "It's nothing to do with that. If he dies before my daughter married, then all of this will have been for nothing. I cannot believe you can't cure him."

The visitor chuckled, and the sound of it made Ellie shiver.

"I didn't say I couldn't. But everything has a price, as I said. If you would like to make *another* bargain with me—"

"I have had enough of your bargains. They have brought me nothing but misery."

The visitor stepped from behind Olivia, but all Ellie could see was a long, dark cloak. He or she was shorter than Olivia by at least six inches. The cloak had a voluminous hood, dousing the visitor in shadows. Ellie's skin broke out in gooseflesh, and she was suddenly overcome by a strange chill.

"As I've explained, you got exactly what you wanted. I fulfilled my end of the contract to the letter."

Olivia straightened her shoulders and jutted out her chin, standing her ground with the visitor. "If you will not help me, then this will be our last meeting. You are no longer welcome in my home."

"*Your* home?" The visitor's odd voice sounded even stranger now that Ellie could hear it without the door between them. She—Ellie had decided it was a she—chuckled again. "Are you sure about that?"

Olivia puckered her lips in a look of white-hot anger that Ellie well recognized. "Leave now."

The visitor headed for the stairs. Ellie almost burst from her hiding place, demanding to know what she knew about her father's illness and how she could help. But the words and her muscles turned to ice as the visitor turned and faced Olivia. Two glowing eyes, bright as stars, pierced the darkness of the hall. For a moment the visitor hesitated in Ellie's direction. Thinking she was caught, she slid deeper into the shadows.

"Do not dismiss me so lightly," the visitor hissed. "You do not understand the depths of my power."

Ellie remained where she was, unable to move, until she heard both the front door and her stepmother's bedroom door close. She climbed the stairs and felt her way across a cleared space to the small wooden table and lit her tiny oil lamp. Its bright, warm glow did nothing to stave off the chill, either from the air or inside Ellie's heart.

What had she just witnessed? A meeting between her stepmother and who, or — she didn't relish the idea — what? When she was young her grandmother had told her stories about the Fae and their strange and tricky ways, their eyes that glowed like fireflies. She tried to tell herself that the visitor's glowing eyes were only a trick of the light and her imagination running away with her, but was not able to convince herself completely. Believing in magic was one thing, but Ben was right, faeries were just for stories.

All of the old junk had been moved to the far end of the attic, leaving a cleared space at the top of the stairs. To one side was Ellie's bed, a flattened feather mattress resting atop a battered iron frame, covered in old quilts. She bypassed her tiny sleeping space and headed toward the piles at the back. There wasn't much more here than there was when she was a child. Her stepmother had sold all of her mother's furniture to pay for a houseful of new, expensive and ridiculously uncomfortable furnishings. But what remained in the attic looked as if it filled much more space than it should.

Ellie dropped to her hands and knees and crawled forward, the book and package in one hand, pushing the lamp along with the other. She squeezed through a hole in the pile of junk, just big enough for her small frame. The roof was made of trunks and books, bridged between two old leather portmanteaus.

A rabbit hole.

She emerged on the other side, the soft light flickering over a little cluster of furniture arranged around a low, chipped marble-top table. Fortunately her stepmother couldn't be bothered to clear out the attic, only shoving things around to make room for Ellie's sleeping quarters. She never came upstairs so Ellie had been able to create this place without any trouble.

She straightened and set the lamp on the table, sitting on the dusty love seat, the book and muslin-wrapped package in her lap. Sleep had been driven from her mind, though it clung to her body. The conversation between her stepmother and the strange visitor echoed in her mind, and she tried to make sense of it. Her stepmother had made some sort of bargain, signed a contract with the visitor. Ellie put aside the fact that her stepmother could not sign a contract without her husband's consent, as the law required. Whatever the bargain was, it had to do with Ellie's father's illness. She didn't see how it was possible—how could anyone make another person sick? Poison? No, her father wasn't being poisoned, because Ellie made all of his food, what little he ate.

She turned sideways on the seat, lifting her feet to the cushion, and let her thoughts follow the path of her father's life since she had known him. Ellie's little-girl memory painted him as so vibrant, and devoted to his family. When Mother died, he had been deeply sad, sitting and staring out the window for hours. Then suddenly he was surprisingly happy, and married Olivia. He had turned strange after that, his eyes only for his second wife as he ignored his only child, and finally so ill he could barely sit up and recognized no one.

Olivia seemed to genuinely care for her father, at least at first. Then something had happened, like a pane of glass had slipped between them. Ellie didn't know what it was, only that it had happened about the same time she had turned so cold toward her stepdaughter. Despite that, her stepmother had been concerned when the illness struck. She had summoned a doctor immediately. The doctor had given him a thorough examination but couldn't tell them what was wrong. He had prescribed rest, hot soup, some disgusting sticky syrup, and predicted a quick recovery. No doctor had stepped foot in the house since. With her father's worsening illness, so had Olivia's panic risen.

What could Olivia know about it? Her father's illness wasn't anything strange, though it was resistant to treatment. That wasn't unusual, though. Plenty of people had illnesses, even died from them, like pneumonia or consumption. The thought made a shiver run through Ellie. *Could* that strange visitor really cure him? Though the idea terrified her, she would find it within herself to ask, if only she knew who the visitor was. Her father was more important than her fear. Whatever the price, Ellie would pay it.

Her heart heavy, she lay back and sighed. Morning was only a few hours away, but her mind whirred like a sewing machine. She put *Jane Eyre* aside and placed the package on the table. With two fingers, she pulled the end of the twine, undoing the bow in one motion. The muslin fell off and the item inside clunked against the table. It was a bird, no bigger than the palm of her hand, made completely of metal. Ellie moved her head to look at it from all sides, amazed at the detail Ben had managed with nothing but brass and copper. A small key stuck out from the back, and she turned it carefully with two fingers.

The bird sprung to life. Its head cocked, so that it studied Ellie with a quizzical look. Its beak opened and closed, but there was no sound. The little bird flapped its wings, though it was too heavy to fly, and hopped a few steps across the table before jumping high into the air, turning completely around, and hopping back. It did this three or four times before it slowed and then finally stopped.

Ellie scooped up the wonderful little bird and held it to her chest. What a lovely gift! She would have to hide both the bird and the book, or else her stepmother would take them and destroy them. She sighed and leaned back against the loveseat, the strange turn of events once again clouding her thoughts.

She might not lead the most pleasant life, but until today it had been predictable and stable, like a train, chugging along its designated route, safe on the tracks. Ellie suddenly felt as if her engine had turned into a runaway locomotive.

CHAPTER V

BEN MOVED THROUGH THE CROWD, WHICH WAS PACKED SO TIGHTLY he felt like he would suffocate before reaching the gate. He cursed the people around him for being so slow and at the same time he willed them to move faster. The Centennial Exposition had been going on for six months now — surely most of the people who wanted to visit had already done so, hadn't they?

Apparently not. Ben tried not to let his annoyance show as yet another person elbowed him in the ribs. He was too excited to allow a simple excess of people to spoil this day for him. The weather was crisp but beautiful, he was out in the fresh air, and was about to enter the place that had dogged his thoughts for two weeks. Ever since the girl in the shop had mentioned the amazing machines that were on display here in Fairmount Park, Ben had dreamed of seeing them with his own eyes, especially the giant steam engine. When Ellie had sent him a note two days ago, asking him to meet her there, it was as if Fate had smiled on him.

It had been no easy feat to get to the Exposition. First there was the scheduling issue. Working at both the theater and the bookshop, plus running around in the middle of the night meeting pretty girls didn't leave much time for riding halfway across the city to stroll through the park. Then there was the problem of money. He needed the fare to ride the horse-drawn trolley to the gate, and then there was the admission fee to the Expo itself — fifty cents, which could only be paid with paper scrip, which didn't exactly grow in a garden. It had pained him to do so, but he had dipped into his savings, money he had been hoarding to fund his illusionist career. But if what he had come to see — besides Ellie — was half as amazing as it sounded, it would be worth every penny.

Ben handed his money to the man at the gate, almost crying as he watched it go, and pushed his way inside. He found a spot where he could stop and get a sense of the place. The park was enormous —

hundreds of acres dotted by a series of buildings, their peaked roofs like sailboats floating along on a sea of people. Off in the distance stood a large building with a huge glass dome that sparkled in the weak autumn light.

Ben took it all in, trying not to look as overwhelmed as he felt. Ellie had asked him to meet her, but not for hours yet. So he decided to find the very things he ached to see. He spotted a map nearby, surrounded, like everything else, by a mob of people.

He weaved his way through the throng and got a look. There were dozens of buildings, all over the park. How would he find the right one?

"I believe you're looking for the Machinery Hall," a gentle voice said over his shoulder. He turned around and came face to face with a young woman about his own age. She was on the plump side and looked vaguely familiar.

"Excuse me?" he said. "How did you know...?"

The girl held her gloved hand to her ample chest, her cheeks blooming in a blush. "Oh, I'm sorry. You just look like you might be looking for the giant steam engine. And I happen to know it's in the Machinery Hall." She walked up to the map and pointed to a drawing of a long building on the far side of the park. She faced Ben again, he finally recognized her, and suddenly wondered why God hated him. *A million people in this place, and I run into Rebecca Gibson.*

Ben looked around for Olivia, knowing the mother hen would never stray far from her chick. He spotted the woman a few yards away, looking disgusted at the jostling crowd. Ellie stood behind her. She wore a plain blue walking dress, not as flattering as the evening gown, but still very pretty. Ben's heartbeat sped up when she swiveled her head his way. He caught her eye and she smiled, raising her hand as if to wave. But she must have noticed who Ben stood with, because her eyes expanded like a pair of hot air balloons. She covered her surprise by snapping her gaze down and brushing a speck of dust from the front of her dress. She gazed at him cautiously from beneath the brim of her hat. Ben gave a tiny apologetic shrug, although he didn't know why. It wasn't as if he had planned on starting up a conversation with her stepsister.

Fortunately, Rebecca didn't seem to recognize him. A more pressing problem was that Olivia might see him, and he was afraid she *would* recognize him. Because she was just that mean, and he was just that unlucky. So he put his back to Ellie and her stepmother, hoping the crowd would bar him from view.

"Oh, uh, the Machinery Hall? Thank you."

Rebecca smiled. "You're very welcome. I want to go there myself. I can't believe the stories I've heard, they sound so fantastic. I don't think I'll believe any of it until I see the machines for myself."

"Really?" Ben was genuinely surprised. "You like machines?"

Rebecca nodded and looked at the ground shyly. "I mean, most of them are noisy and smelly, but they fascinate me. I like to know how they work. Gears and steam, and engines that roar." She gazed wistfully toward the other end of the fairgrounds, where a train's whistle pierced the air. She leaned in close, allowing Ben to get a whiff of her lavender perfume. "I'll tell you a secret, but only if I can trust you. Can I?"

Ben shrugged, then nodded. "Of course, I suppose."

"I've taken apart my father's pocket watch and put it back together five times. And it still works." There was a note of pride in her voice, reflected in the glint in her eye and her sly smile. She glanced over her shoulder. "My mother would murder me if she knew."

Ben scratched his head. Unlike the evening at the theater, Rebecca looked happy today, her round face glowing. And now that he was close enough to get a proper look, he realized her childhood plumpness had migrated both North and South, supplying her with a set of womanly curves that Ben could only describe as voluptuous. As much as he would like to continue the conversation — he still couldn't believe a girl had an interest in machines — he couldn't take a chance that her memory wouldn't suddenly return. He needed to make a quick and smooth exit.

"I'm sorry, but I really need to go. My… wife is waiting for me."

Rebecca raised an eyebrow.

"Your wife?" She studied Ben's face, probably trying to figure out how old he was. He was almost offended. There were men his age already married. He was old enough to have children, though the idea made his throat tighten.

"How long have you been married?" Rebecca turned her head right and left, scanning the crowd.

Yes, Ben, that was smooth as glass. Ben mentally slapped himself in the head. "Did I say wife? Uh, no, sorry, I mean, my sister. She's, um…

over there." He pointed vaguely in the direction of the buildings. "Thank you again for your help."

"Oh." Rebecca looked disappointed, as if she had expected them to go to the Machinery Hall together. *There's as good a chance of that as of Hell becoming well-known for its ice sculptures.* It was nothing against Rebecca. She seemed like a pleasant girl, and Ben actually felt bad for lying to her. Under other circumstances Ben might even have enjoyed a walk to the Machinery Hall with her and Ellie, but right now he needed to get and stay as far away from her mother as he could. Rebecca looked up at him with big, brown eyes, and he realized she had a rather pretty face. *Must be from her father's side.*

Ben tried to ease her feelings. "Maybe I'll see you there?"

Rebecca's face brightened. "Maybe you will."

Ben left, thanking God he had escaped unscathed. He moved through the crowd, heading in the direction of the Machinery Hall. Eventually, he relaxed and slowed down enough to see the many marvels along his way. A series of buildings had been erected on both sides of a paved walking path. Each belonged to a country, and each reflected their country's historical architecture. Ben approached the Japanese Building, with its slat-framed windows of paper and a porch topped with a triangular roof that swooped up on the ends. Inside contained displays of Japanese calligraphy, amazing watercolor paintings, and pottery.

A large statue, made of dark, polished stone, sat on a pedestal in the center of the building. Candles covered the lower levels of the pedestal, and the placard said it was an image of the god Buddha. Ben thought he seemed a cheerful fellow and perhaps some of the dour priests, with their talk of fire and brimstone, could take a lesson from him.

He left the country area and went on, where he came upon the strangest thing he had seen by far. A great copper arm, standing free in the middle of an open area. It jutted upward from the earth, as if someone had buried a giant and run out of dirt before the job was finished. The hand held a flaming torch, flames frozen in time. A few people walked around the balcony at the base of the flame, and Ben was stumped as to how they got all the way up there, for there was no ladder or stairs in evidence. He stared at it for a few moments, but could not figure out what it was or its purpose. A tent had been erected around the arm's base, and three men stood inside, selling tickets through an open flap. He walked along one side of the queue and looked up at the sign posted above the ticket window.

"Visit the arm of the Statue of Liberty." Ben read. "Walk the stairs inside and see the spectacular view from the torch's balcony. Admission: Fifty Cents." *That's a lot of money just to walk inside an arm. For the whole body, maybe, but just the arm?*

A tap on the shoulder interrupted his train of thought. Ben jumped in surprise and spun around.

"Hello."

Ellie laughed—she had startled Ben on purpose. He scanned the area, as if searching for someone.

"They're inside." She gave a small nod in the direction of the gigantic limb. She leaned in close to him and whispered. "Between you and me, I think it's very odd."

"So do I," Ben replied. "Why just an arm? Where's the rest?"

"Apparently, it's the only part they could afford. The admission money is all going toward funding the rest of the statue. It's supposed to be a great lady when it's finished, and they're going to erect it in New York Harbor."

Ben crossed his arms over his chest and considered the limb again.

"I see. That explains a lot, but I still wouldn't pay fifty cents to see the inside. Why didn't you go up with... uh..."

"With what passes for my family?"

Ben nodded, and Ellie could see he had been thinking the same thing, only he was too polite to say it out loud.

"First of all, my stepmother could barely part with the whole dollar it cost for the two of them. You wouldn't know it to see the way she and Rebecca dress, but my stepmother can be very tight-fisted. Secondly, I didn't really want to go." Her gaze moved to the copper flame, frozen in time, and traveled down the arm as if measuring every inch. She opened her mouth, then closed it again. "It's a good thing I didn't go, because now we can move up our appointment. Mr. Grimm, would you care to be my escort?"

Ben stepped away. "Are you sure? I don't want to get on the wrong side of the great and terrible Olivia Banneker."

Ellie brushed the question away. "You're being much too cautious. I had planned on slipping away to meet you, so what's six of one is a half dozen of the other, as they say. When she can't find me, perhaps she'll hope I've finally run away."

"But won't you be scandalized, being escorted by a man without a chaperone?"

"We're surrounded by people. Who, besides you and my family, even knows my name? You could very well be my husband, for all these people know, and it's perfectly acceptable for a husband and wife to go out walking together." The words fell from Ellie's lips as naturally as her own name should have, and until she heard herself speak them she didn't realize what implications they might have. Her cheeks burned, though her stomach fluttered. "Oh, unless you don't want to pretend? Would you rather I be your sister?"

Ben, who seemed at a sudden loss for words, pulled on his collar, swallowed hard and shook his head. "I just… don't want to cause a problem."

"You aren't," Ellie replied. "If I get into trouble, I will have caused it myself."

He held out his elbow, and her heart skipped a little when she slipped her arm inside his. He led her away from the Statue of Liberty's arm. "I was on my way to the Machinery Hall."

"Yes, that's what Rebecca said. Stepmother saw her talking to you."

"I guess she didn't recognize me?"

"No, thank goodness, neither of them did." Ellie cast a sidelong glance at Ben, not bothering to cover the mischievous smile that crept onto her lips. "Rebecca seemed quite taken with you, though. She said you were so polite and rather handsome."

She shouldn't be so mean to poor Ben, but it was a *little* fun, like a new version of the teasing they had given each other when they were children.

Ben cleared his throat. "Yes, well, to be honest, she seemed like a nice girl. I don't know about your relationship with her."

Ellie considered it for a moment.

"When it's just the two of us, she talks to me about things besides which dress she wants to wear or to ask me to darn her stockings. We're the same age, you know. This is her debut year, so she's been telling me about the party invitations her mother expects to arrive. It's strange, but she doesn't seem very excited about it."

She shrugged, because there was nothing else to do. "Of course, when my stepmother saw you, she only saw your clothes. She scolded Rebecca for talking to 'someone like you'."

"Like me?" He tried not to sound offended but failed. "What does that mean, exactly?"

"I suppose she means one of the great unwashed of the working class."

Ben snorted a laugh. "Does she forget she once *was* one of the great unwashed of the working class?"

Ellie knew her stepmother's views on class *very* well. "She doesn't consider being a governess working class. And now that she's married to my father..."

"She thinks she's automatically part of the upper class. She's always acted like she was better than everyone, especially my family," Ben said. "Unlike your mother and father, and you, who treated us like we were friends."

Ellie's heart squeezed a bit. "Because you were and are. There's no reason to treat someone who works in your home like they're beneath you. My mother always said that."

"Your mother was an exceptional lady," Ben said. "What in the world possessed him to marry your stepmother?"

Ellie's expression darkened at the word *possessed*.

"She took advantage of a grieving man. I still remember the day Mother introduced her to me as Mrs. Gibson, my new governess."

"I had forgotten that was her name before she married your father," Ben replied.

"And Rebecca. She had just lost her own father, who left them with nothing, and Mother took them in." Ellie looked at Ben. There was a moment of silence, laced with sadness.

Ben waved his hand, brushing away the melancholy that had crept up on them. "Look at us. Here we are, having a lovely walk on a perfect autumn day, and we're spoiling it with talk of that troll you call a stepmother. We should be enjoying ourselves, instead of talking over things we can't do anything about. Look at where we are, will you?" He slowly moved his hand across their field of view. "The wonders of the world are on display, just waiting for us to come and see them."

Ellie smiled. "Of course! And, we have business to discuss. Have you found out anything about the pages I gave you?"

Ben guided her past a group of people gathered around a man standing on a small stage. The man gestured toward a large wooden barrel and touted the qualities of the brown liquid in the glass mug he held in his hand.

"Hires Root Beer!" he cried in a carnival barker's voice. "For the first time ever in public, right here at the Exposition! Come and taste this smooth, delicious elixir!"

While the drink certainly did look to be everything the man exclaimed, the crowd around the man was too large or else Ellie might have stopped to try some.

"No, unfortunately." Ben sounded genuinely sorry for his lack of progress. "I thought about asking some of the people at the theater. Some of them are very superstitious. Some are zealous about it, actually. One actress I know keeps a rabbit's foot pinned to her undergarments."

Ellie feigned shock and surprise, putting a hand to her breast, her mouth falling open. "Mr. Grimm! How do you know about her undergarments?"

Ben's cheeks bloomed like roses, and Ellie couldn't help but be pleased at his embarrassment. "Uh, oh, well, that's what I've heard."

Ellie laughed. "No, I don't think they could help me." She struggled to hide her disappointment, knowing Ben was trying his best.

They entered a shaded part of the avenue, not well traveled. The shadows dropped over them like a curtain, and Ellie shivered.

"Tell your fortune, dear?"

The old woman's croaking voice startled Ellie. She hadn't seen the woman before; it was as if she had appeared out of thin air.

"What? I'm sorry, I didn't hear you."

The woman smiled, and Ellie was surprised again at both the whiteness and straightness of her teeth. The rest of her was old and wrinkled, like a chemise that had been rolled into a ball and stuffed into a drawer. She was thin as an old twig, her tiny arms weighed down with clanging bracelets. A pink shawl was wrapped around her shoulders, and strings of glittering beads hung about her neck. But her gray eyes were sharp as pins.

"Tell your fortune?" The woman had a slight Eastern European accent. "See your future, tell you the past."

"Oh! Uh… no, thank you." Something about the woman made Ellie uneasy, and yet she seemed familiar as well. Had they ever met before? Try as she might, she couldn't place her face. "Although it sounds like fun, I know the past, and no one can see the future." It sounded silly, considering what she *did* believe, but she didn't want to hurt the old lady's feelings. "Besides, I don't have any money. I'm sorry."

"For such a pretty young girl? I'll do it for free." The woman bobbed her head agreeably.

Ellie almost gave in. What would be the harm? But Ben tugged on her arm, pulling her away. His eyes were wary, and he shook his head slightly.

"I'm sorry, I really need to go. Thank you for the kind offer."

They stepped around the woman to continue on their way. The woman's arm shot out, at a speed unsuspected in such an elderly person, and her hand clamped around Ellie's wrist like a shackle.

"You are in grave danger, more than you know. If you want the answers you seek, you must listen. Or else you and your father will both be lost."

CHAPTER VI

ELLIE AND BEN FROZE, HELD IN PLACE BY THE OLD WOMAN'S RAPTOR-grip on Ellie's wrist. Ben would have called out, except that he didn't want to make a scene. Attention would not be welcome for either of them, sneaking around together as they were. Word would be sure to get back to Olivia, and that would be the end of their newly reforged friendship. And he wasn't as cavalier in regard to how her stepmother might punish Ellie as she was. He leaned in close to the woman and growled.

"Let go of her arm, right now."

The woman did not even acknowledge his existence. Her gaze remained locked with Ellie's, storm gray versus glass green. Ellie's face was paper-white, her lips seeming brighter red. To Ben's utter shock, she nodded. The old woman loosened her fingers and slid them down to clasp Ellie's hand, leading her like a child toward a small tent that Ben did not remember seeing before.

"Wait, Ellie, you can't be serious. She's a shyster. No one can tell the future."

Ellie's look was one of patience, mixed with a little hurt at Ben's lack of faith in her judgment. "I know she can't really tell the future. I don't think so, anyway. Obviously, this is important to her, so what's the harm? Besides, she said something about my father."

"Just keep a firm grip on your handbag," Ben muttered. He didn't like the idea of Ellie being swept even further along in her fantasies of magic, not when he thought he might be able to reach out to the reasonable, logical girl he knew was in there somewhere. This side trip to the fortune-teller would not help his cause. With an uneasy sigh, he followed Ellie and the old woman into the tent.

It was musty, the smell of old canvas that reminded Ben of back-drops that had been in storage for a long time. When the flap dropped over the entrance, the tent was cloaked in almost total darkness. A few candles, covered by hurricane lamps, threw sparse and shifting light.

In the center of the tent sat a small, round table covered in a midnight-blue cloth, dotted with silver stars. He half-expected to see a crystal ball sitting there, but the table was empty. A few talismans hung from the ceiling—an Egyptian Eye of Horus, a Star of David, a Christian cross, along with some other symbols he didn't recognize. They shone like they were made of silver and gold, but they were probably only polished copper and tin made to look like precious metals, props in this woman's performance.

The woman sat on one of the two rickety chairs around the table, and indicated that Ellie should sit in the other. Ben stood behind her, hoping his expression indicated to the woman exactly how he felt about her dragging Ellie in here. The woman still did not bother with him, however, keeping her attention firmly on Ellie.

She adjusted her shawl, the light from the lamp on the table making her wrinkled face look as if it had been carved from wood. Ben had to admit that she had done a fine job with the scenery and lighting, creating the appropriately spooky mood. He almost expected two other old women and a cauldron to appear, reciting lines from a certain Scottish play.

"Are you one of those mediums I've heard so much about?" Ellie asked. Ben didn't like the excitement beneath her words. He had also heard about the so-called spiritualists that were becoming more pervasive in polite society—people that spoke to the dead, read the future in tea leaves or on palms and the bumps on one's head. Even he knew about the famous Fox sisters, though he had yet to figure out how their tricks worked. He feared Ellie was getting her hopes up for nothing.

"I have many gifts." The old woman leaned forward, her gaze piercing. "But I have had a message from the spirit world, yes."

"Who? Who contacted you?" Ellie's questions were harsh whispers that Ben could barely hear. "Was it… my mother?"

"I cannot say. There was no name given to me except yours, Eleanor."

Even Ben was impressed. It was easy to say someone's spirit had contacted you and then be vague on the identity, but how did the woman know Ellie's name? And how did the woman know Ellie, when the girl was convinced that no one recognized her but him? Just another reason to believe she *wasn't* under a magic spell.

Ellie gripped the edge of the table so tightly that Ben was afraid she would break the wood, and his heart sank. She had bought this woman's act completely. He closed his eyes and prayed he would be able to repair the damage.

A deck of cards sat to one side of the table. The woman asked Ellie to mix them up, and then she pulled four from the top of the deck and studied them.

"You think you know the past, but there are things hidden. Someone plots against you. Like the moon, she does not show her true face. It is this person that keeps you from yourself, and from your father, and you believe you understand the reason, but it has not yet been revealed."

Ben's suspicion strengthened. It was one thing to find out a name and put it with a face, but the woman was speaking Ellie's fears aloud. So how did she know? There was something other than magic at work here — someone else must know what was going on in the Banneker house, and they were using it to manipulate her. He was nearly ready to make Ellie leave, even if he had to drag her from the table, but the woman grasped one of Ellie's hands, holding it lightly but with urgency.

"You are in such danger, child. More than you know. A cloud of darkness hangs over you, and things are coming to bear. A curse. If you do not stop it, you will lose everything."

"And I'd bet a week's wages that if we have the right coins, you'll tell us just how to solve all of our problems." Ben couldn't help the sarcasm in his voice; this had gone far enough.

The woman's gray eyes finally locked on to him, and Ben suddenly wished they hadn't. Her gaze sent icy fingers down his spine, so cold he was sure she could stop his heart with a glance. She said nothing to him, but he got the message. She turned again at Ellie.

"There really *are* spells on us. I'm right, aren't I?" Ellie licked her lips and let her breath out in a rush. "Oh, please, can you tell me how to break them? I'll pay you, anything. I'll find a way to get the money."

Ben couldn't hold his tongue any longer. He bent down and hissed in Ellie's ear. "Have you lost your mind? This woman cannot help you, she's taking advantage. She's found out a few things about you, to make you think she's got mystical powers. It's a sham."

Ellie turned her head, and Ben again wished he had not opened his mouth. "I just mean that you need to look for real solutions to your problems, not hocus-pocus. The only danger you're in is of being the victim of a confidence artist."

Ellie turned her gaze down, and shifted in her seat. "Ben, what if she's right," she whispered. "I'm not going to turn down an opportunity to find out how to fix this, no matter how far-fetched you think it is. If we really are spellbound, then I need to listen." A bit of uncertainty flitted across her expression, but she turned and faced the old woman again. Ben gritted his teeth. Her stubbornness was maddening.

"What do I need to do?"

The woman glanced at Ben, and he swore there was a smug, satisfied gleam in her eye as she returned her attention to Ellie.

"It will not be easy. The bargain that has been made is powerful, the spells tightly bound. You must gather together these things: a diamond that has been kissed by the sea, the bone of a holy man, a raven's claw. A token, freely given, from the one who holds your heart."

Ellie nodded, concentrating as she committed the ridiculous list to memory. Ben, having learned his lesson, bit his tongue.

"One last item. You will need to retrieve what she took from each of you. Place everything in a white dish and burn a white candle. Visualize the chains around you and your father falling away. The spells will be broken."

"What about..." Ellie looked over her shoulder at Ben, then leaned in close and whispered in the woman's ear.

The old woman shook her head. "That is outside of the curse. I am sorry."

Ellie's face went white. "Thank you." She squeezed the old woman's hand in thanks, and opened her reticule, no doubt to fish out the few coins she had to give them to this charlatan.

The woman held her up her hand, stopping Ellie. "Please, I ask nothing of you. The only payment you can give me is to succeed."

Ellie glanced over her shoulder at Ben and closed her purse, then stood to leave. "Thank you, again."

"One last thing, dear. Your time is running short. You must break the spell before the New Year. If you do not, when the clock strikes midnight, you and your father will be bound forever."

Ellie, feeling shaken to her bones, let Ben lead her from the tent. The rush of fresh air on her face was like a bucket of cold water, but still her nerves jangled like wind chimes in a hurricane. Before she had mentioned the bargain, Ellie might have believed it was all just cleverness, like Ben said. But the woman knew the truth about her and her family. Which meant that she had been right all along — she was definitely bewitched. And now she had a deadline. New Year's Eve was only weeks away! How would she be able to gather those things the old woman said she needed? It seemed like a hopeless task.

"Are you all right? Ellie?" Ben was sweet in his attention, guiding her by the elbow down the avenue and into the sunlight. He probably hoped it would chase away the ghosts he didn't believe in, make her see that what had just happened had all been folly. But the light did nothing to stop her shaking. She looked over her shoulder for one last glance at the medium's tent, and her heart nearly jumped from her chest.

It was gone.

Ben spun around, and even he could not explain how that had happened, though he certainly did try.

"We're probably looking in the wrong place. It was back from the road further, in the shadows, and we can't see it from here." But Ellie could tell he didn't even believe his own words completely. "Are you all right, though? You look as if you've, um, well, you don't look well."

Ellie pulled her shoulders straight and tightened her grip on her handbag to stop the shaking. It didn't help. "I'm fine, but I think I could use some tea."

She led the way to a nearby octagonal building. The sign above the door announced it as a tea room. Ben hesitated at the entrance.

"I, um, I don't have any money."

Ellie took a deep breath, blowing away the cobwebs that clung to her mind, and focusing on her friend. It helped.

"I have a little. It's enough for tea and cakes, I think."

Inside, they were led to a table near the outer edge of the room, and soon a waiter, dressed in crisp black-and-white, took their order of tea and iced cakes. Ellie watched Ben fidget in his chair, and was just about to chastise him when the waiter appeared with a blue-and-white teapot, two cups and saucers, and a plate of cakes.

"I see that the lessons of being a proper society lady have remained intact." Ben smiled at Ellie, and she got the impression that he was making fun of her.

She did not rise to his bait. "That woman. She was... unusual."

Ben's expression darkened and she feared they were traveling toward another argument. "It wasn't real. However that woman found out those things… I can't explain it. A lucky guess. Or maybe she's been watching you, which is much more disturbing. But I know it wasn't magic." He emphasized his point by jabbing the table with one finger.

Ellie sipped her tea, considering her next words carefully. She fixed Ben with her most solemn expression. "If I were you, I would probably say the very same thing. However, I will tell you that the woman knew more than you realize, more than she possibly could have guessed at." She took a deep breath. "The night I met you in the cemetery, my stepmother entertained a very strange visitor." She described the person, right down to the glowing eyes.

Ben nearly choked on his tea. "Ellie… it's…" He mopped tea from the front of his shirt with a napkin. "It's not that I don't believe you. I think you *think* you saw the eyes glowing. It was probably a reflection from the lamp or something."

"No, it wasn't, I—"

Ben stopped her objection with a wave of his hand. "All right, I won't argue with you over it. So, what about it?"

"My stepmother and this woman had an argument, and I heard them mention some kind of bargain. A contract."

Ben tilted his head, and looked as if he wasn't sure what to do with the information Ellie had given him, so she helped him along. "The fortune-teller said, 'the bargain that has been made is powerful.' After what I heard, I believe it has something to do with what's happened to me and my father."

"What kind of contract?" A hairline crack appeared in Ben's façade of disbelief. "Maybe that visitor told the old woman, and that's how she knew about it. They're in cahoots."

Ellie had to give him credit, he was stubborn. And his explanation made sense.

"I don't know what kind of contract. But it proves to me that the old woman knew what she was talking about." She waved a hand, dismissing the subject. "The contract is secondary to the task at hand." She looked Ben right in the eye, almost daring him to look away. "So I guess the only thing left to discuss is whether or not you are going to continue to help me break the spells."

CHAPTER VII

FTER BEN HAD AGREED TO HIS CONTINUED HELP — WHICH HE DID
out of the desire both not to make her angry with him again,
and so that he could make sure she stayed out of trouble —
Ellie paid their bill and asked for directions to the Machinery Hall. The
rest of the walk was blessedly uneventful.

The Hall was huge, but still not as big as the main exhibit hall next
door. The building was long with high peaked ceilings, like a gigantic
train depot. Hundreds of glass windows blinked in the sunlight, calling
people to its six arched entrances. Train tracks ran behind the building,
and a long, high-pitched whistle pierced the air, announcing the next
departure.

If the building was huge on the outside, the inside appeared to be
twice as large. Ben stopped just inside the door, gawking in open-
mouthed amazement, quite possibly looking as if he had recently
arrived in town by way of a turnip truck. Ellie pulled on his arm,
urging him forward. Ben was only vaguely aware that Ellie was still on
his arm, and walked slowly forward, making sure he did not miss a
single thing. Booths lined the walls and ran down the center into the
distance, crammed with machines of gleaming brass and steel, whirring
and chirping and moving in all sorts of ways Ben had never imagined
in his most far-reaching daydreams. One was a sewing machine that
ran without the need to be cranked. Ellie looked at it longingly, amazed
at such a labor-saving device.

They came upon another machine whose purpose seemed to be
doing laundry. A metal tub had been outfitted with paddles that agitated the water, using a belt to turn them. Ben had seen machines like it
before, and all of them used a hand crank. But this one swished the
soapy water and clothes about all on its own. Ben watched it, fascinated,
fighting to keep himself from jumping into the booth and pulling it
apart to see how it worked.

"It's steam-powered," the man in the booth said proudly. "A smaller version of the big ones commercial laundries have been using for years." He glanced at Ellie and pointed toward the ceiling. "We've tapped into the steam power supplied by the Corliss engine."

Ben and Ellie looked upward, where several long pipes ran along the ceiling. Smaller pipes branched out from them, running downward into the booths. The salesman continued. "But at home all you need is a little coal. I'm sure your pretty wife there would love to have one of these."

Ben's head snapped up at the remark. He glanced at Ellie, who was making a concerted effort not to laugh, and failing in a spectacular way. She rescued him from having to lie, however, by jumping in with a quick-witted reply.

"Oh, yes. I can honestly say that something like this would make my whole life much easier."

The man, quite pleased by Ellie's answer, reached out to shake Ben's hand. "You've got yourself a very smart little lady, there, sir. You just write your name and address on the list over there." He indicated a clipboard near the edge of the booth. "And we'll send you a postcard when the machines are available. I'm trying to get them into Wanamaker's department store for the New Year, so it might not be too long before your laundry drudgery is over."

Ben was afraid to ask the next question. "How much?"

"Only one hundred dollars." The salesman winked at Ellie as Ben nearly choked on the number the man had quoted. "Don't worry about the cost. Doesn't your wife deserve to be treated to such a convenience?"

Ben wanted to happily tell the salesman to take a long walk into the Delaware River, but he stuck with a simple thank you. Ellie certainly deserved the very best of things, but buying her a washing machine wasn't his idea of a gift. The salesman tipped his hat to them as they walked away from the booth.

"That was actually very interesting," Ellie said. They walked by a display featuring another steam-powered machine that apparently sheared sheep. The sheep in question was not enjoying it. "That laundry machine looked very useful. Your mother might like one."

"She might, although she would beat my father with a strap if he ever spent a hundred dollars on something like that. I can hear her already saying how the sweat of her brow is good enough."

"I see," Ellie said, with a clear respect for Cora Grimm's practical nature. "I've been thinking about what the old woman said. The list she gave me. A raven's claw, that's obvious, though not simple. The bone of a holy man, which is just disgusting. What Olivia took from me and my father—I put my hair back in hiding, but I can get it again easily. I don't know what she took from my father. But a diamond that has been kissed by the sea? I have no idea what that means. I know what a diamond is, though I don't see how I'm expected to get one. It's not like they're lying around, waiting for someone to take them. I *could* possibly borrow one..." She bit her lip and looked around, as if to see if anyone was listening. "But then what? Do I run to the ocean and dip it in? I can't see how that's practical. How am I supposed to get to the seashore?"

"That sounds very logical," he muttered, barely paying attention.

"Ben? Did you hear me? I asked, how in the world am I going to get to the seashore? It's nearly winter. I don't think the trains or coaches even run there at this time of year."

Ben opened his mouth to answer, but then closed it again, since he wasn't entirely sure what she was talking about. His attention had been diverted to the enormous display in the very center of the hall. There stood a dais two feet high, surrounded by a metal railing. On top of the dais sat a machine unlike anything Ben had ever seen in his life. The machine was five stories tall, with a ladder on either end of the platform that led to the top. Centered in the middle of the maze of pipes and gears was a huge flywheel, whose slow turning powered two cylinders that would crush anyone who was unfortunate enough to be caught beneath their pistons. Steam belched from the beast, and Ben felt the heat of it from thirty feet away. All of the pipes that decorated the hall's ceiling led here, like the center of a giant spider's web. This was the source of power for every machine in the hall.

This was the Corliss Steam Engine.

When Ellie left Ben half an hour later, she was no closer to a solution. She only had more questions, and her friend was not being particularly helpful. He was still chatting away with the tall, mustached man responsible for the monster of a machine on display in the middle of the hall. The minute Ben had seen the huge contraption, towering above them with its gigantic wheel and what seemed like a thousand moving parts, it was as if she had ceased to exist. He had walked to it as if drawn by a magnet, dragging Ellie along until she almost had to run to keep up with him.

Ben spoke with the man, who introduced himself as Mr. Corliss, for a few moments, asking questions full of technical gibberish that sounded to Ellie like a foreign language. The man had apparently been impressed by Ben's knowledge of machinery, because he invited Ben onto the dais to inspect the strange machine. Ellie, half-listening to their conversation but not bothering any longer to try and understand it, wandered around the machine, puzzling over it. She looked at it from every angle, and although she could not figure out what it did or how it worked, it was impressive.

When Ben took off his jacket and rolled up his shirtsleeves, Ellie knew he was lost to her. He looked so happy talking to Mr. Corliss that she didn't even mind the fact he had abandoned her, but it was getting late and her stepmother would be looking for her. Not out of worry, but propriety. Heaven forbid it got around that Olivia Banneker let her niece run around unescorted. Never mind that she was only a "poor relation," such a scandal would tarnish her stepmother's reputation instantly and was therefore almost worth spending several more hours wandering around the fair, making sure every last person she met knew who was responsible for protecting her honor.

She said goodbye to Ben, received a half-wave in reply, and left the Machinery Hall. She stopped just outside the building, realizing she had no idea where her stepmother and stepsister would be. Knowing Olivia, they wouldn't be anywhere near here, even though Rebecca desperately wanted to see it. The hall was filled with noise and machines that either emitted smelly smoke or were used for household chores better performed by servants. Decidedly unladylike. No, she would seek out something quiet and as pretentious as possible. The Horticulture Hall.

Ellie pushed her way through the crowd, which seemed to be growing at an exponential rate, and after what seemed like a day and a half of walking finally stood in front of the Horticulture Hall. It wasn't half as large as the Machinery Hall, but glittered like a jewel with its curved glass roof. The patrons going in and out were mostly women. Ellie joined the short queue and entered the building. Immediately, she was struck by a wave of heat. She moved to one side of the walkway, between displays of plants and flowers, and leaned against one of the roof supports to catch her breath.

Fortunately, her stepmother and stepsister weren't hard to spot. The huge ostrich plumes in her stepmother's hat, even though they were wilted from the heat, acted like a lighthouse beacon. Ellie had already worked out what she planned to say, so she put on her best distressed expression, which wasn't difficult as she still felt a little out of breath, and walked up to them.

"Thank goodness I've found you!"

Olivia slowly turned her head. She was wearing the smile she used only when she was around people she wanted to impress, which made her look as if her face was about to split in two. When she saw Ellie, the smile remained, but her eyes turned from warm and fawning to ice-cold anger. She had seen that look before. Even though they were in a public place where her stepmother would not dare to reprimand her, Ellie took an involuntary step backward.

"There you are, my dear. Wherever have you been?" There was a high-pitched note to Olivia's voice, as if someone had pulled a bow across a too-tightly strung violin. "We've been worried about you."

Clearly. Ellie's thought was supported by the look of abject incredulity that Rebecca wasn't quick enough to squelch.

"I'm so sorry. I waited for you outside the Statue of Liberty's arm, but the crowd was so large I was just swept away like a leaf on the river." Even though it set her teeth on edge, she acted like a simpering fool of a girl. "I've spent the entire time since, searching for you." She amazed herself by squeezing out a few tears, making it appear as if she had been terrified she'd never see her stepmother's face again.

Olivia's gaze shifted quickly to one side and she smiled again, stretching her mouth so wide it looked painful. She put her hand on Ellie's shoulder.

"It's perfectly all right, dear. I'm just happy we've found each other again and you're safe." The ice in her eyes had turned to fire, betraying the lie of her words, and her gloved hand closed like a vice over Ellie's flesh. She did not cry out, but her eyes welled with real tears. She balled her hands into fists, and pressed them against her skirt.

"Such a brave young lady, walking around this huge fairground unescorted," said a deep voice. Ellie turned toward the speaker, and found herself face-to-face with a young man. She had been so focused on making her excuses she hadn't noticed him, and she got the impression the three of them had been in conversation before she interrupted. The young man smiled at her, the warmth of it as genuine as her stepmother's was false. Ellie was suddenly dizzy, positive her corset had shrunk, and had the greenhouse suddenly turned hotter? She was barely able to find her own voice, and when she did it came out as a scratchy near-whisper. "I wouldn't say that I was brave, sir."

The kindness of the man's smile was matched in his voice. "It most certainly was brave. What a terrible ordeal for you, lost and alone in this great mob. You must have been terrified."

Ellie wished she had thought to bring a fan, for she was certain she could cook sausage on her face. How did the gentleman stay so cool, with his waistcoat and jacket, his blonde hair completely dry beneath his derby? She managed to fumble out a simple, "For a while, I suppose. Thank you, sir."

"And just who is this charming young woman?" The man held his hand, encased in a pearl gray glove, out to Ellie. She lifted her own to take it, her stomach turning as if she had swallowed a jar of butterflies. What in the world was wrong with her? Had she come down with a case of grippe? This feeling had hit her so suddenly she felt she must be ill. Just as their fingers were about to touch, Olivia stepped between them. She looked at the man, her sugary smile laced with viper's venom.

"She is my daughter's companion, Mr. Scott. Miss Anna Gibson, my poor, orphaned niece, you see. I've taken her in." She glanced over her shoulder and looked directly into Ellie's eyes. "I'm training her as a ladies' companion and governess."

Mr. Scott lowered his hand and looked at Ellie's stepmother with a tight-lipped smile. "How very charitable of you, Mrs. Banneker." The icy formality that had crept into his voice felt like a slap to Ellie's face. She pulled her shoulders back, indignant. *Why should I care what some high-born gentleman thinks of me? So what if he's handsome and charming, he's also quite a bore.* Suddenly, she wished she had stayed in the Machinery Hall with Ben.

Olivia turned back to Mr. Scott, pinning him beneath her gaze like a butterfly in a shadow box, and took a step toward Rebecca. "Now tell us, please, Mr. Scott, all about the railroad business. Such an innovator your father is, forging new roads to faraway places. It must be terribly fascinating." She tilted her head toward her daughter, drawing Mr. Scott's attention.

Ellie suddenly understood, all too clearly. It was the time of year for the mothers of young women making their debut to start hunting young gentlemen like pheasant, informally introducing them to their daughters, so that by the time of the Assembly Ball, most would have their dance cards already filled. And, of course, a few prospects for marriage. Or so Ellie had heard from maids in other households. Mr. Hamilton Scott was apparently the game that was in-season, which almost made Ellie feel sympathy for him.

Mr. Scott cleared his throat, wilting a little under Olivia's razor-edged gaze. He glanced in Ellie's direction, as if he wanted to include her in the conversation, and her hardness toward him softened a little more.

"I'm afraid it's not all that romantic or exciting, Mrs. Banneker. Right now we're concentrating on the local area. There are already tracks laid from Philadelphia to all the surrounding countryside. The main line of the Pennsylvania Railroad. My father wants more trains to run along that route. He's got some notion that the upper classes are bored with city living, and he's trying to get people to build their country estates out there. Bryn Mawr, Merion, that area."

Olivia held her fan to her breast. "But why would anyone want to leave the city? We have so much here — the opera, the ballet, the theaters. The finest stores and restaurants."

Mr. Scott shrugged. "It's only a short train ride, a fraction of the time it takes by carriage. The lure of fresh air and the space for stables, with the ability to return to the city's culture in an hour. Right now it's all just empty land. Father's building a huge place himself in Haverford. Should be finished next summer."

For the first time, Rebecca spoke. "Do you actually build the trains, Mr. Scott?"

Mr. Scott laughed out loud, a deep, hearty sound that bounced off the glass above them. "Goodness, no, Miss Gibson. Though they're fascinating, I haven't a single clue how those contraptions work. My father just pays the people who do."

Rebecca looked embarrassed, and Olivia's ire-filled smile turned on her own daughter. But she saved the conversation with a twittering laugh of her own.

"Who would want to know how they operate, anyway, when there are so many other worthwhile pursuits?" She put her hand to her chest, ignoring Rebecca's downcast look and red cheeks.

"I don't mean to say that learning about machinery isn't worth-while, Mrs. Banneker, only I do not have the mind for it."

Olivia paused, her cat's grin turning just a shade darker for the reproof. "Of course. Well, we will look forward to the first garden party of the season."

Hamilton made a slight choking sound, but recovered himself quickly, and Ellie suddenly found herself liking him.

"Yes, that will be... pleasant." His shoulders relaxed and he looked at Ellie, this time catching and holding her gaze, a smile flitting across his full lips before he pulled away again. Any remaining coldness she had toward him melted like ice in the sun. "Do you like the country, miss?"

Ellie, enraptured by the timbre of his voice, was about to tell Hamilton she hadn't been since she was a child but would love to see it again. But Olivia bumped Ellie with her hip, nearly sending her flying, but more importantly out of Hamilton's line of view. Ellie's stepmother opened her fan with a snap and waved it, cooling her face.

"Well, Mr. Scott, how sweet of you to ask. Rebecca adores the country. Don't you, Rebecca?"

Rebecca offered a small, polite smile. "Yes, I suppose. It would be lovely to get away." Her tone was flat, and she regarded Hamilton as if he was a piece of furniture rather than a would-be suitor.

How could she not be interested? Ellie thought. She studied Hamilton's profile — the strong, clean jaw line, his long, sloped nose. His eyes crinkled at the corners when he smiled, and suddenly more than anything she wanted to hear him laugh again. She found breath suddenly scarce, her heart beating in a most erratic manner. She focused instead on a nearby display of orchids, understanding at last why she felt so strange. *I'm being a ninny, letting the first handsome gentleman I meet to turn my head.* She let out a shaking breath and tried to control her galloping heartbeat.

"That settles it, then," Olivia said as if she had just solved the problem of gravity. "We will be first in line to purchase tickets on your new railroad."

Hamilton bobbed his head toward them. "I look forward to seeing you there. And now, ladies, you must excuse me. This has been a lovely diversion, but I do have business to attend to. Enjoy the rest of the Exposition."

"Certainly." Olivia stepped closer to Rebecca, as if she were trying to occupy the same space as her daughter. "I expect we'll be seeing you again soon enough. The holiday season will be upon us before you know it."

Hamilton's smile tightened and stretched, as if he were holding it up by sheer force of will. "Yes. It surely will." His tone was cheery, but Ellie had the distinct impression he wasn't excited about the prospect of the rounds of holiday parties that were the talk of every parlor each winter.

Olivia didn't seem to catch on to Hamilton's lack of enthusiasm. "And of course you will be attending the Assembly Ball, won't you? It wouldn't be an event without you there."

"I certainly will be." Hamilton looked as if he would rather have a hot poker jammed into his eye. "My mother would not have it otherwise."

"Then perhaps..." A coy lilt crept into Olivia's voice, and Ellie was sure the woman had batted her eyes at him. "Rebecca might save a space on her dance card for you?"

Rebecca's face once again turned the exact shade of ripe apples. Ellie could only imagine the embarrassment her stepsister felt at her mother's audacity. Hamilton remained a gentleman; his expression did not acknowledge either the awkwardness of Olivia's blatant attempt to throw her daughter at him or Rebecca's discomfort. Ellie was grateful to him for that, and he climbed another notch in her esteem.

"That would be pleasant. I look forward to it, Miss Gibson." Ellie didn't think it possible, but Rebecca's color deepened. Hamilton turned his gaze on Ellie and tipped his hat. "And Miss Gibson, it was *lovely* to meet you." He looked another second, long enough for Ellie's insides to flutter madly once more, before he walked away from them and out of the hall, leaving Ellie breathless.

Olivia watched him leave, and then turned toward her daughter. "Honestly, Rebecca, you might at least act as if you cared what he had to say. Are you still pouting about not being able to go to that horrid Machinery Hall? Hamilton Scott is a good match for you, and a man like him is a rare breed. Handsome, wealthy, and from one of the finest and oldest families in Philadelphia. Believe me, you could do much worse."

"Yes, of course, Mother." Rebecca nodded in agreement, but her shoulders slumped. Ellie wondered why her stepsister was so melancholy. Did she not like Hamilton in particular, or was it something else? Having been on the receiving end of Olivia's ire, she felt a great deal of sympathy for Rebecca at this moment.

"That's my girl." Olivia pulled a handkerchief from beneath her sleeve and handed it to Rebecca. "Now blot your face, dear, you're starting to perspire."

Rebecca took the handkerchief and dabbed at her upper lip and forehead. "Can we go now, please, Mother? I'm tired."

"Yes, my love, if that's what you want. I think we've put enough of an appearance." Olivia threaded her arm through Rebecca's and led her toward the door. "When we get home, we'll sit down and put together your social schedule. I think we're sure to be invited to Sarah James' party, she and I have been playing cards at the club, and then there's..."

Ellie walked behind her stepmother and stepsister, listening in resigned silence as her stepmother rattled off the litany of names that would appear in the return addresses on the stack of invitations that would be finding their way into the postbox. Although she had stopped dreaming of parties long ago, there was still a flicker of disappointment. Her mother had always told her she would attend the Assembly Ball one day, filled her head full of sugarplum daydreams of fancy dresses and dancing. *It is a stupid tradition anyway,* she thought. *Just an excuse for mothers to put their daughters on display like prize ponies, looking for the right stud.* She covered her giggle at the image while her cheeks burned with embarrassment.

Olivia's chatter filled the carriage ride home. Rebecca sat quietly, her chin in her hand as she watched out the carriage window, nodding in all the appropriate places but making no suggestions or comments. She seemed distant, perhaps a little sad as well, and Ellie wished she knew what Rebecca was thinking.

Olivia's total absorption with her plans for Rebecca's future left Ellie to her own thoughts. Ben still didn't believe she was under a spell, but he was willing to help her. With the sun shining on her face, like now, and everything feeling so... normal... she almost believed she *was* mad. Then her father's face appeared in her thoughts and she remembered. She repeated the medium's list in her mind again—a diamond kissed by the sea, bone of a holy man, raven's claw. What Olivia took from each of them. She would have to look for her father's token soon.

She sighed, trying to think of something less depressing. Hamilton Scott's handsome face floated into her mind's eye. She recalled every second of their meeting, conveniently skipping over the parts where her stepmother had intruded, filling them in with a lively, flirtatious, and completely imaginary conversation in which he had asked *her* if she would save him a space on her dance card.

"And just what are *you* smiling at?"

CHAPTER VIII

OLIVIA'S VOICE BROKE INTO HER DAYDREAM, TURNING IT TO SMOKE. The carriage had stopped, and there was her own doorstep. Her stepmother and stepsister stood on the sidewalk, waiting, Olivia's face twisted into impatience personified.

"Oh, was I smiling?" She hadn't realized she had been smiling, though she wasn't surprised. "It was nothing."

Olivia's eyes narrowed in suspicion. "Yes, well, that isn't surprising. Some days I wonder if your head isn't filled with straw."

Ellie, bristling at the insult, followed the other women inside. Olivia didn't drop the subject of her stepdaughter's intelligence, continuing to mutter about how stupid it was for her to disappear at the fair.

She knew it was asking for trouble, but couldn't stand another second of her stepmother's diatribe. "Stepmother, I am sorry. I told you that I was pulled away. It wasn't my fault." She didn't even care that it was a complete lie. She owed her stepmother nothing, including explanations.

The front door clicked shut behind them. Olivia rounded on Ellie, her eyes flashing as her anger unfurled like a ship's sail in a hurricane.

"Not your fault? You ungrateful child." She spat the words as if they were poison. This was the storm that had been brewing earlier, unleashed with such force it threatened to knock Ellie to her knees.

"I don't care if you were abducted by nomads." Olivia pulled off her gloves, tugging at each finger as if it had done her a personal insult. "You should not have moved from the spot until I came for you."

Ellie choked back her rebuttal. There was no sense in baiting her stepmother. It was easier to just let her blow herself out.

"If I had known you were going to be this much trouble I would have left you at home. You should be very thankful we did not have to search for you." Olivia ripped her hat from her head so forcefully that one of the ostrich feathers snapped in half. The broken piece fluttered to the floor. It did not stop her ranting, the ruined hat only fueling her anger. "And speaking to Mr. Scott? You little harlot, I should have slapped your mouth."

Ellie's own temper began to heat like a kettle over a low flame. "He spoke to me first, Stepmother, and I thought it would be impolite to not respond." She knew she would regret the reply, but perhaps a rational thought would cool her stepmother's ire.

It didn't even slow her down.

"Don't argue with me, I know what I saw. And to think of what I have had to put up with from you, for all these years, after all that I have given you."

"All that you have given me?" The words were out of Ellie's mouth before she could stop them. Once they started, they tumbled like a jar of marbles tipped down a staircase. "A drafty attic? To wash your clothes, cook your food, clean my own home? All of that, and to be denied my season as well?" She slapped her gloves against her hand. "I should be grateful?"

Olivia's lips turned white. Her body trembled with cold fury, and Ellie did not care.

"You have no idea, *step*daughter, of how lucky you truly are. You could have disappeared years ago."

"And why didn't I?" Years of frustration and anger burst out alongside Ellie's words. "My father? What would he have done to you if you had sent me away?"

Olivia stopped cold. Her lips turned upward and it took Ellie a moment before she realized her stepmother was smiling. It wasn't pleasant, but a cruel sneer. "Your father?" She laughed. "I have made sure that his only thoughts for the last seven years have been for me and me alone."

It was a thrust for Ellie's heart, but she knew how to parry, and exactly where to stick her own blade. "Is that why he calls out my mother's name in his sleep?" She jutted her chin upward stubbornly. Rebecca, cowering by the parlor door, gasped.

"You bitch," Olivia hissed.

Ellie took a step toward the stairs, not out of fear but self-preservation. Olivia's hand shot out and clamped on her elbow. She dragged Ellie toward the back of the house and stopped at the end of the hall in front of the kitchen door.

"You impertinent mongrel, let's see how you feel after some time in the cellar."

Ellie's heart began to race as panic clutched her chest. She pulled away from her stepmother with all her might, but to no avail.

"No, please! I'm… sorry!" The slick soles of her boots slid across the rug, struggling for purchase as terror gripped her with slender, cold fingers. Her elbow pulled from Olivia's hand, but quick as lightning the woman reached out and grabbed Ellie's hair. Her tidy bun was pulled free, pins falling to the floor, and she screamed as she was dragged into the kitchen to the cellar door.

"Do you honestly think I would accept an apology from you? This is what you deserve after such disrespect. If I'm feeling generous I *might* let you out in the morning."

Olivia twisted Ellie around, pulled the cellar door open and shoved her inside. She stumbled and fell into the dark hole that rushed up to greet her, just able to make out the bare stone wall and the staircase before the door slammed shut behind her, leaving her blind. She threw both hands out to steady herself against the rough wall, barely able to stop herself from plunging headlong down the stairs. The sound of the key turning in the lock was loud as gunfire in her ears, already pounding with the sound of her own heart.

She felt her way to the door and beat her balled fists against the wood. Panic nested in her chest like a snake, coiled tightly and ready to strike. It was suddenly hard to breathe, and her corset felt as if it were crushing her ribs as she gulped air, trying to fill her lungs.

"Let me out, please! Stepmother!"

Ellie cried out until her throat was raw. She leaned against the door and slid to the wooden floor of the landing, her face moist with tears that cooled her burning cheeks. Finally she gave up, knowing her stepmother would not be moved. She covered her face with trembling hands and wept.

She hated that her stepmother knew that this punishment would fill her with fear. This unreasonable terror of dark, enclosed places, stemmed from when she was eleven years old, the first time she had been locked down here. The damp, tangy metallic scent of the earthen floor and stone walls hit her nose and her whole body shook as the memory swept over her. She was serving her stepmother and stepsister tea in the parlor. Ellie tipped the teapot, full and heavy, toward the delicate china cup. The amber liquid flowed into the cup too quickly, and before Ellie could stop it, the cup overflowed into the saucer, onto the table and its lace cover, and dripped onto the rug.

"What are you doing, you clumsy little fool?" her stepmother screeched. Ellie jumped, startled, and dropped the teapot. It shattered, scattering china and hot liquid across the Persian carpet, the stain spreading as the thirsty wool soaked up the tea.

Olivia, rage bubbling over like the tea in the cup, threw her napkin onto the table. "You did that on purpose."

"N-n-no! Stepmother, I didn't, I'm sorry." Ellie stepped back and cowered, tears brimming in her eyes.

Olivia grabbed Ellie by the ear, dragged the weeping girl down the hall and locked her in the cellar. "This will teach you to be so careless." Olivia slammed the door and locked it.

It was a horrible place for a young girl to be trapped, dark and silent except for the scratching of the rats she could not see, the spiders who dropped onto her skin without warning, and the unnerving drip of water that she could not drink. A terrified Ellie had huddled against the door, just as she was now, unable to move and not knowing when or if she would see daylight again.

Since that day, Ellie did not enter the cellar unless she had no choice. She never, ever closed the door behind her. It was her one true fear, even though she was grown and had seen with her own eyes that there was nothing in the cellar that would harm her.

She closed her eyes and listened. The sound of her own breath. The ever-present drip of water. Nothing else. She slumped against the door with a sigh, but a sudden scratching set her heart racing again as she pulled her knees close to her chest, wrapping her skirts around them, protection against the rat that might be bold or hungry enough to approach her. There was nothing she could do about the spiders.

The day she had spilled the tea she had spent only four hours here, though it had seemed like an eternity. How long would her stepmother leave her here this time? A day? More? Ellie's worst fear, then as well as now, was that she would be forgotten entirely. Her despair deepened. No one else knew she existed. Everyone thought of her as either just another servant or a charity case for her stepmother. Both made her invisible.

Except for Ben. He, by some miracle, saw her for who she really was. If something happened to her, he would find out. He would see that Olivia paid for it. She saw his face in her mind, his soft brown eyes and shaggy hair. Her heart swelled thinking about it, and despite herself, she smiled.

Ben raced through the back door of the bookshop, slamming it behind him. Without a word to his mother, who poked her head into the back of the shop to make a comment about a stampede of bulls, he ran down the stairs to his workshop.

His mind whirred with so many thoughts that he barely registered the fact it was dark until his shin connected with something solid. Hopping on one foot and cursing under his breath, he fumbled around the room, looking for the container of matches that was supposed to be at the bottom of the steps. Finally, he found them, struck one, and used the flame to see his way to the lamp. He placed the lamp on the workbench and tossed his coat toward the nail he used as a coat hook. Instead it landed on the floor in a puddle of brown wool. He grabbed a pencil, opened the notebook to the last drawing, and started to work. His head bent over the page, he erased lines and drew new ones, scribbling notes in the margins and drawing arrows.

"Ben, I'm closing the shop now. Are you coming home? It's time for supper," his mother called.

"No, Mother. I'm working."

"You need to eat."

"This is more important."

The sigh that came down the stairs was long-suffering. "All right, but don't be late to the theater, or your father will have your hide. I'll send along a cold meat sandwich with him, so you don't go hungry."

"Alright. Thanks."

The back door to the store closed and everything fell silent except for the scratching of Ben's pencil. When he ran out of space for notes, he continued on the back of the page. Beneath his hand, the product of his imagination blended with the real machine he had seen that afternoon. Something impossible was becoming less so, at least on paper. He still couldn't figure out how he would ever make it real, but Mr. Corliss had been very encouraging.

The clock upstairs chimed the hour. Eight o'clock. Ben froze, his pencil hovering above the page. Even after his mother's reminder, he was late. The evening performance was about to begin. His father would be furious. Even angrier if Ben told him the reason he was late. He looked at his drawing, longing to continue. For the first time ever he considered not going to the theater. But he would have to explain his actions to his father, and that would be a losing battle. He could lie and say he was sick, but his mother had just seen him.

Besides, he didn't want to lie. Even though they didn't see eye-to-eye about his ambitions, Ben respected his father. His heart tugged him in two directions, stretching like taffy in his chest.

He heaved a sigh. "Damn." If he lost his job, not only would he lose his father's respect, he would also lose his only way of making money, and he had precious little left after his trip to the Exposition today. It would have to wait a little longer. Ben took his coat from the floor and pulled it on as he started toward the stairs. Halfway up, he jumped back down. He grabbed his notebook and stuffed it in his pocket, then blew out the lamp, dashed up the stairs and out of the shop.

CHAPTER IX

ELLIE WAS SURROUNDED BY A SOFT GOLDEN LIGHT. SHE WAS IN A grand ballroom. A pair of strong arms held her, guiding her steps in the waltz played by an unseen string quartet. The skirt of her pale blue gown swished around her with the whisper of silk. Beneath her feet was polished marble, and above her head hung a giant crystal chandelier, sparkling like a sky full of stars gathered together. She and her partner were surrounded by other couples. The dancers whirled by, but she could not make out any of their faces.

Was this the Assembly Ball? How had she gotten here?

"Have I told you how pleased I am you agreed to dance with me?" a deep voice rumbled gently into her ear. It sounded familiar, though she could not place it. The closeness of the man and the sound of his voice sent a pleasant shiver down Ellie's spine and caused warmth to pool low in her stomach. Whoever he was, he never missed a step. His tuxedo fit him well, perfectly tailored for his broad shoulders and muscular arms, his white shirt bright in the light. Was his hair wheat-blond, or brown? It was hard to tell. She lifted her chin to look into his face and gasped. Like the rest of the faces, his was a blur. Ellie stopped dancing and pulled away.

"What's wrong?" The man reached for her, but she backed out of reach.

"What is my name?"

The man chuckled. "What silliness is this? Come, dance." The man shook his offered hand, but Ellie put both of hers behind her back.

"Say my name!"

Before the mystery man could answer, someone grabbed her shoulder and spun her around.

Fury burned in Olivia's eyes like coals. "Eleanor, what do you think you are doing? You cannot dance with him, he is Rebecca's partner. *This* is the only name on your dance card." She thrust out her arm, and in her hand was an old straw broom. Ellie looked down at herself. Her fine gown was gone, and in its place was the gray muslin dress she wore to clean the fireplaces. Her hands were covered in soot. She reached up to her hair and found it covered by a scarf. The other dancers encircled her, all of them pointing and laughing. Heat rose in Ellie's face, hot tears rolling down her cheeks.

"No!" Ellie jerked awake. Her eyes opened, but there was nothing to see. She took a deep breath, and the musty odor of mildew hit her nose.

She was still in the cellar.

Her heart pounded anew, terror sticking to her like flour paste. How could she have fallen asleep? She rubbed her scalp, still sore from her hair being pulled, and the argument with Olivia came back in a rush. *Did I really say all of those terrible things?* She had indeed, and moreover she had *meant* them. Even if she had suffered from the inclination to be sorry for her words, she had paid for it with her imprisonment.

Ellie wondered if she had she slept the whole night away, sitting on the dusty landing, or had it only been a few hours?

She felt her way to the door and stood, her muscles crying out with stiffness. A strip of light at her feet bled into the dark — it was day. Ellie ran her trembling fingers along the wood of the door until she came to the round, cold smoothness of the knob. She gripped it, hoping the door would open, not believing it would.

The metal turned easily beneath her fingers. *When did my stepmother unlock it?* That caused her to wonder what time it was, because her stepmother would not do something so generous as to rise early for Ellie's benefit. If she had, she would have already ripped the door open and shouted her awake. It didn't matter. Gratefully, she pushed the door open and light flooded in, blinding her. She stumbled into the kitchen and flung herself into one of the kitchen chairs, taking deep breaths of clean, fresh air. She laid her head onto the kitchen table and wept with relief, feeling stupid at being so afraid of an empty, dark space but unable to stop herself.

Feeling like a wrung-out dishcloth, she looked up at the clock. It was morning, but still an hour or more until her family rose for the day. Enough time for her to clean herself up and change. She stole up to her room. After peeling off her walking dress, which was covered with dust and spider webs, and changing into her plain shirtwaist and wool skirt, she checked on her father. He was awake, his eyes bright and clear. Ellie smiled as she entered the room.

"Good morning, Papa. Did you sleep well?"

Her father turned toward her, his smile widening. "Very well, thank you." His voice was soft, so unlike the robust tone he had before his illness. "And how are you this morning?"

Ellie gulped back the truth. "I am happy to see you, as always." She helped him up so that he could use the chamber pot and then tucked him back into bed. "You just wait right here, and I'll get you some breakfast. Later I'll change these sheets and we'll get you a clean nightshirt."

"Thank you, my darling. I am, I think, the luckiest husband in the entire world."

"I'm your daughter, Papa." She fought to say her own name, to put the sound of it into his ear, but it would not come.

"What? My daughter? No, you're Olivia... or are you Violetta... I don't remember..." He leaned back against the pillow, exhausted. As long as he remembered her mother's name, Ellie had hope; some part of him struggled against Olivia's magical grip.

Back in the kitchen, she lit the stove and let its warmth drive the last of the cellar's damp and chill from her bones. She went to the sink, pumped some water and splashed it on her face, dipping her wet finger into the baking powder and using it to scrub her teeth, which felt as if they'd grown fur overnight.

While Ellie filled the teakettle, she slowly rotated her head, trying to loosen the muscles. She set the kettle on the stove and went to the back door to fetch the milk. The morning was cold, the ground covered with frost, glazing the leaves of her small pumpkin patch. The pumpkins were nearly ready for harvesting and canning, to be turned into holiday pies she would never taste. Her stepmother would put them on the Thanksgiving table, which Ellie would not sit at, and send them to the hostesses of the parties Rebecca was invited to. *She'll probably claim to have made them herself, maybe even say she grew the pumpkins.*

Ellie scolded herself for being so cynical. Her life could be so much worse than it was. She didn't deny Rebecca the chance for happiness, she only wanted some of her own. Above her head, a gray dove cooed quietly in the eaves, as if to say she understood. With a sad sigh, Ellie leaned down to open the milk box.

"What's this?" Something stuck out from beneath the box's wooden lid. It was much too early for the milkman's monthly bill. Curious, she plucked it from its place. It was a cream-colored envelope with her name on the front, written in indigo ink.

"Now who would be writing me a letter?" she said to Clarence, who pranced up the stairs, returning from his night of mouse-chasing and tom-catting. She had no friends except for Ben, and the elegant handwriting certainly didn't look like it belonged to a man, although the only comparison she had was her father's. His had been long and thin, more like the scratching of chickens looking for food than proper writing.

Ellie looked around, thinking that perhaps the letter-writer had stayed close by to be sure their missive was delivered. She saw no one. She clutched the letter to her chest, a little thrill going through her. *A secret letter!* She wanted to tear it open and read it immediately, but hesitated. Whoever wrote the letter wanted only her to read it, or else they would have sent it with the regular post. With the envelope tucked into her apron, she grabbed the two bottles of milk and went back inside.

"Rebecca? Is that you, dear?" Olivia's dulcet tones, much like the squawking of an irritated goose, resonated through the house. Ellie started, clanging the glass milk bottles together. Neither broke, fortunately.

The goose herself appeared in the kitchen doorway and her eyes narrowed when she saw Ellie.

"How did you get out of the cellar?"

Ellie, who had no answer but the truth, shrugged. "The door was open, Stepmother." It made her stomach turn to kowtow to Olivia, but she wanted to keep the peace this morning.

Olivia tucked her chin toward her chest, her mouth falling open. She patted the pockets of her robe, muttering to herself.

"I... could have sworn... I have the key right here." She reached into her pocket and pulled out a heavy brass key. She glanced at Ellie, then stuffed the key back into her pocket and straightened her robe, grasping at the locket around her neck, and then smoothing back a strand of gray-streaked hair that had come loose from her nighttime braid.

"I trust you have learned your lesson? About how to speak to your betters?"

Ellie bit back her first reply, which had to do with the day Olivia becoming her better coinciding with the end of time.

"Yes, Stepmother."

Olivia gave a curt nod.

"Fine, then get breakfast and be quick about it. It will not do for Rebecca and me to be late for church." She left, the kitchen door swinging in her wake. Ellie's shoulders slumped in relief. The note would have to wait until after the women left. She pulled it from her apron and tucked it into the back of the dish cupboard for safekeeping. As she did so, her stepmother's words poked at her thoughts, awaking a realization. Church. They were going to church. Where else to find the bone of a holy man? Ellie knew from attending services with her parents that beneath the stones of the sanctuary lay the bones of several prominent clergy. But dare she?

The letter and her prospective sacrilege continued to absorb her thoughts throughout breakfast.

"What are you doing, you stupid girl?" Olivia screeched. Ellie, looked down. The salt cellar was in her hand, the small spoon filled with salt. Both were positioned above her stepmother's teacup. She quickly moved her hand over the poached eggs and tapped the spoon with one finger.

"I'm salting your eggs, Stepmother." *It was a good thing they hadn't wanted breakfast in bed this morning, or else I might have spent the day scrubbing poached eggs out of the upstairs carpet.*

Rebecca's voice cut through her woolgathering. "Mother, I see that the invitation to the Assembly Ball arrived in yesterday's post."

"Yes, that's right, my dear," Olivia said sweetly, with a sidelong glance at Ellie that was meant to sting. "It will be here before you know it." She sipped her tea, and Ellie wished she *had* dumped salt into it. "This year it will be a masked ball. Which I think to be a little juvenile, but I suppose the Dancing Assembly decided it needed to try something new."

Rebecca dipped the corner of her toast in her teacup, looking thoughtful. "Yes, it sounds wonderful." Ellie thought her words sounded forced. "But I thought, Mother, that since it is such a special occasion, and so important for a girl, that maybe... *perhaps*... Eleanor might accompany us?"

Ellie, who had been trying not to listen to the conversation, nearly dropped the teapot. She kept her gaze fixed on the table, not daring to glance at either of the other women. The silence hung heavy as lead. What if her stepmother, by some miracle, said yes? Visions of shopping for a dress, and slippers, and fans fluttered through her mind like a flock of doves.

Olivia smashed Ellie's delicate hope like an eggshell.

"Why ever would Eleanor go to the ball, dear?" This was the way of things in her home—her stepmother speaking about her as if she were not there.

Rebecca's forehead creased briefly. "Because she's family, mother. She is seventeen now as well. And perhaps she would like to go."

Olivia folded her napkin and placed it on the table, smoothing it with one long-fingered hand. "I still don't see why, Rebecca. She isn't prepared for such social engagements, and her place is here. No, Eleanor will *not* go."

Rebecca wet her lips, as if trying to think of another way to convince her mother without causing her to lose her temper. It was like watching a mouse try and outwit a cat. She opened her mouth, but her mother stopped her with a singsong, "I won't hear another word about it." She picked up her spoon and scooped up some porridge. "I don't want to spoil our breakfast, darling. I have a delicate constitution."

Now Ellie wanted to *hit* her stepmother with the teapot.

"Yes, Mother." Rebecca's gaze dropped to her own bowl, but not before she gave Ellie a deeply apologetic look. Ellie tried to convey how grateful she was for the attempt, however unsuccessful. Olivia, without so much as a glance at Ellie, pushed the remaining corner of her toast off her plate and onto the floor, which of course landed with the buttered side down. Ellie, gritting her teeth so tightly she thought she heard a crack, cleaned up the mess and returned to the kitchen. She threw the bread out the back door for the birds and her dishtowel at the wall. It hit with a smack, and Ellie wished it was Olivia's face.

She had never been able to puzzle out what had she done to make her stepmother dislike her so vehemently. Her stepmother's rejection shouldn't hurt as much as it did, but it seemed it was a wound that would not heal. She wiped her eyes with the edge of her apron. It was silly to cry over a ball. Even if she were to go, she still had to break the spell, and that night was her deadline, so she couldn't spend her time shopping for frilly dresses or ridiculous and probably painful dancing slippers.

An hour and a half later, both women climbed into the carriage and clopped off to church. Finally, she was able to take a bowl of porridge and a cup of tea to her poor father. He was sitting exactly as she had left him, and he allowed her to spoon-feed him, like a baby.

"Thank you, dear. You are always so good to me."

Ellie wiped some porridge from his chin. "It's because I love you."

He patted Ellie's knee. "Of course. And you know I love you as well, Olivia."

Ellie's sigh was heart-weary. "Yes, I know."

Olivia had taken her father from her. Even though they were in the same room, it was as if hundreds of miles separated them. She gave him his medicine and left him to rest, then raced to the kitchen to retrieve her letter. Even though the house was essentially empty, she headed straight for the attic. Wrapping herself in the threadbare quilt, she sat on the sofa, her hands shaking with more than cold.

When was the last time she had opened a letter of her own? When she was young there had been the occasional Christmas card from her grandparents, who were gone and buried, or a note from her parents on her birthday, but nothing since. She lifted the envelope's flap, pulling up the plain wax seal with it. Inside was a sheet of thin, crisp stationary. Ellie unfolded it, the paper shaking in her fingers. There was no monogram across the top, but the writing inside was the same as that on the envelope.

Eleanor,

The answers you seek are inside your stepmother's secretary.

A Friend

That was all. Ellie flipped the page over, but it was blank. She reread the message. Which answers? Every question she had at the moment was about this letter. Who was "A Friend," and how would they know what kinds of things she might find in her stepmother's desk? Searching it was a dangerous idea. A night in the cellar would seem like afternoon tea if she was caught.

She bit her lip. It wasn't an issue of being afraid to snoop in her stepmother's desk. But the church service must be nearly over by now. Not enough time to properly search. She would have to wait. Another chore to add to her ever-growing list. Not to mention how in the world to get into the church and procure a bone. Just yesterday her problems seemed relatively simple and clearly defined. But not anymore.

Ellie threw off the quilt and kneeled in front of the sofa. She reached underneath and wrapped her fingertips around the edge of a particular floorboard. With a little tugging, the board pulled away. She reached her hand into the space beneath and extracted a carved wooden box. When she lifted the lid, it revealed a blue velvet lining and all her worldly treasure. Sparkling emerald earrings and a matching necklace that had once graced her mother's ears and slender neck, rescued from Olivia's purge of the house. The precious few coins she had, the delightful mechanical bird Ben had given her, which she wound up almost every day. Tucked to one side was the copy of *Jane Eyre*. She had managed to read some of it, fascinated by the story of poor Jane and Mr. Rochester. She slipped the note between the pages of the book, and then replaced both the box and the board. She rushed down the stairs, her feet touching the third-floor carpet just as the front door was thrown open.

"Eleanor!"

Ben pushed open the giant doors of the old barn and stepped inside. Dust floated through the air in clouds, filling his nose and making him sneeze.

"God bless." Ron clapped Ben on the back. "You'd better be careful, or you might hurt yourself."

"Oh, shut up, Ronnie." Ben pulled his handkerchief from his back pocket and wiped his running nose.

Ron chuckled. "Just having some fun." He looked around at contents of the barn. "Your father really must be angry with you to give you this job."

Ben stuffed his handkerchief into his pocket. "You have no idea." His father had steamed right past angry and into furious when Ben showed up nearly half an hour late to the theater. It had been over a week, and he still pulled his lips tight whenever he looked at his son.

"Well, if you're going to get into trouble, you might as well do it right." Ron patted Ben on the shoulder. "Being late to a *Saturday evening* performance?" He let out a long whistle. "I didn't think your father knew that many curse words."

"Let's just get started, all right?" He left Ron and walked into the barn. His father's punishment—making him clean out, straighten, and inventory the Properties and Sets warehouse—was not as bad as Ben knew it could have been. At least he still had a job. He lifted a flat that had fallen over. On the other side was the painted image of a garden. He pushed the torn flat back onto the top of a pile that leaned against the wall. His gaze wandered from the rows of tall, sturdy wooden shelves, each full to bursting with a wide array of props, all the way to the lofts that ran around the top of the cavernous building.

"This is going to take months."

"Yep," Ron replied. "Have fun."

Ben spun around, his mouth falling open. "You're not staying?"

Ron's smile widened, showing the gap between his two front teeth. "Nope. This job is all yours. I just came to show you the way and make sure you didn't get lost."

"Damn it." Ben kicked at a pebble, which skittered off into the shadowy depths of the warehouse, bouncing off something that sounded miles away. "That's just great."

"Aw, now, don't be that way. The Properties Master *might* be by later to check up on you. Then again, maybe not." He shrugged. "Have fun, boy-o." He shut the door behind him, and the thud of it reverberated like the closing of a tomb, enveloping Ben in eerie silence. He gazed around him, stunned by the sheer size of the room. Where did he even begin?

"I guess I could start with the cleaning," he muttered. "I can't very well do inventory when everything's all over the place." That was his mother talking. She'd be proud of him, and probably shocked speechless that he had actually remembered her words.

"But first, I think, a tour is in order. Let's just see what I'm up against." He cracked his knuckles and walked down the first aisle. The shelves were stuffed, but there seemed to be at least some semblance of order. One shelf contained a hodgepodge of armor and weapons, swords and shields mixed in with pistols and spears. Another contained vases of all shapes and sizes, but Ben spied a skull resting between them. The further from the door, the larger the props became. The last shelf held miles of rolled up carpets. Just beyond the shelves sat at least a dozen houses' worth of furniture — chairs of all shapes and colors, dining room tables and a mish-mash of chairs and settees. Though it might have looked cozy, none of it was comfortable, with springs that poked and pinched just beneath the fabric.

A gathering of Grandfather clocks caught his eye. Some were nothing but empty shells, never meant to chime an hour, but a couple still had their insides. He wondered if anyone would notice if he scavenged their parts. *This job might not be so bad after all.*

Ben finally came to the back of the gigantic space. It was like a theatrical graveyard, the land of forgotten props. Buried in the middle of a sea of broken tables, bent swords, and cracked flats sat a hulking bulk of something. It was covered in what must have once been a white tarp, now brown with dust.

What in the world could that be? It was by far the biggest single item in the entire warehouse. Ben, curious, picked his way through the debris until he reached the covered object. He glanced over his shoulder. There was no one in this wooden cave but him. *And the rats. A place like this has to have rats.* A shiver raced down his spine.

He grabbed the edge of the cover. It was made of heavy canvas, like a ship's sail. He tried to lift it gently, to keep the dust from flying into his eyes, but failed in the grandest fashion. A thick cloud floated up from the fabric, nearly choking him, making his eyes water. *Maybe it would be better if I just ripped it off.* He turned his head, closing his eyes against the onslaught of dust, then took a step back and pulled the tarp as hard as he could. It slid away and dropped to the floor. Ben waited a moment, and then slowly opened his eyes. Dust still floated above, but it settled quickly, putting a new layer on everything around him. He stared at what lay beneath, unable to believe his luck.

Ben grasped the tarnished brass handle of the old carriage and opened the door, which complained loudly in a voice of rusty hinges. The leather of the seats was dry and cracked around the edges, the old curtains moldering on their rods. The metal of the carriage's frame was riddled with spots of rust, the brass lamps black with age. But when Ben set his foot on the step and carefully put his weight on it, it held. He bounced a little, and the springs groaned like an old man with arthritis. *Nothing a little oil and elbow grease won't fix.*

He visualized the sketch in his notebook, complete with the changes he had made after his trip to the Exposition. He saw where each gear would go, how one would work with the next, and where he could put the tanks. A flywheel underneath, driving the cylinders connected to the wheels. *This is possible.*

Ben's conscience nudged him. This carriage, like everything else in the barn, was the property of the Walnut Street Theater. The coach didn't look like it had been used in ages, though. Who would miss it? He gnawed on his lip. The fact it wouldn't be missed didn't mean he could take it. Who should he ask—his father? That could be problematic, given the current chilly climate of their relationship. The Properties Master might be a better choice, but there was no telling when Ben would be able to speak to him. His fingers itched to pick up his tools and transform this ordinary carriage into something extraordinary.

No one would ever know, his soul, his deepest desire, whispered. It was probably true—he could work here and no one would notice. The lure of the magic in his fingertips was strong. He stroked the metal of the carriage, feeling warmth in the cold iron, a chord of doubt played somewhere inside him. It had taken him so long to get the simple bird cage device to work—how long would this take?

Ben rested his head on the carriage, his stomach queasy from thinking about undertaking such a task. Maybe it was better if he didn't try. If he didn't try, he couldn't fail.

Something fell from the carriage's seat, landing on his foot. He picked up a dusty, bug-chewed playbill. He couldn't read the cover, but the advertisement on the back was in near pristine condition. His heart nearly stopped as he read it, and the voice of the old fortune teller echoed in his mind.

It was a complete coincidence, it had to be. But…what if…? For the first time he considered that Ellie was right about being under some kind of spell or curse. *I must be going out of my mind.* But the paper in his hand was no illusion.

It was leading him to one of the very things Ellie needed at the very time she needed it.

He leaned his head on the carriage and sighed. "Oh, alright, already. I give up." He would help, really help, Ellie find everything she needed. Which meant they would need to take a little journey. He leaned on the carriage, and suddenly had the feeling that it was a gift, sent to help him and Ellie. Who was he to refuse a gift?

From somewhere above, a dove cooed, and he swore he could smell the faintest hint of rosewater in the musty, stale air. The voice of his spirit whispered again, and that was all it took to make up his mind.

CHAPTER X

ELLIE WAITED IN THE SHADOWS, HER STOMACH CHURNING. SHE hadn't asked Ben to come on this expedition, but now she was rethinking that decision. It wasn't that she was afraid, *exactly*, only that she really would rather have someone to talk to other than herself and whatever spirits lurked around Christ Church. But she had already asked so much of him and she didn't want to land them both in trouble.

Her stepmother had not entertained any late-night guests this evening, so she had gone to bed as scheduled. When Ellie had passed her bedroom door, Olivia was snoring so loudly she wouldn't have heard Ellie leave if she stomped down the staircase wearing a man's work boots and playing a trombone. She had all night to run this morbid errand.

Here she stood, in front of the church's door, beneath the shadow of the knife-like steeple, crawling through the shadows like a thief. Which she was, technically, but only out of necessity and not out of malice. Her stepmother had forced her to do this terrible and ghoulish thing. Ellie was glad the burial ground was not within eyesight, so she would not have to look at her mother's grave. Would she be disappointed in her daughter or proud?

There's a good possibility I'm going to Hell for this. She tried one of the double doors at the back of the building. Locked. *Oh well, I guess I'll just have to go home and come another time. Preferably at high noon on a sunny day.* Ellie backed away from the door, wanting to race from this place and not stop until she was in her own bed.

Stop it this instant, you coward. She couldn't run away now, too much depended on her getting what was inside. The crowbar she had brought weighed heavy in her hand. She put the flat end into the gap between the two doors, hoping she would not be struck dead where she stood. Slowly at first, and then with a mighty tug, the door swung open with a splintering of wood. Ellie let the crowbar hang from one hand, nearly slipping from her fingers, and stared into the dark opening.

See? That wasn't so difficult, was it? No, it wasn't, but she still felt sick over the damage. She would just add it to the list of things she would need to be forgiven for after this night was over.

She stepped over the threshold and was swallowed by the darkness inside, cursing herself for forgetting to bring a candle and tinderbox. Holding the crowbar up like a weapon, she stepped from beneath the balcony, suspended over the door, which held the church's pipe organ. Free of its shadow, the sanctuary appeared, lit by streaks of silver moonlight that poured through the huge stained-glass windows.

She hadn't been inside this church for six and a half years, and suddenly memory ran over her like a cold wind. The antique brass chandelier hung above as always, a steadfast guardian. She spotted her family's pew, a quarter of the way from the front, where she had stood between her mother and father on dozens of Sundays, singing hymns, her father's clear baritone mingling with her mother's soprano.

It had all been stolen from them, so maybe it was only fair that she was here, trying to steal it back. She walked up the nave, the path feeling as familiar beneath her feet as if she walked it every Sunday still, ghosts of the past whispering in her ear.

Concentrate!

She kept her gaze on the goal—the floor in front of the altar. It looked five miles away, but she kept moving forward, ignoring the figures in the stained-glass windows, following her progress with stern looks. Late-autumn wind howled as it raced through the steeple, rattling the windows like a specter's chains. She could not shake the feeling that someone was watching her, and a shiver crept up her spine like spiders.

She arrived at her destination, feeling as if she had just run a gauntlet rather than walked the forty feet from the door. Her feet trod on many engraved stones, some with names that had been worn away by time and many feet. They marked the final resting places of the few people important enough to be buried inside the church. As a girl she had memorized the names, and knew exactly which one she wanted. It lay on the floor directly in front of the steps that led up to the altar, just beside the front row of pews.

"Good evening, Bishop White. I'm awfully sorry about this." She thought it was appropriate to apologize to the poor man, who had died a hundred years before she was born. She liked to think that if he knew her predicament, that he would have wanted to help, being a pious man of the cloth. It was a tiny bit of comfort.

She knelt on the cold floor and ran her fingers around the edge, searching for a place where the space between stones was just a little wider. Along one of the long sides of the rectangle was a perfect spot. She slipped the flat edge of the crowbar into the space and pushed down. The metal ground against the stone as the crowbar sunk an inch. Ellie wiped her sweating palms on her coat to improve her grip. She clasped the crowbar handle, and with quick prayer leaned against it as hard as she could.

The stone did not budge.

She pushed again, the only result being burning pain in her arms. A very unladylike word slipped from her mouth, echoing across the sanctuary. Now she *really* wished she had brought Ben. This had seemed like a perfect plan until that moment. There were plenty of graves in the cemetery that belonged to reverends and pastors, but she had thought that digging would be too difficult and too noticeable. This was supposed to have been a simple task—open the crypt, steal a *small* bone, and put the stone back. No one would ever notice or know she had been there. Now what was she going to do?

What she needed was a longer handled instrument, for more lever-age. There wasn't time to go out and look for the tools the gravediggers used, though a shovel might have done the trick. A quick but thorough search of the sanctuary turned up Bibles, hymnbooks, and a half-full bottle of whiskey inside the pulpit. She knelt on the altar steps, her head in her hands, trying desperately not to dissolve into tears.

Suddenly an image came to mind, a memory from watching a hundred Sunday services as a girl. Her head popped up, her eyes wide. *Oh, no, I can't!* At this point, she didn't have much choice. But where would such a thing be kept? There was a door on either side of the altar. Ellie opened the one on the right, but it was only a closet. She grabbed a candle and some matches from one of the shelves and shut the door, then ran across to the other.

The pastor's vestry. Vestments hung in a half-open wardrobe, pointed hats embroidered in gold and silver were lined up along a shelf, and a full-length oval mirror stood in one corner beside a tall bureau. Ellie looked to the opposite corner and her breath came out in a *whoosh* of relief. She pulled the six-foot long pastoral staff from its place on the rack and ran back out to the sanctuary.

The brass-tipped tapered end of the staff just fit between the stones. She reached up and wrapped her hands around the ornate crook at the top.

I am definitely *going to Hell for this.*

Leaning back, she pulled downward. At first there was no progress, but once she lifted her feet from the ground and hung from the end of the staff, the stone grudgingly shifted. She bounced on the balls of her feet and jumped. There was just enough momentum and force that the stone lifted a few inches. Holding on despite trembling arms, she yanked and pulled until the gap had widened enough that she could see inside the crypt beneath. She pushed the staff-lever to the floor and stood on it, then slid her feet down the length of the wood and gripped the stone. With a grunt, she slid it to the side.

The vault was a dark, gaping hole in the floor. Cold air seeped from it, and Ellie had expected there to be a horrific odor, but there was none. The moonlight could not reach inside, so she lit one of the candles she had pilfered from the closet. The smoky yellow light gave little aid, but it was enough. She lay on the floor and reached in. The crypt's walls were lined with brick. The coffin was below the reach of her fingertips. There was room enough to slip down inside, but no way for her to lift the lid if she was standing on it. She picked up the staff, spun it around, and used the crooked end to hook the edge of the coffin's lid. *In for a penny, in for a pound.* The lid lifted upward, revealing the occupant. Fortunately, the candlelight was dim enough that she didn't have a very good look.

She slipped into the crypt, one foot on either side of the coffin. With a deep breath and a hard swallow, she squatted down and snatched a bone from the poor man's hand — the smallest bone she could find. She wouldn't add insult to injury by taking something larger, like his skull, though the idea of carting around a human skull made her giggle, shiver, and want to vomit all at the same time.

"Thank you very much, Your Excellency. You don't know what this means to me." With her prize in her pocket, she hauled herself out of the vault and onto the cold stone floor. She lowered the coffin lid with the staff, sealing up the bishop once more. All that was left was to replace the marker stone. She slipped behind it, her back pressed against the pew, and used her feet to slide it back into place.

It wasn't until the heavy tablet was already moving that she realized her mistake. She watched in horror as the stone tipped sideways and tumbled straight *into* the vault.

Ellie clapped her hands over her mouth to stop her horrified scream as the stone scraped across the vault's brick lining with a sickening crunch, coming to rest at a cockeyed angle. Almost immediately there was a shout from outside.

"Hey, Bob, did you hear that?"

The light of a lantern, swinging on the arm of someone running, moved outside the stained-glass windows. Ellie looked around for another way to escape, but all she saw was the door she had broken to enter.

"Bill, c'mere quick! Someone's broken into the church!"

Ellie scooped up the candle and ran into the pastor's changing room, leaving the pastoral staff lying on the floor. Once inside she leaned against the door and listened. Bob's and Bill's voices loudly exclaim their shock at the damaged church door. Soon enough they would find the staff and the desecrated tomb. Ellie looked around her, and suddenly realized her second mistake.

She was trapped. There was only one door in and out of the room, the same one she had used to enter.

"Saints in Heaven! Bob, will you look at this? Bishop White's crypt's been broken into! Run and get the police, and wake the pastor! I'll search the church, see if the culprit's still here."

Ellie had only seconds before Bill made his way back to the vestry. The door had no lock, of course. She grabbed the one and only chair in the room and wedged it beneath the doorknob, which would at least slow down anyone trying to get inside. Hopefully, it would be enough. She held the candle high and scanned the room again. There were two mullioned windows, too high to reach. With the chair previously engaged, the only thing left to stand on was the bureau.

The doorknob rattled, and someone pushed against it. "Is there someone in there?"

Ellie rolled her eyes. *Genius, isn't he? As if I'm going to reply!* She slid the bureau across the floor until it was under the window, then grabbed the padded footstool in the corner and stood on it. She hoisted onto the top of the dresser

Bill — or was it Bob? — hit the door with something heavy. The chair wouldn't keep him out for long, and soon she would be good and caught. She unfastened the window latch. The door shook again, and behind it was the clatter of feet on stone, shouting, and dogs barking. Bill or Bob had returned, police in tow. She pushed the window open and scooted onto the sill, just as there was another slam to the door. Wood splintered, and the chair gave way. The door swung open, and Ellie only had a glimpse of the men standing behind it before she jumped.

The following afternoon, Ben walked home, pleased with himself over a good day's work. He whistled as he walked, thinking of a warm supper and a quick wash-up before the evening performance.

On a corner near the brand-new South Street Bridge, the cry of a newsboy caught his attention. He didn't usually pay any mind to the news, since none of it had anything to do with him, but today the headline made him stop and listen.

"Burglary at Christ Church! Bishop's final resting place desecrated! Thieves escape! Read all about it!" the boy shouted at the top of his lungs. He waved an evening edition of the *Philadelphia Inquirer* over his head. "Police believe thief involved in the occult! Read all about it!"

Ben grabbed the paper from the boy's hand and skimmed the article. His eyes nearly popped from his head when he discovered what had been taken and the state in which Bishop White's vault had been left. Fortunately, the article also said they had no leads and no idea why someone would go to such lengths to steal a dead man's finger bone, speculating that it was taken for "dark and nefarious purposes." He, on the other hand, had a very good idea who had done it, and the exact reason why. Once he was done scolding her for doing such a reckless thing, he'd ask why he hadn't been invited.

"Are you going to buy that, mister?"

Ben, grinning from ear-to-ear, handed the paper back to the boy. "Sorry." It wasn't that he didn't want to help the lad, but his pockets were empty. "I already read the best story of the day."

CHAPTER XI

ELLIE PEEKED FROM BEHIND THE CURTAIN AND WATCHED THE carriage pull away, taking her stepmother and stepsister in search of new hats and gloves suitable for the bevy of upcoming social calls that were part of the holiday season for a girl on the verge of coming out. Part of her was wistful, wishing she was the one choosing feathers and bows, but mostly she was grateful for their going.

It had been a week since the burglary, and her stepmother and stepsister hadn't left the house without her once. Preparations for the holidays and the ball required her stepmother to drag her along for use as a pack horse. All the while, the mysterious note burned in her thoughts, and she longed for a stretch of solitude so she could search for the answers her unknown friend thought she would find.

Two minutes after the carriage turned the corner, Ellie stood in front of the study doors. The key to her stepmother's secretary was in one hand, a feather duster in the other. Her heart thrummed like a kettle drum.

The quiet of the house seemed to press down on Ellie as she slid back the doors and crept across the plush carpet. She approached the secretary, which stood along the far wall. With the exception of this wall and the one behind her father's desk, every available inch of space was covered with floor-to-ceiling bookcases. Each was filled to bursting with leather-bound volumes, all favorites of Ellie's parents. She lovingly kept the shelves free from dust, but the books sat undisturbed, silent monuments to two people who no longer existed. Her stepmother didn't read much besides ladies' magazines and shopping catalogs, and she had overheard Olivia telling Rebecca once that reading too often would ruin her eyesight, and that men didn't marry girls who wore glasses.

Ellie laid the feather duster, which she had brought to use as an excuse for being in the room if she were caught, on her father's desk. It looked lonely and strange, the top cleared of her father's clutter. Her father would sit in the creaky leather chair, hunched over the blotter, ink-stained fingers clutching the nib of his fountain pen as it scratched across the page.

Her mind painted pictures of the past. Her mother, seated in front of the secretary. Her father at his desk. The two adults working in companionable silence as eight year-old Ellie sat on the floor, looking at one of the hundreds of books, trying to work out the words on the page. She took the book to her father and asked for his help, not realizing she had chosen *Democracy in America,* written in French far beyond the simple vocabulary of a child. Ellie's father looked into his daughter's inquisitive gaze, then at the book, and let out a loud laugh, the corners of his eyes crinkling as he lifted his daughter onto his lap with strong, capable arms that could take away any of her little-girl hurts.

She came back to the present with tears burning her eyes. Tears for her father, for her mother, and for herself. Her life was nothing like she dreamed it would be. There was no laughter anymore, not in this house of silence and secrets.

Ellie gave each cheek an angry swipe, brushing off the tears. *I'm wasting time with ghosts.* She returned her attention to the secretary. Olivia always kept it locked, and until now Ellie had never had a reason to look inside. She stared at the desk as if it were a wild animal, ready to bite her. *Quit being such a goose. For goodness' sake, you snuck into a church and broke into a crypt! One little secretary couldn't possibly be half as frightening!*

Still, something about it seemed foreign to her. Someone thought there was something inside she needed to see. Knowledge is power, that's what Ellie's father used to tell her whenever she complained about her studies. The memory was like a stab to her heart. He had been stripped of his power. She would take it back, for both of them.

Her backbone steeled, she slipped the key into the keyhole. The latch made a soft click as it released. She pulled open the two small drawers in the front. Papers filled both of them, all ordinary. One held a stack of bills — the milkman, the grocer, and coal delivery service. The other drawer held some personal correspondence, though if Olivia had any friends Ellie was unaware of it. She only socialized with the upper-class wives she was constantly trying to impress, spending her time at the club vying for invitations to play bridge or come to tea. None of them really accepted her, because Olivia Banneker, though she bore a name of status, was not one of them. They all knew she had been a governess before becoming Mrs. Ephraim Banneker. She had no name of her own, not like Ellie's mother did before she had married.

She returned the papers to their places with a disappointed sigh. Nothing here looked out of the ordinary. Perhaps the anonymous note-sender had been mistaken, or her stepmother had moved the incriminating evidence. She lowered the secretary's drop-front. Behind it were a series of pigeonholes, full of assorted bits and bobs. Ellie seated herself in the cushioned chair and peered inside. One cubby held an array of fountain pens, nibs, and bottles of ink, along with some sealing wax and her stepmother's heavy brass seal, monogrammed with her initials. Another housed a box of her stepmother's stationary and calling cards, her name inscribed in beautiful swirling script across rectangles of heavy paper. Everything one would expect to find in a lady's writing desk.

Ellie leaned back into the chair. She didn't know what she expected to find, but was still surprised by the depth of her disappointment. It was her own fault; she had built it up in her mind that there would be some marvelous discovery, some bit of information that would suddenly change her entire life. *I need to get my head out of the clouds. There is no fairy godmother here to wave her wand and bring Mother back or make Father well.*

The windows rattled in their frames, shaken by the brisk autumn wind. Ellie jumped, rattled as well. That was all she needed to remind her that she couldn't spend the day lounging about. Her stepmother could return at any moment.

She pushed herself out of the chair, raised the drop front of the desk, and closed the drawers. As she put the key into the lock, she noticed something sticking out from above the piece of wood between the drawers. It looked like the corner of a piece of paper. She grasped it with two fingers and tugged on it, but it didn't budge. Where was the rest of it? Ellie peeked inside the drop front, but there was no paper in evidence. She pulled one of the drawers out completely and looked inside the gaping hole, but it was solid wood on both sides. Nothing could have fallen out and gotten into the space between.

She replaced the drawer and turned to the paper again. The gap the paper stuck out from was only slightly larger than a fingernail. She grabbed her stepmother's letter opener from the top of the secretary and slipped it into the space to try to pry the paper out. Instead, the entire panel fell open. Panicked she had broken the desk, she dropped the letter opener on the floor and grasped the panel so she could put it back in place. The panel did not come away in her hands, as she expected, and when she looked closer, she saw two small, hidden hinges on the bottom of the panel. It was supposed to open — a secret hiding place. The corner of paper was part of a tidy bundle of folded pages, tucked into the space behind the panel. She snaked her hand into the small space and drew out the bundle, which was tied up with a strip of dark leather.

Ellie took her prize to her father's desk. Releasing the knot, she unfolded the pages. Lines of calligraphy filled the parchment. *Last Will and Testament* scrolled across the top of the first page. She scanned the first few lines and frowned when she saw her father's name. It probably wasn't so unusual for her stepmother to have her father's will, but why was she hiding it? It should be locked in the safe, hidden behind the large oil painting that hung on the wall over her father's desk, or at least in a safe deposit box at the bank.

Ellie's annoyance turned to curiosity. She supposed she realized her father had a will, but it wasn't any of her business. Or was it? She was his only child, after all. Maybe she *should* understand what her father's wishes were for his estate. But the thought of her father's death made her breath catch in her throat.

I'm only being practical, a part of her counseled, sounding quite a bit like her mother. Her father wasn't getting better. What would happen when he was gone? She skimmed over the first page, which was mostly legal bits about her father's sound mind, arrangements for his funeral — Ellie shuddered — and who he named as executor of his will (Mr. McIntyre, a colleague at the bank). Mr. McIntyre had not come by the house since her father fell ill. Like everyone else, he must have believed Olivia's lies that Ephraim Banneker was on sabbatical in France.

Ellie turned the page and continued to read. Halfway down, she nearly dropped the document. She read the lines again and then again to make perfectly sure of what they meant.

"I bequeath my estate, in its entirety, to my daughter, Eleanor Violetta Banneker. If she is not of a majority age when I pass on, I appoint Thomas McIntyre, the executor of this will, as her guardian and the manager of the estate until Eleanor reaches the age of seventeen, unless I remarry, in which case my wife will become Eleanor's guardian. If Eleanor predeceases me, the estate will be sold and all proceeds given to the Wills Eye Hospital in Philadelphia."

She thumbed to the final page of the document. There was her father's signature, strong and clear, made by a hand untouched by illness. Beside it were the signatures of Mr. McIntyre and her father's attorney. On the last line was the date that her father had signed the will. It was just a month after her mother had died, in that small window of time between his grieving for one wife and being forced to fall in love with another.

Ellie took the will and ran into her father's room. He lay with his back to her. She skirted the bed and knelt beside his head.

"Papa?"

Her father lifted his red-rimmed eyes to meet her clear gaze. "Hello, darling."

She showed him the will. "Papa? Do you remember this?"

He wrinkled his brow and studied the paper. "Oh, I haven't seen that in years. Where did you find it?" He paused, thinking. "There was something... someone wanted me to do..."

"What? What was it?"

He shook his head. "I'm sorry, I can't remember."

Ellie kissed her father on the forehead. "It's all right, Papa. Just rest." She left, closing the door behind her, and returned to the study.

The rest of the papers were still on the desk. She unfolded them and found it was another formal-looking document. At first Ellie thought it must be her stepmother's own will, but a second look said told her that it was not.

It was a contract.

With her heart galloping like a runaway horse, she flipped to the last of the six pages and saw her stepmother's signature. The other signature was unreadable, but she recognized it. It was the same spidery scrawl of whoever penned the two spells Ellie had found hidden beneath her stepmother's jewelry box.

The face of her stepmother's curious middle-of-the-night visitor, with eyes that glowed like fallen stars jumped to her mind. She and Olivia had made a deal, this contract in Ellie's hands right now. The stranger had written the spells, told Olivia how to capture her father's heart and erase Ellie from the world.

Ellie scanned the pages, looking for words that would tell her of the deal her stepmother had made. She skipped over all of the standard legal language and pulled her brow low as she concentrated on decoding the long paragraphs. Somewhere around the middle of the third page, she finally came to the point. As the words sunk in, her blood turned to ice, and her stomach clenched as if she were about to revisit her breakfast.

What has she done?

Ellie read the pages, seeing the words but not believing them. As much as her father's will had shed light upon the last few years, so this document cast it in shadow. She held the will in one hand, the contract in the other, feeling as if she held her own life balanced between them.

And now that you know, what are you going to do about it? a voice as cold as the wind whispered in her mind. Confronting her stepmother directly was out of the question. Frankly, Ellie had no idea what to do with the information. But there was someone who might...

She tied the pages up, then clapped the secret panel shut and locked the desk. With singular purpose she ran downstairs and through the kitchen, grabbing her coat and hat from the hook and slipping them on as she walked out the back door, the stolen papers clutched in her hand.

Ben dropped his head in his hand, his eyes heavy. Fortunately, the shop was empty, not unusual for a Tuesday afternoon. The Exposition had closed, taking with it most of the tourist traffic. Ben's mother had commented that while she would miss the extra income, she was glad for the respite before the deluge of holiday shoppers descended. Ben, on the other hand, was bored. The clock ticked behind him, a steady, hypnotic rhythm that did nothing to help him stay awake.

A hand slapped the counter hard, jarring him from his trance and making him jump. "Hey, sleepyhead," Harry chirped, far too cheerily for Ben's liking. "What's the matter with you, anyway?"

Ben rubbed his eyes and stifled a yawn, though his first instinct was to box Harry's ears. "I'm tired."

"Whose fault is that?" Harry leaned on the counter across from Ben and gave him the same chiding look their mother favored. "No one told you to stay out all hours of the day and night."

"I have responsibilities." While he didn't feel it was necessary to explain the details of his life to his little brother, the conversation was better than the quiet. "I'm still cleaning and taking inventory in the Props barn. That takes most of the day. I work at the theater every night. And Father hasn't let me stop helping out here."

"That still leaves time for sleeping," Harry replied in his most logical tone. It grated on Ben's nerves. "You're out the door before the neighbor's roosters start crowing. You have no one to blame for being tired but yourself."

Ben could not answer his brother's argument. To answer would force him to explain that the extra time he wasn't spending in his bed was being spent either in the Props barn, working on his secret project, or in the scrap yards, looking for parts. Except for lack of sleep, he couldn't complain. Things went well. He'd finished the repairs to the frame, and installed an old copper tank he had found in the scrap yard as a perfect boiler. Ben was confident the carriage would be finished very soon. He wasn't as confident it would run, but he would cross that bridge when he got to it.

"I suppose you're right, Harry." He let an unexplained but satisfied smile touch his lips, and gave his brother's hair a good-natured ruffle. Ellie was well worth the lost sleep. When she found out that he had solved the riddle of the first item on the list, and that he had also come up with a way to acquire it, she would be so grateful. She might even be moved to throw her arms around him again. He smiled.

When Ellie herself stepped into the shop half a heartbeat later, as if his thoughts had conjured her, Ben's weariness vanished. The bells over the shop door clanged alarmingly as she charged inside.

"Ellie? What are you doing here?" His realized he sounded as if he weren't happy to see her, and stumbled to try again. "Uh, oh, I mean, hello!" He rounded the end of the counter, but halfway across the shop his smile faded into concern. She looked as if she was being chased by the devil himself—her hat askew, her coat unbuttoned. A sprinkling of the half-hearted snowstorm that had been trying all afternoon to turn into something more menacing lay across her shoulders. Her eyes were wild, round as a clock's face, and her skin was flushed with the cold. She breathed as if she had just run across the city.

"Ellie? What's wrong?"

Ellie met Ben's gaze. She stepped toward him, but the toe of her boot caught the rug and she stumbled. Ben instinctively reached out and wrapped his arms around her. He pulled her upright and toward him, and when she lifted her face and her gaze met his, he jumped back to the proper distance of an arm's length.

"Are you alright?" Ben's throat went dry and his voice came out in a scratchy whisper. He was very glad the shop was empty, even of his mother. *Especially* of his mother. She would have asked far too many questions for Ben's comfort, and then scolded him for being too forward. He glanced at Harry, who stared at them while doing a fabulous impression of a freshly-caught trout. Ben hoped his little brother knew enough to keep quiet. He would have to explain everything later and make him understand.

Ellie turned toward him, and her lower lip trembled. She held out a small, flat bundle.

"I found the answers we've been looking for, Ben. And I really wish I hadn't."

CHAPTER XII

EN STARED AT THE TWO ITEMS ON THE TABLE IN FRONT OF HIM, trying to figure out what Ellie saw in them that he didn't. He had spent the last thirty minutes in silence, carefully examining both, scratching his head over the second.

"Ben?" Ellie sat in the most comfortable chair in the back room of the shop. Her hands cradled an old chipped cup filled with hot tea brought to her by a thoughtful-yet-bewildered Harry.

"Ben, what are you thinking?"

Ben lifted Ephraim Banneker's will and turned to the second page. He opened his mouth, then closed it, thought for a second, and tried again. "What does this have to do with your... problem?"

Ellie folded her hands, set them on the table, and spoke in a slow, patient voice. "I had always assumed that my stepmother's sudden change of heart regarding me was because of something that *I* did. But it wasn't anything I did at all. My father didn't leave Olivia any of his money. Not one thin dime. It's the reason she hated me *and* the reason she never... sent me away. If something happened to him before I turned seventeen, she would need me so she could keep his money.

"Without me, she would lose everything. I can almost guarantee you that there's a copy of that document somewhere, probably at the bank."

Ben rubbed his chin, devious thoughts whirling in his mind. "But you're already seventeen. And your father isn't likely to die anytime soon. He was always been healthy as a bull."

Ellie nearly choked on her tea. Her face turned ghostly white, and Ben was sorry he had asked the question.

"Are you alright?"

She nodded, coughed into her hand, and then tucked her lower lip between her teeth and gazed at the table, a gesture Ben discovered he was fond of.

"There's something I haven't told you. I should have, but it was just never the proper time, and now here we are. Ben, my father is ill."

Ben's mouth fell open just as his body dropped into the seat across from her, which was fortunately placed, otherwise he would have landed on the floor.

"How... ill?" He was sure she wasn't talking about a simple head cold.

"Gravely. And he has been, for almost a year. I don't know what kind of illness. A doctor has been to look at him, once, but nothing has helped. And... Olivia's strange visitor, with the odd eyes? Her and my stepmother argued about my father's illness and the contract. She said something about there being a price."

Gears clicked in place, and Ben figured out where she was going. "You think that your father's health is the price for Olivia's bargain." He picked up the contract and studied it again. He still didn't understand it, but with this new information it seemed more ominous.

"Not just his health," Ellie whispered. "His life."

The words of the old medium from the Exposition came back to haunt Ben, and he felt the blood drain from his face. If Ellie didn't break the spell by midnight on New Year's Eve, they both would be bound forever. If Mr. Banneker died, Ellie would be trapped. The tiny kernel of belief in magic that he had found in the Props barn grew. Any illness that was as bad as Ellie described would surely be contagious — scarlet fever, consumption, measles. Everyone else in the house would have gotten it by now.

Ellie's voice was lifeless as she continued. "My father fell ill with this will in place. I don't know why he didn't change it once he re-married." She paused, her eyes lighting up with understanding. "I think Olivia tried to have him change it, once he was under her spell, but she couldn't get him to do it. Either way, he did not leave any way for her to get her hands on the estate once I was old enough to inherit it myself. And now, if he dies and something was to happen to me..." Her pause was heavy with implication. "Everything would be sold and the money donated to the hospital. She has to get out now."

Ben's eyebrows lifted as he made the connection. "She has to make sure Rebecca finds a husband *this* season."

"Exactly. My stepmother will need someplace to go when my father..." Ellie let her words trail off, leaving the thought unspoken but hanging heavily over them.

"Poor Rebecca." He didn't mean for it to sound as if Ellie's problems were trivial. But Olivia was manipulating her own daughter in addition to everyone else she claimed as family. Rebecca and Ben had only shared a few minutes of conversation, but she seemed sweet. She had certainly been excited about looking at machines, so she couldn't be all bad.

But Rebecca was not his problem. If it was a choice between which of them would be stuck with Olivia, there was no choice.

"If Olivia can find Rebecca a husband *this* season, she'll have nothing more to worry about. She will make sure she is welcome at her new son-in-law's home, so my father's money won't matter anymore."

Ben tipped his chair back and crossed his arms over his chest, letting out a long, low whistle. "She's diabolical, that one. Slippery as a greased pig."

Ellie pressed her lips together, but the smile was unmistakable. Perhaps she, like Ben was imagining a pig wearing Olivia's hat. "Yes, well... she isn't a stupid woman."

"And that's probably the nicest thing you can say about her."

"Oh, you're a horrid boy!" Ellie's smile turned to a laugh that betrayed her words. Ben suddenly wished she didn't have to go back to that place she called home, and would instead stay here with him where he could continue to make her laugh.

The smiles lasted only a moment. Ellie's faded as she glanced at the contract. "Let me see that." She took the document and flipped to one section, which she pointed out to Ben. "What do you think this bit means? I haven't truly been able to make heads nor tails of it, outside of what part my father plays."

Ben scanned the lines. "I can't even begin to explain it. I guess my problem is that I don't understand exactly what it is your stepmother wanted this mystery woman to do for her. It's not clearly spelled out here."

Ellie studied Ben for a moment, her brow furrowed. "I've been turning it over and over in my mind. One moment I think I do understand because it would explain everything. But then I think I can't possibly understand, because the whole idea is just so absurd, and my thoughts begin to chase each other like a dog trying to catch its tail." She pressed her fingers to her forehead. "You must think I'm a raving lunatic. One straight jacket, no waiting." She laughed again, but this time there was no merriment in it.

Ben leaned in toward Ellie, breathing in her delicate rosewater scent. "No, I don't." He wanted to add that he thought she was wonderful, but couldn't make the words come without sounding terribly forward.

"Let's just take it at its word for a moment. In which case, my stepmother contracted with someone for... I can't say it out loud. It's silly, I know, but I'm afraid I'll call something ferocious down on our heads."

"That *is* silly. I'll read it to you." Ben skirted the table and read over her shoulder. "'In exchange for a price, to be decided upon by the first party, the undersigned will receive her heart's desire.'"

Ellie cast a significant look, and Ben pulled his brow low, thinking. "What kind of contract *is* that? Who could possibly provide someone's heart's desire unless it's something you can touch, like a piece of furniture or jewelry, and then why not just say so?"

"You know who could do it." It was all she needed to say. Ben understood. He had not seen the strange eyes of Olivia's visitor, but at this point he was willing to believe there was something not quite right about her.

"All right, let's say she could. What sane and rational person signs a contract with no specific price in writing? Sounds like something my supposed ancestors wrote about."

Ellie did not hear him. "No one ever said Olivia was sane or rational. And we know the price..." She set the pages on the table, her voice trembling. "It all makes sense."

Ben crossed his arms over his chest. "It's a little too Faustian for me. How desperate did your stepmother have to be to agree to this, I wonder?"

Ellie studied the inside of her teacup. "I know it's less than charitable of me to say, but if my stepmother has a soul, I'm sure she'd gladly sell it to get what she desires most — to remain part of high society." She flipped to the signature page again. "Look at the date on the contract. It's a year *before* she married my father. My mother was *still alive*. Oh, dear!" Her eyes grew wide and fearful. "What if her heart's desire was to marry my father?"

"But he was married then, and she was your governess."

Ellie's cheeks turned red, and Ben was sure she was having the same inappropriate thoughts as he. He had spent enough time in the theater to know that just because a man was married didn't mean he couldn't enjoy the pleasure of another woman's company. Secret dalliances were practically a nightly ritual in the dressing rooms below the stage at the

Walnut. But would Mr. Banneker have been unfaithful to Ellie's mother? A mere affair wouldn't get Olivia a fortune or a name, though. Ben cleared his throat and changed the subject.

"Let's assume she wanted to marry your father and take his money. What could this person she made the bargain with do to make that happen?"

Ellie gasped, and her face went from red to the white of old cream. Her voice came out barely a whisper. "She would have had to get rid of my mother. Do you think she…" She couldn't even finish, but Ben knew what she meant.

"I hadn't even considered that. But no, how could she? Your mother's death was an accident. Your stepmother was at home all day. I remember, because she yelled at me for peeking in at your dance lesson. She threatened to beat me with a switch."

"What if it *wasn't* an accident?" Ellie said without looking at Ben. "What if it was some kind of magic that caused the carriage to run off the bridge and fall into the river?"

"It was an *accident*," Ben spoke softly but emphatically. It wasn't that he thought it was completely out of the realm of possibility, especially after the revelations of the last ten minutes. But Ellie was teetering close to the brink of hysteria. "A dog ran across the road and spooked the horses. The police said so."

He tried to steer their conversation back to the subject at hand. "So, if it was your stepmother's desire to marry your father, and then she gave him a love potion to make him fall in love with her, do you think *she* loves *him*? I can't imagine marrying someone I didn't love." Ben glanced sidelong at Ellie, and it was his turn to blush.

She scoffed. "No, of course not. She wanted his money, and to be able to live well and ingratiate herself and her daughter into society." But the words were not spoken with conviction. Ben considered that perhaps she didn't know her stepmother's heart as well as she thought.

"It's all well and good to know the why of everything, but it doesn't solve the problem. I have the white candle, and I have the… never mind." She cleared her throat. "I only have one of the things on the list, and there are only a few weeks until the New Year." She sniffed and wiped her nose again, her eyes filling.

Ben smiled and stood straight. "Wait right here." He ran down to the basement. The playbill from the warehouse sat on the end of his workbench. He grabbed it and the item beside it, and then dashed back upstairs. He placed the second item on the table in front of a confused-looking Ellie.

"What's this?" She looked at the dried bird's claw, her lip curled in disgust and fascination.

"Why, that's one genuine raven's claw, suitable for breaking spells."

She looked up at Ben, horrified. "You didn't... kill an innocent bird, did you?"

He held his hands. "Oh, no! I took it from a stuffed raven that I found in the Props warehouse. I think it was left over from one of those Poe readings the theater management likes to put on at Halloween."

Ellie relaxed. "Oh, well, then. Thank you." She lifted the claw with the tips of two fingers and dropped it into her bag with a shudder.

Ben leaned across the table and whispered. "What? That little thing makes you squeamish, when you've been down in the depths of a crypt and stolen a holy man's finger bone?"

Her eyes bulged and she gasped. "How did you know?"

Ben sat back and shrugged. "I read the papers."

Her face lit up like fireworks on the Fourth of July. "Oh, I'm so embarrassed." She bent her head, but not before Ben caught sight of her bottom lip between her teeth, holding back a smile. "I should have asked you to come with me, but I didn't think you would."

"I probably wouldn't have, because then I would be an accomplice and have to turn you in to the police."

Ellie's head whipped up. "You wouldn't have!"

Ben laughed. "No, of course not. I'm a little sad I missed the adventure. But I have something else for you." With a bit of a flourish, he set the playbill on the table. She wrinkled her brow as she lifted the dusty paper from the table.

"How is this supposed to help me?"

"Turn it over." Ben sat back and waited for her to read the advertisement, which was for a popular seaside resort. Her eyes moved back and forth as she scanned the page, and he knew she had cottoned on to his thinking when her eyebrows shot up and her mouth dropped open.

"This can't be. Is it? Whoever heard of something as absurd as a beach covered in diamonds?"

Ben laughed out loud, unable to help himself, leaning over to catch his breath. "I'm sorry. You believe you've been bewitched, and that your stepmother is meeting with a person who might not be a person, but *this* sounds absurd?" He paused but got no reply except Ellie's surprised expression, which made him laugh harder.

"I didn't mean to make fun. But I asked around, and it's for real. They're not real diamonds, but that's what they're called. Cape May Diamonds. They're all over the beach, washed up by the ocean, just waiting to be picked up. Diamonds that have been kissed by the sea."

Ellie bit her lower lip again, hesitant belief appearing in her eyes. He found he was quite fond of that look too.

"I'm not quite sure that's what the medium meant, Ben."

"I know it sounds strange, but I am sure this is it. I feel it in my gut." He couldn't offer her a better explanation, because then he'd have to admit how the playbill was dropped into his lap, and admit that he was starting to believe in magic. He wasn't quite ready for that yet.

"But… how are we going to get there?" Ellie said.

This is the best part, Ben mused. Or it would be, anyway. "Just leave that to me. Can you be ready to go in, say, a week?" That *should* give him enough time. "I'll find a way."

Ellie stood, her eyes sparkling like emeralds. She grabbed the contract and the will and folded and tied them as they were before.

"I have to put these away before she misses them." Her fingers shook as she tied the leather. As Ben showed her to the front door she bounced on the balls of her feet, like she had when they were nine years old and planning to sneak into the kitchen to steal some sweets. *Some things never change.*

At the door, Ellie turned and pressed the papers to her chest. "I finally feel as if I have a chance. Can't you feel it, Ben? Everything is going to work out and go back to the way it's supposed to be, and all because of you."

She lifted herself onto her toes and planted a kiss on Ben's cheek. Before he could say another word, she turned and rushed out of the shop, leaving Ben staring at the place she had stood, the cold wind blowing through the open door.

A tap on his shoulder made Ben jump and spin around. Harry stood there, fists jammed onto his hips and a look of scrutiny on his face. He lowered his chin and looked at Ben over the top of his glasses.

"Mind telling me what all that was about?"

Ellie had to keep her head down, her face away from the biting wind and flying snow that poked at her like needles. But she felt as warm as spring.

A single spot darkened her mood. Her conversation with Ben about the pages in her hand unwound like a spool, drawing out a thread of disturbing thoughts. Could her stepmother really have planned everything? *If I find out she had anything to do with my mother's death...* She clenched her free hand into a fist, not daring to finish the thought, because she could not even think of what she would do. At the moment, with her face being unrecognizable to the world, there wasn't much she *could* do. Well, there was, but it would be unadvisable to poison her stepmother or push her in front of a moving train. Ellie was so focused on her thoughts that she did not see the black woolen greatcoat that blocked the sidewalk.

"Oh!" she cried as she ran headlong into the very solid occupant of the coat. Her petite frame was no match for the man's bulk, and she stumbled backward, greeting the snow-covered pavement with the whole of her backside.

"Goodness." A familiar voice, smooth as fresh butter, spoke over Ellie's head. She peered from beneath the brim of her bonnet, squinting as flakes of snow dropped onto her face, sticking to her eyelashes. The person she had collided with stood above her, blocking the weak winter sunlight, and for a second Ellie could have sworn she was looking at an angel. She blinked, and when she opened her eyes again, she saw the outline of a man. The cape of his Petersham hung from his shoulders like a pair of wings.

"Are you all right, miss?" The man shifted so that Ellie could see his face, and she wished with all her heart that she could crawl away and hide in the nearest snowdrift. It was Hamilton Scott.

"Yes, I'm fine, thank you," she muttered, or at least she thought she did. She was so stunned by the sudden meeting, followed by the racing of her pulse and the disconcerting sensation that her stomach was ready to leap from its place inside her, that she could not be sure she had actually spoken. It was the jolt of being knocked to the ground, she was sure, and had nothing to do with *who* she had run into.

Hamilton looked at her, blue eyes full of concern and perhaps a bit of amusement. The snow stuck like bits of confectioner's sugar to his eyebrows and the single lock of blonde hair that his bowler did not cover. She caught herself staring and felt her face flush and her breath become scarce. She couldn't blame it on the heat this time.

He reached toward Ellie, and she recoiled slightly, confused as to his intention. She felt ridiculous when he gently grasped her hand, the soft leather of his glove closing around her cold, naked fingers. With his other hand he clasped her elbow, and before she could say that she was perfectly capable of getting up herself, he had lifted her from the ground and set her back upon her feet.

"There now. Are you sure you're alright?"

Ellie, having now completely misplaced her voice, could do nothing but nod. The places where Hamilton's hands had touched her blazed as if they had been exposed to fire. He studied her for a moment, his gaze curious. "I'm sorry if this seems forward of me, but have we met before? You seem familiar." He snapped his mouth closed and pulled away from her. "Please, you must forgive me for my complete lack of manners." He looked at his fingers in an embarrassed and boyish way that was nothing short of endearing.

Ellie realized with growing horror the potential disaster of her situation. First, the thought of Hamilton seeing her dressed in her maid's attire made panic rise in her chest like bread dough. Not that she dared to hope he thought of her at all, but if he did, she wanted him to remember her as he had seen her in the greenhouse at the Exposition.

Her other problem was much more urgent.

"I'm sorry," she said, taking care not to make eye contact. "I don't think we've ever met, sir."

Hamilton's gaze shifted from her face to her clothing. "Oh, no, I suppose not. You must simply remind me of someone." He stepped aside and tipped his hat to her, the gesture cordial but stiff. "I will let you get on with your business, miss."

Ellie dipped a small curtsey. "Thank you for your help, sir." She walked away with quick, purposeful steps that hovered on the edge of a run. She rounded the next corner, even though it was in the opposite direction she needed to go, just to get out of his line of sight. Falling against the cold brick wall of a haberdashery, she closed her eyes and thanked the stars she had escaped before calamity had struck.

While her heart had wanted nothing less than for her to scream to Mr. Scott who she was, her brain had fortunately remained in charge and kept her mouth shut. Not only was she embarrassed about the way she was dressed, the terrible scene that could have come to pass played itself out in her mind — Mr. Scott seeing Olivia at some party or another, telling her with an amused chuckle how he had literally run into her niece on the street.

Ellie couldn't begin to fathom the depth of her stepmother's rage if that happened. All her plans could be torn asunder in an instant. On top of everything else, she just couldn't stand the look on his face when he finally realized the shabby maid *actually was* the same girl he had met before. It would shatter her heart into a million pieces.

She shook her head clear. *Why should I care what Mr. Scott thinks?* She recognized the swooping, fluttery sensation in her chest when she thought of his handsome face, how his strong arms had held her. It was nearly the same feeling she had when she had been in Ben's arms, listening to his laugh, only it seemed to burn brighter. Or maybe that was because he had just left.

No, no, no! You stupid girl! She pressed her head to the brick wall and groaned. *You might as well be in love with the King of France as Hamilton Scott. Never in a hundred years would he ever look my way.* Even if he did, she wanted him to see Eleanor Banneker, not Ann Gibson, the preposterous identity Olivia had thrust upon her.

The clock over the nearby Rittenhouse's Watch and Clock rang the hour, shaking Ellie from her reverie. She pushed away from the wall, angry with herself for letting infatuation get the better of her. That's all it could be, infatuation, because she had only met the man twice. There was no possibility she was actually in love with him. She needed to keep her head about her, and not become distracted by charming and attractive gentlemen.

If her luck held, her stepmother and stepsister would still be out shopping. She would be able get inside and put the papers back into the secret compartment of the secretary with no one the wiser.

The papers.

Ellie looked at her empty hands as if she were noticing them for the first time in her life. Where were the papers? They had been in her hands when she left the bookshop. Somewhere between there and here, she had lost them. Her stomach gave an uncomfortable lurch. She must have dropped them when she plowed into Mr. Scott. With equal amounts caution and hope, she peered around the corner. He was gone. She crept out onto the sidewalk, scanning the area and trying not to look as frantic as she felt, almost willing the bundle to appear before her.

But her luck, it would seem, had run out.

CHAPTER XIII

N OVEMBER EXITED, SENT ON HIS WAY WITH FEASTING AND THE QUIET giving of thanks. December made her grand entrance from stage right, wrapped in a stole of snow and cold, bitter air which forced everyone to go about dressed as if they were wearing every scrap of clothing they owned.

Three days after Ellie burst into the bookshop, Ben entered the Props barn, happy to escape the weather. The air inside did not even have a passing acquaintance with warm, but at least he was protected from the wind and snow.

"Wait for me, will you?" Harry scampered in behind him, breathing hard as if he had run all the way from home.

"It's not my fault you can't keep up," Ben chided.

"Your legs are longer than mine." Harry tried to pull the door shut behind him, but the wind was stronger than his ten-year-old arms, and Ben had to help him.

"Again, not my fault," Ben replied, but he smiled as he said it. He didn't mind that his brother had tagged along. After so many lonely hours in the barn, he was glad for company. Besides, Harry, like a good little brother, had threatened to tell their mother about Ellie if Ben didn't bring him.

"Come on, this way."

Shedding his hat, gloves, and overcoat like a snake shedding its skin, Ben walked down one of the recently cleared aisles, straight toward the back of the building with Harry on his heels.

"Wow." Harry gazed, wide-eyed, at the immensity of the barn and the now-organized piles of props and neatly stacked flats. He picked up a sword and swung it over his head. "This place is amazing."

"It's all right, I guess. Put that down before you hurt yourself." Ben did not spare even a passing glance for the props. The wonder they had held for him had long since worn as thin as the knees of Harry's pants. He still had a long way to go before he was finished cleaning, but he had made enough headway to keep his father and the Properties Master satisfied.

Harry replaced the sword and moved on to an old painting of a vase of flowers, yellowing in its frame. "So, this is where you've been spending all your time?" He had a knack for stating the obvious.

Ben nodded. "But not just cleaning. Wait until you see."

They arrived at the back of the building, where Ben had cleared a space large enough for an elephant to turn around in. In the center, like the main attraction at an art gallery, sat the carriage beneath its canvas cover.

Harry approached it carefully, eyes wide. "What is it?"

"Just watch." Ben grabbed the canvas with both hands, and, using his best magician's flourish, pulled the cover off of the former horse-pulled carriage.

Harry's mouth fell open. He stepped toward the newly made machine, amazed. "It's just like that drawing in your book!"

Ben stood beside his creation, chest swelling with pride, and basked in the glow of Harry's admiration. Not that Ben didn't deserve it — the carriage was the greatest piece of machinery he had ever built — but it was nice to have his work appreciated by someone other than himself.

Harry walked around the carriage slowly. "You built this all yourself? How?"

"It wasn't easy," Ben replied with the smallest bit of exaggeration. "Getting all the parts was the hardest." He ran his fingertips along the side, feeling the smoothness of the wooden panels he had spent hours sanding by hand.

"It's wonderful," Harry said. "Except it looks a bit worse for wear."

"It needs paint, I know. We can do that today, right after the dress rehearsal."

Harry's eyebrows disappeared beneath the shaggy overhang of his hair. "Dress rehearsal? Wait, you don't even know if it works?"

"Well, no." Ben rubbed the back of his neck. "I haven't started it up yet."

"Afraid it won't work?" Harry teased as he hauled himself onto the runner, his hair falling into his eyes. He peered in the window, leaving the smudge of his nose print on the glass.

Ben stumbled over his words. "Uh... er... well, not exactly. In theory, I've done everything right, and it should work." He didn't say out loud what else he was thinking—that if it didn't work, he would only have three days to fix it.

Harry hopped to the floor and dusted his hands. "No better time to try it out than the present. C'mon, Ben, I want a ride!"

Ben lifted his brother's hat and mussed his hair. "Sometimes, Harry, you're not a complete ninny. Just let me double check everything, and I'll start it up." He looked beneath the carriage, reaching in to pull and push on belts and flywheels, giving the once-over to the pipes and valves he had painstakingly installed over the past few weeks. Then he tapped the brass tank under the dickey box. The tank replied with a deep, wet-sounding ring. There was another tank attached to the rear of the carriage, and he triple-checked its connector and the bracing that secured it.

"Everything looks good." He hopped up onto the seat.

Harry jumped up beside him. "What's this for?" He pointed to the carriage's dashboard, which had been fitted with a variety of knobs and gauges.

"That one tells me the temperature of the water in the boiler, which is under the seat. This one, next to it, tells me the amount of pressure running through the system." He slid behind the steering mechanism, which he had fashioned from a discarded bicycle handlebar. "Now, lean over and watch the wheels." Ben twisted the bars back and forth. His brother's gasp echoed into the barn. "The wheels turn! How did you do that?"

"My secret." It was a bit of genius on Ben's part, attaching chains between the wheels and the handlebars, but he wasn't about to impart the idea to Harry. Part of the showman's code was to always leave the audience wanting more.

"Let's go already! Come on, Ben! I want to see it move!" Harry bounced in the seat like a rubber ball, shaking the entire carriage.

"All right, all right, fine. But you need to get out and wait over there." Ben pointed to a place a dozen yards away from the carriage.

"Aw, why?"

"Because there's just as good a chance this thing will blow up as start." He hitched a thumb over his shoulder. "That tank on the back is full of coal gas."

Harry, not needing further encouragement, scrambled from the seat. Ben's hand hovered above the red button just to the right of the steering mechanism. He wasn't surprised that his fingers trembled, but didn't know if it was from fear or anticipation. Sweat beaded on his brow and he wiped it away with the back of his hand.

"Just do it!" Harry called. "Don't be such a chicken."

Ben laughed, releasing the tension inside him like an open valve.

"Just hold your horses. And cross your fingers." With a prayer and a squeeze of his lucky gear, he closed his eyes and pushed the button. The hiss of gas being released was followed by a few loud clicks as the striker snapped across the flint, then a whoosh as the lamp burner beneath the boiler under his seat caught.

So far, so good. He hopped down and examined the undercarriage, watching the blue flames lick the bottom of the water tank.

"Is that it?" Harry called. "Pretty disappointing. I was hoping it would blow up." His giggle echoed around the barn.

"Ha, ha, so funny. Maybe you should join a vaudeville act. No, that's not all. It takes a few minutes for the water in the tank to boil. Then I can start the engine."

Ben hauled himself back into the dickey box and watched the gauges climb. When the temperature and pressure were both just right, he pressed a second button beside the steering mechanism.

The machine roared to life. The engine, constructed of pilfered leather belts, a flywheel, and some makeshift pistons, along with assorted gears, springs, and clockworks, sounded like a giant cat. If the cat was coughing up a fur ball. The entire carriage vibrated with the energy of it, and Ben vibrated as well, shaking with the excitement of his accomplishment. Harry shouted and clapped, galloping around in a circle, using his hat like a riding crop.

"Come on," Ben called. "Let's take a little ride."

Harry practically flew into the seat beside him.

"Ready?"

Harry's head bobbed up and down with such ferocity Ben thought for certain it would roll off of his shoulders. He pointed to the brass rail on the far side of the box. "Then hold on. This might be a little bumpy."

Ben reached for one of the two levers to his left and pushed it forward. The carriage rocked a little as the brakes released. The other lever he pulled all the way back, letting the steam into the mechanism that turned the wheels.

The carriage shot forward like a wild animal released from a cage. Ben gripped the steering handle and kept the wheels straight as they raced toward the wall.

"Look out!" Harry shouted as if Ben could not see they were on a collision course. Ben wrenched the handlebars right and the carriage careened away. It rocked dangerously to the side, and Ben was afraid for a moment that it would tip over, but he managed to round the corner with all the wheels still on the ground, only clipping a pile of wooden crates as he went by.

Unfortunately, in his panic he had turned away from his cleared space and now they headed up one of the aisles, toward the center of the barn, picking up speed. Ben, his knuckles white as he gripped the handlebars, maneuvered the carriage through the warehouse, up the wide rows he was very thankful he had cleared. Another right turn brought him face-to-face with a huge flat, painted with trees and flowers. It completely blocked the path.

"Turn!" Harry yelled.

"There's nowhere to go," Ben yelled back. "Just hang on."

The sound of tearing canvas was almost louder than the engine as they crashed through the middle of the flat. One more hairpin turn positioned them once again toward the back of the warehouse. Ben pried his stiff fingers from the handlebars and grabbed the brake lever just as they burst into the empty space where they had started. He pulled as hard as he could, and the carriage skidded to a stop. He reset the other lever, cutting power to the wheels, and even managed to keep his hand steady enough to turn the key and shut off the engine.

He leaned on the handlebars, his breath coming in deep gulps, and waited for his heart to stop pounding. Harry sat still as a statue beside him, clutching the edge of the seat with white fingertips.

"That was... exciting," he said, his face as pale as a freshly laundered sheet.

Ben grinned. "I suppose that's one way of putting it."

Harry turned his head slowly and looked right at Ben, and at once they both burst out laughing. Ben fished his handkerchief out of his pocket and mopped his sweaty forehead and his leaking eyes.

When their laughter subsided, they were holding their stomachs. Harry clapped Ben on the back.

"I'm pretty proud of you." He tapped the floor with his foot. "This thing, this... what do you call it anyway?"

Ben pushed his hair back from his forehead and rested his hand on his head. "I haven't thought about it. What do you think we should call it?"

Harry's eyes lit up. He knitted his brow, undoubtedly trying to think of some weighty and intellectual-sounding name.

"A horseless carriage?" He shook his head. "No, that's no good. Perhaps... a motorcar?"

"Motorcar?" Ben planted an elbow on one knee and considered it. "I like the sound of that."

Harry started to laugh. "The motorcar works, Ben. We might have almost been turned into pancakes, but it works."

"Hey, that's right." Ben lifted his hands and let out a whoop of triumph that echoed to the very roof of the barn and beyond, possibly reaching Heaven itself. "It works!!"

Ellie waited in the alley behind her house, the cold wind biting through her coat. She pulled it closer, wondering how much longer Ben would be. Little Harry Grimm had appeared on her doorstep this afternoon, bearing a note that said she should be ready to leave at nine o'clock that evening, when he would come and meet her in the alley. She had tucked her father in for the night and shipped her stepmother and stepsister off to the first of many holiday balls, so it was no trouble to leave the house. She only had to make sure she was back before they got home. Ellie had no idea what Ben had in mind, and couldn't imagine how he was going to get them eighty miles from the city at this time of night and then back in time. *Maybe he's invented a flying machine.* Her heart beat faster, anxious for Ben to arrive and put her curiosity to rest.

It wasn't Ben, but Harry that appeared in the alley. He greeted her with a tip of his cap and a most solemn expression on his face. It was all Ellie could do to not to laugh.

"Good evening, Miss Banneker."

Ellie dropped a small curtsey, still fighting a smile. "And good evening to you, Master Grimm. Where is your brother?"

"He's waiting. Follow me." Harry turned on his heel and strutted down the alley. Ellie's curiosity flowed like a swollen river — had he stolen a carriage? Hijacked a locomotive? She hoped he hadn't committed a crime on her account. There had been enough of that already.

At the end of the alley, Harry turned left, and at the next corner, they made a right. Two more blocks brought them to a small park. On the far side, she could just make out something near the sidewalk. Whatever it was, it was between streetlamps, cast in shadow. It was the size of a carriage, but it was oddly shaped. As they approached it, Ellie was able to see more clearly.

She stopped ten feet away, her mouth hanging agape. It *was* a carriage, shiny and black, with polished brass trimmings and gleaming wooden wheels. It looked perfectly normal, except for the fact that there were no horses hitched to the front. A strange, low hum came from within it. She was almost afraid to ask, but she had to know, especially if she was expected to ride in it, which she assumed was the general plan.

"What *is* that?"

Ben puffed up his chest proudly. "Do you like it? I built it myself. Well, I made it so that it works without horses, anyway. It's steam-powered."

Ellie understood. "The giant steam engine at the Exposition?"

Ben nodded. "It's the same basic principle, just smaller. Almost like that clothes washer and a train smashed together."

She pressed her lips together, not sure how to phrase her thought. "I don't want to be rude, but is it safe?"

He scratched the back of his neck. "I did have a little trouble at first," he admitted. "But with a few adjustments, it's all very safe. I drove it over here without any trouble."

Ellie didn't mention that they were going a bit further than from wherever he kept this mechanical beast to the park. He was so proud of himself, and to be honest it was a wonderful invention. Even though she still held some reservations about climbing into a carriage where the source of power didn't eat hay, she put her hand on the smooth side and felt the vibration. Powerful and strong, like a hundred horses. Suddenly she couldn't wait to climb inside and start their journey.

"What do you call it?"

"We've named it the motorcar," Ben replied.

"A motorcar." Ellie let the word roll around in her head for a moment. She turned toward Ben and Harry, standing together on the sidewalk, and put a hand on her hip.

"Well, are we going or not?"

CHAPTER XIV

BEN SHIFTED THE LEVER, LETTING MORE STEAM INTO THE ENGINE; AS the motorcar picked up speed, he grabbed his hat before it blew off his head. If he was going to make a habit of this, he needed to get a hat that wouldn't fly away. And goggles, he thought as he squinted to see through the dust that assaulted his face. He was glad he had made Harry ride in the carriage with Ellie. It was not only freezing up here, but it was dangerous. Every time he hit a bump in the road, he feared he was going to fly right out of his seat.

The city had been reduced to a few specks of light on the other side of the Delaware River. The ferry had taken longer than he thought it would, and he had to make up for lost time. They had passed through Camden, New Jersey half an hour ago. Unfortunately, leaving civilization meant they also left behind proper roads and lighting. The dirt track that dared call itself a road was barely visible in the dim, unfocused light from the motorcar's swinging carriage lanterns. He made another mental note to add some lamps to the front of the vehicle, like the headlamp on the front of a steam engine.

He had studied a map he found in the bookshop, to familiarize himself with the route, but it was a whole different game to follow it in the dark. There were signposts, to guide the stagecoaches, but they were hard to see. He missed the first one, which had jumped out at him from the shadows, and had had to turn around. Once he knew what he was looking for, he kept one eye out for them, while with the other tried not to run them off the road and into a ditch.

They passed through a few clusters of buildings that Ben wouldn't call towns except that he had no other word for them. Most of them consisted of a church and a few tiny houses. Between these barely-towns, the road was long and lonely, lined on both sides with pine trees that loomed over them like giants.

After what seemed like days but had only been about three hours, he smelled the tang of salt on the air. A few lights appeared in the distance, across the canal. The city of Cape May, its streetlamps lit for the few year-round residents. Ben pulled on the brake lever and the vehicle slowed so he could guide it over the narrow wooden bridge that crossed the canal. The bridge, used to horses and coaches, complained and shook as the mechanical contraption rolled over it. Ben was afraid, more than once, that it might not hold, dumping them into the freezing water. Snow started to fall as they rode through the silent and thankfully paved streets. Ben passed through the middle of town and came to a stop. He put on the brake.

One of the motorcar's doors flew open, and Harry's head popped out. He looked around, eyes wide. "Are we there?"

"Sort of." Ben looked around. To his right stood a row of large and fancy homes, with gingerbread trim, turrets, and giant front porches. Some of them had signs that proclaimed them to be Bed-and-Breakfast establishments. They were all shuttered tight for the winter. On his left, the land rose in a small pale hill. It took Ben a moment to realize that it wasn't covered in snow, but that it was a sand dune. Long grasses grew in clumps, waving in the wind. Not far from where he stood were a set of wooden steps, and in the near distance, a low, steady roar.

"Why have we stopped?" Ellie's head appeared beside Harry's in the open doorway.

"Because I'm not exactly sure where to find what we're looking for." He pulled the playbill out of his coat pocket. "This says that Cape May diamonds can only be found on the beach at Cape May Point. I was looking for something that might tell us where that might be." He hadn't studied a city map, only road maps.

Harry hopped out onto the street and looked around for a moment before he took off running.

"Where are you going?" Ben shouted, his voice getting lost in the wind. The tail of Harry's coat flapped behind him as he ran around the corner. Ben waited a minute, to see if he'd reappear, but there was nothing.

"Wait here, Ellie, I'll get him and be right back." Ben had only run a few yards when his brother reappeared.

"Where did you go?" Ben tried not to sound angry, even though he was furious. If he lost his little brother, his mother would never forgive him.

Harry's grin was wide and smug at the same time. "I found out where Cape May Point is."

"Really? How did you do that?"

"I found a sign. A great big one down the street. We must have driven right past it."

Ben's mouth fell open. "Uh, well, it's hard to see with sand blowing in your eyes," he mumbled. He crossed his arms over his chest and huffed, just a little. "Doesn't matter, at least we know where to go." He moved toward the front of the motorcar. "Let's not waste any more time."

Ten minutes later, the carriage jerked to a stop. Ellie sat inside alone, because Harry had insisted on riding on the driver's box with his brother, so he could navigate. She leapt from her seat and jumped from the carriage before Ben could come around and open the door.

The moon hung like a limelight. The road ran right onto the beach, which was flat. Beyond it, the ocean seemed to go on forever, moving as if it were alive in a constant rhythm of crashing waves that pulled back before crashing again. It was the most beautiful thing she had ever seen in her life.

"Oh, my goodness, it's freezing out here." She wrapped her coat closer around her. "Just look at it. I wish we could see it in the daylight. Wouldn't it be thrilling to just sail across it and see what's on the other side?"

A jetty poked into the ocean like a long finger of rock. Off to the right a landing jutted twice as far into the water as the jetty. If Ben's description was correct, this was definitely the right beach—there was no sand here, only pebbles, covering every inch of the shoreline.

"Which are the right ones?" The light of the moon and Ben's lantern, which he had detached from the motorcar and brought down to the beach, reflected the surfaces of millions of stones of every color and size imaginable, glittering bits of rock polished by the sea. She was sure they weren't *all* so-called Cape May Diamonds!

She could barely hear Ben's reply. "Uh... I'm not sure."

"What?" Ellie spun, sending pebbles flying, and faced him. "I thought you knew!"

"Wait, wait, just a second." Ben pulled something from his back pocket—the playbill. Holding his light under the crook of one arm, he scanned the back. He slowly lifted his head, looking at Ellie with apologetic eyes and a solemn shrug.

"Let's just grab as many as we can and sort it out later!" Harry's voice rang across the beach. He danced on top of the jetty, water spraying up on either side of him like rain.

"Get off of there!" Ben yelled. "Before you slip and fall in. You know you can't swim!"

Ellie fell to her knees, sifting through the stones. Without proper light, it was nearly impossible to tell one from another. Some were as small as a grain of rice, others as large as a goose egg. Most were white or pink or striped, all were smooth and beautiful as jewels, but not one looked like a diamond.

"Damn it, Harry! What did I say?"

Ben set the lamp down beside Ellie and chased after his brother. She ignored the boys' argument and dug deeper, pebbles falling through her fingers, still not seeing something she could say even resembled a diamond.

"What kind of a name is that for a plain rock, anyway? Why would you call something a diamond if it doesn't look like a diamond?" She picked up two handfuls of pebbles and threw them in frustration.

"Watch where you're throwing those things, will you? That stings!"

Ben's booted feet appeared, followed by a smaller pair. Both were soaked. Ellie's gaze traveled up, taking in two pairs of drenched pants. "What happened to you?"

Harry gave a sheepish shrug. "I fell in."

"Fortunately, it wasn't very deep, and the current wasn't strong, so I fished him without too much damage." Ben gripped his brother by his coat's collar. "He's lucky he didn't crack his skull on the rocks."

Ellie sat back on her heels and studied the two boys, their dripping coat tails, and hangdog looks. She couldn't help but laugh. "You two look ridiculous. And you're going to catch your death, standing here in those wet clothes."

"Well, that's not my fault," Ben said. "I couldn't let the little rat drown, could I?" He looked at the hole Ellie had dug. "No luck?"

Ellie sifted through the stones. "No. I can't tell which of these would be a diamond. None of them look like..."

Something at the bottom of the hole caught her eye. She only noticed it because Ben had picked up the lantern, shifting the light. It was the size of her palm, and clear as glass. She lifted it out and held it up, turning it one way and the other, watching it shine. Like a diamond.

Ben let out a long whistle. "I'd say that fits the bill nicely." He held his hand out and helped Ellie to her feet. The stone was heavy and cold, but it warmed quickly in her grip.

"That's it then? We're finished?" Harry said through chattering teeth.

"Yes, we can go," Ben replied without a trace of sympathy.

Harry ran across the beach, pebbles flying behind him, and dove into the motorcar.

Ben shook his head. "Sometimes I wish I was an only child."

"You don't mean that," Ellie said sadly as she slipped the stone into her pocket.

"No, I don't." He took his watch from his pocket and flipped the lid open. "Uh, oh."

Ellie stopped, her stomach swooping and flipping at his tone. "What is it?"

"This took longer than I thought it would. We don't have much time." He showed her the watch face. It was one in the morning.

"Olivia and Rebecca will be home at three." Ellie paused just long enough to make sure her heart was still beating. "It took us three hours to get here — we'll never get back in time." She raced toward the motorcar and jumped in beside Harry, who was wrapped up tightly in a wool blanket. She leaned out the open door and saw Ben disappearing into the driver's box. A few seconds later, the engine growled to life.

"We won't make it, Ben."

Ben's face appeared around the side of the carriage, leaning over to look at her, a huge grin on his face. "Maybe we will. We're going to take a shortcut." He disappeared from view again, leaving Ellie to wonder just what *kind* of shortcut he meant. There was only one road, and everything else was water and beach.

There was a change in the sound of the engine, and Ellie shut the door just as Ben shifted the motorcar into gear. They took off, like a racehorse from the starting gate, and she was jerked back into her seat. It wasn't long, however, before she felt them slowing down. They turned left, then a quick right. Suddenly, the road turned rough. But it was a strange kind of rough, where the bumps produced a regular, steady beat. Ellie leaned out the side window. All she could see were shadows whirring by. She glanced out the back window, and then turned her whole body around and stared.

"Oh, dear Lord. Harry, your brother has completely lost his mind. He's going to kill us all."

CHAPTER XV

BEN LEANED FORWARD IN THE DRIVER'S SEAT LIKE A JOCKEY, URGING the mechanical horse forward. This was a brilliant idea, really. He had studied the road map for days, to make sure he knew the way to get here. He had also taken note of the rail lines. These tracks ran through Cape May up to a junction at Schellenger's Landing, and from there he could make the turn onto the line that ran straight to Camden, where they would catch the ferry. They wouldn't have to worry about getting lost, since there was nowhere to make a wrong turn. It would shave at least an hour off of their travel time. They would just make it.

It was such a good idea he was mad at himself for not thinking of it earlier. He pushed the lever forward, squeezing just a little more speed from the engine, his heart pumping faster in response. The ties whizzed beneath the wheels, a blur of wood.

Fifteen minutes later, Ben eased the motorcar through the empty junction and pointed its nose into the dark, and, somewhere beyond, Philadelphia. With a Cheshire cat's grin, he opened the valves as far as they would go, and slid the lever forward. They shot forward again, faster than before, crossing the canal, and leaving the shore behind.

Ellie jolted awake. She couldn't believe she had fallen asleep, but the rhythmic rumble of the motorcar's wheels over the railroad ties had been like a lullaby. Harry lay curled up on the opposite seat, still wrapped in the blanket, fast asleep.

She looked out the window, thankful that they were still in one piece. Maybe Ben wasn't mad after all, only clever. They were passing through a town, larger than the ones they had seen on the way. As quick as a wink, the sleepy town was behind them, never knowing what strange contraption had passed among them in the night. She looked at the sky, wondering what time it was. For all his good intentions, she was certain there was no possible way for her to make it back before Olivia and Rebecca came home.

What would her stepmother do to her? She remembered the look of cold fury in her stepmother's eyes when they had returned from the Exposition. Olivia was capable of much more—she was still sure that the wicked woman had quite possibly arranged for her mother's death, no matter what Ben and the official record said. But would her stepmother commit murder with her own two hands? Ellie was not willing to bet her own life she wouldn't.

Light outside the window distracted her from her thoughts. She peered out and was surprised to see they were approaching Camden. The lights of the city seemed extra-bright after so much darkness, and she squinted against them. In fact, they were *too* bright. A soft sound behind her made her look over her shoulder.

She jumped from her seat and turned completely around, kneeling on the bench, fingers digging into the leather.

"Oh. No. No no no no no!"

She fumbled for the door latch and turned it. The wind caught the door as she opened it and pulled it from her hand, slamming it back against the carriage. With her hand wound through the loop that hung from the roof, she leaned out to Ben, using all her breath to call him.

His face appeared around the edge of the box. "What are you doing? You're going to get hurt! Get back inside!"

"Can you make this go any faster?" Ellie screamed.

"I know you're in a hurry, but I'm doing my best. We're almost to the ferry, and then home! We'll just make it."

"That's not what I'm worried about!"

Ben glanced forward, than back at her again. "Then what?"

"The train!"

Ben wasn't sure he heard Ellie properly. She couldn't have said there was a train coming—trains didn't run this time of night.

Except for freight trains. He had forgotten about the freight trains, which ran all times of day and night. He looked past Ellie, still leaning out of the carriage, and saw what looked like a small moon, rocketing straight toward them. The headlamp of a locomotive.

With his stomach turning to a ball of lead and his heart trying to abandon ship, he looked at his gauges. All of them were almost at full capacity, the needles straining to the right. He was using all the power the motorcar had. If he pushed the machine anymore, the tank on the back might explode. Then again, if the train hit them, the same thing would happen. He looked back again, and wished he hadn't.

There was no choice. With a deep swallow and a quick prayer, he carefully turned the knob that increased the pressure, watching the needle rise even further. A noise behind him made him jump, and he wasn't sure if it was the train's whistle or Ellie screaming. As if the seat of his pants were on fire, Ben shoved the lever forward, releasing the pressure and forcing the steam into the engine.

The motorcar sped up just the tiniest bit. Or maybe Ben was only hoping they had sped up. It had to be enough. There was a crossing ahead, but it was half a mile away. He willed the machine to go faster, not daring another look back. A quarter mile left, and the train's whistle deafened him.

The crossing was within reach. He braced his feet on the side of the box, and leaned left, wrenching the wheel as hard as he could.

The motorcar took the corner at full speed, leaning dangerously to the left. He was sure he felt the right-side wheels leave the ground, and heaved himself to that side. They landed with a crash, the motorcar careening down the road. Ben got control and pulled the brake, bringing them to a halt full of screeching and jarring and a loud thump from inside, followed by an "Ow!"

The train went on its way, clacking down the track as if it hadn't almost crushed three people and a brand-new motorcar. Ben leaned his head on the handlebars, waiting for the earth to stop shaking, then realized *he* was the one shaking. That thundering sound was his heart, beating in his ears.

Ellie jumped from the carriage and stomped her way over to Ben.

"What were you thinking?" She punched him in the arm, and pain shot through his shoulder, adding to his misery. "You could have killed us."

"That wasn't the idea. I was just trying to make good time." He wiped his sweating brow with his sleeve and pulled out his watch. "And we did too. It's 2.15." He showed her the watch. "We have forty-five minutes to get you home."

"We'll never make it," Ellie yelled. "We're still on the wrong side of the river! It wasn't worth our lives, Ben!"

Ben understood she was upset, but she didn't have to be ungrateful. "Excuse me, then. I was only thinking of keeping you out of the fire. I—"

"What's going on? Are we home yet?" Harry appeared in the doorway, and hopped to the ground. He rubbed his eyes and yawned, then looked from Ellie to Ben and back again. "Did I miss something?"

"Get back inside, both of you. We can just make the next ferry, if we go right now." He heard a boat's whistle in the distance. "As in, right this very minute."

Ellie flopped back against the seat. As predicted, they had just barely made the ferry. It was full of dock workers, heading across the river before their very early shift began. Ben had insisted she sit inside the carriage, being the only woman on the boat. She had reluctantly agreed, mostly because she wanted to be out of sight of the leering workmen and not because she wanted to admit Ben was right about anything. Besides, she was still angry with him for their near brush with death, and not ready to talk to him civilly just yet.

She put her hand in her pocket and rubbed her fingers over the stone they had almost died to get. Slippery smooth and polished only by the ocean, it was as fine as any jewel in a shop. She pulled it out and looked at it, amazed at its beauty.

"You were a lot of trouble, do you know that?"

All she needed now was what Olivia had taken from her and her father. The lock of her hair would be easy to steal. Though she hadn't figured out what her stepmother had taken from her father, she still had a little bit of time to find it. Even if it took until New Year's Eve, as long as she found it before midnight, she could break the spell.

Her breath caught in her throat and she sat up straight as she remembered the old woman's words. There was something else she needed. Oh, how could she have forgotten!

A token, freely given, from the one who has your heart.

Her heart sank, heavy as the stone in her hand. *Who* held her heart? Hamilton Scott, worry in his kind eyes as he helped to her feet outside Grimm's bookshop? The man whose look had made her flush and feel dizzy in the Horticultural Hall?

Or was it Ben? She certainly did not have the same feelings for him that she did for Hamilton. Or did she? She was angry with him now, but there was no denying the easy way they were together, and how close they had become in just a few short weeks. It was a different feeling than she had when she was with Hamilton, but no less strong. If Ben was the one, getting a token from him would be as simple as asking. But what if she was wrong? She could not be wrong about this, or else it could mean her enchantment would last forever.

She would have to get a token from both of them.

But how? There was no possible way she would ever get close enough to Hamilton, let alone expect him to just hand her something of his. Just when she thought she had everything in order, the world suddenly seemed dark once again.

The motorcar's engine started, and the door opened. Harry hopped inside, his cheeks pink with cold, his smile as wide as the river.

"We're almost to the dock. And we've still got fifteen minutes. Plenty of time on these streets. Or that's what my brother says anyway." He looked at Ellie, eyes bright as stars. "That was some adventure, wasn't it? When can we go on another one?"

Despite herself and her new troubles, Ellie laughed. "Harry, I sincerely hope, in all my life, to *never* do that again."

Ben was never happier to see Philadelphia than he was that morning. When the ferry docked, the crowd parted to let him off first. He knew the men were staring at his machine, a mixture of awe and suspicion, and he couldn't help but feel proud of himself. Despite a few mishaps, he had pulled off a veritable miracle tonight. He tipped his hat to the dumbfounded ferryman as he rolled past, and set the motorcar running on a blessedly smooth, paved city street. All he had to do was get Ellie home in the next fourteen minutes.

He blazed a trail down Walnut Street, past shuttered shops and restaurants. A few people wandered the streets, turning their heads to follow the strange vehicle's progress. There was at least one extremely surprised policeman on duty, because he blew his whistle and shouted at them to slow down. Just a few blocks left, and more than enough minutes to get there.

That was when the motorcar spluttered to a stop.

"Why are we stopped?" Ellie made no effort to hide her panic. They were just a few blocks from home. "What's wrong?"

Ben pushed the button and tapped the gauges, pulled and pushed levers. "I'm not sure, I mean… oh, wait." He glanced down at Ellie, his face chalk white. "We're out of gas. Outrunning the train burned through it faster than I thought. Ellie, I'm so sorry. I thought we could make it."

Ellie stepped back. "I still can. How much time is left?"

"About nine minutes, but… Wait, what are you doing?"

She barely heard him, because she had started running. Halfway down the block, she shouted over her shoulder. "Thank you, Ben!"

With her head down, she ran as fast as she could, cutting through alleys where the motorcar wouldn't have fit, taking shortcuts where she could find them. Finally, she came to Delancey Place.

And there was her family's carriage, just turning onto the street.

Ellie raced for the alley that ran behind the houses, her feet slipping on the wet leaves plastered to the sidewalk. She rounded the corner, nearly falling but not stopping until she reached her own gate. She threw it open, reaching into her pocket for her door key as she leaped up the stairs. The key seemed to be working against her, not wanting to find the hole the first three times she tried. Finally, it slid home, and Ellie burst into the kitchen. There was no sound in the foyer, which means her stepmother and stepsister had not yet gotten inside. She tossed her coat onto the rack and ran up the servants' stairs, taking them two at a time.

She stepped onto the second floor and stopped, trying to catch her breath. If Olivia saw her now, she would know that Ellie had been up to something. She gulped air, trying to slow everything down to normal.

"Wasn't that just the loveliest ball?" Olivia cooed so sweetly it gave Ellie a stomachache. "The Purcells always throw the most elegant affairs, though that Katharine is a bit too flirtatious, if you ask me."

"It was fine." Rebecca's voice was barely audible. "I didn't notice about Katharine. She seems like a nice girl."

"Oh, don't be such a pooh. You were wonderful tonight, my dear. Gracious and beautiful, everything a young man could want. Why didn't you dance more? You were asked, weren't you? Your dance card should have been filled."

"I don't know, Mother. I was tired."

"Hamilton Scott looked especially dashing tonight, didn't he?" Olivia's hint was about as subtle as an iron tossed through a window. Ellie's stomach clenched at the sound of Hamilton's name. Though part of her knew he was going to be at all the parties, dancing with other girls, she hadn't realized how incredibly jealous she would be about it.

Rebecca sighed. "I suppose."

"Oh, you don't have to play coy here with me, my darling. I could tell he was interested in you."

"Mother, I don't really think he was."

"Nonsense, you just didn't see it. You're so young, and you don't know what to look for."

"If you say so, Mother."

"Oh, Rebecca, why are you so miserable? This is your chance to find the perfect husband. Someone who can take care of you, and provide a good life — the life you deserve. I only want the best for you, my sweet."

Rebecca answered with a sigh.

Ellie could not stand it any longer. She thudded down the stairs, hoping she looked like she had just woken from a deep sleep and not like she had been dashing about the countryside, digging in the dirt, and being chased by a locomotive.

"Good evening, Stepmother, Rebecca. I hope you had a nice evening."

CHAPTER XVI

CHRISTMAS MORNING ARRIVED BRIGHT AND COLD. THERE WAS NO holiday for Ellie, however. It was just another day, save for one tradition that Ellie alone would keep later today. There were still fires to be tended, and breakfast to be made. She lay in bed, looking at the bare wood and beams of the attic ceiling by the dim light of the barely risen sun. As was usual of late, her night had been anything but restful. Breaking the spell commanded her every waking thought, and it chased her through her dreams as well.

The last three weeks had not brought her any closer to solving the problem of how she was going to get a token from Hamilton Scott, and her prospects looked dim. She had exactly one week left. Ellie shuddered to think what would happen if she failed. The walls were closing in, crushing the breath right out of her.

The day would not wait any longer. She eased off her quilt, emerged into the freezing air and dressed herself as rapidly as possible, then hurried down into the relative warmth of the third floor. She went into her father's room. He slept peacefully, thank goodness, but his breathing was louder than she had ever heard it. Something rattled in his chest like a ball bearing in an old can, another reminder of how time plotted against her. Before Ellie lit the fire, she put a hand to his head and breathed a thankful sigh that it was cool.

Her stepmother and stepsister were both still fast asleep when she went into their rooms to light their fires. They hadn't returned from the Worthingtons' Christmas Eve party until well after midnight. Ellie had been asleep on the damask settee in Rebecca's room, waiting to help them undress. Mr. and Mrs. Worthington had been friends of her parents, and Ellie remembered them as a cheerful couple who always had a kind word and something sweet for Ellie. Rebecca had, with some prodding, regaled Ellie with stories of her evening.

"You should have seen the look on Mrs. Pennington's face!" Rebecca giggled like a much younger girl. "She was as red as the tablecloth!"

She looked over her shoulder at Ellie and her expression fell. "Oh, I'm sorry. I don't mean to go on so. It's not very nice of me, when you..."

Ellie waved her apology away. "No, no, no. I asked you, didn't I?" She gave her stepsister a reassuring smile as she folded Rebecca's stays. "Thank you for telling me. It sounds wonderful."

Rebecca sat at the vanity and began to brush her hair. She glanced up at her stepsister in the mirror. "Ellie? Do you remember Benjamin Grimm?"

Ellie froze halfway across the room. "Who?"

"Benjamin Grimm, that little boy who belonged to the old cook."

Ellie pretended to think hard. "Oh, yes, I remember. Whatever made you think of him?"

Rebecca looked away, brushing her hair with renewed effort, spots of color on her cheeks. "I don't know. He just popped into my head. You were such good friends then, and he was such a... and anyway, I guess I wondered if you had spoken to him."

Ellie busied herself putting away Rebecca's gown. "No, not in years. When would I have?"

"He must be a young man. I wonder what he's doing now." There was a dreamy quality to her words that made Ellie's stomach twist a little.

"No idea." Ellie finished helping her stepsister and quickly left.

Fortunately for her, her stepmother had been too busy with the holiday party season to notice that the will and contract were missing from her secretary. Or at least she thought not, since there had been no eruption from Mount Olivia. It was yet another problem for which Ellie had no solution. Without breaking the spell, the will was useless to her. Without the contract she had no proof of Olivia's treachery.

She moved along to the second floor and lit the fire in the morning room, then moved downstairs to the dining room and the parlor. The Christmas tree stood in front of the bowed front window of the parlor, where everyone who passed by could see. Every available branch of the eight-foot-tall spruce was covered with velvet bows, sparkling glass balls in deep jewel tones, gingerbread men, or angels fashioned from crocheted lace. Ellie gently stroked one of the angels, remembering how her mother would spend hours making lace ornaments. She had loved the Christmas season, more than any other time of year, and decorated the house from top to bottom with garlands of green.

Ellie dropped her hand, her heart aching with longing, and scolded herself for dwelling yet again on the past. It never did her any good. She glanced at the packages beneath the tree, boxes perfectly wrapped with exquisite paper and tied with festive ribbon, marked with tags written in flowing script. There were three to her stepmother from Rebecca, and a good dozen for Rebecca from her mother.

What else would there be? No one had given her a Christmas gift in years. Ellie knelt in front of the tree and looked over the packages, trying to guess what was in each: a new fan, a pair of gloves, a hat in a large one with a green bow. All the things necessary for a girl on her way to becoming a lady. All things Ellie should have but did not.

She returned them all to their places. Something rubbed against her feet and she jumped, her head hitting the lower branches of the tree. Fortunately, none of the glass ornaments had been hung that low, to keep them out of reach of—

"Clarence, you wicked cat! Are you trying to scare me to death?"

Clarence looked up at her with wide innocent eyes and let out a small cry.

"Oh, you're hungry, aren't you? I'm sorry, I've gone and let myself become distracted. Come on, then, let's go into the kitchen. I've got to get out for my holiday visit and be back before those two drag themselves from bed."

Clarence followed Ellie down the hall. She shut the kitchen door and poured a bowl of cream for the cat, then raced through the rest of her morning chores. With the sweet roll dough rising on top of the warm stove, she pulled on her coat and slipped out the back door. The streets were virtually empty, save for a few souls on their way to early church services, or the delivery people who, like Ellie, never had a morning off, not even on Christmas. The lamp lighters had been and gone, up at the break of day to douse the lamps. At least they would be home for Christmas breakfast.

Ellie pulled her coat tighter around her as she walked through the alternating patches of light and shadow. In summer, she would have been grateful for the shade, but now she rushed through it to the next sunny section to soak up the little bit of warmth the sun cast down on her. She entered the burial ground, the gate creaking like an old woman's bones behind her. It was quiet, but there were traces that other visitors had been here. Bunches of greens tied with red ribbons decorated several graves, and potted poinsettias graced others. The scent of the fresh pine cuttings almost covered the smells of the city.

The hazel tree beside her mother's headstone seemed to bow to her in greeting, pushed by particularly strong gust of wind. Ellie settled herself on the bench.

"Good morning, Mother. It's Christmas Day. I'm sorry I didn't bring you any greens this year, but I just didn't have a chance to get any. Things have been so busy." She heaved a deep sigh. "Another year has come and gone, and I still miss you." She pulled an old, stained handkerchief from her pocket and dabbed at her leaking eyes. Suddenly, her grief flowed over like a too-full washbasin, turning into anger. She jumped from the bench, her hands balled into fists.

"Here I am, talking to your grave, when I should be talking to you! Olivia will pay. For all of it." She stopped and shook her head. "Listen to me, ranting like a lunatic! These are not the glad tidings I should be bringing you on this day, are they?"

She sat on the bench again, her backside freezing on the stone. "I've been working so hard to get everything I need to break the spells. I didn't think I would be able to, but Ben — remember little Ben Grimm? He's all grown up now, and you wouldn't believe how helpful he's been. I just wish I could find a way to bring you back to me, so that everything would be the way it was. The way it's supposed to be. I wish…"

A sound caused Ellie to look up from her lap. A gray dove perched on top of her mother's headstone, head tilted to the side with a quizzical look.

"Were you listening to all of that, little bird?" The dove hopped to the right side of the stone, and then off the edge, landing on the coarse brown grass beside a small, rectangular box covered in gold paper and tied with a green ribbon.

It was Ellie's turn to tilt her head. She was sure the box had not been there when she sat down. Or had it? She looked around, but she was still alone. No one could have put it down while she wasn't looking. Maybe someone had dropped it. It would be a shame for someone to lose what was obviously a Christmas gift. She lifted it onto her lap, hoping there might be some clue as to who it belonged to so she could return it.

Her head began to spin when she read the attached gift tag. It bore *her* name. Ellie glanced over her shoulder, looking for the perpetrator of what was obviously someone's idea of a prank. *Perhaps not.* Maybe Ben had left her the gift, knowing she would come here today. She took a closer look, to make sure her eyes were not the ones playing tricks. No, there was her name. The *from* part of the tag was filled in as well, and Ellie's breath stopped when she read it.

Mother.

Now she knew she was being played for a fool. Who would be so cruel? Tears sprang into to her eyes and she nearly threw the box from her lap. But something stayed her hand, something small and quiet, speaking in the back of her mind. A whisper, lighter than a spring breeze. It said only one word: *Perhaps.*

This is the season of miracles, after all. Ellie believed in magic, didn't she? If it could work against her, why couldn't something good come from it as well? The dove, who had retreated to a low-hanging branch of the hazel tree, cooed softly.

Licking her lips, which had turned paper-dry, she slid a finger beneath the edge of the paper. She lifted it slowly, just a little at first. Then, unable to stop herself, she ripped the paper off and threw it to the ground. The box beneath was battered gray cardboard with no markings. She lifted the lid with both hands and gazed at the contents in disbelief.

A pair of golden slippers nestled inside, wrapped in white tissue paper. Ellie took one out and turned it over in her hands, wonderstruck. The golden silk was embroidered from toe to heel with intricate, swirling designs of flowers and vines in gold and silver thread. Tiny crystals formed the centers of the flowers, glittering in the sunlight. The shoes were made for dancing, and she didn't need to try them on to know they would fit her perfectly.

She returned the shoe to its mate and shut the box. What was her mother—if that was indeed who they were from—trying to tell her? She had no use for dancing slippers, even a pair as beautiful as these. Where would she possibly wear them?

The answer dawned on her like sun breaking through the heavy clouds overhead. Of course, why hadn't she thought of it before! But her happiness dissolved as quickly as it had come. How could she possibly do it in only a week? It didn't matter; it was her last chance. Perhaps Ben would have an idea. She was sure he would help her. It wouldn't be the first mad plan they'd hatched together. A twinge of guilt pulled at her. How could she ask Ben to help her meet another man? He didn't know about Hamilton or her uncertain feelings for each of them. It was all so confusing, but she couldn't chance that either boy was the one who truly held her heart.

"Thank you, Mother." A breeze blew through the branches of the hazel tree, uncommonly warm for December, and Ellie was almost certain she heard an answering whisper. With the box tucked firmly beneath her arm, she gathered up the wrappings and headed home.

She entered the kitchen as silently as she had left. It was almost 9:30, but after her stepmother and stepsister's late night, she was sure they would sleep until at least ten. She put the box with the slippers in the pantry, on the topmost shelf behind some canned tomatoes, and then gathered what she needed for breakfast and shut the door. The dough had risen nicely, and Ellie set to work punching it down. With the rolls in the oven, she went to the icebox to retrieve butter and eggs. When she turned around, Rebecca stood in the doorway.

"Oh!" Ellie jumped, almost sending the eggs to an early demise against the kitchen floor.

Rebecca blushed, and Ellie wondered why she had never noticed how lovely her stepsister was when she was embarrassed. "I'm so sorry. I didn't mean to frighten you."

"It's all right. I'm fine. I just didn't expect... I thought you would still be in bed. Breakfast isn't ready yet, but if you'll give me a minute, I can make you some tea."

Rebecca took a hesitant step into the kitchen. "Please don't go to any trouble. I'm not hungry. I just wanted to be up before Mother, so I could give you this." She held out a package wrapped in pretty mauve and gold-striped paper.

"You didn't have to get me anything," Ellie's voice was thick. "I don't have anything for you."

"Oh, don't worry about that. It's just a little thing, nothing really." Rebecca set the box on the table and stepped back out into the hall. "Happy Christmas, Ellie."

Ellie had trouble making her voice work, but she managed to get out, "Merry Christmas to you, too, Rebecca."

She sat at the kitchen table, staring at the box. Rebecca had never given her a gift, not for a single birthday or Christmas, in all the time they had known each other. Finally, Ellie opened her gift, not really caring what was inside, only glad for the thought behind it.

Under the lid of the white box, stamped in gold with the name *Wanamaker's*, lay a beautiful silk fan. Ellie lifted it from the box. It had a turquoise tassel, and one side was painted with the image of a peacock. She opened and closed it, watching the beautiful peacock appear and disappear. Though she wanted to look at it all day, she put it away and discovered something else, wrapped in delicate tissue. She pulled it out, and almost dropped it in surprise. It was a masquerade mask—a white silk half-face with mauve feathers on the ends and small paste jewels glued around the eyes. White satin ribbons were attached to either side, so that it could be tied around the wearer's head.

Tucked into the bottom of the box was another small box. Ellie fished it out and opened it. It was a small watch, heart-shaped, with several sparkling white stones. It hung from a gold bow, which had a back so it could be pinned to the front of a dress.

Ellie put all of the items back into the box, handling her treasures as if they were all made of gold. The idea that had taken root as she stood beside her mother's grave began to sprout. She stowed the box with the slippers, a list of other things she would need racing through her head, like the ingredients for apple cake. If she was going to go through with this, she would need to get started right away.

While the tea kettle warmed on the stove, and the eggs boiling, she pulled a piece of paper from the box on the pantry shelf, along with the pencil. She sat at the kitchen table and began to write.

The day after Christmas, Ben entered the Props barn. Soon his life would be busy once more, working in the bookshop, preparing the theater for the next performance, which would begin rehearsals two days after the New Year. His father wanted the inventory finished before then, which meant he had precious little time to finish the job he had only been doing half-heartedly before now, because he had spent so much of his time working on the motorcar.

He lay on the floor below his contraption, inspecting the engine, making sure everything was in order after their little adventure. He adjusted and greased the valves, and then checked over everything before coming up and standing beside the vehicle.

A beautiful carriage that has carried a beautiful lady. Although he was alone, his cheeks flushed. It wasn't a lie—she was a pretty girl, he had thought so from the moment he saw her in the theatre. *She's my friend, and that's all she is.* Ellie had never indicated, in the slightest fashion, that she had any feelings other than friendship for him, and unless she did, he wasn't going to upset the applecart.

The echo of the warehouse door creaking open stopped his train of thought. He grabbed the canvas and tossed it across the carriage as fast as he could. Shuffling footsteps came closer, and Ben scrambled to pull the cover down.

"Relax, Ben, it's only me." Harry stepped from the shadows between the shelves. He had a strange look about him, as if he wasn't sure whether to be happy or upset.

"Harry, what's the matter?"

Harry pulled an envelope from his pocket. "This arrived for you at the shop. I managed to get it before Mother could see, and as soon as I read it, I ran over here."

"You read it?" Ben tried not to sound angry. "Why would you read it, if it was addressed to me?"

"Because the person who brought it said it was very important. Life and death important."

"Who brought it? Ellie?"

"No." Harry hesitated. "Someone else. I didn't recognize her, but she was pretty. Anyway, as soon as I read it, I rushed right over here."

Ben, thinking Harry might do well as an actor for all the drama he put into his speech, took the envelope from his brother's hand. His name flowed across the front in indigo ink. He leaned against the shelves, and pulled a piece of crisp, clean stationary from inside and opened it.

"It's really that important you say? Life or death? Well, then maybe it's some girl that's taken a fancy to your brother, then, and this is a declaration of her undying love for —" He swallowed his words, and his brows creased deeply as he scanned the two short, and unsigned, lines.

Ellie needs your help. It is of the utmost importance that she attends the Assembly Ball.

"She wants to do what?" Ben thought for a moment, counting in his head. "But that's only six days from now." He looked at Harry, all joking wiped from his expression. "You said a woman brought this?"

"Yes."

"What did she look like?" Ben shook his head impatiently, stopping Harry's already open mouth. "Never mind, it doesn't matter." He put the note into his own coat pocket and headed back the way Harry had come, grabbing his brother's shoulder and turning him around as he went.

"Come on, we've got work to do and you're going to help."

CHAPTER XVII

LLIE SAT ON THE SETTEE IN HER ATTIC ROOM, *JANE EYRE* UNOPENED beside her. She was racking her brains about how she could talk to Ben. Since Christmas, the idea had been in her head, racing around, growing bigger by the minute. She had written him a letter, outlining her entire plan, but had not been able to deliver it. Her stepmother had stayed infuriatingly close to home, as if she sensed that Ellie needed her to leave. She had not even had the opportunity to search the house for whatever Olivia had used to bind her father to the Love Spell.

She sighed and put her head in her hands. Perhaps it was just a crazy plan, without a chance of success, but for now she had no other choice. Her life, possibly literally, depended on its success.

She had to go to the Assembly Ball.

Her mother's gift, and then Rebecca's, had made it seem as if once again serendipity worked in her life. Hamilton would be at the ball, and it was the only opportunity she would have to get a token from him. But when she sat down to think about all of the details, she realized how overwhelming the task truly was. Getting to the ball shouldn't be any trouble, if Ben would drive her in his motorcar again. Next was the issue of her dress. There were a few old gowns of her mother's in one of the steamer trunks, but they were moth-eaten. Despite the fact she was an expert seamstress, even she could not make an elegant gown in five days, especially not since her stepmother was sure to be breathing down her neck more than usual this week, making sure everything was perfect for Rebecca's debut. Then there was the problem of getting in the door when she did not have an invitation. Without that, it wouldn't matter what she wore.

Oh, this would be so much easier if I knew which one of them I loved! She loved them both, but which was the true love of her heart? It was maddening. She leaned her head back, stared at the bare rafters, and tried to untangle her thoughts, the tapping of a light rain on her windows soothing her nerves.

Wait, rain? It had been freezing over the last few weeks. Surely it was cold enough to snow. So what was that sound? Ellie sat up and listened. The tapping stopped, and then started again, and strangely enough it seemed to only be hitting the attic window. It sounded less like rain and more like tiny pebbles against the glass.

She crept to the window and looked down. Harry Grimm stood in the alley. His arm was cocked back, ready to throw the next handful of pebbles. Ellie knocked on the glass and waved, trying to get his attention. He stopped and returned the wave, dropping the stones then indicated he wanted her to meet him at the back door.

"Hello, Harry," Ellie said as she opened the door. "What do I owe the pleasure of your visit?"

Harry giggled at her formality, rocking back and forth on the balls of his feet. "I have a message." He held out his hand. In his fingers was a folded piece of paper.

Ellie took the note and, opened it. She scanned the words, her brow puckering in the center. "What is this all about?"

"Exactly what it says," Harry said importantly. "My brother and I have everything well in hand."

And before Ellie had a chance to ask a single question, Harry bowed from the waist and took off running. She watched him go, then shut the door, stunned. Creeping back into her room and safely into her rabbit hole, she studied the note again, still in disbelief.

Ellie,

Be ready on New Year's Eve. I'll have everything you need for the ball, don't worry. The curtain will rise at 8:30pm.

– Ben

What did that mean? She stared at the words, willing the ink to tell her more. He said he would have everything she needed, but how did he know what she needed, and how would Ben, of all people, get a ball gown and an invitation to the most exclusive ball of the year? She was sure Ben had meant for his note to put her at ease, but it only turned her into a bundle of nerves.

The next five days were the longest of her life. She wanted desperately to sneak away and talk to Ben face-to-face, but her stepmother kept her hopping, running to the milliners, the florist, the bakery, the market. The little time that the women were away from the house was spent searching for the item that bound her father to the spell. It was definitely not with the lock of her own hair beneath Olivia's jewelry box, which Ellie took and stashed with the raven's claw, finger bone, and Cape May diamond. She turned the house upside down in her searching, but came up empty-handed.

The night of the ball arrived, and Ellie was nervous as a mouse in a house full of cats. She could almost feel her time slipping away. With her trust placed in Ben, she concentrated on her plan once she was *at* the ball. Hamilton would need to give her something of his own free will. Just thinking about him made her tongue-tied.

Once she had her token, she would dash home, perform the ritual, and be free. She wondered if she would feel any different. As for her father... she didn't want to think about what would happen if she didn't break the spell. Ellie shook her head, refusing to give in to hopeless thoughts. Perhaps there was a bit of the same magic that had given her the slippers and told Ben about the ball left in the world, enough to help her. It was a slim and fragile hope, but if she did not keep a hold of it, she might not have the strength to finish what she had started. Her father and mother would want her to break the bewitching spell and save herself, no matter what else happened.

Though she wanted to jump from her own skin, she had to act as if everything were normal. She even tried to put on an air of melancholy as she carried Rebecca's gown across her room. It was royal blue, a shade that complimented Rebecca's coloring, with a beaded bodice. She would look perfect in it, and though Ellie knew it must have cost a fortune of her father's money she tried not to feel jealous.

Rebecca sat in front of her vanity table. The barest hint of blush graced her cheeks, but she glowed with inner beauty, even though she did not seem excited for her evening.

"Your hair looks lovely." She tried to balance her compliment with a bit of sadness, still playing her part as the sister being left behind.

Rebecca, who Ellie was certain was *not* acting, heaved a sigh as she set the puff back into the container of powder. She gazed at her own reflection in the mirror, as if she didn't recognize the young woman that looked back at her.

"Thank you, Ellie." She behaved as if she were going to a funeral rather than her own debut. Though Ellie was confused by her attitude, perhaps she also understood. Both of them were being used by Olivia for her own purpose. Rebecca wasn't stupid, and was probably well aware of what part she played in this game. For a moment they were kindred spirits, like real sisters.

"Let's get you into your dress, all right?" She tried to be cheerful, but Rebecca did not return the sentiment. She dragged herself to standing and pulled off her dressing gown, leaving her in her stockings, chemise, and corset. Ellie helped her into her petticoat and bustle, and Rebecca raised her arms when Ellie lifted the gown and dropped it over her body, carefully pulling it into place. Their eyes met. She reached out, grabbed Ellie's hands in hers, squeezing them tightly, and pulled her close.

"Please don't give up hope, Ellie, "she whispered. "It's all going to turn out right in the end. Just... don't give up."

Ellie was too shocked to reply. Another moment passed between them in silence, and then Rebecca dropped Ellie's hands and looked away. Shaken by her stepsister's sudden outburst, she did up the buttons on the gown in silence and slipped out of the room.

An hour later the Banneker family carriage pulled up in front of the house. The driver and footman helped Olivia and Rebecca to pile their cumbersome gowns into the carriage, and then they rolled away. Ellie ran upstairs to tend to her father. He greeted her as usual, calling her by her stepmother's name and then her mother's, and she gently reminded him again that she was his daughter.

"No, you can't be my daughter. She's just a little girl. What kind of silly game are you playing?" He coughed; a wet sound full of phlegm. She waited until the fit passed, then handed him a glass of water and watched him drink it. She told herself it didn't matter that he didn't know her. If everything went well tonight, it would be the last time he called her by another's name.

"Now take your medicine, and get some rest." Ellie spooned the syrup into his mouth, and then tucked him in. In minutes he was snoring softly, and she jumped into action, scrubbing her face and making sure she was ready for Ben's arrival.

At 8:30 exactly by the grandfather clock in the foyer, a knock sounded at the door. Ellie dashed down the stairs.

"Just a moment."

Another knock, this one more urgent, just as Ellie reached the door. She pulled it open with such force that it banged against the chair rail.

There was Ben, wearing a long coat of black leather with gold buttons. He smiled so big Ellie was certain she could see all his teeth. "Good evening." He whisked a strange-looking top hat from his head. Like the coat it was made of leather, but it also sported a large pair of brass-rimmed goggles, resting on the brim. Ben gave a deep, almost comical, bow.

"I am here to take Miss Eleanor Banneker to the Assembly Ball. Is she ready?" He looked Ellie up and down, and his grin changed to a look of surprise. "My goodness, Miss Banneker! You can't go to the ball dressed like that. People will snigger."

Ellie stepped back, smiling though the butterflies in her stomach currently performed a complicated ballet. "Well, Mr. Grimm, I would, except I don't have anything suitable to wear."

Ben jammed his fists on his hips. "Oh, no? Well, then, I guess it's lucky for you that I happen to have just the thing." He pulled a cloth from inside his coat and draped it over his free hand, then waved the other over the cloth, like a magician doing a trick. When he whisked the cloth away, in his hands was a large white box.

Large enough to hold a ball gown.

Ellie's heart skipped a beat. She wanted to know how he had accomplished both the magic trick and obtaining a gown, which was almost as large a feat as far as she was concerned. A million questions leaped to the tip of her tongue, but Ben silenced them all when he handed her the box.

"Go and get ready, and don't dawdle."

Ben stood in the Banneker's foyer, hands behind his back, waiting for Ellie. Her eyes had danced like fireworks when he handed her the box. She had raced up the stairs, the box clutched to her chest. Above him were the sounds of up-and-down stairs, then the shutting of doors, and finally quiet. Ben strolled around the foyer, peeking through the doors on either side. The one to his right was the parlor. His mouth fell open when he saw it.

The room was completely different from the last time he'd seen it. Instead of the comfortable-but-fashionable furniture, the room was filled with chairs so stiff they looked like torture devices. The simple mauve walls he remembered now sported hideous flowered wallpaper. The quiet, subtle decorations had been replaced with gaudy, ostentatious lamps and pieces of art so ugly that he was certain it all cost a fortune. It was more as if the room were meant solely to remind anyone who was invited inside of the owner's status and wealth.

The other door led to the dining room. Ben stepped inside and took a deep breath. The faintest scent of Mr. Banneker's cherry pipe tobacco found his nose, plunging him in memory. He and Ellie had sat on the floor for hours beneath the big table, cross-legged, hunched over a book, or playing with Ellie's toys, hidden by the white linen tablecloth. His cheeks warmed as he recalled the day she had forced him to participate in a tea party with all of her dolls. Mr. Banneker had laughed when he caught them, but had extended his full sympathies to Ben, confiding that he too had once been wheedled into an afternoon tea with dollies.

Ben sighed and leaned against the doorframe. Mr. Banneker had been a devoted father to Ellie. He had surely never raised a hand to her, even when she had been stubborn—a trait she had obviously not outgrown—always seeking instead to reason with her. Ellie and her mother had been his whole world.

"Ben?" Ellie's call pulled him back to the present. He stepped back into the foyer and looked to the top of the stairs, but she was nowhere to be seen.

"Ellie? Are you alright?" He hoped she didn't need help getting into the dress. Not only was it implausibly inappropriate, he wasn't exactly an expert on women's clothing. The thought of all those buttons and ties made his head spin.

"Yes, I'm fine. I'm just nervous. You're going to laugh at how ridiculous I look in all these ruffles. I feel as if I'm both drowning in fabric and half-naked."

Ben hadn't expected such a reaction, but maybe it was normal. Had Ellie ever even worn a formal gown before? He had seen her dressed for the theater, in what he thought was a very fancy dress, but maybe he was wrong. "Don't be silly. I'm sure you look just fine."

"I don't know..."

"You're not going to get cold feet on me *now*, are you? If you won't let me see, how are you going to go to the ball and dance in front of all those people?"

"Dance?" The word came out as if she hadn't even considered the idea until that moment. He still didn't understand her sudden need to attend this ridiculous affair, but the note that Harry had brought him the day after Christmas had made it seem as if the world would end if she didn't. He had not discovered who had sent the note, but apparently whoever it was knew what they were talking about. Ellie hadn't even considered refusing to go. It must have something to do with her breaking the spell, since the deadline was tonight and he could not see her traipsing off to a dance for any other reason.

"I assume dancing will be involved. It is a ball, after all." The clock chimed the three-quarters of an hour. "If we don't go soon, you're going to miss your chance."

A pause. "All right. Here I come. Promise you won't laugh."

Ben swore he heard Ellie take a deep breath, as if she were getting ready to dive into deep water. A second later she appeared at the top of the stairs, and all of the breath rushed from *his* lungs. The mauve silk made her skin glow. She had pulled her hair up on top of her head, accenting her long, slender neck, around which was draped a necklace of sparkling green jewels. One shoulder was covered in silk roses, which trailed down the neckline and across the bodice to her waist. Ben had to keep himself from staring at the space between her head and the top of the *low* neckline of the bodice.

"Ben?" Ellie's brow creased in concern. "Ben, you look as if you're going to faint. Say something. How do I look?"

Wonderful, gorgeous, the most beautiful woman I have ever seen, all ran though his mind, but none of it made it as far as his tongue, which suddenly he had forgotten how to operate. He waved a finger at the area around her neck. "The jewelry... your mother's?" *Really? All of the words in the world, and I talk about her jewelry?*

Ellie touched her necklace and nodded. She watched him for a moment, as if trying to see herself the way he saw her. Finally, her shoulders relaxed and she smiled. "Thank you." She descended, her arms covered in the elbow-length white satin gloves that had also been in the box. Ben caught the scent of her perfume—not her usual subtle rosewater, but something a little heavier, like lilacs. He had to stop himself from inhaling deeply. Her hands held a wool mantle.

"Where did you get that?" Ben pointed to the wrap.

Ellie blushed. "I, um, borrowed it from Rebecca."

"You *stole* it?"

She looked insulted. "After everything I've done in the last two months, *this* is what shocks you?" Her expression turned pensive. "I have a feeling she won't mind at all. And I plan on returning it, just so that you know."

Ben took a quick step back and acted as if he were insulted. "Of course, you are. I never thought otherwise," he said with an air of mock gentility.

"As we're on the subject of borrowing, wherever did you acquire this beautiful gown?" She plucked at the skirt with her fingers and stared at it, enraptured by its beauty.

Ben winked at her. "Ah, a good illusionist never reveals his secrets." After an accusing look from Ellie, his shoulders slumped. "Oh, all right, spoil my fun. I borrowed it from the Walnut."

Ellie looked shocked. "You didn't just take it, did you?"

Ben put his hand over his heart, as if pledging his words were true. "No, don't worry. I came by it honestly. The Wardrobe Mistress let me borrow it. It was the only place I could think of where I could possibly acquire one, short of stealing one from Wanamaker's window. I was going to ask her to doll up something from the wardrobe. She's a wizard with a needle. But then I saw this and I knew it was perfect. She didn't want to part with it at first, since it's for Miss Fanny Davenport, and—"

"Fanny Davenport?" Ellie's eyes turned bright and wide. "The actress? This is *her* dress?"

"Well, yes. She's coming into town next week, and the dress was set aside for her. It took some wheedling, but I can be very charming when I want to."

Ellie laughed. "I have absolutely no trouble believing that."

"I borrowed these as well." He indicated his coat and hat. "Except for the goggles. Those I made myself. I had to guess that the dress would fit you, since I didn't know your, uh, size." The last bit came out mumbled, and his cheeks flushed.

Ellie narrowed her eyes and put a hand on her hip as she cocked her head. "How did you know I *needed* this dress?"

Ben wagged a finger at her. "Now that *is* my secret." He didn't want to tell her about the note he had received by mysterious messenger, mostly because he didn't want to upset her. They didn't have time for that discussion. "Now, if you would allow me, my lady, I'd be happy to escort you to your carriage." He held his arm out to her.

She turned on her heel and headed straight down the hall.

"Ellie, where are you going? It's this way."

She called over her shoulder just before she disappeared into the kitchen. "Just wait right there. I won't be a moment." The sound of the kitchen door swinging shut was followed by the muffled sounds of her moving around inside. *What in the world is she doing in there?*

True to her word, a moment later she reappeared in the hall, carrying two boxes stacked one on top of the other. She handed the one to Ben and opened the other.

"Where did you get *those?*" Ben had never seen such elegant slippers. Not that he saw many pairs. His mother had no use for the dainty shoes, but he knew enough to see that the pair in the box was something special.

Ellie's gaze flickered up to Ben and then back to the slippers. "I could tell you, but you wouldn't believe me."

With a surreptitious smile and a wink, Ellie set the box on the stairs. She leaned on the end of the banister, lifted her foot and slipped the shoes on. The gold disappeared beneath the layers of petticoat and mauve silk, and Ben thought it was a shame that no one would see them when she danced.

"What's in this one?" Ben said as he gave it to her.

Ellie opened the box and pulled out a fan. She opened it and showed it to him, fluttering it in an alluring way. Suddenly, he realized that other men would be looking at her in that dress. They would touch her, their hands on her waist as they led her across the dance floor. Jealousy flared in his chest, a spurt of green flame that shocked him.

Ellie reached into the second box, as if she had also spent years studying how to pull surprising objects from inconspicuous containers and showed him a white silk mask.

"Where did you get those?" Ben thought that perhaps the fan, like the jewelry, had also belonged to Ellie's mother, but the mask looked brand new.

"You'll never guess." Ellie went to the gilt-framed mirror on the wall and put the mask over her face, tying the ribbons just under the bulk of her upswept hair. She turned to face Ben. "Rebecca gave them to me."

Ben's stomach gave an uncomfortable lurch. "Why would she give you a fan and a mask? Did you tell her you were planning on attending the ball?"

Ellie shook her head. "I certainly did not. In fact, I hadn't even come up with this insane idea until Christmas Day. It was as if she *knew* I needed to go. She tried to convince Olivia to take me with them, a few weeks ago, but my stepmother predictably refused." She tucked a stray hair behind her ear. "Rebecca's been acting so strange lately. What she said to me today..."

"What did she say?" Ben felt as if he would jump out of his skin.

She turned to the mirror again and studied her reflection. "It doesn't matter."

Women, Ben thought. *No matter their station, they can never resist looking at themselves in the mirror.*

"Are you ready now?" he asked with pretended exasperation.

"In a hurry to be rid of me?" Ellie turned, looking over the edge of her fan at him, a teasing gesture that made his throat seem tight.

Ben shrugged, trying to stay nonchalant as he glanced at the clock. "You're not the only girl I'm taking to the ball, you know. I have a queue, and I need to stay on schedule."

Ellie closed the fan and gave him a good-natured smack across the shoulder with it. "One last thing." She reached into the box and pulled out something small and gold. She watched herself in the mirror as she pinned a brooch to the front of her dress. When she had finished, she turned around. "Yes, I'm ready, Mr. Grimm." She took a deep, shaky breath. "At least I think I am. I'm a bit nervous."

"No need to worry. I have no doubt that you'll be perfect." Ben looked closer at the brooch and realized it was a ladies' timepiece. "Was that from Rebecca as well?"

Ellie glanced down. "Yes, actually. It's lovely, isn't it?" She lifted it and looked at the face, and then at the grandfather clock, making sure the times matched. With two gloved fingers, she grabbed the tiny stem at the bottom of the heart and turned it, winding the clock.

Ben thought back to his brief meeting with Rebecca at the Exposition and wondered if the girl had made this herself. The watch casing was gold, but unlike any he'd seen in Mr. Rittenhouse's shop. It was engraved with beautiful filigree and looked like it might have had a previous life as a different type of jewelry. A locket, perhaps? Again, he thought there might be much more to Rebecca than met the eye.

He held his arm out once more, and this time Ellie slipped her hand into the crook of his elbow and let him lead her to the door.

CHAPTER XVIII

THE MOTORCAR SAT BY THE CURB IN FRONT OF ELLIE'S HOUSE, looking just as it had on the night they had driven to Cape May. Harry stood by the door, wearing a smaller version of Ben's duster. Smaller but still too large for him, with the sleeves hanging past his hands and the hem dragging on the pavement. Ellie could not help but laugh.

"What are you doing here?"

Harry attempted a bow, but his long coat made it come out all arms and flapping leather. "Every lady needs a footman, doesn't she?" He reached up, flicking the sleeve back, and opened the carriage door. Sweeping his other arm toward the interior, he said, "My lady, if you please, we can be on our way."

Ellie put her fingers to her mouth to stop another laugh. "Yes, of course." She lifted her heavy skirts and made her way down the front stairs.

"Wait just one second, Ellie."

Ellie looked over her shoulder at Ben, her expression questioning. "What? Is something wrong with my dress?"

Ben shook his head. "Hold on." He reached into the deep pocket of his duster and pulled out something small. Ellie held out her gloved hand and he dropped the item into it. She held it up—it was a small, brass gear.

"What's this?"

"It's... for luck."

"Has it brought you luck?" Ellie held the token in her fingers, her heart leaping. She had nearly forgotten that she needed a token from Ben, too. Had he remembered, or was it just a kind gesture?

Ben shrugged. "Hasn't let me down yet."

Ellie tucked the gear inside her bodice. "Thank you, Ben. I'll take good care of it and get it back to you as soon as possible."

Ben shook his head. "You keep it."

Ellie held his gaze a moment longer, not sure what she wanted to say, and so remained quiet as she climbed into the carriage and slid across the seat. Harry bundled her train up after her, as well as any trained footman, and shut the door.

Ben had spruced up the interior with dark velvet curtains and some bolster pillows.

"All set, Ben." Harry's muffled voice came from the front, up high— he must have been sitting in the driver's box. The carriage shifted a little as Ben climbed up. Ellie, well aware of this machine's unpredictable movements, slipped her hand around the handle attached to the wall and braced herself.

"Ready?" Ben didn't bother waiting for an answer before shouting, "Here we go."

The sound of the engine shifted pitch. There was a small jolt as the carriage moved forward, which turned smooth as they headed down the street. She shifted back as far as her bustle would allow and watched as the houses passed by the window, snow falling gently. The streets were virtually empty, save for a few pedestrians probably on their way to a pub or a party to welcome the New Year.

Ellie was running a little late, although some might call it fashionable. It was probably better she was late, otherwise this carriage might cause such a sensation that no one would want to leave the street. *Ben deserves for people to see his wonderful invention,* Ellie thought with a small smile and swell of pride. *Just not tonight.*

What seemed like only a few moments after they had left the house, Ellie felt the carriage slowing down. She looked out the window and there were the buildings of Broad Street.

The Academy of Music came into view. The building was ablaze with light—it spilled from the enormous arched windows, dwarfing the flames of the street lamps. It illuminated the dark red brick of the building and streamed into the night, a beacon calling everyone to its splendor. As the motorcar slowed, Ellie's heart beat faster. She had arrived at the Assembly Ball.

And now that she was here, she couldn't move. Her legs seemed to have turned to jelly, shaking beneath her voluminous skirts. *All I have to do is get Hamilton to give me something, and I can leave. Simple.* But no amount of convincing would make her muscles relax. She closed her eyes.

"Oh, Mother, I wish that you were here." She wanted to hear her mother's voice, soothing her nerves and giving words of wisdom and comfort. In that quiet moment, Ellie felt a hand slip into hers, the warmth of slender fingers in her own. They gave a quick squeeze and disappeared, leaving her with a feeling of calm.

The queue was short; only three other carriages separated Ellie's from the front. The snow fell harder now, and no one was willing to ruin their fine gowns by getting out before they reached the protection of the awning that stretched from the door to the street. So, they waited. Two carriages, then one. A lovely girl in a gown of pink-and-white striped silk emerged from the carriage ahead of Ellie's, accompanied by a man and woman she assumed were the girl's parents. Ellie's heart gave another tug and she reached for a hand that was no longer there.

The man glanced over his shoulder, looked again, and then turned completely around to stare at the motorcar. He walked backward, toward the Academy doors, and almost bumped into his daughter before he spun around and entered the building. Ellie hoped that Ben had seen the look on the man's face — part astonishment and part admiration.

The family's carriage moved along, and now it was Ellie's turn. Ben piloted his strange conveyance into the vacant spot. The door opened and there stood Harry and Ben, waiting to help her onto the sidewalk. She squared her shoulders, took Ben's offered hand, and stepped down. There was no one behind them — they must be the last to arrive. She pulled her mantle a little closer to stave off the cold air that wanted to touch the bare skin of her shoulders.

"Here you are, as promised." Ben bowed, solemn and respectful, with no trace of his former teasing. He straightened and looked Ellie in the eye. There was something there, something she thought she recognized.

"Thank you, Ben." She leaned forward and kissed his cheek. It seemed like the only appropriate way to show him the enormous thanks she owed him. He opened his mouth, but before he could say anything, Ellie bent down and kissed Harry, too.

"Can I ask you one thing?" Ben said. "Why? You haven't broken the spell yet. So why this—" he used his chin to indicate the building " —and why now?"

"This is... part of it." Ellie swallowed deeply, the rest of the truth stuck in her throat. How could she tell Ben that she might be in love with two men? Now she knew what she had seen in his eyes a moment earlier. If he wasn't the one who held her heart, she could break his with a word. "I promise I wouldn't have come if it wasn't important."

Ben nodded, thankfully not pressing her for more information. They looked at each other a moment, volumes said in silence.

"I have to go," Ellie said quickly.

Ben nodded and slowly lowered his hand. "What time should I come back?"

Ellie blinked, and then looked at the watch on her dress. "I need to be home before midnight, with enough time to break the spell. Is 11:30 all right? That should give me plenty of time to get... what I need." She had left everything else set out on the bureau in her father's room, where they waited for the final items. Or at least most of them—she still hadn't found what her stepmother had taken from her father. It was seeming less and less likely she would be able to break the love spell, which tore a hole in her heart.

"I'll be here. And you'll also need this." He reached into his coat, pulled out a white piece of cardstock and handed it to Ellie.

Ellie scanned it, unable to believe both that she had forgotten about it and that Ben had managed to obtain one. "An invitation. How did you get it?"

Ben rubbed the back of his neck, looking embarrassed. "Um, that's kind of a secret. Even from me. I swear, someone sent it to me. It came in the bookshop's mail three days ago."

Ellie touched the invitation with one gloved finger. She knitted her brow, confused. "But who is Eliza Reed? I know that name from somewhere."

"Well, the invitation didn't have a name on it, so I had to make one up. So, for tonight, Eliza Reed is you," Ben replied. "Even though you're wearing a mask, you can't use your own name, obviously, and you can't use the pseudonym Olivia gave you. I've come up with a whole character for you. You are a socialite from New York City, in town visiting spinster cousins, and they procured you a late invitation."

"And here I am, without a patron? How very scandalous," Ellie replied. Ben's eyes widened—he must not have considered it.

"Don't worry, Ben, I'll be fine." Ellie held up the invitation. She tucked the card into the pocket of her mantle and turned toward the open front door. "Thank you for everything."

"Good luck," Harry said cheerfully. "You look really pretty, Ellie."

Ellie looked over her shoulder at him, unable to control her smile. "Thank you, Harry." She turned from the two boys and walked toward the Academy.

Ben watched Ellie's graceful form disappear into the bright light of the Academy's foyer, swallowed by the world of high society that she had been born to. A place he could not follow. It left him feeling a little empty and sad as he climbed up into the driver's box.

"What are we going to do while she's in there?" Harry asked, climbing up beside him.

"You, my little brother, are going home."

Harry groaned. "Please let me stay with you."

His pleas fell on deaf ears. "Absolutely not. Mother would skin me alive if I kept you out that late."

Harry's rebuttal was a smug look. "What would she do if she found out that you took me to the seashore, I fell into the ocean and almost drowned, and then we almost got run over by a train, and didn't get home until after three in the morning?"

Ben did not rise to the bait. "You did not almost drown. And you wouldn't dare tell her."

"Oh, I wouldn't?"

"No, you wouldn't. Or else I'll have to tell her that you were the one who used her best tablecloth during your one-man production of *Julius Caesar* last summer."

Harry's mouth fell open, forming an O. "All right, fine," he grumbled. "But it's not fair."

"Your complaint has been recognized by the management."

Ben released the carriage's brakes and let steam into the engine. They rolled down the street, headed for home. Ben would drop off Harry, and then he would wait.

He wondered if the girl that entered the ball would be the same one that emerged.

CHAPTER XIX

ELLIE STEPPED INTO THE ACADEMY'S LOBBY, AND IT WAS AS IF SHE HAD walked into a dream. She blinked in the bright light cast by the chandelier, which glittered like fairy dust. A few people milled about, exchanging greetings and guesses about who was behind the masks, laughter echoing across the room for a wrong answer. There were two staircases leading from the narrow room with the polished tile floor, and a group of partygoers climbed the one to the left, headed for the ballroom.

"Excuse me, miss? May I see your invitation?"

Ellie turned to her right. A tall, dark-haired man in a tuxedo stood there, masked like everyone else. He held out his hand, and for a moment she was confused about what he wanted.

"My invitation? Of course." She reached into her pocket and pulled it out, then handed it to the man, praying he would not question it.

He barely glanced at it before handing it back to her. "Very well, Miss Reed. Do you have an escort?"

Ellie's mind raced to find an acceptable answer. "Yes, I do, they're… still outside with the carriage. They should be along shortly. I wanted to get out of the cold."

The man narrowed his eyes behind his mask, but his head bobbed in a short nod. "Terrible weather tonight, completely unsuited to young ladies or their garments. You may leave your wrap in the upstairs coatroom. The dance cards are on the table by the ballroom doors. Please enjoy yourself."

Ellie tried not to smile too broadly as she dropped a curtsey. "Thank you, sir."

She joined the last few stragglers ascending to the ballroom. At the top, she stepped into a long, elegant hallway, painted in buttercup yellow and robin's egg blue. Rows of potted plants stood sentry against the wall, while a series of huge windows on the other side provided a bird's-eye view of Broad Street. Ellie followed a group of ladies into a small, crowded room where she deposited her mantle, and then further down the hall to a pair of tall, arched double doors. The entrance stood open, strains of music pouring out like honeyed wine. Beside the doors, as promised, was a small table covered in blank dance card booklets. She selected one, and using the pencil attached to the card, Ellie wrote the name Ben had chosen for her on the front.

Eliza Reed. She thought again that she recognized the name, but still could not place it. Then she realized — Eliza was Jane Eyre's cousin, a bitter and staunchly virtuous woman who in the end joined a convent. *Just what is Ben trying to tell me?*

She remained outside the doors with her hand pressed against her stomach, trying to quiet the butterflies, waltzing in their own version of what would happen inside the ballroom. A sudden thought jarred her: what if no one asked her to dance?

Dancing is not why I'm here, she scolded herself. *If I end up dancing, it will be because I don't want to draw attention to myself by not dancing.* What she would do once she found Hamilton was another story, one she hadn't yet written the ending to. She couldn't ask Hamilton to dance, it wouldn't be proper, and she had to find a way for him to give her something of his. Her stomach flipped again as she thought about all the ways this could go wrong.

With her card secured to her wrist by a piece of ribbon, she pulled her shoulders back, which unfortunately put the low neckline of her gown front and center. She lowered her shoulders and pulled in her chest, feeling horribly exposed, and faced the doors of the ballroom.

"Ready or not, here I come." Ellie took a long, slow, breath. She exhaled and stepped over the threshold.

Every one of her senses kindled at once. The scent of lilies and orchids filled her nose, mingled with ladies' perfume. The music of a small orchestra at the far end of the room caressed her ears. Women, dressed as if they were the flowers, and flawlessly dressed gentlemen milled about. The rows of drop-crystal chandeliers were reflected by an array of gold-framed mirrors.

Ellie stood in the doorway, unsure what to look at or do next. With a deep swallow, she entered the organized chaos. She skirted the edge of the room, looking for a good place to stand until she could get her bearings, searching all the while for Hamilton's blonde head.

"First dance in ten minutes," someone called over the throng. "Ten minutes. Ladies, get out your dance cards."

Ellie watched as a swirl of activity was put into motion. Gentlemen and young ladies paired, dances were promised, and each moved on to the next. By the time the first dance started, most of the ladies' cards would be filled.

"Yes, my Rebecca is coming out this year, of course. Mr. Scott has agreed to give her a dance, but I know she's promised the first waltz to that lovely Mr. Winthrop."

The sound of Olivia's voice froze Ellie's blood in her veins. Trying to appear nonchalant, she turned her head one way and then the other until she found her. Although her stepmother wore a mask like everyone else, it was easy to spot her gown of chocolate silk. She stood a few feet away, with her back to Ellie, talking with three older women, mothers and patronesses of the girls being introduced tonight. Ellie slunk away, thankful for her own mask, and slipped to the opposite side of the room, where she positioned herself between a group of young ladies and a large potted plant. From this new vantage point, she had a good view of the room. She hadn't located Hamilton yet, but she did see Rebecca. Her stepsister was on the arm of a broad, tall man Ellie had never seen before, but based on Olivia's conversation must be the "Lovely Mr. Winthrop." She tried to remember if her stepmother had ever mentioned the man, but there had been so many names bandied about, it was possible Ellie had forgotten. For her part, Rebecca's smile looked painted on, and she kept more than a respectable distance from her escort.

The group of girls Ellie was using as shelter all wore identical hopeful looks while the gentlemen walked by, appraising each one in a polite way. The scene struck Ellie as familiar, and she was horrified when she realized it was exactly like the market. She and the other girls were the geese, hanging in the butcher's window, waiting to be chosen. The idea was both mortifying and sickening.

"I hope that handsome Mr. Franklin asks me to dance," one of the girls said. She was tall—taller than most of the men in the room—and slender, with a long face and limbs to match. "He was at all the parties this season. Such a charming man, and a wonderful dancer."

"I danced with him at the Adams' party," another girl replied with a touch of superiority. "His parents and mine are the best of friends, you know. He's promised me at least one quadrille tonight." She held up her dance card and showed the tall girl, whose mouth tightened slightly before she put on a grudging smile, which she covered with her fan before turning away.

Ellie didn't know which was worse, the men looking at women like livestock, or the girls themselves sniping at each other like cats over scraps of fish. Did all society girls act so terribly toward each other, speak with their words barbed like fishhooks? An even darker thought came to her — would *she* have been the same if she had grown up within their circle? It suddenly seemed to Ellie that she had made a huge mistake in coming here, where she was so clearly out of her depth. She, who had broken into a church, had no idea how to navigate the much more dangerous waters of a formal ball. Maybe she was better off breaking the spell and then telling Ben that she loved him. It certainly would be easier. Then again, she reminded herself, she wasn't certain which boys' token actually *would* break the spell, and so she promised herself to stay, at least until she saw Hamilton.

Ellie's stomach turned, and when a waiter came around with a tray of champagne, she took one of the crystal flutes and tipped it upward, drinking it as quickly as she could swallow. The drink tickled her nose and went straight to her head, making it seem as if the champagne's bubbles had taken up residence inside.

"Hello, have we met?"

Ellie, startled by the question directed at her, stepped back — right into the potted plant. The long leaves brushed her hair, and she waved them away.

"I'm so sorry, I didn't mean to frighten you." A girl gazed at her, and Ellie, blinking and trying to find her balance, pulled herself from the clutches of the grasping plant and tried to regain her dignity.

"You didn't frighten me; I was just surprised." The girl looked familiar. The pink-and-white striped gown — this was the girl she had seen getting out of her carriage. The neckline of her dress was lower than Ellie's, even with the lace trim, her ample bust line highlighted by both a tiny waist and the long strands of pearls around her neck. She carried herself well, her blonde hair done up high on her head, also decorated with pearls. Even with the mask it was easy to tell she was a real beauty, never left to stand with the wallflowers. So, what was she doing talking to Ellie?

The girl tilted her head one way and then the other. "I thought I recognized everyone here tonight, even with their masks. But I can't quite place you."

Ellie's chest squeezed tight in panic for a moment. She *was* wearing a mask. And she had a false identity. What was there to worry about? She tried to relax and act as if this were not the first social event she had ever attended.

"No, I don't think we have met. My name is Eliza Reed." She covered her mouth with her hand and gasped. "Oh, wait, was I supposed to keep it a surprise?"

The girl laughed. "Well, I suppose so, but almost everyone in this room already knows each other." She touched her mask. "These aren't really very good disguises. And the gentlemen have to put their names on our dance cards, so we'll know who they are. If you think about it, it all seems rather silly. I'm Katharine Purcell," She looked at Ellie curiously. "I thought I knew all the girls in town."

"Oh, I'm from New York. I'm here visiting my cousins." Ellie said a silent thank you to Ben for being so clever.

Katherine looked around, searching for Ellie's imaginary relatives. "Who are your cousins? I don't remember any Reeds on the Register."

"Oh, they're my mother's cousins, so we don't have the same last name." Ellie gave herself a mental pat on the back for her own cleverness, and just prayed that Katharine would not ask for the last name of her mother's cousins. "They're not here tonight, they're older." Ellie cast a glance sideways and held her hand beside her mouth to keep others from hearing. "Bluestockings."

Katherine nodded slowly, understanding Ellie's meaning. Spinsters didn't usually attend formal social functions. Ellie shrugged. "This was a last-minute visit, and they were dears in getting me an invitation so late."

Katharine looked shocked. "They sent you without a chaperone?"

Ellie blushed but hoped Katharine would attribute it to the champagne. She couldn't be certain it wasn't at least in part from the champagne, which was still making a concerted effort to tip her sideways.

"Oh, no, I'm being looked after by one of their friends." The words fell from her mouth, and somewhere in the back of her mind she knew she had always planned to say them. It was her turn to crane her neck and look around. "I don't see her here. Maybe she's gone to the powder room."

Katharine was unrelenting. "What is her name? Maybe I know her."

A word most unbecoming a lady ran through Ellie's mind at Katharine's unrelenting pursuit of the subject. "You know, I only met them this evening, and I can be such a goose about remembering names. When I catch sight of her again, I'll point her out to you."

That seemed to satisfy Katharine, and Ellie breathed a sigh of relief. Hopefully soon some gentleman would come along and sweep her onto the dance floor, leaving Ellie to return to her task. At least she had been able to rehearse her story.

But Katharine stayed right where she was, watching the dancers take their positions, chatting about this one or that. While the girl was kind and pleasant, she hindered Ellie's search for Hamilton. She couldn't even ask Katharine about him, seeing as how she was supposed to be from out of town. She would excuse herself to the powder room and sneak away to continue the hunt.

But before she could speak, several men headed straight for where Katharine and Ellie stood, like bees drawn to a beautiful flower. Ellie tried to step out of the way, but the swarm enveloped her too quickly and she was trapped.

"And I had thought I'd be able to hide from all of you over here," Katharine teased. She was like a queen holding court—calm and poised as the men gathered around her, speaking in low tones while her expression and body language remained that of a modest girl. Ellie, on the other hand, was at that moment most grateful for her voluminous skirt, because it hid her shaking legs. The wallflowers cast dagger-filled glances their way, and Ellie felt as if she should be sorry, though it wasn't her fault.

"Miss Purcell?" A man with glossy black hair and a brilliant smile approached. "I believe my name is first on your card. I have come to claim my dance."

Katharine looked at her dance card and then up at the young man. "Why, so it is, Mr. Cooper." The other men dispersed, heading toward the waiting girls now that their prize had been taken. Katharine took Mr. Cooper's offered arm and started to go with him toward the dance floor. She glanced over her shoulder at Ellie and stopped. Mr.Cooper looked down at her. "Something wrong, Miss Purcell?"

Katharine shook her head. "Well, it's just that, my friend Eliza there—" she indicated Ellie with her head "—is new in the city. Just arrived, in fact. She doesn't know anyone, and I feel terrible leaving her alone. Could you, perhaps, find her a dance partner?"

Oh no. Although it was a kind gesture, it left Ellie embarrassed and annoyed; embarrassed that Katharine had made the request, as if she was some kind of charity case, and annoyed because she could not refuse if Mr. Cooper went to the trouble, and then she would be stuck with whatever man he selected for her, wasting precious time. Ellie tried to relax and not look either embarrassed or annoyed, though it was difficult. Maybe he would refuse, or be unable to find someone, and then he and Katharine would leave her in peace.

Mr. Cooper looked over Ellie appraisingly, which made her feel as if she were a horse at auction. He looked again at Katharine, and she gave him an upward glance through lowered lashes, her bottom lip pushed out slightly. "Please? I would be so grateful."

All of a sudden, it seemed that the collar of Mr. Cooper's shirt had become too tight. He took a deep breath and gave a weak smile. "Of course, it would be my pleasure."

Ellie had to stop her mouth from falling open in amazement. She was not used to the games that women of society had to play, though she had heard of them. Katharine, it would seem, was an expert player. *Women may not be able to vote, but they certainly do have power,* Ellie thought. *Katharine is a veritable force of nature.*

Mr. Cooper scanned the field of unattached young men, which were significantly fewer than a few moments ago. He lifted his chin, looking over Ellie's shoulder at someone behind her.

"I see the perfect man for the job. Wait one moment?"

Katharine nodded and smiled. Mr. Cooper strode past Ellie to somewhere behind her. She silently cursed the man and couldn't bring herself to turn and see who he had chosen for her. If she had to go through with this, she hoped the gentleman was at least a capable dancer. She would not appreciate it if her toes, encased in the delicate golden slippers, were trampled on by the heavy, hard-soled shoes men wore.

Mr. Cooper appeared beside Ellie, a man at his elbow. She couldn't quite see him, and she didn't turn to look, taking slow, even breaths and allowing Mr. Cooper to make the introductions.

I am a well-mannered girl. I will accept the offer with poise and grace.

Mr. Cooper made a small bow to Ellie. "Here we are. Miss..."

"Reed," Katharine said. "Miss Eliza Reed."

"Yes, Miss Reed. May I introduce..."

There's time for one dance, after all. And maybe it won't be such a waste. I can watch the dance floor and see if I can spy—

"Mr. Hamilton Scott. Mr. Scott, Miss Reed."

Ellie was sure her heart had stopped completely. She turned and faced him, only the smallest thread of will keeping the whirlpool of surprise and delight that raged inside her at bay, remembering this was supposed to be the first time they had ever met.

Hamilton wore a small, tight smile as he took her hand and bowed over it. Ellie was a little taken aback at his lack of enthusiasm, but she dropped a curtsey.

"It's a pleasure to meet you, Mr. Scott."

Hamilton's cool gaze traveled over her. It had the exact opposite effect of when Mr. Cooper had done the same, though. Ellie shivered, a pleasant feeling that raced up her spine and settled in her lower belly.

"The pleasure is mine, Miss Reed," he replied, his voice stiff and formal. He cleared his throat. "May I see your dance card?" Ellie raised her left hand and held out the little booklet toward him. He grasped it and thumbed it open. "You seem to have a space open for the first dance. Would you do me the honor of allowing me to fill it?"

Ellie managed to nod her assent and smile. His discretion in not mentioning that he had been asked to dance with her as a favor reminded her of his kindness at the Exposition.

"Of course, Mr. Scott. That would be lovely." He took the pencil, scribbled on the page and showed it to her. "There, now it is official." She was surprised and overjoyed to see that he had claimed not only the waltz, but the quadrille following as well.

Mr. Scott held out his elbow. "Shall we? The dance is about to begin, and we don't want to be late." Indeed, couples had found their way to the dance floor and arranged themselves in the proper fashion.

Ellie slipped her arm through his. He thought he was leading her to the dance floor, but what he was really doing was keeping her tethered to the ground. She was certain if he let her go, she would float away. They found a clear space in front of the string quartet, which bore the allure of being on the other end of the floor, away from both the evil glares of the wallflowers and her stepmother. Hamilton pulled Ellie around in front of him, where she had no choice but to look at him directly. He wore a gray tuxedo with embroidered lapels and cuffs, which matched the fine work on his waistcoat.

He took Ellie's right hand in his. She was glad for her gloves or else Hamilton might have had to wipe his palm dry from all that hers were sweating. His other hand he placed on her waist, which caused Ellie's insides to turn to preserves.

Concentrate, you silly girl! You're right where you need to be! The same feeling came over her as when she had arrived at the ball—now that her plan had come to fruition, she had no idea what to do next. How would she get him to give her a token? Hamilton looked as if he'd rather be anywhere but where he was—his fingers and expression stiff, and he did not look at her. He seemed to detest the idea of dancing, but whether it was dancing in general or with her specifically she could not say. Either way, it was hard not to be at least a little insulted. *What a puzzling man!* If he hated dancing so much, why had he agreed? And if he didn't want to dance with her, then why had he taken two dances on her card?

As the music started, she tried to keep her mind focused on the dance steps instead of the warmth of Hamilton's hands on her body. Fortunately, he was a competent and graceful, if stiff, dancer, for which her feet were thankful. After a few moments, they slipped into an easy rhythm. Just when the silence between them seemed to take on a life of its own, Hamilton chose that moment to start a conversation.

"So, Miss Reed, David tells me you are from New York. How are you finding our fair Philadelphia?"

It took Ellie a moment to realize that David must be Mr. Cooper, which was enough time for her to form a reply. "It's a fine city, Mr. Scott." She paused, trying to think of something to add so that she didn't seem as if she were a poor conversationalist. "I understand that there were some exciting goings on this past year, with the Centennial Exposition?"

Hamilton nodded. "It was rather interesting, the Exposition, but noisy and crowded and dirty, as those things are. My father was interested in the new steam-powered machines, of course. He's in the railroad business, so when he sees any gadget that uses steam, he's like a child with a new toy." He let out a self-deprecating laugh. "I'm sorry, Miss Reed. I must sound like a pompous bore."

"Oh, no," Ellie said. "Did you see the washing machine, and Mr. Corliss' steam engine?"

Hamilton gave her a curious look. "I thought you said this was your first trip to the city?"

Ellie cursed her runaway mouth. She hoped Hamilton didn't notice how her fingers had tightened in his. "Yes, it is, but..." As if a light had been turned on in a dark room, the answer came to her. "Philadelphia does not exist as an island unto itself, Mr. Scott. News does make it as far north as New York. I read about it in the papers. The articles were so detailed, it made it seem as if I had been there."

Hamilton's expression was unreadable. He paused and then nodded. "Of course, how silly of me. I did see the engine, to answer your question. My father is quite the lover of steam-powered machines, as I said. Mr. Corliss' engine is a noisy, smelly beast, though I see the benefits to it. It saves hours of manpower in the factories." He fell quiet after that, his expression stony. Ellie could not stand it any longer.

"Pardon me, Mr. Scott, but it seems to me that you don't enjoy dancing."

He blinked, surprised. "Why do you say that?"

"Your arm is as stiff as an ironing board, and you look as if you've recently sucked on a lemon. I hope it's not the company." She tried not to sound hurt.

He studied her for a second, his mouth falling open. "I am sorry, Miss Reed. It's not dancing I am opposed to, or your company, which is very pleasant. I am only tired of all of these formal affairs. This is nothing more than a well-dressed marriage market, as I am sure you know."

Ellie blushed but said nothing.

"My mother insists that I attend them all, but each and every one is the same. The same people, the same posturing, the same tiring intrigues. Pretty girls with important last names and empty heads that talk of nothing but tea parties and gowns and embroidery, and have no desire to read anything but romance novels and the Society page." His tone made it clear that he found those topics as exciting as mucking out a horse's stall. He sighed. "I apologize for my attitude. I know this is part of the life we lead, our burden to bear. It has nothing to do with you. Actually, this is the most enjoyable conversation I've had all season. I have never met a lady interested in machinery."

Ellie smiled and lowered her head, trying to get from beneath his steady gaze, which made her nearly forget all of her names. "I am interested in quite a lot of things, Mr. Scott. I like embroidery, and novels, like other girls. I don't read the Society page, but I like the newspaper. I find machines and the things they can do fascinating, though I admit

I don't understand how they work and have no desire to take them apart."

"Really?" Hamilton's mouth turned up in a crooked smile, and Ellie's heart flipped in her chest. His pulled his head back and looked at her. "Your voice seems so familiar to me. I've been to New York many times—are you certain we have not met before? We couldn't have, though, because I would have remembered you."

The dance ended before Ellie could reply. While she was relieved at not having to lie to him—again—he also had to release her. Everyone prepared for the quadrille.

Katharine appeared with a new dance partner, a man at least three inches shorter than she, with a shock of strawberry blonde hair and ruddy cheeks. They joined Ellie and Hamilton, as did another couple Ellie did not know.

"You look beautiful," a voice whispered in her ear. Ellie turned her head to see the speaker and her heart nearly stopped.

It was Rebecca. She was no longer paired with the Lovely Mr. Winthrop, but instead with a tall, thin man in his mid-thirties. They glided by her and Hamilton and took their places as the fourth couple in the square.

Rebecca's eyes were hidden behind her own mask, midnight blue with white feathers. Ellie waited for some other acknowledgement, but she gave no sign beyond the proper nod of the head and polite smile. Ellie shut her open mouth, hoping no one noticed her look of surprise.

The orchestra started to play. Ellie curtsied to Hamilton, and the dance began. Twirling and stepping in the complicated patterns with newfound enthusiasm, she enjoyed the dance. By the end, her smile was permanently etched onto her face.

When the set finished, Rebecca and her partner vanished into the crowd. Katharine approached her. "You are a good dancer." She opened her fan and waved it in front of her face and chest, which were both flushed. "I'm so hot, I need a break. Come and get a drink with me." And before Ellie could reply, Katharine had looped her arm through Ellie's and was dragging her away from the floor and Hamilton. With her free hand, she opened her own fan and used it to cool her skin, which was hot from excitement as much as from exertion.

They made their way through the crowd, Ellie just managing to steer Katharine around Olivia before they were spotted. Her stepmother had cornered poor Hamilton. The look of forced politeness had returned to his face, but his eyes followed Ellie, though she pretended not to notice. The next dance started, and Hamilton was paired with Rebecca, the long-promised dance finally fulfilled. She thought she saw Rebecca whisper something in his ear, but too many bodies were between them to be certain.

The girls found their way to the punch bowl and gulped down two glasses a piece as ladylike as possible. Katharine looked over the edge of her third glass, half-full, at Ellie. "It looks as if you've charmed Mr. Hamilton Scott."

Ellie nearly choked on her punch. "Oh, no, I don't think I have." She looked down into her glass. "How could I? We've just met this evening."

Katharine shrugged. "He seemed to enjoy dancing with you, which was unusual for him. I've seen him at dozens of parties this year, and usually he looks bored to death."

"He said something to that effect." Ellie did not reveal the rest of his admission, about how he had complimented her interest in things outside the usual woman's sphere. If he had only been flattering her, she didn't want to seem naïve by mentioning it to Katharine.

"I would watch my back if I were you, though, especially if he asks you to dance again."

"Why?" Ellie refilled her glass.

"Because some of these girls can be vicious, especially when it comes to finding a husband, and Hamilton is the most eligible bachelor in town. I'm probably the only girl in the room *not* interested in him, although my mother wishes it were otherwise."

"Why aren't you interested in him?" Ellie tried her best to make the question sound nonchalant. "He's handsome, and charming, and… a good dancer."

Katharine shrugged. "His family and mine are close friends. He's more like a brother to me. I can't imagine kissing him."

"Oh. I see." Unlike her companion, Ellie had no trouble at all imagining kissing Hamilton. Her impertinent mind began to imagine him kissing her neck, and touching her in outrageously inappropriate ways. Her cheeks burned as if she were on fire. She pushed the image away and hoped Katharine could not tell what she had been thinking.

Her companion sipped her punch and gave Ellie a crooked smirk. "Whatever did you talk about during the waltz?"

Ellie just couldn't stand one more lie. "The Centennial Exposition, and railroads, and machines."

"Oh, is that all?" Katharine said with a laugh. "Well, that explains it. Hamilton cannot stand silly, empty-headed girls. He's always saying how he wishes he could find a girl with a brain and the ability to talk about something other than furnishings." She laughed, as if the idea were ridiculous. One eyebrow lifted as she looked at something behind Ellie. "Whatever you said, you must have impressed him."

"Why do you say that?"

"Because he's coming this way."

CHAPTER XX

ELLIE SPUN AROUND SO FAST SHE SPILLED HER PUNCH ALL OVER THE waistcoat of the man behind her. He was Katharine's dance partner from the quadrille, the man with the strawberry blonde hair. His cheeks were even ruddier than before, from either dancing or drink. Ellie supplied a sincere but rushed apology, her attention focused on the man Katharine had indicated. It *was* Hamilton, and he was indeed coming toward them. Ellie tried to step around the man on whom she had spilled her punch, but he followed her movement.

"Please don't worry about it," he said good-naturedly. "No harm done."

Hamilton had spotted Ellie and Katharine. His steps became more urgent as he tried to maneuver through the crowd. The red-haired man must have noticed her distraction — he cleared his throat to get her attention.

"Miss... I'm sorry, I didn't catch your name?"

"Reed," Ellie replied with a hint of impatience. Her stomach dropped for what seemed like the twentieth time that night. She knew what was coming next.

"I was wondering if you were free for the next dance?"

Ellie opened her mouth, completely unsure how to respond.

"No, she is not free. Miss Reed has promised the entire next set to me."

Hamilton Scott had finally arrived. He stood so close beside Ellie her midsection felt as if it were on fire. He glanced at her with another of those hard-to-read expressions, and the ruddy man's green eyes widened behind his mask. He looked up at Hamilton — it was a considerable distance — and cleared his throat again.

"Oh, I see," the man squeaked. He gave a small bow and backed away.

Ellie turned toward Hamilton, hoping she hid the extent of her pleasure lest it appear unseemly. "Mr. Scott? I don't remember agreeing to dance the next set with you." She hoped the teasing in her voice struck the proper tenor. Unlike Katharine, Ellie had no experience with flirting.

Hamilton's mouth fell open. "Well, I... uh... oh..." he sputtered.

Ellie, partly delighted and partly sorry, saved him from further floundering with a warm smile. "But I would be happy to do so." She held her dance card out to him. He took it gently, returning her smile with one of his own, and wrote his name. Ellie took it back and looked at it. Now it was her turn to become flustered, because he had written his name in for every one of the remaining dances for the evening. What would she tell him when she had to suddenly leave? At least she would have ample opportunity to get her token.

Someone announced that the next set was about to begin. It started with another quadrille, and Ellie was caught up in the spinning and turning, her head whirling almost as fast as the dance. The polka was followed by a Virginia Reel, a Lancier, and a Redowa, and Ellie drank in every moment that she was able to touch her very capable dancing partner, who was no longer moving like he was made of wood.

Finally, it was time for another waltz, and Ellie was glad for the chance to catch her breath. But when Hamilton pulled her into his arms, she found no respite. Had he pulled her closer than he had the first time they had danced? She didn't remember being able to smell his cologne before, but the spicy, slightly musky scent was nearly as intoxicating as the champagne. Mr. Scott's breath brushed her cheek, and she knew she was not imagining their closeness.

"Miss Reed?" Mr. Scott's voice was quiet and strange, a tone that made a pleasant warmth pool in Ellie's belly. She could listen to him speak to her like that forever, though it would likely drive her to do something untoward if it went on much longer.

"Yes?" Ellie matched his low tone.

"I have had the most wonderful time with you this evening." He paused. "More than with any young lady I can recall. I was wondering if I might... call on you."

Was he really asking? Did the beautiful, charming, wonderful Hamilton Scott want to court her? If she thought she would float away earlier, now she was certain she would sprout wings and fly.

"I know it's terribly forward of me to ask you like this," Hamilton went on. "But since you are in the city without your father, and I cannot seem to locate your chaperone..." Ellie tried not to cringe. "I felt I had no other options but to ask you directly."

Ellie wished she had the power to stop time, to let this moment remain forever. But time screamed in her ear, reminding her of her life beyond the ballroom, and her flying spirit crashed to earth. How could she say yes, when nearly every word from her mouth had been a lie? She could not receive him as Eliza Reed of New York, and Ann Gibson was not worthy of him. Even if he would forgive her lies, the spell still prevented her from telling him who she really was. Her heart cracked in two as she came up yet another lie in order to stop his pursuit.

"But Mr. Scott, I live in New York. I am returning there tomorrow afternoon."

His laugh was soft and gentle, as if her words were a charming ploy. "As you said before, Miss Reed, Philadelphia does not exist as an island. Nor is New York the other end of the Earth. It is only a short ride by train. And I happen to know quite a bit about trains. Mrs. Astor's ball is in the next few weeks, is it not? I am sure that a young lady of your caliber is on the guest list, and the Astors are personal friends. I should very much like to dance with you there."

Ellie began to panic. She was trying to be subtle—why was he so persistent?

"I would also like to have you visit us again in Philadelphia. If you haven't been to the annual Horse Show in May, in Devon, you could attend with my family." The implications in such an invitation were not lost on Ellie, and she felt every last drop of blood rush from her face.

Oh dear. For the briefest of moments, she considered throwing caution to the wind and giving her unconditional agreement, but quickly pulled her wits about her, not letting the spell of his charm and her own heart take root. She still needed her token, which she would probably be able to get easily if she led him on for a little longer. It wouldn't be right, and she wasn't sure she had the stomach for it. There had to be another way. Could she let him go without hurting his feelings?

"Mr. Scott, I am sincerely flattered and much honored by your offer. Unfortunately, I am scheduled to leave the country in three days' time. My father is going to London on business, and I am going with him to visit family and participate in their Season. I won't return until fall." Her stomach churned as the falsehood fell from her lips, but hoped it was enough. By the fall he would have forgotten all about Eliza Reed.

Hamilton frowned, and she jumped to add, "I am truly sorry. If things were different, I would gladly have accepted." She tried to make her words, which were the absolute truth for once this evening, into a balm soothing the discomfort of the moment.

"Of course, Miss Reed. I understand." His smile returned, but it had lost some of its warmth. His hand seemed to stiffen in Ellie's, and the space between them increased ever so slightly. To Ellie, it was as if they were a world apart. *And aren't we, really?* The thought was bitter as bile. Though she had been born to it, she didn't really belong to this world of ball gowns and flirtation, of careful steps not always taken on the dance floor. Did she belong to Ben's world, then? She didn't feel she fit there, either, though the look in Ben's eyes said he would welcome her gladly. The room was crowded with people, but Ellie suddenly felt utterly alone.

The dance ended with Ellie and Hamilton still in uncomfortable silence. He escorted her to the edge of the dance floor and left her without a word. Though she couldn't blame him, the gesture crushed the remains of her battered heart to powder. Unbidden, a tear slipped from her eye. There was a buzzing in her chest, pain from her heart breaking. But no, it wasn't. The buzzing was accompanied by the sound of tiny bells. Ellie looked down, and found the little watch chiming. Had it been doing that all night, chiming the time? Or had it only decided to alert her now, as a reminder of her true task? She lifted it to look and nearly cried out loud. It was 11:30! Ben would be waiting for her. She had a mere thirty minutes until any chance of reclaiming her life would vanish. She had spent the entire night getting close to Hamilton, only to push him away at the last moment with her clumsy attempt at playing the debutante, leaving her with no token and only half a chance at breaking the spell.

There was no more time. She would have to hope that Ben's token would be enough to save her. Ellie weaved between the people that blocked her way to the door, turning one way and then the other until she was no longer sure where the exit was. She took a step backward to avoid being trampled by an older gentleman with a red nose, and backed directly into someone.

She turned around, ready to apologize. "Excuse me, I'm so sorry..."

The words turned to dust in her mouth. Even though half of her face was hidden by a mask of chocolate-colored silk, Ellie would know her stepmother's perpetual expression of distaste anywhere. She almost fell again as she took another hasty step backward, this time over her own dress. Her hands shook, from both fear and anger, and she balled them into fists.

Olivia looked Ellie up and down, lips pursed. "I should say. Clumsy girl. Be more careful."

Ellie swallowed but it was difficult with her throat turned dry as sand, and nodded. "Yes, ma'am." It pained her to say the words, but it was the only way to get away from Olivia without a fuss.

Her stepmother did not let her go that easily. The woman's lips pursed in that familiar expression of suspicion. "What is your name? I've watched you dancing all night with Mr. Scott, haven't I? You shouldn't have allowed him so many dances, you know. People will talk."

Let me guess what 'people' those would be, Ellie thought. "My name is Eliza Reed, ma'am." She should have at least dropped a small curtsey, but didn't, purely out of spite. "I am from New York."

Olivia looked down her nose and gave a sniff. "Oh, I see. Besides your reputation, dear, it isn't fair of you to monopolize Mr. Scott's time. There are many other girls to whom he promised dances, long before this night."

Ellie would have cheerfully spit in Olivia's eye, but decided that words would leave a deeper impression. "I had no idea, of course. But Mr. Hamilton is a free man with his own mind, is he not? Those other obligations must not have been very important to him, because he never once mentioned them." She tilted her head, as if she were thinking. "And I don't recall holding a pistol to his head when he filled in the spaces on my dance card, either."

She turned and left, not bothering to see the effect of her words. Olivia would be stewing, probably standing in the middle of the crowd with her mouth wide open like a fish at the market. Ellie felt ridiculously satisfied, but the feeling left as quickly as it had come — it was the last time she would ever be able to speak to Olivia that way. If her stepmother even allowed her to continue speaking at all once her plans were complete.

Ellie couldn't consider that now. Now she needed to get home and be with her father. Fresh tears rolled down her cheeks. All night she had only been thinking of herself, while he was at home, alone and ill. *I have been so selfish, leaving him while I was out dancing! I am no better than those other girls, am I?*

She burst through ballroom doors and fell into the cool and blessedly empty hallway. She stopped just long enough to collect her mantle, and was at the top of the staircase.

"Miss Reed! Please wait."

She was shocked to see Hamilton chasing her down the hall. *What could he possibly want?* She didn't have time for proper etiquette anymore. "I'm sorry, Mr. Scott, I was just on my way out."

Hamilton caught up to her in just a few steps, stopping her with a touch to her shoulder. "I need to apologize for my rude behavior." He pulled off his mask and dropped it to the floor, revealing his eyes of sun-washed blue, like the sky at midsummer. His cheeks reddened a little, and he cleared his throat. "I was impolite to you after you refused my call. You gave a perfectly reasonable answer, and I let my pride get in the way of accepting your refusal as a gentleman should."

Ellie nodded. "Well, there was no harm done, and you've apologized, so if you'll excuse me, I must be going."

"You're leaving now?" Hamilton's voice stopped her mid-turn. "But... it's almost midnight."

"I'm afraid I must. I promised my aunt that I would be home before the clock strikes the hour. You know how spinster aunts can be. My chaperone has gone to get the carriage." She stepped onto the first stair, then paused and looked back at him. "Goodbye, Mr. Scott."

"Please," Hamilton said quietly. "If you won't stay, may I at least see your face before you leave?"

"I'm sorry, but I really must go now."

He pulled his handkerchief from his pocket and held it out to her. "I hope I am not the cause of your tears."

Ellie took the linen cloth, embroidered with his initials, and dabbed at her face. She held it out to him, but he held up his hands in refusal.

"Please, keep it. To remember."

Ellie pressed it to her chest as if it were made of solid gold. It was worth more—she held her own life in her hands.

"No, you may rest easy that you are not." She cringed. "I'm sorry. I didn't mean that the way it sounded. Only that my tears are for something else. And now I may not need them." Hamilton looked confused, and she shook her head, wishing she could explain.

"I'm sorry, Mr. Scott, but I still must go. I'm afraid my time is short."

Hamilton's face fell once more, and Ellie almost couldn't bear it. "Please, just show me your face," he said again. "So that I can remember you."

Ellie paused for half a breath, the handkerchief like the beat of her heart in her hand, before reaching up and pulling the end of the satin ribbon tied behind her head. The mask fluttered to the ground, and she looked at him, both afraid and bold.

Hamilton paused, smiling, then his eyes widened.

"We *have* met before. I remember. You're—"

"Please don't tell anyone that you have seen me. I don't have time to explain, but it's very important that no one know I was here. Now I really must go." She resumed her descent, and then paused again. "Mr. Scott, if I could have accepted your offer, I would have. With all of my heart."

"Wait, come back! I don't understand!"

His words chased her down the steps. She nearly stumbled over the hem of her dress, sliding as she hit the marble floor. It was cold and strange beneath her feet, but her only thought was for getting home. Ellie pulled open the door and hurtled out into the snow.

Ben checked his watch. 11:40. Where is she? He had arrived ten minutes before he had told Ellie he would be here, waiting inside the motorcar instead of out in the snow, which still fell steadily. Ellie hadn't yet emerged from the Academy's doors, which worried him. What if she lost track of time? She was cutting it close. He brushed some dirt from his boots and glanced at the doors, his nerves on edge.

She'll be out any second. We'll get this spell business all taken care of, and then we can get back to our lives. He had no idea what that would mean tomorrow, or where it left their friendship. After tonight, she would be Eleanor Banneker, socialite. A thread of fear ran through him, that once she had regained the life of luxury and status, that she would no longer have time for him. *That's ridiculous. She's not like these other snobs, who barely acknowledge the existence of the people whose hard work makes their lives easier.* But no matter how he tried, he could not shake the feeling.

What would happen if she couldn't break the spell? If her father died, she would have nothing left here. Would she want to join him when he left the city to build his career? The pleasant vision of Ellie on his arm as they toured the cities of Europe warmed him right to his toes. So much mattered on what happened in the next twenty minutes.

Make that ten. Ben opened the door and hopped to the sidewalk. He dusted off the driver's seat, and watched the Academy doors in anticipation, willing them to open. The silence of the snow falling seemed to stretch out like an uncoiled spring.

With a sound like a gunshot, the door flew open. Ellie burst onto the sidewalk, running toward him as if a pack of hounds were at her heels.

"There you are. I was just starting to wonder what—"

Ben's words died in his throat. Ellie's mask was gone. Her skin was blotchy, her nose red, as if she had been crying. She ran past him and jumped into the motorcar with no regard for the back end of her dress.

"Go!"

Ben shut the door and jumped into the dickey box. Pushing the button to start the engine, he then pulled the lever to release the brakes. As they pulled away from the curb, he glanced back at the Academy. A man had come through the door behind Ellie. He ran to the edge of the sidewalk and stood in the snow. There was something in his hand, small and golden. The man looked first one way, then the other, as if searching for something, and when he saw the motorcar, he ran after them, calling something Ben could not quite make out.

Ben pulled his goggles over his eyes, put more steam into the engine and sped off into the night.

Ellie sat on the edge of the seat, the handkerchief pressed to her chest, barely feeling the bumps in the road as the city went by in a blur. Her mind whirred as fast as the motorcar's wheels, thoughts flying by before she had a chance to dwell on them. Dancing with Hamilton, the look on his face when he realized who she was. He had been hurt by her refusal, and confused, but what was done was done, and none of it mattered as much as getting home to her father before the clock struck twelve.

As if responding to her wish, the machine slowed and then stopped. There was her own front door. Ben silenced the engine, leaving her with nothing but the sound of her own heart. She threw the door open and leapt to the sidewalk before Ben was out of the driver's seat. One of her feet was cold, but she barely felt it as she ran up the front steps.

"Ellie? Are you alright?" Ben jumped to the sidewalk beside her.

"Ask me again tomorrow," she called as she dashed inside, leaving the door hanging open. "Thank you for everything, Ben!"

Grasping her skirt with both hands and holding it high, she took the first-floor stairs two at a time. When she reached the top, the grandfather clock began to chime, marking the midnight hour.

CHAPTER XXI

BEN STOOD IN THE OPEN FRONT DOOR, HIS HAT IN HIS HAND, wondering if he should wait or if he should go. Uncertainty twisted his stomach into a knot. He should wait, he decided. If this did not work, and the spell held, he would get Ellie out of the house before Olivia came home. She wouldn't want to go, but he realized the danger she was in, even if she did not. He would bundle her into the motorcar and drive away.

The clock's bell rang over and again, the chime reverberating through the house like a cathedral bell. Was it nine, or ten? He couldn't stand it any longer. Forget good manners, he was going up. He jumped up the first four steps just as the clock stopped ringing, its message delivered for another hour. The silence that followed felt as if time itself had stopped, the air pressing on him. Ben was afraid to move, afraid to breathe.

There was a thunderous crash. A second later, a tremor shook the house and knocked him down the steps.

"Ellie? Are you alright?" He was already on his way upstairs again, not waiting for an answer.

"Nooooooooo!"

Ellie's heartbroken scream cut through the silence like broken glass.

Ellie came into her father's room as the clock rang for the fourth time. He was sleeping, just as she had left him. Everything else was also just as she had left it — the white bowl and candle, the lock of her own hair, the Cape May Diamond, the bone, the raven's claw. But there was something else as well. An envelope leaned against the front of the bowl. Ellie grabbed it, and was surprised by its weight. There were only two words written across the front in indigo ink:

Open Me.

She turned the envelope over, and Olivia's locket slid out and into her palm. Ellie fumbled with the latch and opened it, and then nearly dropped it when she saw the curl of brown hair, tied neatly with a red ribbon, tucked inside. Her father's hair.

The clock chimed again, and Ellie realized she had lost count. She dropped the locket on the floor and with shaking fingers, she tried to light the candle. The first time, the match did not light.

"Damn it!"

She tried again and succeeded. Into the bowl, she put the bishop's finger bone, the raven's claw, and the sparkling crystal. Another two chimes. She dropped her own hair into the bowl, then kissed her father's lock of hair and put it in as well. All that was left were the tokens. Ellie held the handkerchief in one hand, the brass gear in the other. Images of both faces floated across her mind. Ben, kind eyes and open smile. Hamilton, his gentle voice and sun-washed blue eyes. There was no time to decide, and she could not get it wrong. Another chime jarred her bones. She dropped both into the bowl and hoped it would work.

She looked into the mirror above the bureau. There were herself and her father, reflected. She concentrated on the candle's flame, picturing the two of them bound in chains, and then seeing those chains falling away, just as the old woman directed. The last chime rang, its sound fading away slowly.

Ellie held her breath, and it seemed as if the rest of the world stopped with her. The room went dark, the gas lights extinguished. The candle's flame shot upward until the heat licked her skin. She looked at her reflection. The flickering light made her eyes look hollow and her cheekbones stand out like some kind of ghoul. Something pressed against her chest, as if trying to push her to the ground. She struggled against it with all her might, fighting for her very breath.

"I want my life back. I want my father's memory returned. We want to be free. I *demand* that we be freed."

There was a crash like thunder that shook the whole house. Then the pressure disappeared, and there was the sensation of weight slipping off her shoulders, like a heavy cloak falling to the floor. The candle went out, plunging the room into darkness for a second, and then the gas lamps leapt to life once more. She forced herself to look in the mirror again, half-expecting to see someone else's face staring back at her. It was her own face, as always, but there was something different about it that she couldn't quite put her finger on.

"We're free," she whispered. "Papa, we're free. Oh, please wake up so you can see me."

The reply came in the form of a sudden retching and coughing from the bed behind her.

"Noooooooo!" She ran to her father's side. Sweat poured down his face and soaked his nightshirt, heat radiating from his skin like fire. His body bucked like a horse as a second fit of rattling coughing came over him—he nearly threw himself from the bed with the force of it. Ellie poured water from the pitcher on the table by his bed into a porcelain basin, soaked a rag in it and used the still-sopping cloth to mop her father's burning forehead. He moaned in pain, and clutched at Ellie's hands, gripping them with a nearly inhuman strength.

"Papa, it's all right, just calm down. It will be all right if you just relax." Ellie tried to pull her hands away so she could continue to tend to his fever, but he would not release her.

Ben appeared in the doorway, his face lined with worry. "What happened?"

Ellie shook her head. "I... don't know. I did everything, exactly as the old woman told me. Didn't you feel the earth move?"

Ben nodded.

"When it was over, he started coughing. He's burning with fever—he needs a doctor right now."

"I'll drag one from bed if I have to." Ben's gaze lingered for a moment, and then he was gone, the door slamming behind him. Another fit of coughing came over Ellie's father, and she held a cloth to his mouth. When she pulled it away, flecks of blood decorated the white linen.

The door slammed again. Had Ben found someone so quickly? Two pairs of footsteps thundered up the stairs.

"Thank goodness you're here! Please hurry!"

"What's happening? What are you doing, you wretched girl?"

It was not Ben and a doctor that appeared in the doorway, but Olivia and Rebecca. Olivia took in the scene, her gaze coming to rest on Ellie.

"You! It was you at the ball?" She stepped inside the room, her fury an icy wind that swept the room. "How dare you!"

"Is that all you have to say?" Ellie wiped her father's mouth again. There was more blood. "Can't you see he needs help?"

Olivia finally looked at her husband, and face drained of color. "What's wrong?"

"I don't know, but look." Ellie showed her the blood-stained handkerchief.

Ephraim's coughing slowed, and he finally caught enough breath to speak. "Where... is my wife?" He was so pale, clammy with sweat. Ellie looked into his shining, sunken eyes.

"Papa?"

His voice was like a rusty hinge, his dry throat giving a loud click. "My wife. I need to see her."

Olivia stumbled into the room, leaning on the bed with one knee, the skirt of her ball gown filling up half of the bed. Rebecca pressed herself against the wall, the knuckles of one hand against her mouth, her face white.

"I'm here, Ephraim."

Ellie had never heard her stepmother speak with so much kindness. Ephraim turned his glassy gaze toward Olivia, but there was no spark of recognition.

"No, no. My wife."

"I am your wife. It's me, Olivia." She pulled his hands away from Ellie and clutched them to her chest. "I'm right here." Her voice trembled with the threat of tears. Ellie could barely believe it. Did Olivia actually *love* her father? All of these years, Ellie believed that Olivia had only married her father for his money.

"No, no." Ephraim became more agitated. "My wife, where is my wife?" He pulled his hands from Olivia's grip. "I must see her."

"Papa, calm down, please," Ellie begged. This was the most he had spoken in almost a year, and she wished he would stop. He was obviously delirious, as usual, but she had never seen him so upset. His head swiveled slowly in Ellie's direction, and when his gaze fell on his daughter's face he stopped struggling. His head fell back, sinking into the pillow, and he lifted a hand to Ellie's face.

"There you are, my love."

Tears flowed down Ellie's face at his tenderness. She had long ago forgiven him for not recognizing his only child. Had the spell not broken after all? "Papa, I love you so much."

"And I have always loved you." He stroked her skin again and but his hand shook and then, unable to hold it up any longer, fell to the bed. "My Eleanor."

Ellie was unable to stem the tide of her tears, a new wave washing her cheeks. "You know me?"

"Of course, I do." He seemed lucid for the first time in recent memory. "How could I not know my own daughter? You look so like your mother. I love you both so much."

He looked past Ellie and to the wall, as if someone else were in the room. "Violetta?"

Ellie turned her head to look, knowing of course that her mother would not be there, only driven by the certainty in her father's voice.

He continued to speak to the faded wallpaper of his bedroom. "My dearest love, you've been away too long." He reached toward the person only he could see and started to cough again. This fit was much more violent than before, the rattle in his chest louder than ever. He struggled for every breath, his face turning the color of beets.

"Papa! Breathe, Papa, please!" Ellie begged, helpless to do anything else. Her father was suffocating before her eyes. Olivia sobbed beside him, tears running freely.

The coughing stopped. There was no wheezing afterward, no gulping as the man tried to fill his lungs. Only a single long, slow exhale. As the final breath of Ephraim Banneker left his body, a single word was whispered on the back of the escaping air.

"Eleanor..."

The silence that followed nearly crushed Ellie beneath its weight, squeezing her chest so that she could not even gather the strength to cry out. The broken heart she had endured earlier seemed like a paper cut compared to the gaping wound that opened within her, threatening to swallow her whole. She held her father's too-still hand, and begged him in fervent whispers to return to her.

"Papa, no! You can't leave me, Papa."

His eyes were still open, but the light had gone from them, flickered out like a candle. Ellie was aware, in a detached way, that Olivia still sat on the opposite side of the bed and that she was weeping. The woman's cries had nothing at all to do with Ellie or her nearly unbearable pain.

"It is finished."

The voice, with its strange, ethereal timbre, cut through the fog of Ellie's grief. She turned her head slowly, fighting to focus on the figure that stood in the doorway.

The hall was well-lit tonight, and Ellie had a full view of the visitor. The woman was slight, nearly as tall as Ellie, and carried a carved walking stick topped with a blue-glass sphere. Her hair was silvery-white, twisted into a knot on top of her head, tendrils hanging down to frame her oval face. Her features were delicate, her cheekbones prominent beneath large blue eyes that Ellie had seen shine in the dark like fallen stars

"What are you doing here?" Olivia leapt from the bed, standing defiantly between the visitor and her husband's body. "I told you never to set foot in my house again." Misery and anger appeared to fight for control, neither gaining the upper hand.

The visitor, unfazed, pulled off her gloves and tucked them into the pocket of her striped walking dress. "And I believe I reminded you that this was not *your* house. You do not have the power to refuse me entrance." Her sparkling gaze fell on Ellie. "I am here because our contract has been fulfilled. I have been paid in full, to my satisfaction."

Ellie rose slowly, anger building in her chest as she rounded the end of the bed, lunging toward the stranger.

"You did this." Her voice was low, walking the minute ledge between hysteria and rage.

"Why did you take my father, you—"

"Witch? Not exactly." The stranger's detached coolness made Ellie want to beat the woman with her own walking stick. "But believe me, Miss Banneker, it was nothing personal. Just business."

"You could have cured him! I heard you say so!" Ellie's voice was raw with crying and anger.

The woman shrugged. "I could have, yes. Your stepmother was unwilling to enter into another contract. She did not like my terms."

"I would have!" Ellie curled her hands into fists. "I would have given anything."

The stranger gave an enigmatic smile. "Don't be so sure, child."

"But I broke the spell! I did everything right! Why did you take him?"

The visitor's reply was gentle. "You did indeed break both the Love Spell and your enchantment. His illness was not tied to either. It was payment. Your stepmother bartered with me, and this was the price. She made her choice."

It was hard for Ellie to breathe. She looked at her stepmother. Olivia bent her head, surprising Ellie for the second time that evening with the look of shame she wore. Tears dropped from her stepmother's eyes, hitting the silk skirt of her gown, leaving dark stains.

"I never meant for this to happen."

"You went into the contract with full understanding." The stranger showed no trace of sympathy. "Both of what it was you wanted and my nature. If you remember correctly, I tried to warn you that requests such as yours could have unforeseen ends, but you insisted. You signed the contract." Something appeared in the stranger's hand, as if from thin air—a copy of the contract Ellie had found in the desk. "Here it is, in black-and-white, complete with the appropriate signatures, all in proper order. You wanted your heart's desire, Olivia, and I provided it." An odd look crossed the visitor's face. "You were unconcerned with the cost, probably because you thought I wanted to be paid with something common, like money." She made a derisive sound. "That was your mistake."

Her strange gaze turned to Ellie again. "Do you know, my dear, what it was the drove the heart of Olivia Gibson? Besides providing her with the two spells she used on you and your father, do you know what I did to fulfill my end of the bargain?"

The stranger snapped her fingers once. The contract disappeared, and the globe on her walking stick began to glow. Ellie thought her vision was failing as the stranger's form blurred around the edges. The glow brightened and grew, and the stranger began to shrink. Her dress changed—the fabric pulled close to her body and became coarse. Her nose elongated, the end turning black, while her fingers pulled close together, the nails growing into claws. She fell onto all fours, and a medium-sized white-and-brown spotted dog stood before them. It sat and barked, turning around and jumping up on its hind legs. As quickly as it had changed into a dog, it changed back into the odd visitor.

Ellie's mind reeled, overwhelmed by the amazing illusion. That's what it must be, Ben's voice said in her mind. *Just an illusion, making me see what she wants me to see.* But what did it have to do with her father or Olivia? Puzzled by the shift in the conversation, Ellie tried to piece it together. The stranger responded only with a cold, knowing look. Ben's voice whispered in her mind again, this time from memory.

It was an accident. *A dog ran across the road and spooked the horses.*

Ellie's horrified gasp must have been enough to convince the stranger that her point had been made. With a small, crooked smile, the visitor bobbed her silver-white head once, and then turned and walked down the stairs. No one bothered to show her out, and the sound of the front door closing never came, but she was gone. She left absolute silence in her wake, the three women standing as still as wax mannequins in a department store window tableau.

Ben pulled onto Delancey Place and stopped. The Bannekers' carriage sat in front of the house. Olivia and Rebecca were home, though why they had left the ball so early, Ben didn't know. They should have been gone until dawn. He waited, a block away, until the driver snapped the reins and the carriage was out of sight. He crept the motorcar along and stopped a few houses from Ellie's.

He had gone blocks and blocks, not finding a doctor, even interrupting a raucous New Year's Eve party looking for one. *Most of them,* he thought bitterly, *are probably at the Assembly Ball, and very drunk.* He had been about to head back to the Academy when something made him turn around, an urgent and terrible feeling that Ellie needed him.

Ben ran to the house. He tried to open the door, but it was locked. When he heard wailing coming from inside, he beat on the front door with his fist, demanding entrance. Either no one heard him or they were ignoring him, because the door remained shut. There was more shouting, and then silence. He waited, leaning against the door, but there was nothing more.

"I'd go home if I were you, Mr. Grimm."

Ben jumped, startled, and turned around. A woman, who looked young but had silver hair, stood on the sidewalk. She carried a walking stick topped by a blue ball.

"Where did you come from? How do you know my name?"

The woman shrugged. "I know many things. Where I come from is not important."

"I need to get inside. Ellie might need me."

The woman nodded. "She will need you, and soon. But not tonight. Tonight, you should let her mourn in peace."

"Mourn? He's..."

The woman nodded. "Yes. It is regrettable that it turned out this way. But..." The woman shrugged. "Business is business. Oh, and one last thing, Mr. Grimm. You shouldn't be so quick to dismiss things you don't understand."

She snapped her fingers, and there was a sudden bright light. When it faded, the woman was gone. In her place stood another woman, this one vaguely familiar. Ben stumbled backward, feeling like he had been punched in the stomach, when he realized it was the fortune teller from the Exposition.

"You said that if Ellie broke the spell, she and her father would be saved."

The old woman's smile was enigmatic, but not cruel. "No, I said if she did not break the spell by tonight, they would be bound forever. In the end, though, she did save him. He died a free man."

"And what was in it for you? I thought you had a contract with Olivia?" Ben could barely believe he was talking to this creature who could apparently shape-shift. If it was an illusion, it was stunning, but he had seen enough the last few weeks to know better. This was real magic.

"I did. And I lived up to my end of it. To the letter. Nowhere in our agreement did it say that I could not speak to Eleanor, or tell her how to break her bonds. As for what I was looking for?" She looked up at the Banneker house, to the solitary window where a light flickered.

"Redemption. Have a good evening, Mr. Grimm." She glanced at the motorcar and lifted an eyebrow. "Excellent. You will go far, I think. Yes, yes. Very far."

She turned and walked away, her walking stick tapping out the beat of her steps. Ben watched her go, then tried to open Ellie's front door once more, without success. When he looked up the street again, the woman was gone.

Ellie felt as if her heart had been ripped from her chest, leaving behind a sharp, excruciating pain. Her father was dead. Her mother was dead. Most painful of all, Olivia's machinations and her meddling with whatever forces the visitor represented had been responsible for it all. The woman who stood beside her father's bed, tears still dripping onto her dress, had turned Ellie into an orphan as surely as if she had taken a knife and murdered both of her parents in their sleep.

She did not return to her bed that night. Olivia regained her composure, hiding whatever she felt about the death of her husband and the revelations of the visitor beneath her usual icy facade. As if nothing had happened, she ordered Ellie to help her and Rebecca undress.

Ellie said nothing, but the look in her eyes and the guttural sound that formed in her throat made Olivia stumble backward, catching herself on the door frame with a trembling hand.

"I suppose under the circumstances, you may be excused for this evening. Come, Rebecca."

She exited, head held high, but Rebecca remained for a few moments longer. Tears spilled down her face, leaving streaks of makeup behind.

"Rebecca!" Olivia called from the hallway.

"Ellie, I'm so sorry." The words were whispered, but reverberated through Ellie's head as if she had shouted. "You didn't deserve... any of this." She put a gentle kiss on Ellie's cheek and slipped from the room, closing the door behind her.

Ellie remained in her father's room all night. She felt numb, and hollow as a dry well. Still in her ball gown, she curled up in the upholstered chair in the corner of the room, just as she had when she was a little girl. At some point she realized that she had lost one of her golden slippers along the way, but only as a distant observation, like it was a stranger's problem. She was exhausted but could not bear to close her eyes. She took deep, shuddering breaths as pain and grief collapsed in on her, and after hours she finally fell asleep.

CHAPTER XXII

EN TOSSED THE HAMMER ONTO THE WORKBENCH, FRUSTRATED. ONCE again, he couldn't concentrate, and again, it was because of Ellie. Three days had passed since the ball, and he had heard nothing from her. He was going mad with worry, hearing her cry echo in his mind. It was the sound of a broken heart, and it kept him awake at night.

Knowing what he did about Olivia and Mr. Banneker's will, he wasn't just worried about Ellie's state of mind. The day after the ball he had gone to the kitchen door, not caring if Olivia was home or if she saw him. But no one answered. The house was quiet and the door locked, which made Ben even more nervous. He had tried the next day as well, with no better result.

The bookshop was quiet as a graveyard, the theater not yet ready to resume, and sleep illusive, so he tried to keep himself occupied in his workshop. He had finished the disappearing bird cage, and had started to build the cabinet for the Vanishing Assistant. The Orange Tree's parts were set up on his workbench, but it wasn't going well. Everything seemed so dull after building the steam-powered motorcar. The machine was currently sitting in the properties barn, covered by the dirty canvas. He had no idea what he was going to do with it, but it seemed like the safest place to keep it until he could figure that out.

He rubbed his hands through his hair, leaving the Orange Tree and turning his attention to the task to which he was most inspired — the dancing couple automata. He chose the gears and springs he needed from a pile on the bench and put them together. This was complicated enough to keep his focus, though while he was placing gear and springs he kept thinking of Ellie, dancing in the arms of the man that had chased her out of the Academy. It stirred the flame of jealousy he had felt on the night of the ball. He pushed it away, only to have it replaced by the sound of Ellie's cry as her father died in her arms, tearing his own heart a little more each time.

Harry announced himself in his usual manner, by thudding down the stairs as if he were carrying sacks of bricks. Without asking if he could stay, he flopped onto the floor, crossing his legs in a tailor's seat, and staring at Ben.

His little brother's unmoving gaze made Ben squirm. "All right, what do you want?" he said with a sigh. "I'm busy, so whatever it is, make it quick."

Harry looked down, suddenly bashful, and started doodling in the dirt on the floor with one finger. "I was just wondering... when we were going to see Ellie again."

Ben tried not to laugh at his brother's obvious attempt to not be obvious. "I don't know, Harry." He shrugged and turned away, so that his brother wouldn't see how worried he was. "Soon, I hope."

Harry picked up a bent gear from the floor and played with it. "Me too. She's... nice."

Ben focused on the automaton, setting a spring and tightening it to keep it in place. "Yes, she certainly is." He did not reveal to his little brother the revelation that had come over him just a moment ago.

He was in love with Ellie Banneker.

The last three days had passed in a complete and total haze. Ellie had spent the first day after her father's death in his room, curled up in the chair, unable to move or speak. Her father's body remained on the bed. Ellie had closed his eyes, so it appeared he was sleeping. She vaguely recalled Rebecca coming in, but whether it was morning or afternoon she had no idea. Her stepsister had brought fresh clothes and helped her out of the borrowed gown, neither girl saying a word. She had returned at least once more, bringing a tray with a bowl of steaming porridge and some toast, begging Ellie to eat. But she did not move, and eventually Rebecca took the food away.

The third day, Olivia marched into the room.

"That will be quite enough of this behavior, Eleanor. Today you will return to your duties." Her voice was strong, but her eyes were wary as she made the pronouncement. She made a concerted and deliberate effort to not notice her husband's body. "We have a lot to do."

Ellie had not spoken since the night of her father's death. It was as if she had been struck mute, the pain of her grief paralyzing her voice and numbing her spirit, turning her heart to a lump of ice. She rose from the chair and shoved her stepmother from the room, slamming and locking the door behind her.

There had been no mention of arrangements for her father's funeral. She was sure she should care, but her father was gone and she had already said goodbye. What difference did it make if there was a funeral? There would only be a hole in the ground, surrounded by well-dressed society people who had not laid eyes on or spoken to Ephraim Banneker in over a year, people weeping who had no right to weep. The hypocrisy of it should have thrown Ellie into a fit of absolute rage, but the numbness made it impossible.

The morning of the fourth day began as the others. When Ellie overheard Olivia and Rebecca talking on the second-floor landing, however, something about the tone of her stepmother's voice penetrated the cocoon she had wrapped around her.

"Here is a list of things I need from the butcher, the grocer, and the pharmacy." Ellie heard the crinkle of a sheet of paper. "Make sure you get *everything* on the list. Oh, and stop at the bakery also. Buy a dozen raspberry tarts, the small ones? And some tea cakes."

"This is an odd sort of list," Rebecca remarked. "Whatever do you need henbane for?"

"Because I do," Olivia snapped, and then softened her tone. "It's out of season now, so you'll have to get dried. It will be more dear, but that can't be helped."

There was the jingle of coins, and a pause before Rebecca spoke. "Not that I'm incapable of running errands, Mother, and I certainly don't mind going, but why aren't you sending Eleanor?"

Olivia's response was sharp and immediate. "That's my business, Rebecca. Just do as you are told, and let your mother take care of everything."

"Yes, Mother, of course."

Ellie rose from her seat and crossed to the door. Olivia had never sent Rebecca out shopping for anything as mean as food, and certainly had never sent her alone. She turned around and noticed Ellie standing at the top of the stairs.

"I see you've finally emerged from your stupor, Eleanor. Good. I have an important task for you." It was not said with any kind of affection or concern. Olivia climbed the stairs, and something churned in the pit of Ellie's stomach at the way she had said the word *task*.

She arrived on the third floor, and her gaze was cold as she looked at Ellie. "Your father's body must be taken care of. Now."

The strange churning divulged itself to be a broth of fear that threatened to make a hasty escape through Ellie's mouth. She swallowed hard, pushing it down, and pressed her hand to her stomach. Her vocal chords finally loosened, shocked from their self-induced paralysis by Olivia's request.

"What?" Her voice was rusty from disuse, and the words barely made it from her mouth.

Olivia faced Ellie, her face a mask of cruelty. "I am glad to see you aren't mute after all, but are you going deaf instead? Your father's body must be cared for until... well, never you mind. Wrap him in the bed sheets, tightly. Use lavender to mind the smell. When you are finished, I have another job for you."

Everything began to shake so violently that Ellie was certain the house was falling down around her ears. It took her a moment to understand that it was she that shook. The blood rushed from her face and hands, and she reached back and clutched the doorframe to keep from falling. Olivia remained impassive, as if she had just asked Ellie to sweep the floor.

"No!" Ellie shouted. "He needs a proper burial." The tears she had been too numb to cry rushed up all at once. "I thought you loved him!"

Olivia's face still betrayed no emotion. "*I* do what I need to in order to survive. *You* will do as you are told, Eleanor."

The only question Ellie wanted the answer to fell from her mouth like sour porridge. "Why?"

"Why?" Olivia leaned in close, her bitter breath adding to Ellie's queasiness. "Because you almost ruined everything, and now I have to fix the mess you've made. And to do that, I need to keep your father's death a secret for just little longer."

It took Ellie a moment to think what Olivia was talking about. Then it came to her.

"What did I almost ruin... Is this because I went to the ball?" She couldn't believe it, but knew it was true as soon as the words left her mouth. There was something dangerous in her low, tempered tone, and Olivia stepped back.

"*I* ruined everything? What I did was go to a ball that I had every right to attend, that my own mother had planned for me to attend since the day I was born." Ellie stepped toward Olivia, her legs finding new strength in the anger that boiled inside her. "If I ruined your plans, what did *you* do to my life?"

"I have given you food and shelter, provided you with clothing and meaningful work." Olivia crossed her arms over her chest and lifted her chin, as if posing for the statue she obviously thought should be erected to her magnanimousness.

"And you *took* everything else." Ellie barked a laugh. "You stripped me of my identity, and kept my father from me. Though I might thank you a little, because at least I'm not an empty-headed snob that only cares about the next party or new gowns and would drive a knife into her best friend's back for a handsome face."

She rolled her eyes up to look at her stepmother, her gaze sharp enough to cut flesh. "What bothers you more, Stepmother? That I went to the ball, or that I danced *all night* with the man I know you were most hoping for Rebecca to marry?"

Olivia didn't seem to have an answer readily available, so Ellie continued, the words rushing out as if a dam had burst inside her, seven years of pressure released with the flood. "He *chose* me. He could have danced all night with any girl in that room, including Rebecca, and yet he chose, of his own free will, to spend his time with me. Did you know that he chased me into the hall?" She took great satisfaction in rubbing it in Olivia's smug face. "He asked if he could call on me, almost begged me in fact."

Her stepmother did not back down, though her face paled. "You lie! What would he ever want with a dirty little housemaid?"

Ellie pulled herself as tall as she could, nearly looking down on Olivia. "I am *not* a housemaid! I am Eleanor Violetta Banneker, daughter of Ephraim and Violetta Banneker." The moment her own name spilled from her mouth, it was like an anvil had been lifted from her chest. It was the first time she had said it aloud in seven years. A shudder went through the house, as if it were sighing in relief.

Olivia shook with rage. "How dare you speak to me in such a way!"

"I should have dared long before now," Ellie yelled back, right in her stepmother's face. "But I couldn't, not as long as the spell bound me. But no longer. I am myself and the whole world can see it. My father is dead, and I will bury him properly. Then I will throw you out of *my* house."

Olivia's eyes narrowed. "And how, exactly, will you do that? Do you have any proof of your father's wishes for his estate?" Her smile was cold and merciless. "I do, but you will never see it."

Ellie almost laughed out loud. Olivia still didn't realize the will was gone from her hiding place. "Are you certain about that? I'd check that secret compartment in your secretary if I were you."

Olivia's smile faltered, slipping from her face.

"So, you've taken it. Fine, then show it to me."

Ellie wished she still had it so she could throw it into her step-mother's face. She couldn't tell her the truth, that she had lost both the will and the contract. The lie sprung forth, fully formed.

"Do you think I'm stupid? That I'm going to hand it to you? It's safe for now, hidden, along with your treacherous contract, and that's where they will stay. Once I announce my father's death, I will take it to the courts and make sure his final wishes are honored."

Olivia pursed her lips, and the wheels of her mind were almost audible. A small smile appeared on her lips, cold and conniving. "I hope something doesn't happen to you before then, my dear. Because if it does, and the will is never found, the law says that everything will come to me. As it should have in the first place."

Ellie fought back the fear that crept up from her belly. She knew the threat was far from idle.

"There's a copy of that will at the bank." She was through letting Olivia intimidate her. "And I am certain that Mr. McIntyre knows it. Even if I'm gone, you will get nothing."

Olivia clucked her tongue. "Oh, that? I destroyed that copy years ago. Do not think me so stupid, girl." She moved her face close to Ellie's. "I've been at this much longer than you. Now do as you are told, and be finished before Rebecca returns. She does not need to see such... unpleasantness."

Ellie desired nothing more at that moment to wrap her hands around Olivia's throat. "No. Call the pastor, to give him proper final rites. Call the funeral director to come and attend to him with the dignity he deserves."

Olivia shrugged. "If you will not do it, then I will have to do it myself." She stepped around Ellie, toward the bedroom, but Ellie jumped in front of her, blocking her path.

"You will not touch him."

Olivia licked her lips and stared at Ellie. "Either you will get out of my way, you impertinent bitch, or I will force you. One way or the other, that body will be shrouded and out of sight until after my plans are completed. Whether you remain breathing until that time is up to you."

Olivia's wicked look left no room for debate. She could push Ellie down the stairs and feel not the slightest bit of remorse when her neck broke. That would tie up her plans nicely, and she wouldn't have to worry so much about when or who Rebecca married. Her body would lie beside her father's. She just needed time to think.

"I'll do it myself." The least she could do was be sure that her father was well and lovingly tended. "Now go and leave us in peace."

Ellie, feeling trapped once more, shut her father's bedroom door behind her.

Ben stood at the bookshop's counter, wrapping brown paper around three new romance novels for a pretty young woman. Her husband stood nearby, trying not to look embarrassed over his wife's choice of reading material. They were the only two customers in the shop, and no wonder: winter had gripped the city in full force, the wind howling as it raced by, on its way to chill the few unsuspecting people on the sidewalk. Ben handed the package to the woman, who took it with a smile and a thank you. The man, visibly relieved his torture had ended, hustled his wife from the shop, both of them bundling themselves tightly against the weather. They did not shut the door firmly, and the wind took the opportunity to grab a hold of it and smash it against the wall, rattling the glass panes and causing the bells above to ring out in alarm.

Muttering curses beneath his breath, Ben crossed the shop for the fifth time that morning to shut the door. With a shiver, he headed back to the counter, but hadn't gone two steps when the bells clanged again, the wind biting into his hands and the back of his neck. He spun around to close the door and nearly collided with a boy entering the shop.

"Sorry," Ben said. "I didn't see you there."

"S'all right." The boy looked a little older than Harry. His brown wool coat hung on him as if he was a coat rack instead of a person, and the pants covering his stick-thin legs had seen better days. He didn't look as if he had money to spend in a bookshop.

"Can I help you?" He gave the boy a stern look that said he had better not even think of stealing anything.

The boy peered from beneath the brim of a battered blue wool cap and his lengthy bangs, looking around Ben as if he were searching for someone. "I don't think so, unless you know a Mr. Benjamin Grimm. I was told he would be here."

Ben knit his brows, surprised and confused. "I'm Benjamin Grimm."

The boy looked Ben up and down, as if deciding whether or not he was telling the truth, and then sucked his teeth. "You sure?"

Ben crossed his arms over his chest. "Of course, I'm sure. What do you want?"

The boy appraised Ben for another second and then gave a short nod. "I have a letter for you." He reached with hands covered by moth-bitten gloves into one of the pockets of the large coat and pulled out a bulky, cream-colored envelope, which he handed to Ben.

"Who sent it?" He hoped it was from Ellie, but recognized the handwriting. Beautiful and flowing, his name in indigo ink. It was from the same mysterious note writer that had told him about Ellie wanting to go to the Assembly Ball.

The boy shrugged. "Don't know a name. Was stopped by a lady and given fifty cents to bring this here and give it to Benjamin Grimm. *Fifty cents*, can you believe it? Easiest money I ever made."

Ben barely paid attention to the exorbitant sum the mystery woman had paid for a courier. He was already pulling up the flap on the envelope, his stomach performing feats of acrobatics. With mumbled thanks, he showed the boy back out into the wind, making sure the door was closed tightly before running into the back room. He hoped — no, he knew — that this letter had to do with Ellie, and after four days with no word, the envelope in his hand was the most precious thing in the world.

Too nervous to sit, Ben paced the room. He turned the envelope upside down. Out fell something that looked like a key. The pin end and shaft were like any other key, but the bow looked like the inside of a watch. It was flat and round, with several gears and springs set inside. A button stuck out from the end. Puzzled, he pulled a single, folded sheet of paper from inside the envelope. Holding it between his fingers, his lips were suddenly dry as dust. The dryness spread to his throat as he opened the page and started to read. Just as with the previous note, there was no signature. The words, written in the same beautiful script as the envelope, at first made no sense to Ben, but when he read them a second time, fear and anger rose up within him.

"Benjamin Grimm!" Ben's mother burst into the back, her son's name a vehement hiss. "What is going on?"

But it was too late, Ben ignored her, already out the door.

CHAPTER XXIII

ELLIE BANGED HER FIST AGAINST THE CELLAR DOOR, CALLING WITH ALL of her strength for someone to let her out. She had almost finished the nearly unbearable task of caring for her father's body, gently wrapping his frail body in a shroud of clean sheets, when she realized she had forgotten to get the lavender. There were some of the dried flowers in the basement, to be used as a pomander for the drawers.

It had taken all of her will to enter the damp cellar. Her insides quivered as she forced herself to descend to the bottom of the steps.

She grabbed the lavender as quick as she could and turned to leave. Her breath caught in her throat when she looked to the top of the staircase.

The door was closed.

Ellie ran up the stairs, her heart clanging like a fire alarm against her ribs. In her panic, she dropped the lantern she had used to light her way down. It shattered and went out, plunging her into darkness. She hoped it was just a mistake — that Rebecca had come home, seen the door open, and closed it. But when she turned the knob, her blood turned to ice. It was locked. She tried not to panic, but fear quickly overwhelmed her, and she began beating on the door in earnest. No one responded, so she knocked harder and called louder.

"Will you stop your noise!" Olivia's voice boomed.

Ellie paused with her hand in the air, ready for another assault on the door. She tried to remain calm, but it was impossible. "Stepmother? The door is locked."

"I know. I locked it." Olivia's tone was so matter-of-fact she might have been explaining why the weather was cold in winter.

Ellie took an instinctive step back. In her grief and concern for her father, she had let her guard down. *How stupid can I be!* Not willing to give Olivia the satisfaction of hearing her panic and anger, she forced her voice to remain steady.

"Why did you lock me in the cellar?"

"Because I need to keep you out of the way. I have invited a special guest this afternoon, and I cannot have you gumming things up."

The edge of Ellie's panic turned into curiosity. Who could Olivia have invited today? She pressed her hand flat against the door, willing her heart to stop pounding. "I promise I won't tell anyone what you've done. Who would believe it? I... I'll stay in the attic. Just let me out, please."

"I don't believe you, but that's not even the point. With the spell broken, you are of no use to me as a servant, not when you look so much like your mother. I can no longer use the ruse you are my niece. And if I let you out, how can I be sure you won't run away?"

"I won't, I promise."

There was a pause, as if Olivia considered the proposition. "No. You're already out of the way, and you're going to stay right where you are. Mr. Scott is coming for tea, *specially* brewed just for him, and I can't have you spoiling it, can I? Not when I want him to focus on my darling Rebecca."

Ellie was shocked into silence. The rest of Olivia's words sunk in and her heart turned to stone, plunging to her stomach.

"You wouldn't *dare!*" The words nearly choked her. "Leave him alone!"

"Why should I? I have the recipe for the Love Potion, and it's already cost me... I might as well get my money's worth. Hamilton Scott is a perfect match for Rebecca, and it's not as if he is *otherwise* engaged." There was venom in Olivia's words. Her poison arrow was true — the thought of Hamilton falling in love with another girl, whether by use of a potion or not, was like a stab to the heart. Ellie slumped against the door, weeping.

"But Rebecca doesn't love him! Shouldn't she be able to choose for herself?"

"Perhaps she does not love him now," Olivia drawled. "But many women marry for duty instead of love. And most of them end up quite content. Rebecca will learn to love him, especially once he suddenly becomes completely and utterly devoted to her, just as your father was utterly devoted to me." The low chuckle that came through the door made Ellie's breath freeze in her lungs. "But, just to be sure, I might have to help her along as well."

"No!" Ellie began her pounding anew, using all of her strength. She beat her hands against the wood, throwing her body against it a few times for good measure, but it was no use. The door did not budge. She finally stopped, her hands bruised, her shoulder feeling like a slab of beef. Olivia would not open the door, and Ellie could not break it down, so she would wait. When Hamilton arrived, she would start again.

"I won't let you do this. I'll just keep pounding. Hamilton will hear. So, you might as well let me out."

Ellie could practically hear Olivia's smirk. "Be my guest, beat the door until your hands fall off. *No one* will hear you once the kitchen door is closed, and Mr. Scott safely ensconced in the parlor." There was a pause, and the sound of Olivia's footsteps. When she spoke again, it was muffled.

"Ah, there you are, my dear Rebecca. I'll take the packages, thank you. Why don't you go upstairs and rest. We're having a guest later, and I want you to look your best. That's my precious dove."

Ellie began to scream anew, calling to Rebecca to help her.

"Mother, what is that noise?"

Ellie's hope kindled, a tiny spark that only needed a little air to turn into a flame. She continued to shout, straining her voice.

"What noise, my pet?"

"It sounds like someone is calling, from the kitchen."

"Oh, that's probably just that infernal cat, crying to be let in."

A pause. "Where's Eleanor?"

"I sent her on an errand. Now you run along and rest."

The kitchen door creaked open again, and only one set of footsteps tapped across the floor. Then the sound of pots and pans clanging against one another, and movement around the kitchen. Olivia started to hum as she brewed the tea that would ensnare Hamilton Scott. There was no sense in yelling or pounding now. If the woman was willing to give her own daughter a love potion, she was beyond reason.

And once Olivia's plan had succeeded, what was she going to do with *her*? Ellie, feeling as if a house had been dropped on her, leaned against the door as a wave of hopelessness washed over her.

Ben lifted the brass door knocker and banged it against the Bannekers' front door again, taking his agitation out on the poor wood. Ellie was in trouble, if the note was to be believed. If he had to break down the door and physically remove her from the house, then that's what he would do. He lifted his fist, ready to bang upon the door again, when it flew open. Olivia Banneker stood there, her face a wall of stone.

"What do you want? I don't give to vagabonds and I have no handyman work."

Even though Ben hadn't expected a warm welcome, he still bristled at the tone of her voice, as if he were something distasteful.

"I am here to see Miss Eleanor Banneker, please." He should have given his name as well, but didn't want to run the risk of Olivia slamming the door in his face. Obviously, she still didn't recognize him, or that probably would have happened already.

Olivia narrowed her hawk's gaze. "There is no one by that name here." She started to shut the door, but Ben stopped her with one hand. "This is the house of Ephraim Banneker, is it not? He has a daughter named Eleanor, and I'm sure that she lives here."

"Listen to me very carefully." Olivia, seething beneath her cultured exterior, leaned down close to Ben's face. "There is no Eleanor Banneker here. And you would do well to forget that name, young man." She straightened up and stepped inside. "Do not darken my threshold again, or I will call the police." And with that, she slammed the door in his face.

That was all it took for Ben to know that Ellie really was in trouble. If Olivia had realized who he was and all he knew, she never would have threatened him with the police. It would be no use to try knocking again.

"So much for the direct approach," Ben muttered. "Now I'll just have to do it the fun way." He rubbed his hands together and hopped down the steps, nearly colliding with a gentleman on the sidewalk. He was as tall as Ben, around the same age, and wore a greatcoat and derby over his blonde hair.

"Excuse me," Ben said, genuinely sorry.

"No harm done." The gentleman looked at Ellie's house and then at Ben. "Did you have business with Mrs. Banneker?" He didn't exactly frown, but his expression made it clear exactly how the gentleman saw the boy before him — brown wool trousers, patched and moth-gnawed peacoat, old hat. A nobody. The gentleman looked familiar, but Ben couldn't quite place him. *Looks like every other dandy, maybe that's why I think I know him.* He probably had seen him at the theater.

"I, uh, no, sir, just looking for work." No sense in telling the truth, and even less sense in trying to disabuse the man of his notions. He went on his way before the conversation could continue any further. Once he rounded the corner he broke into a run, darting down the alley behind the houses. He stopped just outside Ellie's gate. Quietly he opened it, and crept across the silent courtyard and up the back steps. The kitchen door window showed an empty room. He shifted his head so that he could see the doors on the far left—the pantry, the basement, and the one that led to the rest of the house.

Ben grabbed the doorknob and turned it slowly. With his other hand pressed against the door itself, he pushed gently. The door did not budge. He tried the knob again, more forcefully this time, and that's when he figured out that it was locked. *Of course*. He thought about finding a rock to break the glass, and hope the key was in the lock on the other side, but that would cause too much noise.

Ben leaned his head back to look up at the house. There were no windows open on this bitter day in the middle of winter. He rubbed his head in frustration. He had to find a way inside. He could shimmy up the drainpipe and break an upper window. No one would hear him if he broke one on the third floor or the attic. Probably.

Having no better idea, Ben grasped the copper drainpipe, turned green from years in the weather. He bent his knees, ready to hoist himself up when the soft clink of metal on stone stopped him. When he glanced over his shoulder to see what had caused it, there was the strange key that had come inside the note, sitting on the top step. It must have fallen from his pocket. In his worry about Ellie, he had forgotten all about it. He plucked it from the stone—it was cold in his bare hand. What were the odds that it would fit the lock? Another sound, this one small and gentle, made him look up. Above the door, hiding in the eaves, was a small, gray dove. She caught Ben's eye, and there was something in the bird's gaze that struck Ben as familiar.

Under the dove's watchful gaze, Ben put the key into the keyhole below the knob of the kitchen door and turned it. It stuck fast. He pulled it out and looked at the key. The button on the end seemed significant. With two fingers, he pulled the button out, like the stem of a watch. He turned it, and watched the gears and springs turn and tighten. When he let it go, he watched in amazement as the mechanism went to work. There was a ticking, like a clock, but instead of hands, the gears moved the pin at the other end of the key back and forth. Something connected the gears to the pin—the cylinder must be hollow. He wondered what the purpose of this was and then, as the strange key slowed down and then stopped, he understood.

He pushed the pin end into lock on the kitchen door, and wound the mechanism again. He heard the pin scrape as it went back and forth, then felt it catch as it fit itself to the lock. With a whispered prayer and a bit of disbelief, he turned the key. There was an amazing and satisfying clunk as the tumblers turned and the deadbolt retracted. The knob moved freely and Ben pushed the door open.

He crept inside.

Ellie sat on the top step in the dark cellar, weeping. Her hands ached from beating on the door, her heart ached from grief. There had been no sign of life from the kitchen since Olivia had left. If Hamilton had arrived, they were already in the parlor, well out of hearing. It was over, then. Olivia had, after everything Ellie had done and sacrificed, won. She was at this moment taking the very last bit of Ellie's soul and crushing it beneath her expensive heel.

"Hello?"

The voice was so soft Ellie thought she had imagined it. She pressed her ear against the door, feeling ridiculous for answering her own hallucination. "Is... Is there someone out there?"

"Ellie, it's me."

"Ben?" Now Ellie was certain her mind deceived her, giving her false hope. After all, how could he *possibly* be here? How would he even know to come? Her mind finished the daydream, allowing her to picture the broad-shouldered boy standing in her kitchen.

"Don't worry, I'm going to let you out." The knob rattled, but the door did not open.

"The key to the door is usually on a nail beside the door." Ellie called out, her voice muffled by the door.

Ben glanced up at the vacant nail. "It's not there."

"Olivia must have taken it with her. You'll have to find another way."

"Just give me a second, I'll have you out."

"There's no time, Ben. Please, you have to warn Ham... Mr. Scott. He mustn't drink the tea."

"What?" Ben answered. She wasn't making any sense. Who in the world was Mr. Scott and what was wrong with the tea? He didn't much care. His only concern was Ellie. "I won't leave you."

"Please, Ben, you have to—"

"Hold on, please?" Ben slipped the mechanical key into the lock on the cellar door and wound it again. Just like it did before, the key's pin adjusted itself to the lock. When it caught, he turned the key and again heard the deadbolt slip back into the door.

"Ellie, try the door now."

The knob spun and the door opened, just a hair, and then it flew open, nearly knocking Ben on his backside. She stepped into the kitchen, accompanied by the aroma of lavender

"How did you do that?" Ellie asked.

Ben held up the mechanical key.

Ellie looked confused but didn't ask for further explanation. "Thank you. I just hope I'm in time." She headed straight for the door that led to the rest of the house.

Ben caught her by the wrist. "Where are you going?"

"I have to stop Olivia. Ben, she's about to do something terrible."

"She's done enough already. What we need to do is to go." Ben took her hand. It was battered, black and blue as if someone had beat it with a hammer. He held it gingerly. "I know about your father, Ellie. Come with me, right now, and you'll never have to see Olivia or this house ever again." He didn't think it was the right time to profess his love— he would get to that once they were away from this madhouse.

Ellie hesitated, but only for a second, before she pulled her hand away. "Ben, I have to go." She turned around and walked through the door, leaving Ben standing in the kitchen, stunned.

Ellie burst into the parlor, pushing back the pocket doors with such force they rebounded in their frames. She took in the scene in front of her. Olivia's best tea set was on the low table. The woman herself sat in her overstuffed wingback chair, a sycophantic smile on her lips. Rebecca was positioned on the settee, sitting as if someone had stuffed an iron- ing board down the back of her dress. Beside her sat Hamilton Scott, a full tea cup raised halfway to his lips. Just like the first time Ellie had seen him, she felt as if all the air had been sucked from the room. All three heads turned toward the door, three sets of eyes locking on Ellie.

She could only imagine what she looked like in her maid's clothing, covered in dust from the cellar, her hands looking like pounded veal cutlets. Anger bloomed in her chest.

Time started again, and Olivia's expression shifted to one of abject horror. Ellie stormed into the room, headed straight for Hamilton. "Stop!"

CHAPTER XXIV

HAMILTON STARTED, SLOSHING HOT, AMBER LIQUID OVER THE SIDE of the delicate china cup and across the sleeve of his tailored jacket. "Excuse me?"

"Mr. Scott, you must not drink that tea," Ellie said, more softly this time.

Olivia's voice walked the line between of painfully polite and murderous. Her gaze flickered to Hamilton and back to Ellie. "Dear? What is the meaning of this?"

"You know very well the meaning of it." Ellie was no longer playing Olivia's game. "That drink is laced, Mr. Scott."

Hamilton looked at his cup, then at Ellie. "What nonsense is this? Laced with what? Mrs. Banneker, what is going on here and who is this woman?"

Ellie had almost forgotten that Hamilton would not recognize her now that the spell had been broken. She would have to convince him that everything she said was true, and it would have to come to him from someone he believed to be a total stranger. "Mr. Scott, please forgive me, but I am —"

Olivia rose from her seat, and Ellie could practically feel the heat of anger radiating from her. "She is my stepdaughter, Eleanor."

Ellie stared, amazed. Her amazement turned to disbelief at Olivia's next words.

"I know that I've said to everyone for years that she's been at boarding school in Europe. But I'm afraid the truth is that she's mentally unstable. I just haven't the heart to send her to the asylum, and so I keep her here, under lock and key."

"I am *not* a lunatic!" Ellie shout came out strangled, dangerously close to denouncing her own denial. "I *am* Eleanor Banneker. Mr. Scott. But you, I'm afraid, have been brought here for nefarious purposes. That tea is laced with..." She stopped, pressing her lips together. Hamilton *would* think she was a lunatic if she said the word *potion*. "A drug."

"This is outrageous," Olivia seethed. "Why would I try to drug Mr. Scott?" Her gaze flicked to Hamilton and then back to Ellie with a sympathetic smile. "I'm so sorry for this, Mr. Scott. Now, my dear, go back to your room like a good girl." She grasped Ellie's elbow, squeezing so tightly that pain shot up her arm, and dragged her toward the foyer.

"Wait just one moment." Hamilton set the teacup down on the table, pushing it as far from himself as he could, and stood. "This young lady has made some serious accusations, and she seems perfectly lucid to me." He approached Ellie. "What proof do you have of this, and why would Mrs. Banneker try to do me harm?"

Ellie tucked her bottom lip between her teeth and swallowed. What had made him stop Olivia, made him willing to listen to a girl he had just been told was not in her right mind? She didn't care, but she wasn't about to waste the opportunity.

"The only proof I have is her own words. She locked me in the basement to keep me from telling you. The drug in that tea wouldn't harm you… exactly… only make you more amenable. She's trying to get you to marry her daughter, because my father left her nothing in his will and she's afraid of being thrown onto the street."

"Mother, what did you do?" Rebecca spoke for the first time.

"Nothing, my sweet. Nothing. You know how your stepsister can get." She gave Rebecca a pointed look that said she had best not speak again. "You see how ill she is. The ravings of a diseased mind. First, she accuses me of trying to drug you, now this ranting about my husband's will. As if my husband was in danger of dying anytime soon, or that a man would do such a thing to his own wife. The poor dear doesn't know what she's saying." She dug her fingers a little deeper into Ellie's arm.

"I know that none of this makes any sense to you, but please believe me. I can prove to you that everything I've said is true. We've met before. My stepmother introduced me to you at the Exposition as Ann Gibson, her poor niece. But I am and always have been Eleanor Banneker."

Olivia's grip increased and Ellie was afraid that her bones would crack. "You see? Now she thinks she's my niece."

Hamilton turned a look on Ellie that made her blood run cold. "I remember Miss Gibson *very* clearly. You are not her, so what game is this?"

Tears pricked at Ellie's eyes. It had been a mistake to reveal who she was. She shouldn't have expected Hamilton to believe her, especially not when he was so clearly taken with "Ann."

"If I'm not the same girl, then ask her to call her niece into the room, right now."

Hamilton turned to Olivia, hope and fear in his eyes, eagerness playing at the edge of his voice. "Mrs. Banneker, I don't think that's too much to ask."

Olivia's face blanched, and Ellie saw a glimmer of victory. But her stepmother was not about to be defeated that easily.

"My niece is not here, I'm afraid. She's taken employment with a family in New Jersey, as their governess. She left the day after the Assembly Ball."

Hamilton looked crestfallen. Ellie felt terrible for him, but couldn't deny how happy his disappointment made her. He felt something for the girl at the ball—for her.

Ellie, her anger renewed, pulled her arm from Olivia's grip. "Oh, stop it, Stepmother. The game is ended." She turned to Hamilton. "We were introduced in the Horticulture Hall at the Exposition, and you talked about your father's expansion in the railroad. Then we met again, when I ran into you on Chestnut Street, just outside Grimm's bookshop, though you did not recognize me." She paused, not sure if she should say anything more about the rest of their short relationship. But if she was going to make him believe her, she needed to reveal everything.

"We met one other time—at the Assembly Ball. We danced, and you asked if you could call on me, but I refused. I told you I was going to London. You followed me to the staircase and I showed you my face. I was there under the name—"

"Eliza Reed." Hamilton's expression shifted from suspicion to surprise, and his words were almost a whisper. "How do you know that?"

"Because I *am* that girl. We talked about the Corliss steam engine during our first waltz."

Olivia snorted a laugh. "Fine topic of conversation for a young lady."

Hamilton brushed off Olivia's remarks. "You look nothing like the girl I met at the ball. Except..." He paused. "Your eyes." His face changed as he realized she was telling the truth. "But how...?"

"It's difficult to explain." She was not about to tell Hamilton that she had been bewitched, or else they would be right back to Olivia's claim that she was soft in the head. "And not important at the moment. Just understand that because of events that have nothing to do with you, my stepmother would practically poison you to make a match for Rebecca and secure her own future."

Olivia straightened her bodice. "This is all ridiculous. Nothing but fairy tales." She grabbed Ellie's arm again.

"Get your hands off of her, you bitch."

Ben stood in the foyer just outside the parlor doors, his hands balled into fists. He had been there for a few minutes, listening until he couldn't stand it any longer.

Olivia's face went white. "You're the vagabond I sent away. How did you get in here?"

Ben shrugged. She still didn't recognize him, and he wasn't about to illuminate her. "Doesn't matter. But imagine my surprise when I found the mistress of the house locked in the cellar?"

"*I* am the mistress of this house."

"No, you're not." Ben reached into his coat and pulled out a sheaf of folded papers, tied together with a leather thong. He held them up for Olivia to see. "Not anymore."

Olivia released Ellie and grabbed for the papers, but Ben pulled them out of reach.

"Give them to me!"

"Absolutely not." Ben gave Olivia a shove. She stumbled backward, crying out in surprise as she sprawled on the carpet.

"Hold on there!" The gentleman, whom Ben surmised was the Mr. Scott Ellie was so concerned about, approached him, a look of righteous indignation on his face. He was the same man Ben had collided with outside the Bannekers' front door. "You cannot come into someone's house and treat a lady like that. I'll personally throw you out on your ear."

Ben barked a laugh. "First of all, *she* —" he pointed at Olivia " — is no lady. Secondly, I'd like to see you try to throw me out." Ben had three inches and at least twenty pounds on Mr. Scott, but to his credit the man did not back down.

"Stop it, both of you." Ellie stepped between them and elbowed them apart. She turned to Ben.

"Where did you find those?" She nodded at the papers in Ben's hand.

Ben did not hide how proud he was of himself. "The day you brought them to the shop, you must have dropped them on the sidewalk. About five minutes after you left, a man brought them in to see if they belonged to anyone inside. So, I kept them."

To Ben's shock, Ellie's green eyes flashed in anger. "And you didn't *tell* me you had them? I was going out of my mind, thinking I'd lost them!"

His collar suddenly felt very tight. "Uh, well, I was going to return them right away. Then I thought I'd better keep them, because I knew they might not be safe here, and I wanted you to be able to have them when you needed them. And then, uh… to be honest, I forgot about them for a while."

"You forgot?" Ellie growled. "How could you forget?"

Ben withered under her razor-sharp gaze. "Well… we were so busy, you know, with our —" he glanced at Mr. Scott " — project, that I didn't think about them again until the night your father died. Then I knew you would need them, because that old crow would never just hand over everything, not if she saw the chance to keep it all for herself." He glared at Olivia, still on the floor.

"*I* brought them into the bookshop." Mr. Scott's mouth hung open in surprise, not a good look for a refined gentleman. "I thought they might have belonged to the young lady who ran into me on the sidewalk." He bobbed his head at Ellie, still confused. "When I turned around you were nowhere to be found. I saw you come out of the bookshop, so that's where I took them." He looked at Ben again, his eyebrows lifting. "You. Yes, I gave them to you."

"Brilliant deduction, Scott. Mind like a steel trap." Ben turned to Ellie. "I'm sorry your father is gone. But with these, at least you can be taken care of, and have everything he wanted for you." He handed the papers to Ellie, almost hoping she wouldn't take them, and instead she would take his hand and walk right out the door.

Ellie wrapped her fingers around the bundle and pressed it to her heart. "Thank you, Ben."

Hamilton, always on top of things, stepped back, and Ben could hear the rusty gears of his brain, working it all out. "But I thought Ephraim was in France. I've heard he's been on sabbatical for his health."

"My father has been ill for over a year, but has never left this house. He finally succumbed to his illness a few days ago. My stepmother was keeping it secret for the same reason she tried to drug you — to serve her own ends."

She breathed a sigh of relief. All the secrets were out in the open.

Olivia's expression turned dark, and something like a growl erupted from her throat. "No."

Ellie flew backward, hitting the parlor wall with a hard thump that pushed the air from her lungs. There was a weight on her chest and a sudden, searing pain in her left shoulder. Olivia had pinned her against the wall, a murderous gleam in her eye.

"You harlot! After all my hard work, all my sacrifice. You, with your pretty face and your name, just walk in and ruin it all."

Ellie's left arm felt like a wet dishrag. She tried to use her bruised right hand, but Olivia's arm pressed across her chest, pinning her arm. Her stepmother clenched a letter opener in her free hand, the same one Ellie had used to pry open the secret compartment in the secretary. The pointed end, like a miniature sword, dripped red, and Ellie's stomach heaved when she realized it was her own blood.

Ben and Hamilton appeared behind her, wearing matching looks of terror. Olivia held the blade to Ellie's throat, the point almost touching the soft flesh beneath her jaw. Ellie's heart beat faster, her rapid pulse making her jugular a better target.

"Let her go, Olivia. Or so help me, I will make you sorry you ever set foot in this house." Ben's tone even frightened Ellie.

Hamilton tried a subtler approach. "Mrs. Banneker, please. I know you don't want to hurt anyone." Ben gave a derisive snort.

Ellie looked into Olivia's eyes, but they were as empty as a doll's. Olivia licked her lips and pressed her harder against the wall. "You don't understand. I'll be an outcast, I'll have nothing. This is only fair, after everything I've suffered."

"I'm sure that's not true. You're an honorable woman, Olivia. You don't want to do this." Hamilton continued trying to coddle her into submission. "Please, just let her go."

Olivia shook her head. "I'm sorry. I can't. I have to."

Ellie fought the tears and fright she would not let Olivia see. She could barely breathe for fear of accidentally pushing the letter opener into her own throat. "Olivia, it's not fair, I know. None of this is fair. I'm sorry."

"Be quiet!" Olivia's scream was manic. "All of this is your own fault. If it had been you to get sick instead of Ephraim… If he had only just changed the will. I loved him once, did you know that? I truly loved him. But he never looked at me the way he looked at Violetta. And so… I *made* him see me."

"But it wasn't real," Ellie said softly, hoping not to enrage her stepmother further. "If you loved him, you should have let him go."

"No!" Olivia pressed the arm across Ellie's chest further against her. "I couldn't. He was our chance, mine and Rebecca's." She pulled in a shuddering breath. "And then, he cared more about you than us, his new family, so I had to make you disappear too. If he had only just done as I asked… once you're gone, I'll burn that will, and I'll stay here, secure. Little consolation, but it will be something. Rebecca can get married and we will be happy forever."

Olivia pulled the blade back, just slightly, but it was the chance Ellie needed. She drove her knee upward, pushing her stepmother back. The blow knocked Olivia off balance, freeing Ellie's arms. She grabbed her stepmother's wrist.

"After all you've taken, I will be damned if I'm going to let you take my life."

She twisted Olivia's wrist, forcing the weapon from her grip. Hands grabbed Olivia by the shoulders and pulled her away. It was Rebecca, her face white and her lips trembling.

"What are you doing? Let me go! She has to pay, Rebecca. Let me go!"

Ellie brought herself toe-to-toe with Olivia. "I am no longer the little girl you can threaten and treat like garbage."

Olivia pulled free of Rebecca, but this time Ellie was ready. With her good arm she shoved her stepmother and she fell into her chair. She started to rise, but Rebecca pushed her mother back down.

"I'd stay put if I were you," Ben said.

Ellie's head spun. She touched her shoulder and found the wound. It wasn't large but it was deep. Blood soaked her blouse. Ben ran from the room, and in seconds he returned with a cloth from the kitchen, which he pressed against her injury.

"We'll have to get a doctor to look at that."

Ellie pushed Ben's hand and the cloth away, her anger burning brighter and hotter than her shoulder. She pinned Olivia with her gaze, and the woman squirmed in the chair.

"I had wondered if you were capable of killing me to reach your own ends. I didn't think you had the stomach." She leaned down and into Olivia's face and tried not to show the pain it caused her. "But I guess I shouldn't be surprised, after what you did to my mother and father."

"I *loved* your father," Olivia whispered the words this time. "Even when I found out about the will, I still loved him. His illness was not my doing. It was that creature. I had no idea what she planned to do to your mother, either. I didn't want her to die, only to go away. When that... being... accosted me on the street I had no idea what she was. She said she could help me, and I believed her. It wasn't my fault."

"You forced your love on him, took his free will like you took my name. His death might not have been by your hand, but it *was* your fault." Spots danced in front of Ellie's eyes. "You might have loved him, but you were blinded by your own selfish desires."

Olivia's cheeks flushed, and she swallowed but did not speak. Rebecca put a hand on her mother's back and looked up at Ellie.

"I'm so sorry, Ellie. I should have done more to stop this. I... tried. When I found the papers in her desk, I knew what she had done, but not how far she had gone."

"It's not your fault, Rebecca." Ellie didn't know what else to say. Olivia grabbed her daughter's hand. She looked just as she had on the night Ellie's father died, small and fragile.

"I did this all for you, my love." She stroked Rebecca's hand gently.

Rebecca pulled it away. "You did it for yourself, Mother. I know you think you had to protect us, but it's not Ellie's fault that Daddy left us poor."

Rebecca bit her lip, arranging her thoughts. "When my father died, he left us with nothing. He gambled and drank it all away. We were destitute when Violetta took us in. When she died and your father fell in love with my mother — and I swear to you that I had *no idea* how my mother was involved in that until quite recently — I thought we'd be a family and my mother would stop being so bitter."

She glanced at Olivia. "But when she found your father's will, all those years ago, it was like my father's betrayal all over again. She blamed you, because she couldn't bear the idea that Ephraim still loved you more than her. She spent years trying to get him to change his will. But every time, something stopped him. Then he got sick last year, and she grew desperate. I never thought she'd take things so far."

Her cheeks flushed with embarrassment. "Mr. Scott, I am so sorry about that. I had no idea my mother put something in your tea."

Hamilton cleared his throat and straightened, trying to act as if he knew what was going on. "Apology accepted, Miss Gibson."

Ellie, despite the fact the woman had just tried to murder her, felt a little bit sorry for Olivia. "I wish things had been different. I wish..."

She shook her head. The past was over. She needed to think about the future. "I'm sorry you have so much hate in your heart. If you had treated me like a daughter, it wouldn't have mattered who my father left his money to, because we would have been family, and I never turn my back on family." She stood straight, ignoring the pain. "But you chose your path, and now you will have to pay for it."

Olivia sunk back into the chair, eyes widening. "What are you going to do with me?"

"I know what I'd like to do," Ben chimed in.

Ellie could imagine what inventive ideas ran through Ben's mind, and she knew she had every right to seek retribution for all the heartache Olivia had caused. Part of her relished the idea of turning Olivia over to the authorities. To feed her to the wolves of the society she was so desperate to impress.

"I can't prove she had anything to do with either my mother or father's death, even though we know the truth. The police would never believe it. They will, however, believe that you tried to kill me today. There are three witnesses." Ellie was focused and in control, and for the first time since her father's death had true clarity of thought. "You are too dangerous to leave free, Olivia. You might not have to pay for all your crimes, but you will pay for this one."

Olivia bowed her head. Rebecca held her mother's hand. "I understand, Ellie."

"Rebecca, you are more than welcome to stay. I wish you would. You're the only family I have left." Ellie watched the mother and daughter, one devoted to the other in different but no less fierce ways. "But if you choose to go, I understand."

Rebecca seemed surprised at the offer. "I love my mother very much, despite what she's done. But she does need to be punished, and I'll have nowhere else to go. Thank you."

The hurt in Olivia's eyes was obvious. "I only ever wanted the best for you, Rebecca. For you to be a lady, and never want for anything."

"But you never asked me if it was what *I* wanted, Mother." Rebecca knelt beside her mother. "I am not upper class by birth. I am not tethered to their rules. All I've ever wanted was to be free, to see the world and to make my own choices, for good or bad."

Olivia did not seem to understand a word. "You deserve to be treated like a princess, my love. Always."

Rebecca helped her mother to her feet. "Come, Mother. You are going to stay locked in your room until the police come for you." She walked behind her mother as the woman left the parlor, but paused for a moment, her gaze focused on Ben.

"I knew I could count on you, Benjamin Grimm. May I have my key back, please?"

Ben's mouth fell open, and he spluttered some incoherent syllables, but nothing that sounded remotely like the English language. He reached into his pocket and pulled out the strange key that he had used to free Ellie from the cellar. With an enigmatic smile, Rebecca took it and followed her mother up the stairs.

"What was that all about?" Ellie demanded.

"I have a vague idea." Ben shook his head, still wearing a confused expression. "But, it can't be right. She couldn't have..."

Ellie, her anger diffused, flopped into the chair recently vacated by her stepmother. The pain in her shoulder began to scream, radiating from her shoulder to her fingers.

Ben moved immediately to her side. "Are you finished playing the brave one now? That shoulder needs attention." He came at her with the cloth again.

She stopped him with a hand. "Are you done playing nursemaid? I'm fine for the moment. I just need to rest. I'll see the doctor soon enough." He was a good friend, being so attentive, but at the moment he was driving her mad.

Ben handed her the cloth and she pressed it over her wound. The bleeding had slowed a little. "Well, I see your stubbornness is still intact." He scooped up the bundle of documents, dropped and forgotten when Olivia attacked, and placed them in her lap. There was a look in his eye, the same look he had worn on the night of the ball. *Oh, Ben.*

"It's all yours now. Your name, your house. Yours to do with whatever you please."

Ellie rubbed the leather thong between her fingers. It seemed such a hollow victory. All the scheming and planning, nearly being run over by a train, committing grave robbery, all for a piece of paper that said she owned a pile of things. She wanted her father and mother back, but all the money in the world could never give them to her.

Hamilton cleared his throat, pulling her attention from her thoughts. "I'm sorry, Miss Banneker. I still don't understand much of what's happened, but I'm sorry."

Ellie sighed. "It's a very long and complicated story, and none of it truly matters now." He deserved an explanation, but he wasn't going to get it today. She just didn't have the strength. "I'm so sorry you had to be pulled into all of this intrigue. My stepmother had designs on you for a son-in-law, and she wasn't playing fair about it."

Hamilton's brow wrinkled, but he didn't look any less confused. "Yes, I believe I understand that part." He sat on the sofa, his expression unreadable. "Are you truly the woman I danced with at the ball?"

Ellie laughed. After everything he witnessed over the last half-hour, *that* was the most pressing thing on his mind? "Yes, I am. And I'm very sorry for all of my deception, Mr. Scott. I had no choice. If you walked out of this house right now and never returned, I would not blame you."

Hamilton regarded Ellie for one excruciating moment before he turned and walked out of the room. She closed her eyes and braced herself for the sound of the slamming door.

"I believe this belongs to you."

Ellie opened her eyes. Hamilton stood before her, his blond eyebrows pulled together, his posture suggesting uncertainty and hope. He held something in his hands, glittering and gold, the crystal centers of the embroidered flowers catching the light and casting rainbows into Ellie's eyes. Her missing slipper.

"Where did you get that?"

CHAPTER XXV

A FEELING OF DREAD DROPPED OVER BEN AS ELLIE TOOK THE SLIPPER. The look on Hamilton Scott's face was enough to make him want to shove the proper gentleman right out the door.

"You dropped it on the Academy stairs on the night of the ball. I've been carrying it ever since," Hamilton's tone was much too intimate for Ben's liking. "I have been thinking about you every day since. No, that's not the truth. I've been thinking about you for months, since the day we met at the Exposition."

Ugh, could he be any more ridiculous! If Ben's facial muscles tightened any more his jaw would crack. This was getting out of hand; he needed to speak with Ellie alone.

"How could you have known?" Ellie replied, and her tone made Ben's insides turn to lead. He couldn't stand it any longer.

"Mr. Scott, I think your business here is concluded. May I show you out?"

Hamilton's head swiveled around, and when he met Ben's gaze, he wore a completely different expression than he had for Ellie. Cold and sharp.

"Pardon me, but who are you?"

A muscle in the corner of Ben's eye twitched. "Benjamin Grimm's my name."

Hamilton crossed his arms over his chest and cocked his head. "And are you a relative of Miss Banneker's?"

Ben took a step closer to the gentleman and shook his head slowly, just once. "No."

"Are you her guardian?" Hamilton raised an eyebrow.

"No, not as such," Ben growled. "Though I have been watching out for her for a while now."

"Then, please tell me what gives you the right to speak for Miss Banneker? Or, for that matter, the right to speak to her in such a familiar manner?"

"She is my… friend, Mr. Scott. And I think she has been through enough. She could do with some peace and quiet." Ben's tone was tempered with annoyance. "That shoulder needs tending."

Hamilton stepped toward Ben so that the two men stood nearly nose-to-nose. "I will go, Mr. Grimm, when and if Miss Banneker asks it of me, and not one moment before."

Both men turned and faced Ellie

The pit of Ellie's stomach soured like curdled milk as the two men turned toward her. Ben and Hamilton looked at her with anticipation and expectation in their eyes, each wanting her to decide the dispute in his favor. But the real issue wasn't whether or not Hamilton should stay or if Ben was speaking out of place. What they really wanted was for her to *choose*.

Unable to meet the eyes of either man, she looked at her lap, at her father's will, and that was when it hit her. She was *free*, not just from Olivia, but free to make her own life. Olivia could no longer squelch her desires, and her father was gone. She had no other relatives. Ellie was an orphan.

Not an orphan — an heiress. One unknown to polite society, and not yet bound by its rules. For the first time in her entire life, she was able to make her own choices, and the first one that presented itself was nearly impossible. She could no sooner decide between them than she could choose to breathe. Why couldn't she keep them both? She reached into the pocket of her apron with her uninjured hand and felt the two items there. They had been there since the night of her father's death, pulling her heart in two different directions. She rubbed the handkerchief between her thumb and forefinger, her other fingers finding the rough edges of the brass gear. She looked between the boys — the *men* — that stood before her. One would race across the city to save her, the other would scoop up a slipper dropped at a ball in hopes of seeing the girl who wore it again. She loved them both, but realized at that moment she loved them differently.

Standing here all day, staring at each other, would not solve the problem. "Mr. Scott? Would you please excuse us?"

Ben's face brightened, though he tried not to look too pleased.

Ellie continued. "If you'd like, you may wait in the dining room."

Hamilton, trying hard to hide his crooked grin, bowed to Ellie. "Of course." He looked directly at Ben. "I'll be right across the hall if you should have need of me."

"Please shut the door on your way out?" Ellie asked.

When he had gone, she turned to Ben, her stomach and heart dancing like chorus girls.

"Ben, please sit down."

Ben was not sure what to make of the flat tone with which Ellie asked him to sit in the gaudy chair beside hers. The look on her face was not exactly happy, the way he imagined a woman should look when she was about to tell a man she loved him. She almost looked like she was going to be sick. Was that normal, or was it her injury?

Ellie folded her fingers and placed them in her lap, deep furrows marring her forehead.

"Ben... I... I want to thank you for all that you've done for me over the past few months. It means the world to me, you know that, don't you? "

Ben's stomach gave an uncomfortable lurch. He was unsure of the direction this conversation was taking, but something did not seem right. "Sure, I do. And I was happy to do it, Ellie. Because I'd do anything for you." It was now or never. He had to tell her, but now that the moment was here, he wasn't sure he could get the words out.

"I love you. I'm *in* love with you."

Ellie's shoulders slumped and she closed her eyes, as if his words had hurt her. Ben was positive that was *not* the reaction he expected. He waited for her to respond, a strange pressure building in his chest.

"Are you alright? I told you, you need a doctor."

Ellie shook her head. "I'm... It's fine." She paused, her lips pressed together, and then looked directly at him.

"I love you too, Ben. And I always will. You saved me, that night. I put your token into the bowl." She held out Ben's lucky gear. He held out a trembling hand while she dropped it in.

"I remembered, later," Ben said softly. "What the old fortune teller said. That you needed a token. I thought..." He didn't dare finish the thought aloud, that he hoped the token meant she loved him, too.

"But it wasn't the only one that I used." Slowly, she reached into her pocket again and pulled out a fine linen handkerchief. "I couldn't decide which of you held my heart, and so I used both. I didn't know which had broken the spell, until just now when I realized that *both* of them did."

Ben's heart warmed at that, except the word *both*. "I don't understand."

"Ben, we have known each other since we were children. We have shared our dreams, and you have done everything in your power to save me. Of course, I love you. You hold a place in my heart, just as if you were my own brother."

A moment passed before the meaning of Ellie's words sunk in. Ben stood, the pressure turning to pain. "I know you've just been through a lot. You've lost your father, you're injured. You need some time to sort through things. I shouldn't have said anything until you were ready to hear it. I'll wait as long as you need."

Ellie pulled her brows together and turned her face to the ceiling, her eyes bright with tears, her voice thick. "No, Ben, that's not the problem. I love you so much—I hope you know that. You are my best friend."

Ben fell back on the words he had been reciting for days. "We could go away from here, start a new life, wherever you want. London, Paris. I know you have money, but we won't need it. I'll start my career, and we'll see the world. You'll be the toast of Europe."

Ellie closed her eyes and two fat tears rolled down her cheeks. "It sounds like a wonderful dream, Ben. But I'm sorry, I can't."

Like the revelation of an illusion's secret, something suddenly became clear to Ben, and anger surged through him. "So, you love this Scott, is that it? Is that his handkerchief?"

Ellie shook her head. "I... I... It's just that..."

A beast inside of Ben took over and he stood, poisonous thoughts turning to words. "That's it, isn't it? You danced with him at the ball, and his pretty manners and fine clothes have turned your head. I'm just a poor man who earns his money by the sweat of his brow. Scott wouldn't know a hard day's labor if it ran up and bit him in the ass. Now that you're able to mingle among the society idiots, I'm not good enough for you."

The words tumbled from his mouth, unchecked. "I've seen his kind before, Ellie. Don't be surprised when your precious Mr. Scott abandons you for the next pretty girl in a ball gown and tight corset."

The slap was loud, but felt much worse than it sounded. Ellie had jumped from her seat before Ben realized it. She winced in pain, her lips pursed in anger.

"How dare you. I *do* love you, Benjamin Grimm, but right now you are making a complete jackass of yourself."

Ben held his stinging cheek, ashamed.

"I can forgive you, because I know you really didn't mean those words." She looked at him kindly, and he felt exactly like the jackass she accused him of being. "You deserve someone who can give you their whole heart. I want that for you, but she's not me. When you do find that girl, tell her she's very lucky."

The lump in Ben's throat was the size of an apple. He tried to swallow but couldn't. He tried to speak but there were no words. Both the beast and Ben's heart were silent. He gripped the gear in his hand so tightly the teeth bit into his flesh. He gave a single nod and walked away and out the front door, leaving Ellie standing alone in the parlor.

The door slammed with such force that the glass in all the first floor windows rattled in their frames. Ellie went to the parlor window, but Ben had disappeared into the snow that had begun to fall in big, fat, flakes. Part of her wanted to run after him, to make him understand and repair their broken friendship.

"Miss Banneker?" Hamilton's voice spoke soft and gentle. She faced him, her heart jumping in her chest. What had to come next might even be more difficult. Today had been full of difficult, so what was a little more?

"Yes, Mr. Scott?"

"I'm sorry about your friend. He seems to care for you very much."

Ellie replied quietly, turning back to the window. "He does, but I hurt him deeply."

Hamilton shuffled his feet. "Well... perhaps this is not the best time to ask, but since you have the maddening habit of disappearing, I feel that I had better speak up while I have the chance."

Ellie did not turn around. "Yes, Mr. Scott?"

"First of all, please, please, *please* call me Hamilton. Secondly, I would like to ask you, or actually ask you again, if you would allow me the privilege to call on you?"

Ellie's heart cried out for her to accept, as she had wanted to on the night of the ball. But her head remained firmly in charge, and she had made her decision. She clutched his handkerchief to her heart.

"Hamilton, I ..."

A terrible scream from above stopped her speech. It was quickly followed by a nauseating thud outside. Footsteps thundered down, and Rebecca appeared in the foyer.

"I couldn't stop her!" Her face was chalk-white. "Oh, my God!" She ran out the front door, leaving it open.

Ellie held her injured arm and ran after her stepsister. The wind that blew in the open door was freezing, but the scene in the street outside was what chilled her to the bone.

Olivia lay on the sidewalk. Her broken body lay on the bricks, her eyes open but unseeing, a pool of crimson beneath her head. Rebecca knelt beside her mother, tears turning to ice crystals before they struck the fabric of Olivia's dress.

Ellie stepped out, barely feeling the snow that landed on her cheeks. "Rebecca, what happened?"

Rebecca wiped her dripping nose on her sleeve. "We were in her room. She said it was stuffy and she wanted some fresh air, so she opened the window. Then she stood there, rambling about what the women at the club would think? I told her that it could be so much worse." She let out a sharp, humorless sound. "She said there was nothing worse. I looked at her and... I knew. I knew what she was going to do. I tried to stop her, but before I could reach her... she jumped."

Tears burst forth afresh, racking the girl's shoulders with sobs. Ellie could not move, her feet fixed to the spot, unable to close her eyes and blot out the miserable scene. Hamilton came and tried to pull her away, but she remained. One thought ran through her head, the voice of the mysterious stranger, like a macabre fortune-teller.

It is finished.

CHAPTER XXVI

T HE FUNERAL OF EPHRAIM BANNEKER WAS HELD FOUR DAYS LATER. The newspapers reported the official cause of his death as a brain injury he suffered after taking a fall walking along the French coast. Ellie and Rebecca had concocted the story together, and Hamilton, who was still confused but handling everything exceptionally well, had somehow procured the appropriate documents. Ellie had agreed to the lie, not to spare Olivia's reputation, but because it wasn't anyone else's business.

Olivia's death was a much more public affair that involved police and more inventive storytelling. After repeating the story a few times, the idea that she had killed herself out of grief, after receiving the news of her of her husband's death, even sounded like the truth to Ellie. She was buried in a quiet, private ceremony, with no pomp and no circumstance. Though, for Rebecca's sake, Ellie did pay for a small, plain grave marker.

Once word spread that one of the city's most prominent, if lately reclusive, citizens had died, friends of Ellie's parents seemed to appear as if conjured, bringing gifts of food and sympathy. She accepted them with a cold and detached politeness, not inviting any of the callers inside and only answering questions regarding her European education with vague, short, and often curt responses. Not one of them had bothered to look any further than Olivia's lies, which meant Ellie felt absolutely no obligation to them whatsoever to be hospitable.

Every last caller commented on how much Ellie resembled her mother. The bewitching spell had hoodwinked them all, except for Ben, which she had never been able to figure out. She wondered if it was because he was the only one who had truly ever seen her to begin with.

Ephraim's daughter was talked about all across the city, over cards and tea and in smoking rooms over bourbon, and the general consensus was that the girl's strange behavior had been brought on by grief. Rumors abounded, but she ignored all of them, just as she tried to ignore the looks of those around her on the few occasions when she went out, to make arrangements for her father's service or shopping at the market. The gawkers and tongue-flappers were fortunate that Ellie did not have the energy or desire to unleash the anger she felt upon them.

When the day of the funeral came, the streets around Christ Church were crammed with black carriages. All of society stuffed themselves into the pews, dressed in their most fashionable black attire, doing their best to appear properly grief-stricken. Ellie sat in front, with only her stepsister beside her, her heavy black veil covering her face so she did not have to see the hypocrisy that surrounded her.

When the service was over and Ephraim Banneker's body committed to the ground, Hamilton brought his mother and father through the receiving line and introduced them to Ellie.

"Oh, my dear, I am so sorry." Mrs. Scott, a handsome woman with graying hair and perfect posture, pulled Ellie into a solid embrace. "Hamilton's told us everything," she whispered in Ellie's ear. "Your secret is safe with us." She pulled her head back to look at Ellie. "Your mother was such a joy. Once you're ready, you'll come to the house for dinner, all right?"

Ellie was glad for her veil, because she didn't want anyone to see how she cried at Mrs. Scott's genuine kindness.

Ephraim was buried beneath the hazel tree, beside his wife. Long after the rest of the mourners had left, Ellie sat alone on the stone bench. For the first time since her mother's death, she said nothing, just listened to the contented cooing of a pair of doves sitting in the branches of the tree until twilight descended and it was too cold to stay.

Mr. McIntyre, the executor of Ellie's father's will, was the only person besides Rebecca and Hamilton that Ellie was willing to permit inside the house. His condolences were the sincerest of all her father's friends. He was able to help Ellie make the arrangements for the funeral, to the specifications of her father's will. Two days after the funeral, he took her to her father's bank, sat her in the most comfortable chair in his office, and went over all of the assets that were now hers. The house, the carriage, an impressive stock portfolio, and a bank account that held a sum of money larger than Ellie had ever seen. Mr. McIntyre suggested that someone at the bank be assigned to help her to manage it all, and she agreed.

Mrs. Grimm sent flowers and a tin of home-baked tea cakes on the day after the funeral. Hers was the only gift for which Ellie wrote a thank-you note. Ben, however, did not appear nor correspond. Ellie sent letters, but there was never a reply. A week later, she went to the book-shop, where Mrs. Grimm greeted her with a motherly embrace and a cup of hot tea. But Ben was not there; in fact, his mother hadn't seen him in days. It was as if he had performed a great illusion and simply vanished.

Ben shook hands with the man, who looked like he was only a few years older than himself. Which seemed remarkable considering how much money the man and his brother had offered him. The brother, who was an identical copy of the man Ben had been speaking with, stood a few feet away, looking over Ben's motorcar with a practiced and skeptical eye, stopping when he came to the dashboard. He rubbed his chin and smiled.

"Yes, Freelan, I think the boy's definitely got something here. It will need some modifications, of course, but he's done a fine job."

Ben acknowledged the compliment with a nod of his head, but was careful not to look at the carriage. He loved it dearly, but what was he going do with it? Drive it around the city? Cart it off to Europe with him? No, he needed to leave the city behind, so the motorcar was more useful converted into money. With the large sum the brothers were talking about, Ben would be able to finance his plans easily. Besides, the machine reminded him of Ellie, and that wound had not yet healed. He had been watching the newspapers for an engagement announcement, but as of yet, none had appeared. He tried to tell himself it didn't matter, but that was a lie. He would always love Ellie, but he needed to move on. Europe would have to be far enough to do that.

It was just his good fortune that the famous brothers had somehow heard of Ben's invention and contacted him by telegram a few days ago. He had been a bit anxious that they would find some fault with the carriage and pull out of the deal. But it looked as if everything was acceptable, and all Ben wanted now was to finish the transaction and leave this part of his life behind.

"All right, then Francis. I trust your judgment." Freelan, the brother who shook Ben's hand, reached into the inside pocket of his jacket and pulled out a folded slip of paper, which he handed to Ben. The cheque was for the full amount they had discussed. More money than he could have earned in two years working at the theater.

"Thank you, sirs."

"No, no, thank you, Mr. Grimm. This will give us something to tinker with when we've had enough of photography for the day." Francis came to stand beside his brother, which made Ben feel a little dizzy. It was impossible to tell them apart. "And please thank your business manager for contacting us." He held out his hand to Ben.

"My... business manager?"

"The other Mr. Grimm? It was he that contacted us regarding your motorcar." Freelan pulled a piece of paper from his pocket and handed it to Ben. He scanned the telegram, and the name on the bottom made his mouth drop open. *Sincerely, Mr. Harry Grimm.*

Ben tried not to laugh as he handed the telegram back, vowing to use some of his new fortune to buy Harry a present. "Thank you, I will be sure to convey your message. Now I must be going." If he didn't appear at the bookshop soon, his mother would likely send out a search party. He tipped his head toward each of the brothers. "Mr. Stanley, Mr. Stanley." He started up the aisle toward the door, then stopped. "Just one bit of advice. Be careful when you open the steam valve. Let it out slowly, or she might just run away on you."

Rebecca stood on the sidewalk outside the shop on Chestnut Street, reconsidering the idea she had thought was so brilliant this morning. People walked around her, in a hurry to be out of the biting February wind, but Rebecca barely felt it, nor did she hear the complaints of a few of the people who were irritated she was blocking the path.

January had seemed interminable, full of sadness that at times threatened to crush her, and she had been glad to leave it behind. With a new month, she had decided on a new path, and for weeks had thought about how to begin. The answer had struck her like a thunderbolt, just yesterday, and so here she was, taking a chance she would find what she needed.

Cold had frosted over the windows of the shop, but she could see people moving inside.

It's now or never.

Taking a deep breath, she pulled open the door of Grimm's Bookshop and stepped inside. She went to the counter, where an older woman was busy sorting receipts.

"I'm looking for Benjamin Grimm."

The boy himself appeared in the doorway behind the counter. He looked at Rebecca and turned away.

"Wait, please!" Rebecca called after him. "I'm not here about Ellie."

He paused, then turned around and looked right at her. She could see he was still so deeply wounded by Ellie's refusal. She took his remaining in her presence as a queue to continue.

"I'm here, um, well..." She wished she had rehearsed this beforehand. "I came to talk to you. I uh... I think we have some things to talk about."

CHAPTER XXVII

ELLIE THREW OPEN THE FRONT DOOR, HER FACE FLUSHED FROM excitement and the afternoon heat. She pulled the wide-brimmed hat from her head.

"Sarah? Sarah, I'm back!"

The kitchen door swung open and a tall, lean girl came into the hallway. Her brown hair was tucked beneath her white cap, and she wore her usual uniform of domestic's apparel and a serious expression. Ellie had not wanted a maid, but Hamilton had convinced her that it was necessary, if for no other reason than to have someone else in the house. A woman living alone, he said, was asking for trouble. He had pestered her until finally she had agreed.

"Hello, miss. How was your trip?"

Ellie handed the hat to Sarah and, beaming, pulled off her gloves. "Glorious! New York City is so much bigger than Philadelphia. The streets are crammed with people and carriages, everyone moves so quickly. The theaters on Broadway! So many I lost count."

"And Mrs. Astor's summer party?"

"Dull as dirt, like all the rest of them. Boring conversations about nothing, all the while trying to keep eye contact with gentlemen who were more interested in the neckline of my dress than what I had to say. I would much rather have spent time walking in Central Park or visiting a museum. The next time I go, that's what I'll do. Pooh on parties."

Sarah tried not to look horrified. "It sounds lovely, miss, but I hope you'll go with a chaperone. I was afraid for you, all alone in that big city. And if you took someone along, like Mr. Scott and his mother, then perhaps the gentlemen wouldn't think of looking at you that way. If you don't mind my saying."

Ellie waved off Sarah's admonition. "I was *fine*, Sarah, though you're a dear to think of it. You should have seen the looks I got on the train, riding by myself." She glanced at the maid to see her reaction and was rewarded with a second look of dismay.

Sarah went to put the hat away in the closet, muttering something about proper ladies.

"I'm not a proper lady, Sarah, and you already know that." Ellie adored Sarah, but she was taciturn in her adherence to propriety, and Ellie liked ribbing her, just a little.

Sarah shut the closet door. "Shall I prepare some tea, miss?" Ellie traveled often, and when she returned it was always the same routine. Tea and company.

"Yes, please, something simple. And sweet, I could use something sweet, if you don't mind. Hamilton should be arriving shortly. I'll just freshen up a bit."

Ellie dashed upstairs to her newly-furnished bedroom, splashed cool water on her face and wrestled her hair back into place. She closed the door and glanced across the hall to Rebecca's room. She would have to have Sarah dust in there soon, she was sure, just in case her stepsister should return. It was a little sad, not to have her to talk to, but she had her own life to live. When she left, Ellie promised her that she would always be welcome, and always have a home. So, the door across the hall stayed shut, the room exactly the way Rebecca left it.

On the second floor she stopped in the study. There was a stack of letters on her father's desk, mail that had arrived while she was away. The desk and the secretary were the only two pieces of furniture that had remained in the house. She had sold or given away every last thing her stepmother had bought, spending weeks redecorating until she had scrubbed away every hint of Olivia Gibson.

Ellie lifted the stack of mail, which sat beside the mechanical bird Ben had given her last winter. There was an invitation to dinner at the Coopers on the fifteenth. She put it aside, not sure if she would accept. The only reasons she had been invited were because she was a Banneker, and because David and Hamilton were close friends. But it was David's new wife's first dinner party, so she might go after all, to help bolster the girl's confidence.

I do not envy any of those women, whose whole worth lies on how well they set a table.

The next was a note from Katharine Purcell-Adams, thanking Ellie for having her to tea last month. Katharine had not been upset to learn of Ellie's deception at the Assembly Ball, especially after Hamilton explained everything to her as best he could—the whole truth was much too outlandish, even for Katharine. She had jumped at the chance to help Ellie, staving off the wolves and curiosity seekers, and been genuine in her sympathy. The two women had become thick as thieves, much to Hamilton's dismay.

Hamilton. They had been interrupted on that dreadful day, and it wasn't until two weeks after the funeral that they had been able to speak again. She had accepted his suit, with a single condition: that there be no talk of marriage for an entire year. She needed the time to discover who Eleanor Banneker was, without anyone else defining her. For the last six months, she had explored life—paying the bills, having tea, reading books, being invited to dinner. Taking train rides to New York City and going to the theater. He had accepted her terms, though he, like Sarah, didn't like her going off on her own. Which was ridiculous. When she was a maid, she had been allowed to go through the streets unchaperoned, so why shouldn't she continue to do so? Hamilton hadn't had an argument for that—not one that he could win, anyway.

The first flutterings of her heart had grown to genuine affection, and she already knew that when the year was over, she would be ready to be Hamilton's wife, which would make Hamilton's mother breathe a sigh of relief. The woman was kind and gracious, but lately she had been hinting that a year was much too long for a courtship and kept dropping hints about her age and grandchildren.

She put Katherine's note aside so she could write a reply later, and sorted out the bills. At the bottom of the pile was a cream-colored envelope. Ellie saw the familiar handwriting, her own name and address flowing across the stationary in indigo ink. Her heart soared.

"Rebecca!" The postmark said she'd arrived in London. As Ellie tore the envelope open and pulled out the letter, a smaller scrap of paper, a newspaper clipping, fluttered to her lap. It was an advertisement:

The Astounding Grimalkin!
See him perform great Feats of Illusion
~The Orange Tree~
~The Vanishing Woman~
And the never-before seen
~Great Escape~
You will be Amazed!

At the very bottom were show dates, times, and the name of a venue in London. She set the clipping aside and took up the letter, letting the summer sunlight illuminate the words. It was dated nearly a month ago.

21 June, 1877

Dearest Ellie,

We've finally arrived in London! The crossing was rough in places, but was overall pleasant. The city is so beautiful, brimming with people! We're staying in a little hotel called the Wingate, but hope to find some permanent rooms soon. Ben's gotten us a week's engagement at the theater in the clipping, and we open tomorrow night. We've been practicing so hard, you know, but this will be our first time in front of a real audience. I'm nervous, but at the same time it's all so exciting.

This is what I've wanted my whole life, Ellie. Not necessarily to be an Illusionist's assistant, though it is fun (and I adore the costumes) but to see the world, to do as I please. To use my hands and make things. I am sure this is what birds feel like when they fly, and I'm not going to waste one more moment doing what others want. I wore that corset long enough, and it nearly suffocated me.

Ben is doing well. He's thrown himself into his work. He always has a pencil and that notebook in his hand, his brow furrowed in concentration. I've been helping him with some new designs, and learned so much about how things work. Can you imagine? My mother would have been scandalized! We're also working on a new and better motorcar. But it's still just a dream.

He's also quite the businessman, and knows so much about the theater. I think we'll do well here. He hasn't mentioned you very often, but whenever your name comes up, he smiles. I miss you so much, and I think he does too, in his own way.

Ellie, I love him. I hope that doesn't upset you. I think that he loves me too, but he's being very cautious. I don't blame you, my sister, because I know that you followed your own heart, and you were honest, which is always best. We are happy, and I hope you are as well. I expect to find a wedding invitation in "the post," as they say here, sooner rather than later. I hope you and Hamilton are as happy as I.

Please write often — tell me every bit of gossip and everything that goes on in your life. It's all your own now, Ellie, as is mine.

All my love,

Rebecca

Ellie wiped the tears from her eyes before they fell on the page and caused the ink to run. Ben and Rebecca were a good match; she didn't know why she hadn't seen it before. She missed Rebecca so much, missed the camaraderie and understanding that could only come from someone who has survived the same experience.

Ellie's shoulder gave a twinge. She bore a scar beneath the fabric of her dress, a permanent reminder of what she had been through. She and Ben had not spoken since that horrible day.

Rebecca, on the other hand, had gone to Ben and admitted that she had recognized him at the Exposition. She had sent him the mysterious notes, as well as the one that had directed Ellie to the papers hidden in Olivia's desk.

Rebecca was fascinated by Ben's workshop, especially the automatons. Over the following months the two spent a lot of time together. Becca, it seemed, was very clever with her hands. She had also admitted, over tea and biscuits one day, that she had built the strange key that had freed Ellie from the cellar on that fateful day, and also had made the little ladies' watch she had given to Ellie, created from an old locket and other bits and pieces she had gathered, including her father's pocket watch.

One day in April she came home, cheeks flushed and bursting with excitement.

"We're going to Europe."

"Becca, you can't be serious." Ellie hadn't meant it to sound mean; it was just such a surprise. "What are you going to do in Europe?"

Rebecca hadn't even hesitated. "I'm going to be Ben's assistant. Every good illusionist needs one. He's come into some money unexpectedly, and he's almost finished constructing his equipment. We should be able to leave in a month."

Those thirty days passed in a whirl of preparation and excitement. Then the day came. A hack came to the house to take Rebecca to the port. Hamilton loaded Rebecca's trunk into the carriage and the two stepsisters, who were like true sisters now, embraced and said goodbye. Ben hadn't come—he would meet Rebecca at the dock. Ellie had hoped to see him once more, to not have the last words they ever said to one another to be that horrible argument. But he had stayed away.

The doorbell rang, pulling Ellie from her the letter and her thoughts. Hamilton. She made it to the bottom of the stairs just as he walked into the foyer, carrying a large wooden crate.

She was almost afraid to ask. "What is that? Not a gift for me, I hope." She didn't hate presents, but Hamilton tended to spoil her. After the first few much-too-extravagant tokens of his affection, she had insisted that he stop, or at least ask before he bought her anything more than flowers.

"No, I've learned my lesson, thank you. This was on your step. It's addressed to you."

"But I only arrived twenty minutes ago, and it wasn't there. No one rang the bell or knocked, did they, Sarah?" The maid shook her head.

Hamilton set the crate on the floor and studied it. "No return address." He looked at Ellie. "Were you expecting a package?"

"No." Ellie studied the box, and then clapped her hands. "A mystery! Let's open it." She sent Sarah to fetch the brand-new crow bar, and Hamilton pried the lid from the crate. It was stuffed with sawdust and scraps of fabric.

"Whatever is inside, it must be fragile." Ellie pulled out the packing materials, putting it all carefully into the wastebasket Sarah held out for her. Finally, she reached whatever was inside. "Oh, my, it's heavy."

Ellie tried again, but finally gave in and let Hamilton lift the item from the box. He set it on the dining room table.

"It's beautiful." Ellie ran her fingers over a giant music box. Two wooden figures—a man and a woman, both exquisitely carved—were positioned as if dancing on top of a large, polished wooden box. The dark-haired woman wore a dress of mauve silk with roses across the shoulders, and the blonde man was dressed in a fine gray suit. Both figures wore white silk masks.

Ellie, a lump in her throat, lifted the skirt of the woman's dress. Golden slippers cradled her tiny feet. A brass key hung from her arm, dangling on a piece of ribbon. Ellie slid it free, then found the keyhole in the side of the box. Fingers trembling, she inserted the key and turned it carefully.

A waltz began to play, a music box's chime. The man and the woman started to move. They twirled and stepped, dancing across the top of the box in perfect time to the music.

"Oh, miss. It's like magic."

Ellie laughed. Though she had had enough of magic to last her a lifetime, she was inclined to agree.

"This was in the bottom of the box, miss." Sarah handed Ellie a small, cream-colored envelope. Ellie opened it, and out slipped a small brass gear. There was no signature and no greeting on the card, but the words said everything she needed to know.

"Darling? Why are you crying?" Hamilton took the card from her unresisting fingers and read the single line of text. "'And they all lived Happily Ever After'? What does that mean? Ellie, do you know who sent this?"

Ellie, her eyes still on the dancing couple, smiled as tears rolled down her face, and nodded.

AUTHOR'S NOTE

MANY OF THE EVENTS THAT TAKE PLACE IN THIS STORY ARE historically accurate. The Centennial Exposition took place in Philadelphia in 1876, and it was held in Fairmount Park. It was a very special event, because it was the first World's Fair ever held in America. The only building that remains at the Centennial Exposition site is Memorial Hall, with its glittering glass dome. Today it is the home of the Please Touch Museum.

Yes, the telephone was introduced at the Expo by Mr. Alexander Graham Bell, as was Hires Root Beer. The Corliss Steam Engine did indeed power all of the other machines in the Machinery Hall, and the arm of the Statue of Liberty was also on display, the fifty cents it cost to walk inside of it was a princely sum in those days. I must thank the Free Library of Philadelphia for maintaining a wonderful website on the Exposition, including a map and photographs, on which I spent many hours clicking and reading, as well as the Please Touch Museum, who maintains an entire exhibit dedicated the event, complete with a scale model.

Likewise, the Assembly Ball was a real event. It was the oldest debutante ball in the country until it stopped in the late 1950s. It was hosted by the Philadelphia Dancing Assembly, a group which can trace its beginnings to colonial times. The Assembly dances were held as a series of several galas, reduced to two or three grand balls held over the winter months, finally concluded to a single ball held in December — the debutante ball. They were held in the Academy of Music for many years, until they moved to the Bellevue-Stratford hotel.

In Philadelphia, it was not about how much money one had, as in New York society, but who you were related to. Your name would open many more doors than any amount of cash. Helen Montgomery Scott (no relation to Hamilton), the main character played by Katharine Hepburn in A Philadelphia Story, was presented to society at an Assembly Ball.

Wanamaker's department store also opened in 1876, though not in the iconic building that stands on Market Street most people associate with it. Instead, it opened in a huge empty train depot down the street, closer to the Reading Terminal.

As for the names used in this story, all of the first names, with one exception, came from my own family tree. I have been studying my genealogy for some time, and after reading the diary of my great-grandmother, Cora, I decided to dig up more family history. The last names are all my own choosing, except for Hamilton Scott, which I put together from bits of the tree, a first name here and a last name there, because I just thought it was a fabulous name. Benjamin, Oscar, Harry (who was my great-grandmother's little brother and died at an early age from a tragic accident), Ephraim, Violetta, even Clarence the cat, are all named for people related to me, and this story is a tribute to them and the world they knew. My great-great-grandfather, Benjamin Schrack Russell, worked at the Walnut Street Theater as a stage manager, as did his son, Oscar, and his son-in-law, Clarence, who eventually moved up from stagehand to Master Carpenter of the Academy of Music.

Freelan and Francis Stanley, identical twins that looked so much alike even as adults that no one could tell them apart, did in point of fact invent a form of steam-powered motorized car, called the Stanley Steamer, a predecessor to Henry Ford's automobile. The Stanley brothers gave up motorized vehicles for another career, and you might know them better for that contribution to the world—they founded a company that made cameras and film, called Kodak.

ACKNOWLEDGEMENTS

THIS IS A REPRINT OF THE ORIGINAL EDITION, WHICH WAS FIRST published by another publisher after the FIRST publisher to want it suddenly closed. This poor book has been through it all and hopefully now it is in your hands, dear reader, and you love it as much as I do. It's been a journey.

This is the page that everyone who knows the author rushes to look at when they first pick up the book. The one where the author thanks everyone, like a written-down version of an Oscar acceptance speech. They wonder if they'll be mentioned, and if not, why not?

I apologize in advance if I forget anyone.

Dozens of people have contributed toward the final product, and along rather long and arduous trip to get here. Of course, I have to thank my family, because I think it's a rule that you have to do that (and they're pretty great). They put up with a great deal of Annoying Things and weekends without me and hours with my nose buried in the computer screen. I love you guys.

Even in this republished edition, this wouldn't have even had a hope if not for all the people who shaped it and helped me to get it to the point where it would be considered at all: Steve Meltzer, who didn't have to listen to a 45-minute pitch, but gave me great advice. Twice.

Danielle Ackley-McPhail, who always has been a cheerleader and now my publisher. You've given this book a second life — thank you!!

For the Free Library of Philadelphia: THANK YOU. Without your website, parts of this book would have been really hard to write or would have been just plain wrong. You made it so easy and fun. The Please Touch Museum, for maintaining one of the last remaining buildings from the Centennial Exposition and an exhibit dedicated to the event. You keep the past alive and it gave me such joy to see that others are as excited about it as I am.

To the city of Philadelphia, for just being as awesome as you are. It's a Philly thing.

Finally, to the readers: of course, I love you all. Without you I'd just be shouting in the dark. Thanks for listening.

ABOUT THE AUTHOR

ONCE UPON A TIME, CHRISTINE NORRIS THOUGHT SHE WANTED TO BE an archaeologist but hates sand and bugs, so instead, she became a writer. She is the author of several speculative fiction works for children and adults, including *The Library of Athena* series, *A Curse of Ash and Iron*, and contributions to *Gaslight and Grimm* and *Grimm Machinations*. She is kept busy on a daily basis by her day job as a school librarian in New Jersey. She may or may not have a secret library in her basement, and she absolutely believes in fairies.

CPSIA information can be obtained
at www.ICGtesting.com
Printed in the USA
JSHW081636100323
38761JS00002B/9